A Deadly Legend

The truth behind the myth could lead to murder

LM Milford

Readthrough Press

For my brother-in-law Paul
Gone but definitely not forgotten – RIP

Chapter One

A chilly breeze raised goosebumps on the back of Dr Jayne Winter's neck. She didn't believe in ghosts, but the rumours about Old Manor Hall being haunted swam in her brain.

There was a noise behind her and she spun on her heel, half expecting to find Simeon Burns' ghost sweeping towards her. But her torch showed only an empty corridor. Heart pounding, she shook her head. 'Don't be so stupid,' she muttered under her breath. 'It's being back in this place, it's unsettling you.'

A quick glance at her watch in the torchlight showed it was only four-thirty in the afternoon, but already dark on a gloomy November day. She took a deep breath and squared her shoulders.

You know it's here – you just have to find it. Then you can get the hell out, she told herself.

Flashing the torch beam along the corridor ahead, Jayne sighed. Old Manor was a shadow of its former self. Vandals had smashed everything they could find and graffitied the walls. Pictures she'd seen of the house back in its heyday showed parquet flooring, beautiful portraits of the family and elaborate ceiling plasterwork. Back in her school days, the halls teemed with her fellow students all buffeting against each other, laughing and shouting. More often than not, she'd been alone, but that was fine. She didn't need anyone else then, and she certainly didn't need them now.

Broken glass crunched under her feet as she continued, and the torch beam wobbled as her hand shook. This place was super creepy at night.

It's the only way. I have to be first. She took a deep breath and clenched her free hand, hoping to still it. *I'm not backing out now. I'm too close.*

Arriving at what she knew was the principal's office, she pushed open the door, wincing at the horror film-style screech its hinges gave.

Then she heard something else. The crunch of a footstep on broken glass. That wasn't Simeon Burns. Heart skipping a beat, she paused, swinging her torch beam back along the corridor. It was time to get what she needed and get the hell out of here.

The worn carpet almost tripped her as she crept across the room to the bookcase. She began running her hands quickly across the fake books. *It must be here somewhere, it must.* Then she froze as her fingers encountered a slight space between two books. Yes, this was it! But, stiffened by age, it wouldn't move.

Jayne gave a small snort. *I didn't come this far to stop now.*

Yanking her house keys from her coat pocket, she selected the supermarket saver card token and inserted it into the gap between the books. A few wiggles, a satisfying click, which seemed very loud in the quiet room, and the bookcase swung forward to reveal the room behind it. Jayne exhaled, trying to control her racing adrenaline. She'd found it. *I might be the first person in here since Simeon Burns died.*

But as she stepped inside the space behind the false wall, the office door gave another horror-film creak and Jayne froze. *Maybe if I stay really still...*

A voice called, 'I know you're in there. You might as well come out.'

Recognising the voice, Jayne stepped back into the office and swept her torch around the room. The beam landed on a face.

'What are you doing here?' she demanded, taking two steps towards the figure. 'Did you follow me?'

A smile. 'I knew you couldn't resist the bait.'

Jayne stared. 'What are you talking about?' she snapped. 'I don't have time for this.'

'I knew you'd fall for it. Arrogant as ever.'

Jayne watched as the figure walked past her and blocked her from the secret room. 'You're talking rubbish,' she snapped. 'Get out of the way. I need to get into that room.'

The figure shook their head. 'You're not going anywhere. You know what you did.'

Jayne felt her stomach clench. 'What are you talking about? I haven't done anything.'

'Yes, you have, and now I'm going to make you pay for it.'

As the figure advanced towards her, Jayne took two steps back, fingers fumbling for the mobile phone she knew was in her pocket.

'I wouldn't do that if I were you. No one can help you now.'

Jayne turned and tried to run, but her foot caught on the uneven carpet and she crashed to the ground, hearing her mobile clatter to the floor. As her fingers scrabbled to find it, the figure loomed over her, flashing a torch beam directly in her eyes.

Blinded, she said, 'We can share it. I'll say we both—'

A harsh laugh. 'It's too late for that now. It's payback time.'

Chapter Two

Detective Inspector Jude Burton strode towards the entrance of Old Manor Hall swinging her car keys from her index finger. She shivered as the cold wind made its way down the back of her tracksuit top, wishing she'd put on a coat. Glancing up at the building, she took in the solid brick facade and the large windows set symmetrically on either side of the front door. It had once been grand but now looked very sorry for itself.

Detective Sergeant Mark Shepherd, waiting on the front steps between the columns on either side of the door, grinned and gestured to her tracksuit bottoms and trainers as she came within earshot.

'Is it dress-down day and I missed the memo?' he asked, flicking the end of his tie.

Burton grimaced. She would never usually be seen in a work situation without her stilettos. 'I was on my way to the gym when I got the call. Tuesday night is body pump.' She gestured towards the building. 'And why have we been called out for trespassers?'

Burton followed Shepherd's finger as he turned and pointed to a uniformed officer, speaking to three teenage boys.

'Jack was first on the scene after those three called it in at about quarter past five. They'd snuck inside to look for a ghost that haunts the building.'

Burton rolled her eyes. 'Oh, for God's sake. There's an excuse for "came to break some windows" that I've never heard before.' Then she frowned, registering Shepherd's words. 'Called what in?'

Shepherd pointed to the upper floor of the house with his pen. 'They were in the upstairs corridor looking for Simeon Burns' bedroom when—'

'Simeon Burns?' Burton asked, frowning and huddling into the neck of her tracksuit top, wishing she could put the hood up without looking unprofessional.

'The guy who owned this house back in the eighteen hundreds or something,' Shepherd said, consulting his notebook. 'Apparently, he died in the bedroom and it's supposed to be haunted.'

Burton rolled her eyes. 'Give me strength...' She gestured for Shepherd to continue.

'They went into one room – which may or may not have been his bedroom – and found a massive hole in the floor. A quick peek and they saw the body of a woman lying on the floor underneath it.'

'We've got a dead body? You maybe should have led with that bit,' Burton said, irritated. She glanced at the teenagers. 'It can't have been fun for them, finding her. Had she fallen through the ceiling?'

'We're not sure at the moment.'

Burton frowned. 'Did they check if she was dead?'

Shepherd shook his head. 'They bolted outside and called an ambulance. Jack attended along with that and got the full story from the youngsters. He called me.'

'At least they called it in,' Burton said, glancing towards the three young lads. 'I'd have expected them to leg it.'

Shepherd nodded. 'Me too, but it seems they have a social conscience.'

'Good on them.' Burton shoved her hands into her tracksuit jacket pockets.

Shepherd nodded towards the building. 'Brody's inside. It's not much warmer though,' he added, pointing at Burton's hands with his pen.

'Anything is better than the wind out here. I'll talk to her. Tell Jack to get them home and make sure nothing goes on social media,' Burton added. She pointed to the development of flats and houses at the perimeter fence. 'Has anyone canvassed the area?'

Shepherd shook his head. 'I've just sent a couple of bods round there.'

Burton turned and headed into the building. Following a colleague's directions, she found her way to the office, stepping carefully across the broken glass that littered the floor. Thank God she was wearing sensible shoes.

She arrived in the office to find Dr Eleanor Brody, the local pathologist, kneeling on thick foam pads beside the body of a woman who appeared to be in her early thirties. She was wearing skinny jeans, and a brown leather jacket lay open, showing a pale-blue woolly jumper. Brody pushed back the brim of the orange hard hat perched on her brown curls.

Burton opened her mouth, but before she could speak, Brody said, 'I haven't got anything for you yet.'

Burton laughed. 'How did you know it was me without turning around?'

'Expensive French perfume means only one person around

here,' Brody said. She glanced up. 'I certainly wouldn't have known you by those,' she said, pointing to Burton's trainers with her pen. 'Dress-down day, is it?'

Burton rolled her eyes. 'I've just had the same conversation with Mark.'

Brody gave a rare smile. 'It's weird seeing you without the stilettos,' she said, 'but probably safest with the decor around here.' She sat back on her heels and gestured at the glass on the floor. Burton was about to step forward, but Brody held up a hand. 'Stay in the doorway.' She pointed to the ceiling where plaster hung down from a hole. 'That lot isn't very secure. First impressions, as you're gagging for information, are that Dr Jayne Winter here—'

'She's a doctor?' Burton asked, surprised.

Brody nodded. 'That's what it says on her driving licence.'

'Do doctors usually break into abandoned buildings?' Burton asked, looking around the room. *Was this really just a trespassing case*, she wondered, *or was there more to it?*

Brody shrugged. 'Indiana Jones would, I suppose, and he's a doctor. Anyway, she was in here when the ceiling came down and landed on her.'

'It fell on her?' Burton asked. 'She didn't fall from up there?'

Brody shook her head. 'Nope. Even at a first glance, there don't seem to be any wounds consistent with a fall. Of course, that's only early speculation until I do the post-mortem.'

Burton frowned at the ceiling. 'So, a building that has been standing for God knows how many years just randomly collapses when someone who shouldn't even be here is standing under it?'

'It's been on its last legs for ages,' Brody said.

A hand clapped on Burton's shoulder, and she gasped.

'Did you think I was Simeon Burns?' Shepherd asked, appearing beside her. When Burton glared at him, he chuckled. 'We've probably disturbed him with all this racket.'

'What else do we know about her, apart from her name?' Burton asked, pointedly ignoring Shepherd's comment and looking down at the body.

Brody held up a plastic bag containing a set of car keys and a purse.

Burton took it from her and peered at the keys. 'She drives a Toyota Yaris. Any sign of a car nearby?'

Shepherd nodded. 'We've searched the immediate area, but nothing yet. No sign of anyone else either.'

Burton tilted her head on one side. 'Anyone else? A second trespasser?'

Shepherd nodded. 'Our ghost hunters found a footprint in the mud outside the window they climbed through. It looks like it's a man's, just based on size.'

'So someone was here with her.' Burton chewed the inside of her mouth, looking around the room.

'What are you thinking?' Shepherd asked.

Burton scratched her head. 'If you were with someone and a ceiling fell in on them, would you not call for help?'

'They were trespassing,' Shepherd said. 'Maybe they didn't want to get caught?'

Burton wrinkled her nose. 'But still, you'd make the call anonymously, wouldn't you? Something doesn't add up here.'

Brody gave a slight intake of breath, making Burton and Shepherd stare at her.

'What?' Burton demanded.

'I think there's something here. I can't—' Brody began. There was a shower of plaster dust and she glared upwards. 'Hey,' she yelled. A face appeared, looking down at her. 'Be careful up there.' The man waved an apology and disappeared.

Brody turned back to Jayne Winter's body. 'We need to get her out of here quickly. The rest of the ceiling could come down with them stomping about.'

'OK,' Burton said, 'get cleared out as soon as you can. We don't want anyone else hurt.' Then she stopped and stared at the bookcase on the far wall.

'What?' Shepherd asked, following her gaze.

'Is it just me or is that bookcase not flush against the wall?'

Brody glanced over her shoulder, eyes narrowing behind her wire-rimmed glasses. 'You might be right,' she said. 'Good spot. Stop,' she added, as Burton went to step forward. 'I'll get one of my guys to do it when they look at that section of the room.'

Burton nodded. 'Let me know what's behind it,' she said, turning her attention to the plastic evidence bag in her hand.

'Have we tracked down any family yet?' Burton asked Shepherd.

Shepherd shook his head and held up the driving licence in a separate plastic bag. 'Her address on here is in Gravesend, so we'll start there. Here's hoping we find them soon.'

Burton puffed out her cheeks. 'What the hell is a doctor doing in a derelict building in Allensbury if she lives in Gravesend?' She shook her head, frowning. 'Right, find the family. They might know why she was here. We also need to know whether there was anyone else around in the area who might have seen her.'

Shepherd was scribbling in his notebook. 'Appeal through the media?' he asked.

Burton shook her head. 'Not until we've found the family. I'd rather her relatives found out from us than the *Post*.'

Chapter Three

On Wednesday morning, Dan Sullivan walked into the *Allensbury Post* office nursing a takeaway coffee. It had been a very boring on-call shift for him the previous evening, but he'd not slept well. Too much on his mind.

'I wouldn't mind if there was something happening,' he'd moaned to his flatmate, Ed Walker. 'But I just have to sit here waiting and watching that.' He'd jabbed a finger at the on-call phone, making Ed laugh.

'You can't blame the phone.' Ed had sat down on an armchair to fasten his shoelaces. 'What's that saying about watching pots?' He'd had to duck quickly as Dan threw a cushion at him.

'Where are you going?' he'd asked, watching Ed.

'That would be telling, Danny boy,' Ed had said, getting to his feet and grabbing the jacket he'd draped over the back of the chair.

'Ah, come on, take pity and give me some good news,' Dan had said, observing the shiny shoes and smart jeans Ed was wearing instead of his usual trainers. 'She must be special to get the dress-up treatment.'

Ed had grinned. 'No comment,' he'd said, turning away to the door. 'You've got the football to keep you company.' Then he'd turned back. 'No word from Emma?' Seeing Dan's face, he'd added, 'Never mind, say no more.' He'd waved and disappeared down the hall. Dan had heard the front door slam and sighed heavily. He'd glared at the phone, which remained annoyingly silent.

Now, as he walked across the office towards his desk, Daisy, the news editor, waved him over. She had her telephone receiver clamped to her ear, listening intently.

'An interesting voicemail message from late last night,' she said, pressing a few buttons. Her tone immediately put Dan on alert. What had he done wrong now?

A voice came from the speakerphone. 'The police are crawling all over Old Manor Hall.'

Dan rolled his eyes. 'Tell me something new. The police are always at Old Manor.' He turned away, but the next part of the message stopped him.

'I 'eard they found a body and it could be murder.' There was a click and the message ended.

Dan sighed heavily, irritated that he'd been sitting at home while all this was happening, then noticed Daisy staring at him, eyebrows raised.

'Hey, wait a minute,' Dan said, going on the defensive, 'that didn't come through to the crime phone, otherwise I'd have—'

Daisy held up a hand to stem his flow and glared at the deputy news editor. 'Someone forgot to divert his phone when he left last night.' The man winced and did his best to make himself smaller. 'Anyway,' Daisy continued, 'I haven't seen or heard this anywhere else, so hopefully we're the only ones the tipster phoned. See what you can find out.'

Dan headed to his desk, stomach flickering with excitement.

He picked up his phone without taking off his coat and dialled a familiar number.

'You're slipping. I was expecting a voicemail from you when I got to my desk this morning,' said the cheery voice of Suzy, the police press officer, when he'd explained why he was calling.

'Our tip didn't come 'til this morning, so we're slower than usual,' Dan replied, untangling himself from his messenger bag with one hand and grabbing a pen and notebook that sat on his desk. 'What's going on?'

'Not much, but I'll give you everything I've got at the moment,' Suzy said. 'OK, you got a pen in hand?'

'Always.'

Suzy began speaking in her giving-a-statement voice. 'Police officers were called to Old Manor Hall in Allensbury at about seventeen fifteen hours yesterday after three teenagers found the body of a woman inside the building.'

'What was she, or they, doing there?' Dan interrupted. 'That place is a death trap.'

'They were ghost hunting. What she was doing isn't clear yet.'

Dan laughed. 'Looking for Simeon Burns, were they?'

'Who?'

'Simeon Burns. He's the guy who owned the house back in the day. He died there, and rumour has it his spirit decided not to leave.'

'Anywaaaaay,' Suzy continued, dragging out the word, eye-roll almost audible, 'an investigation is underway to establish what happened to this woman.'

'No sign of how she died?' Dan asked, pen flying across the page.

'Nothing we can reveal now,' Suzy replied, 'and before you ask, I can't give you an ID yet.'

'But you know who she is? Is she local?'

Suzy made an exasperated noise. 'You know I can't tell you, no matter how much you beg. It's under wraps until we've been able to inform the family.'

'Are they local?'

An exasperated laugh came down the phone. 'You don't give up, do you? I can't tell you anything else until I get permission.'

Dan clicked his pen a few times as he tried to make sense of the story.

'Hello? You still there?' came Suzy's voice.

'Oh, yeah, sorry. I was just thinking it's weird that an adult was trespassing. Kids I can understand, but why a grown-up woman? It doesn't make sense.'

'I'm sure it'll all fall into place once we know who she is.'

'Could she be anything to do with a housing developer or something like that?' Dan asked, rapidly tracking through his mental filing cabinet of recent news stories.

'Why do you say that?'

'Since it closed down as a school, my school coincidentally, it's been earmarked for demolition and development, but nothing's ever stuck.'

'It was a school?' Suzy asked.

'Yeah, Old Manor Sixth Form College.'

'Why was it never developed?' Suzy asked, in a voice that suggested she was making notes.

Dan shrugged. 'There have been a few planning applications, but they always fall apart. There's an entire housing estate around it, but that bit hasn't been touched. I think Simeon Burns must be protecting his house.'

Something was niggling at the back of his brain, but he just couldn't bring it to the surface. He thanked Suzy, extracted a promise of an update later in the day and hung up.

'Well?' Daisy was standing behind him.

Dan recounted his conversation with Suzy and Daisy puffed out her cheeks.

'So a trespasser was found dead in the building? I'm not surprised. That place is a death trap. Why would someone say it was murder?'

Dan nodded. 'I'm sure I saw something about Old Manor recently, but I can't think what it was.' He sighed and got to his feet. 'I'm sure it'll come to me.'

'Where are you off to?' Daisy asked, as he stuffed his notebook and pen into his coat pocket.

'Old Manor. See what I can see. Somebody in that housing estate must have heard or seen something.'

***

But the Oxton Estate proved to be a disappointment. The streets of executive homes wound into dead ends at every turn and there seemed to be no one about. During the working day was not the best time, Dan thought, on an estate like this. But he decided that luck was on his side, when a woman with long blonde curls parked a BMW on a nearby drive. He parked up and darted across the road to where she stood reaching for some supermarket carrier bags in the boot.

'Hello,' he called when he was about six feet away from her.

She whipped around, a hand flying to her chest. 'Oh my God, you startled me.'

'Sorry,' Dan said, turning on his most charming smile.

She gave a breathy laugh. 'I'm a bit on edge. We had the police round yesterday.'

'Was that about the woman found at Old Manor?' Dan asked, gesturing toward the building that stood behind the woman's house.

She nodded. 'You've heard about that?'

'I'm from the *Allensbury Post*. I was wondering whether you saw or heard anything last night?' He pulled out his notebook.

The woman looked awkward. 'You won't give my name, will you?'

Dan shook his head, hoping that his smile was reassuring.. He hated anonymous quotes, but if it meant getting something, he was prepared to run with it.

Relaxing, the woman took a step towards him, and he could smell a spicy perfume. 'We were just watching TV when the police knocked on the door. Obviously we hadn't heard anything, but I had noticed the car.'

'What car?' Dan asked, head cocked to one side as he tried to work out where this was going.

'Yes. It was a white Toyota Yaris and no one in the street drives one so it caught my eye. Plus, it was parked in a really inconvenient position on that corner.' She pointed towards the T-junction at the entrance to her street. 'It was there at four o'clock when I came home. I nearly crashed into it because it was blocking half the road.'

'Was that why the police came round?' Dan asked.

Her brow furrowed. 'They said there'd been an incident at Old Manor Hall, but you can't really see from our garden because we have quite a high fence. Do you know what happened?'

'They found a woman dead inside,' Dan said. 'I'm guessing the police thought she might be from here.'

The woman's eyes widened. 'Do you think that might have been her car?' she asked.

'Did the police take it away?' Dan asked.

'I don't know. I mean, once I'd spoken to them at the door, I went back to our living room, which is at the back of the house. It was gone this morning, so maybe they did. Or maybe the owner came back and moved it.' She shrugged, then glanced back at the boot of her car. 'Is that all you need? I've got frozen food in here and I have to put it away.'

Dan nodded, then reached into his pocket and pulled out a business card. Handing it over, he said, 'If you think of anything else, will you call me?'

The woman nodded and Dan turned away.

Had the woman found at Old Manor parked her car in the street and then approached on foot? He was sure the gates to the property were padlocked. Maybe she'd parked as close as possible and then somehow got through the boundary fence. But why? What had she been looking for? And had she found it or had someone found her first?

Chapter Four

Burton strode along the CID office, stilettos clacking on the floor. Shepherd looked up from his computer and gestured for her to join him.

'Talk to me,' she said, flopping down in the swivel chair at the desk next to his and twisting to face him.

Shepherd leaned his large frame back in his chair, making it creak loudly. 'I asked the guys over at Gravesend if they'd swing by her flat. They went quite early this morning, the before-work time they called it, and there was no one home. They spoke to a neighbour who said that she lives alone, but they'd not seen her since last week.'

'She's been missing for a week?' Burton asked, incredulous. 'Has her family not reported it?'

'So far nothing, but I searched her online and tracked down her employer. She's a doctor of history and works at the University of North Kent. I've left a message for them to call me back. They might know her family or, at least, where they are.'

Burton sighed. 'Anything else on her?'

'Not so far, but—' The ringing phone interrupted him.

'Keep me posted,' Burton said, getting to her feet as he reached for the receiver.

Her office windows looked out over the main office, and she watched as Shepherd spoke into the phone, pen flying across his notebook page. His forehead creased and she tapped her fingernails on her desk, willing it to be someone with good news. She hated delivering a death message, but keeping a family waiting was worse. When Shepherd replaced the receiver and got to his feet, he was smiling, albeit slightly grimly.

'She's local originally,' he said when he arrived in her doorway, 'and he was happy to give me her family's address.'

'And it's definitely the right Jayne Winter?'

'I described her to him and he said it sounded like her, so I think we're safe to go round and see the family.'

Burton sighed, got to her feet and picked up her handbag.

'I hate this part,' she said, following him out of the door.

Chapter Five

Burton and Shepherd followed Della Winter as she manoeuvred her wheelchair through the specially adapted door and into the living room. A young man rose from the sofa to greet them, and Della introduced him as her son Jordan. Even without being told, Burton reckoned she'd have known that he and Jayne were related. They had the same shade of blonde hair and matching eye shape that set them out as being brother and sister. His hair was longer and he swept his fringe from his eyes as he looked at them. Della gestured for them all to sit down. She parked her chair beside Jordan and he took her hand.

'Has something happened to my sister?' he demanded, leaning forward, body tense and braced for bad news.

Burton sat back slightly, which was Shepherd's cue to take the lead. She knew his experience of being on their side of the fence when his wife died in a hit-and-run several years ago gave him extra insight into what it was like to receive this news.

He spoke gently. 'The body of a woman was found at Old Manor Hall last night and she was carrying Jayne's driving licence. We'll need you to do a formal identification, but we believe it is her.'

Della gasped and tears slid down her face. Jordan passed her a box of tissues and she smiled at him gratefully as she took one.

'Do you know what happened?' he asked, perching on the edge of the sofa.

'We're still trying to figure it out,' Shepherd said. 'Can you think of any reason why Jayne would have gone to Old Manor?'

Jordan sighed. 'Simeon Burns,' he said, sounding tired.

Burton, expecting a negative answer, sat forward, slightly taken aback. 'Your sister was looking for a ghost?' she asked, wondering where this was leading.

Della smiled. 'I don't think she believed in those rumours,' she said. 'She was far too rational.'

'Why was she interested in him?' Burton asked.

'She went to Old Manor when it was a sixth form college,' Della said, patting her face with a tissue. 'They all have to do a research project about the Burns family and she spent hours on hers.'

'And she has a PhD in history now?' Shepherd asked.

Jordan nodded. 'Her research was on medieval social history and not in Allensbury.'

'So nothing to do with Simeon Burns?' Burton asked, struggling to bring the threads together in her head. Jordan shook his head. 'Jayne lived in Gravesend. Do you know why she was in Allensbury?' Burton added.

Della wiped her eyes on the tissue and tucked it up her sleeve. 'She just turned up on the doorstep on Friday saying she needed to stay.'

Burton stared at her. 'She hadn't told you she was coming?'

'No, but that wasn't unusual. She rarely told us what her plans were.'

Burton could see that Shepherd was as puzzled by this family as she was. 'She just said she had some research to do and she needed to be here,' Della added.

Remembering the footprints at the scene, Burton asked, 'Did Jayne have any friends who might have gone along to Old Manor with her?'

Jordan gave a slight snort and Della glared at him.

'Please, it's important that we know these details,' Burton said, feeling frustrated.

Jordan sighed. 'My sister didn't really have any friends. Oh, come on, Mum,' he said when Della cleared her throat meaningfully, 'you know that's true. She lacked people skills,' he said, looking at Burton and Shepherd. 'She could be single-minded and didn't suffer fools gladly, or people who she perceived as fools.'

'So, is there anyone who you think would hurt your sister?' Burton asked, an uncomfortable feeling settling in her stomach. 'Anyone she'd upset in the past?'

'Well, if you're looking for people she'd upset, you'll need a bigger pad,' Jordan said, gesturing to Shepherd's A5 pocket book. 'She had a habit of rubbing people up the wrong way, but I can't imagine anyone would kill her.'

Burton's stomach clenched. Was it a possibility that Jayne hadn't been a lone trespasser at Old Manor as she'd thought the previous evening? Had there been someone there who meant her harm?

'When was the last time you saw Jayne?' Burton heard Shepherd ask.

'Yesterday morning at breakfast,' Della said. 'She made tea and toast and then said she had to go out. She wouldn't tell me where.'

'Did she take anything with her?' Burton asked.

'She had a little shoulder bag. I didn't see what she put in it, but I assumed it was her purse, keys and mobile phone as usual.'

Shepherd leaned forward and Burton knew he was trying to be gentle. The next question was never an easy one to ask.

'Can you both tell me where you were on Tuesday between three and six o'clock?' he asked. As expected, both Della and Jordan looked shocked.

'You're actually asking for our alibis?' Jordan demanded, leaning towards Shepherd.

'Purely routine,' Shepherd said calmly, raising a hand. 'It's a formality.'

Della sighed. 'I was here. My carer Paula came round to check that I was OK and bring me some shopping.'

Shepherd turned to Jordan, eyebrows slightly raised.

'I was at work,' Jordan snapped, 'until five-thirty as usual and then I drove straight home.'

'Thank you,' Shepherd said, clicking away the nib of his pen.

His ability to diffuse angry family members was impressive, Burton thought. 'Does Jayne have a bedroom here?' she asked.

'Not as such,' Della said. 'I had to move out of our family home the year before last when this happened,' she gestured at the wheelchair, 'because I couldn't manage in such a big house, but I was lucky enough to find a bungalow that we could adapt. I have a spare room, so Jayne slept there.'

'Could we have a look at it?' Burton asked, wondering what Jayne had brought with her on a seemingly impromptu research trip.

Della nodded. 'Of course. She travels light, so it won't take you long. Jordan, can you show them?'

Jordan nodded and got to his feet. 'Sure, follow me.' He led the detectives out of the room.

***

Jayne Winter's room was spartan with just a double bed, wardrobe and a wooden table with a matching chair. Somehow Burton thought this mirrored a woman who didn't seem to have a personality yet in their investigation.

'Jayne moved the table in here when she arrived,' Jordan said, jamming his hands into his trouser pockets. 'She needed somewhere to work in private.'

His emphasis on the word *private* caught Burton's attention.

'Was your sister's work confidential?' she asked, her thoughts shifting like jigsaw pieces. Was there more to this woman than just historical research?

Jordan snorted. 'No, that's just how she was. Making a big deal of her stuff being so important. She was terrible for it when she was younger. Wouldn't let me or Kayleigh – that's our sister – anywhere near her room. I don't think she had anything particularly interesting in there. She just enjoyed winding us up.'

'Where is Kayleigh?' Burton asked, frowning.

'She's on a business trip in New York. Mum called her and she's trying to get a flight back.'

Burton opened the wardrobe and stepped back, surprised to find it empty.

'Jayne obviously wasn't staying here long,' she remarked, turning to Jordan, raising a questioning eyebrow.

Jordan nodded. 'She was acting really weird. I mean, more weird than normal.' He spoke in a way that suggested to Burton that there was no love lost between the two siblings.

'Acting weird, how?' Shepherd asked, lifting a black holdall onto the bed. He unzipped the bag and looked inside. A tangle of clothes greeted him.

'I got the impression that she hadn't wanted to tell us she was in town.'

'Not tell her family she was here?' Burton asked, puzzled. As soon as she thought a picture of Jayne Winter was building in her mind, it shifted like a kaleidoscope.

'I'm not sure she even liked us very much,' Jordan said. 'She could be really selfish. It was typical, really. She's not spoken to Mum for months and then turns up demanding a bed without saying how long for.'

There was definite animosity there, Burton thought, but was that normal sibling rivalry or something more?

Burton was about to ask something when Shepherd finished fishing about in the holdall and pulled out a laptop computer.

Jordan looked surprised. 'I'm amazed that it's not locked away,' he said. 'She was always really protective of her laptop.'

'We'll have to take that with us,' Burton said, and Jordan nodded.

'We didn't find a mobile phone at the crime scene,' Shepherd added. 'Do you know if she usually carried one?'

Jordan straightened up and stared at him. 'You didn't find her phone? She was surgically attached to it. She'd never have left it behind.'

'Can you ring it?' Burton asked, and Jordan quickly pulled his own phone from his pocket. But the call went unanswered.

Burton watched as Shepherd took a last scan around the room. Jayne Winter was still something of an enigma. A single-minded career woman who didn't care if she offended people, even her own family, who she hadn't wanted to tell that she was in town. Why? Was her work really confidential or was she just private? Either way, something was going on.

She looked up sharply as Shepherd cleared his throat and found him and Jordan both staring at her.

'I think that's everything for now,' she said crisply, and Jordan led the way back to the sitting room. Della looked deep in thought, staring at a photograph of her daughter on the mantelpiece and shook herself when they entered.

'We'll be off just now,' Burton said. 'We've got Jayne's laptop, which we'll need to investigate, and we'll arrange the formal identification.'

'I'll do that,' Jordan said quickly, but Della shook her head.

'We'll both do it. I owe her that much.'

'There'll be a post-mortem as well,' Burton said, bracing herself for the reaction.

Della gasped. 'Do you have to cut her?' she asked, bottom lip wobbling.

Jordan crossed the room and sat down beside her. 'They have to, Mum, to find out what happened to her.'

Della looked like she was going to argue, but then nodded, a tear falling down her cheek.

'We'll see ourselves out,' Shepherd said, but Jordan followed them to the door.

'Jayne could be difficult, but surely not enough to make someone kill her,' he said in a low voice.

'We're still working out what happened. It may have been an accident, but we need to keep all our options open.'

'You'll let us know what you find?'

'As soon as we know, you'll know,' Burton promised. She glanced back when they reached the car to see Jordan still watching them, an odd expression on his face. A feeling stole over her. Did he know more about his sister's activities than he was letting on?

Chapter Six

As they walked through the doors to the morgue early on Thursday afternoon, Shepherd gave a shudder.

'Don't be so dramatic,' Burton said with a laugh, trying to keep her own shiver under wraps.

'I'm not. It's freezing in here. It gives me the creeps. Like someone walking over your grave.'

'You say that every time,' she said, glancing over her shoulder, 'and you know what Eleanor will say.'

'Eleanor will say stop moaning. I can't turn the heating on just for you,' Brody said, appearing at their elbow making them both jump.

Burton started, making Shepherd laugh and earning him a glare. The pathologist seemed to be set permanently in stealth mode as she moved around the room. 'So what do you know?' she asked, trying to cover her surprise.

Brody walked to the work surface and picked up her clipboard. Shepherd pulled out his notebook.

'As you suspected, the ceiling fall was not accidental,' she said.

'Someone brought the plaster down on her?' Burton asked. She could feel her heart beat faster. She'd been right.

'Yes. They've used a pole or something to loosen it so it caved in, but that's not what killed her.' Brody turned to the computer on the work surface and clicked the mouse a few times and some pictures appeared on a whiteboard.

Shepherd looked impressed. 'Wow, new technology,' he said.

'I got fed up with trying to show people images on a small screen, so I squeezed some money out of my budget, An interactive whiteboard has many uses.'

'What am I looking at?' Burton asked, stepping closer to the screen.

'These are photos taken during Dr Winter's post-mortem,' Brody said. She expanded one picture and indicated for Burton to look. Burton wrinkled her nose, but then widened her eyes as she realised what she was looking at. 'A head wound,' she said.

Brody nodded. 'And, as I suspected, not consistent with a fall from the upper floor or from the plaster falling from the ceiling.'

'She died from a blow to the head? With what?' Burton asked, her brain whirring.

'Looks like it was made of wood, so probably something that was lying around in the room. Something cylindrical, a chair leg maybe.' Brody shrugged. 'The crime scene team is still down there so they're checking to see if they can find it, but I'm not hopeful. That place is a mess.'

Shepherd looked up from his notebook. 'Your theory that there was someone else there bears out,' he said to Burton.

She smiled grimly. 'Did she die quickly?' she asked Brody.

The pathologist nodded. 'There are two blows, but the internal damage suggests she likely wouldn't have survived after the first one, even if help was summoned.'

Burton rubbed her forehead. 'Someone definitely didn't want her getting back up again. But why was she, or indeed they, at Old Manor in the first place? She must have been looking for something, but what? The place is derelict.'

'Her family didn't seem to know what she was up to,' Shepherd said, 'but it didn't sound like she took people into her confidence.'

'Apart from the person she was with?' Burton asked, tilting her head to one side and looking at Brody. 'They came with her, or they followed her and caught her out?'

Brody shrugged. 'Nothing in my evidence to tell you that, I'm afraid.'

Burton ran a hand through her long blonde hair, which was not in its usual ponytail. Not enough time this morning with her girls playing up before school. 'They bashed her over the head and then brought a load of plaster down on her to hide what they'd done. Then they left her there to die, so they obviously weren't friends.' She sighed. 'This is making my head hurt.'

'Any indication of time of death?' Shepherd asked.

Brody consulted a clipboard lying on the nearby work surface. 'Probably about thirty minutes to an hour before officers arrived on scene.'

Burton and Shepherd stared at her.

'How can you be so precise?' Burton demanded. 'You usually tell me off when I ask for that.'

Brody smiled. 'The blood had only just started to coagulate when I was looking at the body in situ.'

'Anything else?' Burton asked, looking back at the images on the screen.

'I may have saved the best 'til last,' Brody said, looking slightly smug.

Burton made a rolling motion with her hand, indicating to Brody to hurry up.

'Fingerprints,' Brody said.

Burton and Shepherd both frowned.

'But you said there's no murder weapon, so where are the fingerprints?' Shepherd asked.

'That bookcase you spotted' – Brody pointed at Burton – 'turned out to be the door to a secret room.'

Burton's eyes widened and her chest tightened. 'A secret room?' she asked.

'That's a bit *Famous Five*, isn't it?' Shepherd asked.

Brody raised a hand to stop their interruptions. 'Let me finish. As you'd expect, Dr Winter's fingerprints were on it, but there were two other sets, and they're male, judging by their size.' She smiled at their shocked faces. 'I do love it when I can surprise you.'

Burton grinned. 'Me too.' Then her mobile phone burbled in her pocket. She pulled it out and groaned. 'Suzy Press Office,' she said.

Brody glanced around the room. 'Is this place bugged? So she knows exactly when to call you for an update?'

Shepherd laughed. 'I think she actually has some sort of spidey sense.'

'Whatever tracking system she's got,' Burton said, pressing the button to answer, 'at least we'll have something to tell her. This is a murder enquiry.'

Chapter Seven

The afternoon rolled around and, still waiting for a police update, Dan sat at his desk, squinting down at the scribbled shorthand notes in his book. It was almost illegible because of numb fingers and a steady drizzle when he'd interviewed the hospital director at the ground-breaking of the new ward. Why they were starting building work in November, Dan would never know. What was wrong with nice, warm indoor projects?

With no way to protect the page, neither pen nor pencil had really worked on damp paper. He could just about decipher what the man had said and began typing up his notes. His hair, which had also been drizzled on, stuck up in its usual clumps, with no attempt made to calm it down. No hair products in the world had ever made it look tidy, so he'd given up trying.

Daisy cleared her throat and Dan held up three fingers, indicating the number of minutes he needed. She turned back to her computer, but he could feel the eyes that he was sure existed in the back of her head staring at him. Computer keys rattling, he finished with a flourish and pressed send. He gave a sigh of relief and rubbed his eyes. That was all his copy done for today's edition of the newspaper.

He jumped as the editorial assistant strode past, thumping a package in front of him. He scrambled to move his keyboard out of the way and opened his mouth to complain, but she was already halfway across the office. Dan picked it up, weighing it in his hand. The parcel was lighter than it had sounded. He tugged hard at the padded envelope, still wet from the rain, but when it didn't open, he grabbed scissors from his drawer and attacked it. A leather-bound notebook slid out of the package and Dan just managed to grab it before it hit the floor. The battered cover had almost split along the spine and the corners of the book looked like they'd been chewed. He recognised the damage caused by it being repeatedly shoved in and out of a bag or pocket. He flipped open the cover and stroked the first page. Tiny, cramped ballpoint pen handwriting covered it. He squinted down at the page. The handwriting was almost as illegible as his shorthand. The pages that followed were crisp with hand-written scribbled notes and photocopied documents and photographs stuck to them.

He was so engrossed that he jumped when the phone rang and dropped the notebook on the floor. Behind him, he heard the junior reporters sniggering. Treating them with the contempt they deserved, he grabbed the phone and was pleased to hear the voice of the police press officer.

'I have an update for you,' she said without preamble.

Retrieving the notebook from the floor, Dan scrabbled on his desk for his pen and reporter's notebook. 'Go ahead.'

Suzy switched into her giving-a-statement voice. 'Police investigating the death of a woman at Old Manor Hall have today launched a full-scale murder enquiry. Dr Jayne Winter, thirty-three, was found on Tuesday by three teenagers trespassing on the site. Dr Winter was—'

'Wait a second,' Dan interrupted, scribbling in his reporter's notepad. 'Did you say Jayne Winter?'

Suzy paused. 'Yes, why?'

'I know a Jayne Winter.'

'How?'

Dan rubbed his forehead. 'I went to school with her at Old Manor, but I've not seen her for years. Do you think it could be the same person?'

'No idea. That'll be part of the investigation,' Suzy said. 'Shall I continue?'

'Yes, sorry.' Dan felt a bit discombobulated by the news. He hadn't particularly been friends with Jayne, but had sat next to her in their A Level history class.

'Dr Winter was found at around seventeen fifteen in the afternoon. She had suffered a fatal head injury, caused by a blunt instrument. Officers are appealing for information as to why Dr Winter was at Old Manor and would like to hear from anyone who saw her in the area.' She paused. 'All OK so far?'

'Yup,' Dan said, scribbling furiously to keep up.

'OK, so, Detective Inspector Jude Burton, Senior Investigating Officer at Allensbury CID, said, "This was a savage attack, which left a young woman dead. At present, we do not know why Dr Winter was at Old Manor Hall and we would ask anyone who saw her or her white Toyota Yaris in the area on Tuesday to come forward. Any detail, however small you think it may be, could be vital, so please call the incident room. Dr Winter's family has been informed and they would much appreciate your help in finding out what happened to her".'

'A Toyota Yaris?' Dan asked. 'Is that the one they found in

Oxton Estate?'

'How do you know about *that*?' Suzy demanded.

'I went for a look and bumped into the woman who reported the car,' Dan said. 'Sometimes it's all about luck.'

'I'm sorry about your friend and that you had to find out from me like this,' Suzy said, suddenly serious.

Dan shrugged. 'She wasn't really a friend, but when it's someone you know, who you saw every day at school, it's a bit weird.'

'Do you know if she had any friends locally?'

Dan shook his head, even though Suzy couldn't see him. 'I don't think she had any friends at school. It sounds awful, but she wasn't a very nice person. Considered herself too clever for the rest of us.'

'There's always one,' Suzy said. 'The family hasn't been asked about doing a tribute piece, but shall I see whether they'll speak?'

'Yes, please,' Dan said. 'I don't know them, but it would definitely be of interest.'

'I'll send you over a photo of her as well,' Suzy said. 'If you can run it alongside the article, it might help jog people's memories if they've seen her. Obviously, if you think of anyone from your school days who could help us, get them to call the CID office.'

Dan thanked her and hung up. He stared into space for a moment. It was bizarre but, now he thought about it, he remembered Jayne Winter so clearly.

'Hey, mate,' came a voice and a thud as a rucksack landed on a nearby desk. Dan started and almost dropped his pen.

'Sorry,' said Ed, as he stood at the desk opposite Dan's, shaking water off his coat. 'It's bucketing out there.' He saw Dan's puzzled face and asked, 'What's the matter?'

Dan recounted what Suzy had told him.

Ed screwed up his face. 'I don't remember her at all, but how sad. Her poor family.'

'She did A Level history with me. Short, slightly tubby, always scowling and being unpleasant to people.'

'That rings a vague bell, but I can't picture her.' He pointed at Dan's desk. 'What's that?'

'Is it stating the obvious to say a notebook?' Dan asked, grinning.

Ed rolled his eyes. 'Yes, it is, but it was a bit of a rhetorical question, wasn't it?' He laughed too. 'Whose is it?'

'I don't know, it just came through the post. No note with it.'

Ed opened his mouth to speak, but before he could say anything, a loud cough from Daisy made them both look round.

'Ed? Court copy? We do have a deadline.'

Ed winced. 'Sorry, Daisy, on it now.' He pulled a face at Dan as he returned to his desk and sat down. 'Tell me more at home later.'

Chapter Eight

'So we know that apart from Jayne Winter, two people – both male – have also been to the murder scene,' Burton said slowly as Shepherd drove them back to the police station. 'Those fingerprints were too big for our three ghost hunters, so who was it?'

'And was one or both of them with Jayne when she found the secret room?' Shepherd asked, eyes fixed on the road.

Burton frowned. 'I suppose they could have been. The question is whether one of them killed Jayne Winter and why.'

'And what the other one was doing while the attack was taking place,' Shepherd added.

Burton stared out of the window, then turned to look at him. 'I have more questions now than I have answers.' She counted them on her fingers. 'Why was Jayne there at all? What was she looking for and did she find it? Were the two other people there at the same time? Did they find it?'

She hated loose ends and Shepherd looked as puzzled as she felt.

'Her mum said that she has an interest in Simeon Burns,' Shepherd said. 'Maybe she was looking for his ghost, too.' When Burton glared at him, he laughed. 'Only kidding.'

'What about that room behind the bookcase?' Burton asked. 'What's that all about?'

'If that was the principal's office, maybe it was for locking up naughty children?'

Burton laughed. 'I wouldn't mind taking another look at it. If Jayne was interested in it, maybe it'll help us work out why she was looking for it.'

Shepherd nodded. 'I'll get Topping or Madison to check when the building will be safe for us to go back there.'

Burton's phone beeped and she pulled it out of her bag, checking the screen. 'Good news,' she said. 'Jayne's boss at work has emailed to say he's free tomorrow if we want to see him.'

'Her laptop has gone to the tech team,' Shepherd said, 'so hopefully there'll be some answers there.'

Burton rested her elbow on the window sill and stared out of the car window, her brain whirring with ideas. Then she sat up straighter. 'Right, I want to go back to the office and see if we can build a timeline of what Jayne Winter was doing and who she came into contact with since she came back to Allensbury.' Her mobile rang in her hand. Looking at the screen, she groaned. 'Suzy Press Office again,' she said. She sighed and answered the call. She listened in silence for a moment. 'You're sure? That's what he said?' When she hung up the phone, Shepherd glanced sideways at her.

'What?' he asked.

'We've got another stop to make,' Burton said. 'You'll never guess who knows Jayne Winter.'

***

37

Burton's fingers were tapping on her knees as they waited in the car outside Dan and Ed's flat.

'What time did they leave the office?' she demanded.

'When I called, they'd only left about ten minutes ago so they'll be here shortly. It's not a long walk.'

'Hmmm, unless they go via the pub,' Burton said, glowering, 'which wouldn't surprise me.'

Out of the corner of her eye, she saw Shepherd open his mouth and then close it again. Just then she spotted the two journalists strolling across the car park towards the block of flats. 'There they are,' she said, quickly opening the door and stepping out of the car. Dan and Ed both stopped abruptly when they saw her and glanced at each other.

'What are you doing here?' Dan asked, approaching. 'I just spoke to Suzy and the update will be in tomorrow's paper.' His eyes widened. 'Is there more already?'

Burton shook her head. 'I spoke to Suzy as well and I understand you know Jayne Winter.'

Dan frowned. 'Well, sort of. I mean, we both went to school with her but we weren't friends as such.'

'Shall we talk inside?' Burton pointed towards the building. She followed the two men as they let themselves into the building and climbed the stairs to their floor, Shepherd bringing up the rear. Once inside the flat, she and Shepherd were ushered into the living room.

Dan pointed them to seats. 'Do you want a cuppa?'

Burton shook her head. 'No, thanks.'

Dan and Ed sat side by side on the sofa, looking like naughty children outside the principal's office, Burton thought. She seated herself on an armchair while Shepherd fetched a chair from the dining table at the other end of the room.

'So,' Dan asked, looking from one to the other, 'what's up?'

'Jayne Winter,' Burton began. 'How well did you know her?'

'Well,' Dan said, 'like I told Suzy, we didn't really know her. I sat next to her in A Level history, but I hadn't seen or spoken to her in nearly twenty years.'

'She didn't get in touch with you when she was coming into town?' Burton asked.

Dan shook his head. 'I don't know why she would.'

Burton frowned. 'Can you think of anyone she would have contacted?'

Dan and Ed exchanged a glance. 'No, I mean, I don't think she had any friends at school,' Ed said. 'That sounds mean, but she wasn't a very nice person.'

Burton felt her shoulders slump. The lack of information about Jayne Winter was frustrating her.

If Jayne had no friends, then who were the men with her at Old Manor? she thought. *Could those fingerprints just be a coincidence?*

'Any idea why she might have gone to Old Manor?' she asked, leaning forward in her seat.

Dan shrugged. 'That place is a death trap. I'm surprised that it's never been knocked down and redeveloped.'

'It's the curse, mate. I've told you,' Ed put in. He looked at Burton. 'Simeon Burns cursed it. He's the guy who used to own it.'

Dan rolled his eyes. 'I don't think a ghost whacked her on the head,' he said.

Ed looked like he was about to retort, so Burton jumped in.

'Is there anyone else from school who you think might know anything about Jayne?' She watched Dan frown.

'There's a Facebook group for our year,' he said. 'I can post a message in there, if that would help?'

'If you could,' Burton said, feeling a flicker of hope, 'that would be great.'

'How's her family doing?' Ed asked.

'As well as can be expected,' Shepherd said.

'Suzy said she's going to ask about a tribute piece,' Dan asked.

'And if they say no, you leave them alone,' Shepherd said sternly.

Dan looked reluctant, but nodded in agreement.

Burton chewed a thumbnail. Jayne must have contacted someone. Maybe it had been through social media.

She realised that Dan, Ed and Shepherd were all staring at her.

'OK, that's all for now,' she said, unable to think of anything to ask. 'If you can post in your group and see if anyone else has heard from her or knows why she was here, that would be great. Likewise, if you get any tips after the article gets published, let us know straight away.'

Dan nodded and showed them to the door. 'Any help we can give,' he said.

As Burton and Shepherd got back into the car, she slapped a hand on the dashboard.

'This case is really getting up my nose,' she snapped.

Shepherd nodded. 'It seems like Jayne really kept herself to herself. Even her family doesn't know what's going on.'

'Right,' Burton said, clipping her seatbelt into place. 'I want a timeline of what Jayne's been doing since she got back, who she's been in touch with. Get onto tech and get her laptop and phone. They must have finished by now. Someone has to know what she was doing, and we've got to find them.'

Chapter Nine

Dan walked back into the living room and stared at Ed. 'I can't believe Jayne Winter was murdered,' he said. He flopped down onto the sofa, feeling slightly queasy. 'It's weird when it's someone you know of, but don't really know.'

Ed frowned. 'I just wish I could remember her.'

Dan pulled out his mobile and opened the Facebook app. He tapped the screen several times and then turned the phone to face Ed.

'Our final year photo,' Ed said gleefully, taking the phone. He peered at the screen for a moment. 'What the hell is my hair doing in this?'

Dan laughed. 'Three people along from the left in the second row as you're looking at it. That's her.'

Ed tapped the photo and zoomed into Jayne Winter's face. Then he clicked his fingers and sat back. 'Yes, I vaguely remember her. Always grumpy, never spoke to anyone?'

'Suzy's getting me an up-to-date photo to go alongside the article, so we'll soon find out what she looks like now,' Dan said, taking back the phone.

Ed's stomach rumbled loudly. 'What are you making for my dinner?' he asked.

Dan glanced at his watch. 'Oh crap, is it that time already?' He put his phone down on the coffee table and got to his feet. 'What do you fancy? Pasta?'

'As that's about the level of your cooking and we've not been to the supermarket yet this week, it'll have to do,' Ed said with a grin.

Dan glared at him and went into the kitchen. He filled the kettle with water and switched it on. As he bent to the cupboard to get plates, he remembered the notebook. He went into the living room and found his bag.

'What are you doing?' Ed asked. 'I'm hungry. Back to your kitchen, slave.'

Dan dug his hand into the bag and pulled out the envelope containing the notebook. He held it up.

'Oooh, I'd forgotten about that,' Ed said, leaning forward with his forearms on his knees.

Dan grinned and pulled out the notebook. A sheet of paper fluttered to the floor and he leaned down to pick it up. He read it and then looked at the postmark on the envelope. Immediately, his stomach started flickering.

'What? What is it?' Ed demanded.

Dan held out the letter to him without speaking.

'"Hi, Dan, you probably don't remember me, but I need your help,"' Ed read aloud. '"I've made a discovery and someone is trying to steal it."' He looked up at Dan.

'Keep reading,' Dan said, pointing at the page.

'"I've almost found what I need. Keep this notebook safe, don't read it and I'll call you in a few days. Don't tell anyone about this. That's very important. Don't tell anyone,"' Ed read. He peered down at the signature at the bottom of the letter. 'Does that say...?'

'It says Jayne Winter,' Dan said.

Ed stared at him. 'You mean—'

Dan held out the packaging and Ed took it.

'And check out the postmark.' He paused while Ed examined the plastic bag and then looked up, eyes widening.

'That means—'

Dan nodded. 'She posted it on Monday, the day before she died.'

Chapter Ten

Dan watched as Ed read the letter again and then held his hand out for the notebook. In silence, Ed flicked through a few pages, stopping at one in particular, looking up at Dan wide-eyed. He turned the book around and showed Dan a floor plan, drawn neatly.

'That's Old Manor,' he said. 'Shit, Dan, what the hell's going on? She sends you this notebook and then gets killed in the building?'

Dan nodded, his stomach flickering wildly. 'Sounds like it.'

'And you've definitely not heard from her recently?' Ed asked. 'Before this, I mean,' he added, holding up the notebook.

Dan shook his head. 'Like I told Burton, it's gotta be about twenty years since I saw her.' He scratched his head, trying to remember his last encounter with Jayne Winter. 'It was probably our leaving assembly.'

'So why has she contacted you? And how did she know where to find you?'

'Clearly she reads the newspaper,' Dan said. 'That's why she sent the book to the office.'

'Posted it rather than brought it by hand?' Ed asked.

Dan was frowning. 'That's a good point. Why not bring it herself?' He held out a hand and took the letter. 'She sounds frightened, doesn't she?' he asked, scanning the contents again. 'Maybe she was worried someone was following her.'

'What could she have found that someone would want to steal?' Ed asked.

'There's one way to find out,' Dan said, 'and that's reading her notebook.' He heard the kettle click off. 'Once I've fed your stomach, of course.'

***

After dinner, Dan sat down in the comfy armchair in the sitting room, his legs slung over one arm. He started reading the first page in the notebook.

Two articles from a Georgian newspaper about Allensbury's influx of workers from the rural areas into the town during the seventeen sixties were stuck to the second and third pages. The handwritten notes on those pages were scribbled in the margins and almost illegible.

Dan stared at the articles. Something about the font used seemed very familiar, but he couldn't place it. He turned the page and found some notes where the handwriting was slightly clearer and started reading.

'"Simeon Burns was a rich silk mill owner, who inherited the Old Manor Hall in eighteen forty-one after the death of his father and lived there until his premature death in eighteen fifty-eight,"' he read aloud.

Then he sat up slightly. Underneath, Jayne had written 'not death, but murder', and underlined it three times.

He wracked his brains, remembering being made to do a project about Simeon Burns while he was at Old Manor, but his recollection was that the man had died of cholera. The rumours said that his ghost haunted the building because he'd cursed it as he lay dying, but he couldn't remember anything that implied murder. Did Jayne think someone had given him cholera on purpose? Was that even possible?

Ed came in from the kitchen, rubbing his hands together. 'Washing up is done,' he said. When Dan looked up and rubbed his eyes, Ed added, 'You'll do yourself a mischief trying to read that.' He flopped onto the sofa and reached out to take the book from Dan.

'She says Simeon Burns was murdered,' Dan said.

Ed looked up from the page. 'I'm not surprised. Simeon Burns was a pretty unpleasant fella as I recall. He sounded like he'd be on a lot of people's hit lists.'

'But that's just it. I don't remember there ever being anything about him dying of anything but natural causes.'

'It was cholera, wasn't it?'

Dan nodded. 'And he cursed the family as he was dying and so haunts the building, blah, blah.'

Ed looked up. 'That curse is real, mate. Why do you think the site hasn't been developed into houses? Simeon Burns is protecting his property.'

Dan rolled his eyes. 'There's no such thing as a curse,' he said. 'What worries me more is that Jayne says she found out something that someone wants to steal, so she sent it to me for safekeeping. Now she's dead. What could she possibly have found after all this time that would be worth killing over?'

Chapter Eleven

Sophie Madison was standing at a whiteboard in the office's corner when Burton and Shepherd arrived. She was tapping a marker pen on her palm and frowning. Burton dropped her coat off in the office and then joined her. A red line ran across the board, broken up into smaller sections.

'What have you got, Soph?' she asked, looking at the red pen markings. Clearly, she and Madison were on the same wavelength because she hadn't even issued the instruction yet.

'I thought I'd make a start on Jayne Winter's timeline,' Madison said. 'Not that we have a massive amount to go on at the moment.' She pointed at the start of the timeline. 'She's last seen at her home about a week ago by the next-door neighbours.'

'Then turns up at her mum's on Friday,' Burton said, pointing to one of the smaller marks.

Madison nodded. 'After that, there's a gap until she's found dead on Tuesday afternoon.'

'And we've got no idea what happened to her – what she was doing during that time?' Burton asked, frowning.

'Nope.'

'She didn't meet anyone? Speak to anyone?'

Madison shook her head. 'We don't know.' When Burton's eyes narrowed, she continued, 'We don't have her mobile, so we don't know if she called anyone.'

'Has that not shown up yet?' Burton snapped. Then, seeing Madison's expression, she said, 'Sorry, have you tried calling the forensic team?'

'They say there wasn't one at the scene. I also tried tech, and they say they're working on the laptop but there's a backlog and they're not sure when they'll be able to get back to them.'

'We'll ask Mark to use his charm on them,' Burton said, looking at Shepherd slyly over her shoulder. 'He seems to have an impact in getting stuff through tech.'

'That's exploitation,' Shepherd remarked, making Madison giggle.

Burton stood back, arms folded. *How did you find out what someone had been up to when they have no friends to speak to?* she thought.

'She leaves home, arrives in Allensbury but won't tell her family why, and then does what?' Burton asked, gesturing towards the board and then shrugging.

'Goes to Old Manor Hall and gets killed,' Shepherd said.

'But why?' Burton folded her arms. 'We know she was into this Simeon Burns fella, but why wait until after dark to go to his house?'

Shepherd frowned. 'She was looking for something and found that secret room, whether by design or accident, we don't know.'

Burton growled. 'But what was she actually looking for if it wasn't that room?'

'She obviously didn't find it,' Madison remarked. Burton and

Shepherd both turned to look at her.

'What makes you say that?' Shepherd asked.

'Well, she didn't have anything in her pockets barring her purse and car keys,' Madison said with a shrug. 'If she'd found something, then it would have been there.'

'Unless,' Burton said slowly, stepping towards the board, 'we were right and there was someone there with her.'

'And they killed her and took whatever it was?' Shepherd asked.

'It makes sense,' Burton said, 'but how the hell do we find out who it was and why they left her there to die?' She glared at her watch. 'I need to brief the boss, and then I think it's time we headed home. Tomorrow, Mark and I will speak to Jayne's boss at work. Sophie, I want you and Gaz to get onto her social media accounts, if she has any. See who she's been in contact with and what they've been talking about. Someone must know why she was here. We need to track them down now.'

Chapter Twelve

When Burton and Shepherd arrived at the University of North Kent the following day, Gregory Welch, Jayne's line manager, was waiting for them in the history department front office.

'I thought it was easier than you trying to find me,' he said. 'Shall we get a coffee? Let's find somewhere where we'll be able to chat in peace.'

He led the way into a silent room that contained some low wooden armchairs decorated as if they were from the seventies. The air was musty, and the silence hung like a heavy blanket. Burton wrinkled her nose, hoping she wouldn't start sneezing.

Give me a noisy office anytime, she thought.

Welch directed them to sit and Burton's armchair sank beneath her, making her worry whether she'd be able to get up again. She glared at Shepherd, who had smirked as he sat on the low wooden table arranged between the armchairs instead. Welch joined them, bringing coffees from the vending machine in the corner of the room, and they accepted gratefully. Perching on an armchair opposite them, Welch poured two sugars into his coffee, stirring it with a wooden stick that masqueraded as a spoon. He put it down on the table and looked up, mouth pulling down at the corners.

'Such sad news about Jayne,' he said. 'I couldn't believe it when you called me. Her poor family. How are they?'

'In shock and wondering who would have killed their daughter and sister,' Burton said, shortly. They needed to get something useful out of this conversation and pleasantries weren't going to do it.

Welch seemed not to notice her sharpness. 'Pass on my best to them, won't you?' He sighed. 'In fact, no. I'll have some flowers sent instead. That seems more appropriate.'

'How well did you know her?' Burton asked.

Gregory puffed out his cheeks. 'We'd worked together for about six years, on and off, but I don't feel like I knew her at all. She was very much a closed book, kept herself to herself. She seemed to find conversation difficult unless you were discussing her work.' He gave a mirthless laugh. 'I hope I'm not doing her a disservice, but she had a very prickly personality.'

Burton nodded, and Shepherd scribbled in his notebook. 'We've heard from several other sources that she could be difficult. Did she have issues with any other staff members or students?'

Gregory ran a hand through his short, grey curly hair. 'She could be downright obstructive and very single-minded. It didn't really endear her to other members of the department. We kept her away from teaching duties after the first year she was here because she had such critical reviews from students.'

'Reviews?' Shepherd stared at him. 'Like books or restaurants?'

Gregory smiled. 'Sorry, bad choice of words. Evaluation is probably more accurate. It's so we can give feedback and support lecturers who are struggling. Jayne's scores were appalling. She made one student cry by mocking her in a seminar for asking what she considered to be a stupid question.'

'And was it a stupid question?' Burton asked, raising her eyebrows.

Gregory shook his head. 'There's no such thing, in my opinion. Jayne could be quite cruel when she felt someone wasn't up to standard – her standard, not everyone else's – and I could never work out whether or not she knew she was doing it.'

Burton paused. She was getting an uncomfortable feeling in her stomach about Jayne Winter. The pool of potential suspects seemed to widen the more people they spoke to. 'So, you pulled Jayne away from teaching. What did she think of that?'

'She was more than happy. In fact, I wondered whether her behaviour was deliberate to get her out of teaching. She said at least she was away from idiots who didn't know what they were talking about, although she still had to work with others in the department.'

Shepherd grimaced. 'Ouch. She actually said that about her colleagues? Did they know she thought like that?'

Welch wrinkled his nose. 'Generally speaking, I don't think so, but she had a row with another staff member, Davis McKenzie, after she called him an amateur and said he should give up researching because he'd never had an original thought.' He nodded at the surprised expressions on the detectives' faces. 'Exactly.'

'We were told that she didn't suffer fools gladly, but that's way over the line. Did you discipline her?' Burton asked, watching Shepherd make a note of Davis McKenzie's name.

Welch nodded. 'Yes, but it was like water off a duck's back. She just didn't care. Said the only thing that mattered was her research and I couldn't take that away from her.'

'When did this happen?'

'About eighteen months ago.'

'And what happened after that?'

'Well,' Gregory said, 'I secured a one-year secondment for her at Allensbury University. An old friend in the history department owed me a favour and—'

'Wait a minute, she was in Allensbury all last year?' Burton demanded, glancing at Shepherd. Jayne's family hadn't mentioned this at all.

Gregory met Burton's eye steadily. 'It was the only way I could see to get her and Davis away from each other. I hoped it would give time for things to blow over.'

'Do you know who she was working with?' Shepherd asked. Burton was glad he had a question to ask, because she was desperately trying to process what Jayne's being in Allensbury might mean.

'No one in particular. She was there as a senior researcher, and I recommended she be given as little teaching as possible.'

Burton frowned. 'What was she researching?'

Gregory looked surprised. 'Her usual subject: she was writing a paper on a new document on display at the British Library in London.'

'It wasn't anything to do with Simeon Burns?' Shepherd asked.

'Who?' Gregory asked, looking puzzled.

Burton changed tack. 'Had things blown over with Davis when she got back?'

Gregory winced. 'Unfortunately, Davis isn't one to let a grudge go. He made the effort to find her and tell her what he thought of her. I warned him I'd end up having to discipline him if he didn't behave, but he said—' Gregory stopped suddenly as if he'd said too much.

Burton leaned forward. 'He said what?' When Gregory didn't answer, she said, 'Dr Welch, this is a murder enquiry. There's such a thing as obstruction of justice and that can mean a minimum of a year in prison.'

'He said if I didn't get rid of her, then he would,' said Gregory miserably.

Burton exchanged a look with Shepherd, who requested Davis McKenzie's address from Welch. The other man nodded, his mouth turning down at the corners. Then he frowned.

'Actually, Davis isn't the only person she argued with recently,' Gregory said, sitting up as if inspiration had just struck. 'I saw her with another man last week – or was it the one before – either way, they were shouting at each other.'

Burton sat forward, feeling her pulse quicken. 'Did you see who it was?'

'I didn't recognise him,' Gregory said, brow furrowing, 'but he was tall with blonde hair. He was calling her selfish, said she needed to remember where her loyalties lay.'

'What did she say?' Burton asked.

'She slapped his face and said she was perfectly aware of her duty and she didn't need him reminding her. She had other priorities just now. Then she turned to walk away, but he grabbed her arm. He said she would be sorry if she didn't come good on her promises. At that point, I thought it best to intervene. He stormed off and I asked if she was OK. She just said, "What can you do when even your own family doesn't understand why some things are more important than them?"'

Chapter Thirteen

Dan was queuing in the Italian café and yawning repeatedly, when someone prodded him hard in the back. He jumped and spun around to find Ed grinning at him.

'You got away from your desk,' Ed exclaimed. 'I thought you'd be chained there all day, waiting for a police update.'

Dan rolled his eyes. 'I've not even had time to think about it. Daisy's been burying me under stuff while I wait.'

'What time did you go to bed? You look wrecked.'

Ed was lucky that the woman at the counter asked for Dan's order so he couldn't deliver a death glare.

'I do *not* look wrecked,' Dan replied as they waited for his sandwich to be made. Then he caught sight of himself in the mirror on the wall. 'Ooh, actually, you know I'm surprised I've not scared any small children or dogs.'

Ed laughed and ordered for himself. 'I thought you'd swallow the room with that last yawn.'

'I didn't sleep very well. Too much going on in my head.'

Ed nodded. 'Took me a while to settle. I kept thinking about Jayne Winter.'

Dan nodded, but in reality it had been his stomach flickering that kept him awake past midnight. He was sure the notebook was going to reveal why Jayne died. He just needed to figure it out. Then he realised Ed had asked him a question.

'What?'

'I said ... What do you think Jayne had found out that someone wanted to steal?'

Dan puffed out his cheeks. 'All I can see so far is that Simeon Burns was murdered, but why would someone care about that now?'

Ed frowned. 'Yeah, I mean Simeon Burns died in, what...' he stared off into space, 'eighteen fifty something. How could something from two hundred years ago be so important that Jayne would get killed over it?'

Dan turned as the woman called his name and took his sandwich and coffee with a smile. He stepped over to a nearby table, out of the way of other queuing customers. Ed joined him a minute later, also armed with food.

Dan picked up his panini and then put it down again. 'If Jayne was researching Simeon Burns, then that would explain why she went to Old Manor.'

'She thought there was proof at the school after all these years?' Ed asked, mushing baked beans and cheese into a jacket potato.

Dan puffed out his cheeks. 'I think I'm clutching at straws, but maybe we need to—'

'No,' Ed said immediately.

'You don't even know what I was going to say,' Dan protested.

'I know exactly what you were going to say. You were going to suggest going to Old Manor, and it's a flat no from me. It's too dangerous.'

Dan sighed heavily. 'I suppose you're right. I went down a bit of a rabbit hole last night researching Jayne after you'd gone to bed.'

'And?' Ed asked, adjusting his chair to allow a large woman to pass him.

'Her normal research has nothing to do with Simeon Burns. It's usually medieval social history.'

Ed stopped with a forkful of potato halfway to his mouth. 'Are you going to tell the police about the notebook?'

Dan thought for a moment. His stomach was flickering, which was a good sign for any investigation. 'I suppose I have to, but I want to see what's in it first. I need to find out what happened to her.'

'You really want to hang onto something that might have got Jayne killed?' Ed asked, eyeing him doubtfully.

But Dan felt he was on a roll. 'Yes, I might find something that could help them.'

'Enough of the I,' Ed said. 'I want in on this investigation too and Emma will kill you if you cut her out.'

'I think she's in the mood to kill me, investigation or not,' Dan said glumly.

Ed groaned. 'Have you guys not patched things up yet?' When Dan didn't answer, Ed pointed at him with his fork. 'Em's solid and you guys make a great couple. You both want to move in together, so why not just do it?'

'You know why. She wants me to move into her place. I think we should get somewhere of our own.'

'Both very valid points. And neither of you will give in? So typical of you two. You're as bad as each other.'

'I'm not. I'm just—'

Ed rolled his eyes. 'Dan, if you weren't so stubborn, you guys would be living together already. I get it,' he said, holding up a hand to stop Dan's interruption. 'It's a big decision, but will you at least try to talk to each other without having a row? You'll have to find a compromise.' He glanced at his watch. 'Ooops, we need to get back. Daisy will be on the warpath after my court copy.' He scoffed the rest of his potato including the skin in a few mouthfuls while Dan finished his sandwich and coffee. 'When is Emma back from that secondment?'

'Next week,' Dan said, downing the rest of his coffee and piling the cup and saucer on top of his now empty plate.

'Promise me you'll talk about it then, without it turning into a row,' Ed said sternly as they got to their feet. 'I want this sorted out by the end of the month, or I'll kick you out myself.'

As he followed Ed out onto the high street, Dan thought about what Ed had said. It was true that he and Emma were both stubborn. But a compromise had to be found and he didn't know whether he was ready for that.

Chapter Fourteen

'So that's two things Jordan Winter lied to us about,' Burton snapped when they got back into the car. 'He failed to mention a stand-up argument with his own sister, and that she was working in town for a year.'

Shepherd started the engine and pulled on his seatbelt. Looking both ways, he pulled the car out of the space and drove out of the car park.

'Not so much lied as just didn't tell us,' he remarked, 'but I'll admit it's very suspicious that he didn't mention it. Her mum didn't say she'd been living in town either.'

Burton was thinking hard. 'What if,' she said, 'they didn't know? She might not have told them.'

Shepherd glanced at her. 'You think she kept it to herself?'

'That might explain him saying she was being selfish and for-getting where her loyalties lie, particularly with their mum being disabled and maybe needing help.' She sighed. 'But is that enough for him to hurt her?'

Shepherd was silent as he negotiated the roundabout onto the road back to Allensbury. 'We need to speak to him. Gaz was doing a background check, so he'll know where Jordan works.'

'Good point,' Burton said, pulling her phone from her handbag. She tapped a few buttons to put through a call. When Gary Topping answered, she asked him for the address and an update, putting the speaker phone on.

Topping reeled off the address of a solicitor's firm in town. 'You may want to query his alibi, though,' Topping said.

Burton held herself still. 'Why?'

'I spoke to his boss and apparently Jordan left at about three-thirty for a dentist's appointment.'

Burton smiled grimly, thanked Topping and hung up. 'Right, let's see what Mr Winter has to say for himself.'

***

'I don't know what else I can tell you,' Jordan Winter said as he led Burton and Shepherd into a small meeting room at the solicitor's office where he worked.

Burton waited until they were all seated before leaning forward on the table. 'Why didn't you tell us you had a row with Jayne?' she asked, fixing him with a beady stare. Jordan shifted in his seat and said nothing. 'You also failed to tell us that Jayne was in Allensbury for an entire year on a university secondment.'

Jordan took a deep breath and exhaled. 'I didn't know about the secondment,' he mumbled. 'Not at the time. Mum still doesn't know. If she did, it would kill her.'

'When did you find out?' Burton asked, resting her elbows on the table and cradling her chin on her hand.

'Just after it finished. A friend saw her coming out of a flat

61

complex down near the university and found out that she'd been living there for the entire time.'

Burton frowned. 'I thought she lived in Gravesend.'

Jordan nodded. 'She was renting a flat here to save on travelling, apparently. To give her more time in the library, I assume,' he said bitterly.

'It must have made you angry to hear what she'd done,' Burton said, hoping that some button pushing would get some results.

'Of course it did. To have a friend come to me and ask why I hadn't mentioned Jayne was back was embarrassing. I mean, my friend knows what she's like, but even she was shocked that I knew nothing about it.'

'So why wait until last week to shout at her about it, calling her selfish?' Burton asked. When Jordan looked uncomfortable, she said, 'Don't deny it. Jayne's boss has already told us what he saw.'

Jordan's head drooped. 'I was going to say something at the time, but I was so angry. I thought I'd let it go, but then Mum needed help with some hospital stuff and I asked Jayne to come over. She refused and I lost it. It's bad enough that she doesn't spend any time with Mum, but she'd gone too far by being back in town for a year and not telling us. When I asked her why, she just said that she hadn't needed to tell us.' He snorted. 'Hadn't needed to tell her own family she was living and working three miles from our mum's house. And then she has the audacity to land on Mum's doorstep last week and expect to stay with her.'

'Did you argue with her about that?' Shepherd asked, looking up from his notebook.

'I waited until Mum was out with her carer and then went over there on Sunday. She didn't even want to let me in the house. Said she was busy. Too busy to speak to her own brother, I ask you.'

'You said she was acting weird when you saw her. Did she say what she was working on?'

Jordan shook his head. 'She would never tell me anything about what she was doing. Made a big deal about keeping it private.'

Burton frowned. Did Jayne Winter have a good reason for so closely guarding her work? Could the academic profile be a cover for something else, something more sinister?

'Your alibi is falling apart too,' she said, glaring at Jordan. 'Apparently you left work at three-thirty for a dentist's appointment. Did you forget about that?'

Jordan shifted in his chair. 'I left for the appointment but then it got cancelled so I just went home.'

'Anyone see you return?' Shepherd asked, looking up from his notebook.

Jordan shrugged. 'I didn't speak to or see anyone, if that's what you mean.'

'Since the post-mortem took place, we now know that Jayne died from a blow to the head from a blunt instrument,' Shepherd began, using his gentle voice.

Jordan's bottom lip wobbled.

Shepherd continued, 'We also found two sets of fingerprints at the scene, both male, and—'

'You think that was me?' Jordan fired up immediately, and Burton could tell from Shepherd's slight smile that was exactly what he had intended.

'Not necessarily, but you can understand our suspicion when you have no alibi for the time of her death.' Shepherd paused. 'Do you recognise the name Davis McKenzie?'

Jordan shook his head. 'No. Who is he?'

'A colleague of Jayne's,' Shepherd said. 'Can you think of anyone else who might have wanted to hurt your sister?'

Jordan suddenly slapped a hand to his forehead. 'I forgot. There was a guy, Professor Sir Stewart Randall. I think he works at Allensbury University.'

Burton leaned forward on the table, relieved that they seemed to be getting somewhere. 'How do you know about him?'

'When I went round at the weekend, her laptop was open on the coffee table. She snapped it shut when she saw me looking, but I saw an email from Randall and the subject was "You'll be sorry you crossed me"'

Burton raised an eyebrow. 'What was it about?'

Jordan shook his head. 'I didn't really see it, but when I asked, she said they'd had an argument about an article and he'd threatened her.'

Shepherd exhaled slowly. 'He threatened her? How?'

'I'm not sure. She just said he was trying to stop her from publishing and that he'd do it by any means necessary.'

'Weren't you worried about that?' Burton asked, sitting forward and resting her elbows on the table.

Jordan shrugged. 'She said he was an old gasbag who didn't know what he was talking about and that she could handle him.' He sighed. 'So I let her deal with it herself. I was so angry.' He sniffed. 'Maybe if I'd done something, she'd still be alive.'

Leaving Jordan in the meeting room, Burton marched back to the car and leaned against it as Shepherd opened the doors.

'How does someone live in the world and leave so little evidence of their life, other than to make other people angry?' She frowned. 'I want Professor Sir Stewart Randall next. If he was issuing threats, then maybe he went further than that. I want to know if he's seen her since she's been back in town.'

Chapter Fifteen

Burton flung open the door to the CID office, making the people sitting nearest to it jump in surprise and papers blow off one desk onto the floor.

'Sorry,' she said in a perfunctory manner before storming away into her office. She saw Topping raise an eyebrow at Shepherd, who stopped and spoke in a low voice. Clearly he was explaining her bad mood, caused by being unable to find Professor Sir Stewart Randall. 'On a research visit', they'd been told at the university, and the door of his house – as well as his mobile – went unanswered.

She was hungry and that never helped her mood. Pulling open her desk drawer, she reached for the packet of emergency biscuits. A sugar boost was what she needed. A quiet cough made her look up. Topping stood in her office doorway, shifting from foot to foot. She gestured for him to come in and offered him a biscuit. He stuffed it into his mouth almost whole and chewed.

'That's no way to treat a chocolate Hobnob,' Burton said mock sternly, breaking hers in two and biting into one half.

'You'll understand when you hear my report from my interview with Davis McKenzie,' Topping said with a grin.

'Will I allow you a second Hobnob?' Burton asked, waggling the packet at him.

'Oh yes.'

She grinned and waved for Shepherd to join them. He eyed the biscuits and Burton offered the packet. He dispatched his biscuit in two bites and brushed the crumbs from his hands into the bin.

'So?' Burton asked, looking at Topping. 'What did Davis McKenzie have to say for himself?'

'He is one angry man,' Topping said. 'Apparently, even though Jayne was exiled to Allensbury University, she didn't go quietly.'

Shepherd smiled. 'Was "exiled" his word or yours?'

'Mine, but he made it sound like she was sent to the gulag or something. I was a bit offended on behalf of our lovely town.'

Burton waved at him to get on with the story, feeling her irritation levels rising again. A second biscuit went some way to quell it. 'What was she doing?'

'She managed to find time to review *all* his books, questioning his methodology, quality of research, referencing of sources, even alleging plagiarism, which is like a death sentence for an academic, apparently.'

Shepherd rolled his eyes. 'We've heard that before,' he said. 'So, what impact did all this have?'

'Well,' Topping scanned his notes, 'it meant that four papers he'd submitted, just before all this started, came back with suggestions that he check his sources and resubmit. When he did, they would be examined stringently before deciding to publish.'

Burton frowned. 'That doesn't sound too onerous.'

'It is when they're each thousands of words and there are hundreds of sources to be checked. They said he had to get his head of department to review them and sign an affidavit that he'd checked everything and it was all correct before they would even consider them.'

'Blimey, how long did that take?' Shepherd asked.

'Nearly four months and he couldn't submit anything until they were all done. Gregory Welch had his own work to do, which naturally he prioritised, so Davis had to wait. In the meantime, he's trying to carry on with work and putting up with snide comments from colleagues in the university and online.'

'She tried to ruin his career?' Burton asked, sitting forward and resting her elbows on the arms of her chair. 'That's an excellent motive for him.'

Topping nodded. 'Well, it was more like seriously dented than ruined. But it put a lot of stress on him at home, and his wife walked out for a few months and took the kids. They're back together now, but she was there when I interviewed him and I got the feeling she thinks he could be capable of it.'

'She said as much?'

'No, it was just that she didn't seem surprised I was asking him questions. There was a definite atmosphere.'

'Alibi?'

Topping grinned. 'That's just it. He was in Allensbury on the afternoon she was killed. Says he was at some event at the university, but I've checked with them and it's one of those things where you collect your ticket at the registration desk, but you don't have to speak to anyone after that. So he could easily have got his ticket and then left and no one would be any the wiser.'

Shepherd frowned. 'Is there anything to place him there, anyone he spoke to?'

'He said there wasn't anyone specific, but I've asked for CCTV footage from the building and surrounding area and also to speak to the students who were helping at the event. Hopefully that'll give us something.'

'Excellent, Gaz,' Burton said, and the DC beamed. 'So, we have an angry colleague in town on the night she died and who so far can't fully account for his whereabouts.'

'Gaz, can you see if automated number plate recognition can place his car anywhere near Old Manor,' Shepherd said. He sighed. 'Academics are such troublemakers.'

'And she seems like the worst of them,' said Burton, rubbing her chin. 'I'm seeing why she was so disliked if she goes to such lengths to destroy a colleague. Reading all those papers must have taken her ages, if she even genuinely read them. I would have thought she'd rather focus on her own work.' She sighed. 'OK, while we're waiting to hear back from Professor Sir Stewart Randall, let's see if we can set up interviews with some other Allensbury colleagues and find out what they know about the falling out between him and Jayne.'

Chapter Sixteen

Reading tiny cramped handwriting in tatty notebooks wasn't Dan and Ed's usual Friday night activity, but after a quick dinner, they settled back at the dining table. Dan's eyes were stinging as he tried to decipher Jayne's notes.

'Her writing is atrocious,' he grumbled, almost wishing he'd never started this.

'What does that say?' Ed asked, trying to hold the page up to the light.

Dan leaned over and screwed up his eyes. 'No idea,' he said.

Ed groaned. 'This is impossible.' He squinted at a photocopy of a handwritten document and then gave an 'Aha'.

'Aha what?' Dan asked, trying to peer at it.

'I can just about read this one. It's a letter from the doctor who was treating Simeon for cholera,' Ed read, the notebook almost against the end of his nose. 'He's written to another doctor saying, "Mr Burns claims that his suffering is greater than anyone who has contracted this disease, but he is prone to exaggeration and his temper so irascible by habit that his agitation is not taken seriously by his family. But, as one medic to another, this is beyond my skills.

He screams in pain from muscle cramps and swears that he is losing movement in his feet. I can do nothing to ease his torment. Please advise what I ought to do.'"

'What's his name?' Dan asked, pulling his laptop towards him and opening an internet browser.

'Oh God, no idea. His signature is totally illegible.' He flicked to the next page and back again. 'It doesn't look like Jayne knew either.'

Dan frowned. 'I thought cholera was mostly sickness and diarrhoea.'

Ed looked up at him. 'What do you mean?'

'Well, the doctor says he's complaining of muscle cramps and something wrong with his feet. Are they symptoms as well?'

Ed shrugged. 'I dunno. I'm not an expert on diseases.' He blinked several times and then rubbed his eyes.

'Stick to reading the printed articles for now,' Dan said, eyes fixed on his laptop as he entered search after search into the internet browser. Then he groaned. 'All I can find on cholera is what we know – nothing about muscles or feet.'

Ed handed him the book and then got up and walked away from the table, rubbing his eyes. 'I'm going to go blind staring at that,' he said.

Dan tilted the notebook towards the light and leaned closer to it. He ran his eye down one particular passage of Jayne's writing and then flipped over the page.

'Hang on,' he said. Then he read it again. 'Look at this.' He held the book up to Ed. 'Doesn't that look like it says something about a fire and Simeon Burns being blamed?'

Ed frowned. 'I don't remember anything about a fire.'

Dan screwed up his forehead. 'Was it something about Simeon

Burns' silk mill?' He grabbed his phone, tapped at the screen and then started typing.

'What is it?' Ed asked.

Dan grinned and held up the screen. 'I know somewhere else we should be able to find everything we need to know about Georgian Allensbury.'

Chapter Seventeen

When the Museum of Allensbury opened the next morning, Dan and Ed were standing on the doorstep. The woman who swung open the door jumped back and squeaked when she saw them, a hand flying to her chest.

'Sorry,' she said. 'I wasn't expecting anyone to be waiting.' They moved back as she stepped outside the door, bringing an A-frame advertisement board, which held a poster about a fundraiser.

'It's the museum's anniversary?' Dan asked, pointing at the poster.

The woman looked at him as if he should already know that and nodded. 'Allensbury Historical Society is raising money to have a permanent collection of Georgian Allensbury exhibits, so they're having a grand black-tie event in a few weeks. Tickets are fifty pounds, if you're interested.'

Dan whistled. 'A bit too rich for me,' he said, 'plus I don't have a tux.'

'Or a long frock?' Ed asked, and they both laughed.

The woman paused, looking at Ed, eyes narrowing.

'It's Ed, isn't it? Ed Walker?' she asked.

Ed's eyes widened. 'Yes. Why?'

'You don't remember me, do you?'

Ed's blank expression answered her question and Dan suppressed a laugh.

'Sorry, I don't.'

'Gracie Lincoln. I went to Old Manor Sixth Form with you. And you,' she said, looking at Dan. When neither spoke, she laughed and ran a hand through her short elfin-cut blonde hair. 'I look a bit different these days, now I've got contact lenses and have lost about five stone.'

As she turned back into the building, Dan tried to picture her at school, but a glance between him and Ed showed he couldn't conjure up an image either. The woman waved a hand airily as if it didn't matter, but Dan saw the corners of her mouth twitch downwards. When she stood behind the ticket office counter, her smile had returned.

'Anyway, you look great,' Dan said, smiled back at her. 'I'm guessing we look pretty different, too.'

Gracie tilted her head on one side. 'No, not really. A few more lines round the eyes, but your hair definitely hasn't changed.'

Ouch, thought Dan, resisting the urge to check out his reflection in the glass front door.

'How've you been? Worked here for long?' Ed asked brightly.

Dan winced. Clearly Ed felt bad about not recognising her.

'About two years.' She looked around. 'I've always wanted to work here, but there weren't any jobs when we left school. I studied history at university and lived in London for a good few years, but I always wanted to come back.'

'You finally achieved your dream,' Ed continued in a slightly too-jovial voice.

Dan tried to nudge him to stop over-compensating, but couldn't reach him.

Gracie smiled. 'What brings you two here on a sunny Saturday? Shouldn't you be out playing football or something?'

Dan glanced at Ed. Did Gracie think they were all still sixteen-year-olds? 'Er, no. We actually wanted to see the Georgian Allensbury exhibition,' he said, pointing to the poster on the wall.

Gracie's eyes narrowed slightly, but then she smiled. 'It's certainly been one of our most popular exhibitions.' She pressed a few buttons on the till and said, 'It's free to get into the museum, but the special exhibition costs ten pounds each.'

Dan glanced at Ed, who held out his hands to show he had no cash on him, and pulled out his wallet. He handed Gracie a twenty-pound note and she briskly tapped some buttons on the till. 'You'll probably want one of those as well,' she said, pointing to some red-fronted paper booklets on the counter. 'It's a guide written by the Allensbury Historical Society about the exhibition.' Dan picked one up, and she continued, 'They're three pounds fifty.'

Dan dug a hand in his pocket for the coins and handed them over. *This is proving to be an expensive day*, he thought.

Gracie handed over the tickets and directed them towards the entrance of the exhibition. As they turned away, she remarked, 'I tell you who hasn't changed since school days: Jayne Winter.'

Dan and Ed turned slowly back to face her. Gracie was rearranging the already tidy pile of guidebooks with a smile on her face, but it wasn't a happy smile.

'When did you see her?' Dan asked, feeling his stomach tighten.

'She was in here last Saturday. She looks different, but she's still the same unpleasant cow she was back then.'

'What did she want?'
'Same as you. To see the special exhibition.'

Chapter Eighteen

Dan stared at her. Did that mean Jayne had found something here at the museum? He became aware that Gracie was speaking to him. 'What?' he asked.

'I said, I don't know what she was doing here. Does she still live in Allensbury?'

Dan shrugged. 'I've no idea where she was living. Did you hear she was found dead on Tuesday?'

Gracie nodded. 'I saw it online. She was at Old Manor, wasn't she? I don't know why she'd want to go back there.'

'Did she say what she was looking for when she came here?' Dan asked.

Gracie snorted. 'She would never tell me anything,' she said. 'We were never friends at school.'

When they made their excuses and moved into the exhibition space, Ed whispered, 'So Jayne was here, too.'

Dan nodded. 'And two days before she died,' he replied in a low voice. 'The last piece of the puzzle could be here as well.'

But Ed was shaking his head as he pushed open the glass door. 'In the letter, she said she was still looking for the last piece.'

Dan sighed. 'Damn, I forgot about that.' He thought for a moment and then said, 'But she might have found whatever led her to the last piece in here.'

Ed laughed. 'Ever the optimist,' he said.

'You know me, glass half full and all that.' He looked at the rows and rows of glass cabinets. 'Wow, it's really creepy in here when it's so quiet. Being first in, at least we've got peace and quiet. Right, there's a lot of ground to cover. Let's split up.'

He turned to the left and Ed turned to the right. Dan wandered along the first bank of cases. Maps of Allensbury showed its growth from a small village in the middle of the eighteenth century to a bigger town in the nineteenth century. The second map of the town was more detailed, showing several mills had sprung up. Dan ignored the sign and snapped a couple of photos.

Ed appeared at the end of the row of cases and hissed loudly. Dan jumped and turned. 'Come here. I think I've found something.'

Dan hurried over to him. 'Why are you whispering?'

Ed shrugged. 'It's so quiet,' he said. Then he pointed at a display case. 'You were right about a connection between Simeon Burns and mills. He owned a silk-making mill, inherited from his father.'

Dan skimmed the information and looked at the picture of Simeon Burns hanging in the glass case. 'He looks really smug, doesn't he?'

Ed grinned. 'No wonder. The mill was making a fortune. He was paying his workers a pittance in terrible conditions and they had to be grateful for it. Sounds like business was good.'

'Then what?' Dan asked, wishing Ed would hurry up.

'An outsider, Franklin Tudham, moved to Allensbury and built another mill. He decked it out with loads of new equipment, made it all safe and started paying people more money. So Simeon started losing workers.'

'I'm guessing he didn't like that?'

'Nope, look here.' Ed pointed. 'A fire destroyed Tudham's mill and twenty workers died after being trapped inside.' He was silent for a moment. 'Two of them were under the age of ten. How awful.'

Dan read the card beside the diagram of the mill. 'Was Simeon involved?' he asked.

Ed shrugged. 'No one was ever caught, but it's too much of a co-incidence that this guy turns up, starts stealing Simeon's business and miraculously his mill gets burned down.'

'What happened to Tudham's family?' Dan asked.

Ed was peering at the next information board. 'Apparently they went bankrupt, so presumably they ended up in the workhouse or something like that.'

Dan chewed the inside of his cheek. 'We have one motive for Simeon Burns to be murdered.' He opened the note-taking app on his phone and tapped in some names and dates.

'You mean Tudham?'

Dan puffed out his cheeks. 'Possibly, but there were also twenty people killed. Any of them could have family who would want revenge.'

Ed was rereading the display board. 'But where do we start to prove it?'

'It's a shame because Jayne might have known.' Dan and Ed spun around to find Gracie standing behind them. Dan wondered how long she'd been standing there.

'Sorry?' he asked.

'She was in here for about two hours. I found her sitting on the floor just here scribbling in a notebook. I asked her if she needed help, but she just snapped at me to go away. Like I said, she hasn't changed.'

Dan glanced around the room. If Jayne had spent two hours in the exhibition, did that mean there was more information to be gleaned? He was about to ask more when Ed spoke. 'Gracie, do you think you could show me the other exhibition you've got on?' he asked. 'It looks really interesting.'

Dan stared at him, but Gracie blossomed from Ed's attention and led him away, asking, 'Are you looking for anything in particular?'

Once they were out of earshot, Dan snapped some pictures of the information about the fire. Then he looked around. Jayne had spent two hours in here. What else had she found?

He walked up and down the remaining glass cases, not sure what he was even looking for. Then he sat down on the floor and pulled Jayne's notebook from his coat pocket. Maybe sitting where she had been might bring inspiration, he thought, but he felt nothing. Then he heard voices and quickly got to his feet. But Ed and Gracie appeared before he could fully stuff the notebook back in his pocket.

'Is that Jayne's notebook?' Gracie asked, her eyes fixed on Dan's pocket. 'She had one with her the other day.'

'No, it's one of mine,' he lied.

But Gracie wasn't convinced. 'Why have you got Jayne's notebook?'

Dan opened his mouth to speak, not sure what he was going to say, but Ed cut in. 'Gracie, I'm really sorry, we've got to go,' he said, glancing at his watch, 'but I'd love to have a proper catch-up. Shall I call you?' Gracie smiled and recited her phone number for Ed to save it on his phone. He grinned. 'I'll be in touch.' Then he grabbed Dan's arm and dragged him outside. 'You're going to bloody owe me for that,' he said.

'What about your new girlfriend?' Dan asked with a grin.

'Not a girlfriend yet, but I'd like her to be, so let's hope she never finds out about this.'

'That was a good save taking her to the other exhibition.'

'It wasn't just a save,' Ed said with a grin. 'I had a feeling it might be useful and I think I've found another piece of the puzzle.'

***

'What did you find?' Dan asked once he'd paid for the beers in the Old Tavern. It was the first step to making it up to Ed for having to see Gracie again and left his wallet feeling much lighter.

Ed took a deep swallow from his pint glass. 'I spotted the other exhibition on the way in, but it didn't click until later. It was about diseases and medicines.'

Dan wrinkled his nose. 'That sounds lovely.'

'Not the way I'd usually want to spend my Saturday morning, but it made me think of something about Simeon Burns.'

'Which was?' Dan asked, sipping his beer.

'He died of cholera, right,' Ed said, 'but how? He lived in a clean home with good sanitation. So, how did he get cholera?'

Dan stared at him. 'You think it was something else?'

Ed grinned. 'Exactly. Jayne said Simeon was murdered and I thought that was odd. I mean, unless someone gave him cholera on purpose. I'm not sure how you would even do that.'

'You think it was something else that killed him?' Dan asked, warming to the theme. 'But what?'

Ed nodded. 'We need an expert on Simeon Burns who might know more about him.'

Dan grinned. 'What better place to look for one of those than at the university? And fortunately, we have a contact who kinda owes us a favour.'

'From when you saved his life, you mean?'

'Indeed.' He pulled out his phone. 'Let's see what Harry can do to help.'

Chapter Nineteen

Professor Harry Evans was more than happy to help Dan and Ed find their expert.

'I reckon Stewart Randall is the guy you want,' he said. 'What he doesn't know about Allensbury history isn't worth knowing, to be honest.' He'd given them Randall's office number with a word of caution: 'If you're quoting him, do not forget to give him his full title. He's the type that likes that kind of thing and takes himself very seriously.'

Much to their surprise, Professor Sir Stewart Randall answered the phone in two rings when they called on Saturday afternoon.

'You're lucky to catch me,' he said. 'I'm supposed to be on a research trip, but I came back early. Come to my office tomorrow morning at ten o'clock and I'm happy to tell you anything you need to know.'

When they arrived at the history department building, they found him waiting outside. He was a tall man, bulky around the middle and with grey hair that was probably usually quite wild but which he had clearly brushed in their honour. He looked at the space behind them and Dan imagined his disappointment there was no photographer.

'So, why am I having the pleasure of a visit from the local newspaper? You were vague on the phone,' he asked as they followed him up the stairs to the second floor. Randall was puffing when he heaved himself up the last few stairs and glanced over his shoulder as he tried to catch his breath. 'Sorry,' he said, 'I'm trying to lose some weight and I was advised to take the stairs.'

'Fine by us,' Ed beamed as Randall led them into his office, his breathing sounding equally uneven.

A floor-to-ceiling bookcase stuffed with books lined one wall. A battered and worn Georgian-style mahogany pedestal desk took centre stage. Randall cleared his throat several times as he sat down behind the desk. He opened a desk drawer, looked inside and closed it again, without putting anything in or taking it out. Then he looked at Dan and Ed, who took the uncomfortable wooden chairs opposite him.

'Have you come to report on my new book?'

Dan glanced at Ed. 'No, we wanted to ask you something about Simeon Burns,' he said. At first Randall looked disappointed, but then another look came over his face that Dan couldn't quite interpret.

Ed nodded. 'We're trying to find out more about how he died.'

Randall looked puzzled. 'He died of cholera. That's widely known.'

'That's what I'd read, but do you know how he caught it?' Dan asked. 'He would have had to drink dirty water, wouldn't he, and if that was the case, surely his whole family would have caught it as well?'

Dan wasn't wrong. There was definitely an odd expression on Randall's face.

'Why are you asking about this?'

Dan pulled out Jayne's notebook and opened it to the page of the doctor's letter. He held out the book, and Randall took it. 'You see, there's this letter from his doctor saying that he was more ill and—' Dan stopped speaking, seeing Randall's hands shake slightly as he looked at the notebook. His stomach flickered and he got an uncomfortable feeling.

'Where did you get this?' Randall demanded.

Dan exchanged a look with Ed, suddenly worried about the way Randall was looking at them.

'From a friend,' Dan said, trying to keep his tone light.

'This is an interesting letter,' Randall said, 'but it doesn't really tell us anything new. The symptoms he's describing are typical of cholera.'

'But the bit about the numb feet,' Ed persisted, 'that's not cholera, is it? What could that be?'

'Are you suggesting that Simeon Burns was murdered?' Randall asked. Dan felt his chest tighten. He nudged Ed to prevent him from saying anything else.

Randall closed the notebook and tapped it against his other palm. 'There is no evidence anywhere that suggests Simeon Burns died of anything other than natural causes.' His fingers tightened on the notebook. 'But if you like, I could authenticate some of these sources for you.'

'No, that's fine,' Dan said, getting to his feet and holding out a hand for the book. There was a pause and it seemed Randall was going to refuse to return the book. But he handed it back with slightly bad grace. Dan felt his chest relax as his fingers closed over the leather cover.

'Do you know Jayne Winter?' Randall asked. His voice sounded casual, but Dan could sense tension in the air.

'Why?' he asked.

'That's her notebook,' Randall said, getting to his feet.

Ed stood up as well.

'You know her?' Dan asked, edging back towards the door.

Randall shrugged. 'We worked together last year. I haven't seen her recently.'

'You won't see her again,' Dan said. 'She was killed on Tuesday.' He saw Randall's eyes widen and then his face relaxed.

'What sad news. I didn't know about that. Where was she?'

Randall's tone was light, but there was something about it that Dan didn't like.

Dan frowned at him. 'It was at Old Manor Hall, if that really matters to you.'

Randall took a step forward and moved around his desk. 'Had she found it?' he demanded. 'Was that why she'd gone there? It's at the hall, isn't it?'

Dan had pulled open the door and Ed was halfway out of it. It seemed imperative to get away from Randall as quickly as possible.

'It's in the notebook, isn't it? I'll give you a hundred pounds for it,' the professor said, holding out a hand.

Dan looked at Ed and then back towards Randall. 'What?'

'Two hundred? A thousand? Whatever it takes.' Randall sounded desperate.

Dan stepped back. 'What? Why would you want the notebook?'

Randall reached towards him, but Dan slapped his hand away.

'Run,' he said, pushing Ed into the corridor and they dashed down the stairs and out into the fresh air. They didn't stop until they reached Dan's car. He leaned against it, panting.

'What the hell was that?' Ed demanded, sagging against the passenger door.

Dan looked at him across the car roof. 'I have no idea, but we need to get out of here. I should never have shown him the notebook.'

'He clearly knows Jayne well enough to know it was hers,' Ed said, taking it from Dan, who started the car and threw it into reverse.

'And he was prepared to pay to get his hands on it,' Dan said, checking both directions before pulling out of the car park onto the main road.

'Do you think Jayne was trying to hide the notebook from him?' Ed asked.

'I bloody hope not,' Dan said, 'because we've just shown him where it is.'

Chapter Twenty

Burton and Shepherd both got out of their cars in the station car park at the same time on Sunday morning, the latter yawning widely.

'Late night, was it?' Burton asked with a grin.

'Dinner with my sister and her husband. And a friend.' He emphasised the word *friend*.

Burton grinned. 'They're still trying to set you up with someone?' she asked.

Shepherd rolled his eyes. 'I mean, she was a pleasant woman and everything, but not really my type.'

'Not Stacey?' Burton asked, referring to Shepherd's late wife.

He nodded, looking down at his feet. 'No one's ever going to match up,' he said.

Burton took a deep breath. 'You need to judge on their own merit, not against her,' she said.

Shepherd shrugged. 'Maybe.'

Burton knew when to let it go and led the way to the office. There they found Jayne Winter's laptop on his desk with a sticky note saying 'all yours, you owe me a beer' and a smiley face. Shepherd laughed as he picked up the note.

Looking over his shoulder, Burton said, 'Bribery and corruption within the police force? You paying for favours?'

Shepherd grinned. 'It's one way to get things done quickly.' He sat down and opened the laptop. Then he logged into his own computer and checked his email. 'Aha, password,' he said, reading an email. He tapped the sequence of letters and numbers into the laptop and sat back as the home screen popped up.

He leaned back towards his own screen and read aloud, 'Nothing untoward on here, although a few internet searches about how to poison someone with arsenic.'

Burton raised an eyebrow. 'And they don't think that's untoward?' she asked. 'Why would she be researching how to poison someone?'

Shepherd laughed and continued reading. 'As you'd expect, it looks like there's a lot of documents, notes for writing a book.'

'She's writing a book?' Burton asked, turning her chair to look over Shepherd's shoulder.

Shepherd pointed to a document icon on the screen. 'It looks like it's called The Curse of Simeon Burns.'

Burton frowned. 'Curse? That's what those teenagers who found her body were chuntering on about. They said he cursed the house. Would anyone want a book on that?'

Shepherd shrugged. 'She obviously thought so if she's writing one.' He fell silent as he read the note from the tech team. 'Tech says her emails make for interesting reading.' He clicked the mouse to bring up Jayne's email account. 'What was the name of the guy Jordan said was threatening Jayne?'

Burton picked up Shepherd's notebook and, after flicking through a few pages, said, 'Professor Sir Stewart Randall.'

Shepherd's fingers rattled on his keyboard. 'Woah,' he said when a list appeared, 'two hundred emails from him just in the past year.'

'Since she finished working at the university?' Burton asked.

Shepherd nodded as he opened one. 'And not very nice emails either.'

Burton sat down and scooted her chair closer, leaning forward to look at Shepherd's screen. 'In this one, he does actually threaten her,' she said. 'He says if she doesn't stop working on the Simeon Burns book, then he'll stop her. That was the latest email. Well, she's certainly been stopped now, hasn't she?'

Shepherd nodded. 'In this email, he says he's got a contract for a book and he won't let her ruin his career by publishing before him. But they're being really vague about what the research actually is.' He sighed and sat back in his chair. 'I can't believe we're back in the position of asking whether someone would be killed for the sake of some research. I realise it could be money-related, but how much would a publisher pay for a textbook contract? It doesn't sound like a big money spinner.'

'Maybe someone with a track record like Stewart Randall would get more money than someone like Jayne Winter, who's a newbie in that subject area. Maybe she was threatening a lucrative stream of income for him. He's written a few Simeon Burns books already, so maybe his track record is important.'

Shepherd frowned and scanned back through the emails. 'There's nothing in the emails showing that he knew she was in town, but the last one is from two days before she died and she hasn't responded to it. In fact, she doesn't seem to have even opened it.'

Burton rubbed her face with the palms of her hands. 'Three questions we need answered – did he know she was back in town, had he seen or spoken to her in person and did he know she was going to Old Manor?'

Chapter Twenty-One

'And here we are again in the hallowed halls of Allensbury University searching for a lesser spotted academic in its natural habitat,' Shepherd muttered to Burton in the style of a narrator from a TV nature programme. She tried not to laugh. It was Monday morning and they were following a serious-looking office manager along the corridor to Professor Sir Stewart Randall's office. She'd called Randall from the reception desk and got no response.

'I don't understand. I saw him go up there about an hour ago,' she said. 'Do you have an appointment?'

Burton nodded, feeling a sense of foreboding. 'Yes, we left a message telling him we were coming.'

The woman smiled indulgently. 'He's probably forgotten. I'll walk you up.'

Following the woman upstairs and along a corridor, Burton asked, 'He's been away on a research trip, hasn't he?'

The woman nodded. 'He might not have checked his messages yet.'

But as they arrived in the corridor, they were just in time to see a man sliding quietly out of a door.

'Professor Randall, there you are,' the secretary called, startling the man into dropping his keys. He looked up and Burton was pleased to see that he looked uncomfortable. Shepherd's message had not said why they wanted to speak to him, but his decision to run spoke volumes.

'Didn't you get our message?' Burton asked, glaring at the man.

'Oh, no, I'm sorry I didn't, erm...' Randall began.

'Well, I'm glad we've caught you,' Burton replied quickly. 'Shall we step inside?'

Randall looked like he was going to refuse, but Burton's steely gaze made him think twice. He opened the door and they followed him inside. Shepherd thanked the office manager for her help. She smiled and disappeared away down the corridor.

'What can I ... er ... do for you?' Randall asked, sitting in the chair behind his desk, which creaked ominously. Burton sat on a chair opposite, while Shepherd leaned against the filing cabinet next to Randall's desk. His presence seemed to put Randall on edge.

'We need to speak to you about Dr Jayne Winter,' Burton said without preamble, pleased to see Randall shift awkwardly in his seat. 'I'm sure you've heard the news despite being away.'

Randall nodded. 'Well, yes, I was told about it.'

'How well did you know Dr Winter?' Burton asked.

Randall shifted in his chair and folded his arms. 'Not at all.'

Burton watched the man squirm. 'I thought you worked together for a year in the same department. Are you telling me you didn't cross paths with her?'

'Well, erm, I, erm, we attended a few department meetings together, I suppose. I don't really have much to do with junior members of staff.'

Burton didn't like the way he emphasised the word junior. She had no time for elitists.

'Did you get on?' she asked.

'Of course, we're fellow academics.'

Shepherd smiled. 'In my experience, it doesn't always follow that academics get along.'

Randall gave him a sharp look. 'What are you implying?' he demanded.

'Well, we've got Dr Winter's laptop and we've seen the emails between you in which you threaten her,' Shepherd said.

Randall's eyes widened. 'What? That's nonsense.'

Burton reached into her handbag and pulled out a printed page. She leaned forward, placed it on the desk and pushed it towards him. 'What about this?' she asked.

Randall's eyes scanned down the page and he shifted awkwardly in his chair again.

When he said nothing, Burton leaned forward. 'I think your intentions are clear here,' she said, tapping a finger of the page.

The man cleared his throat. 'It isn't what it looks like,' he said.

'Isn't it? See, to me it looks like you're threatening Jayne Winter and now she's been killed, so I'm sure you can understand our questions.'

'You said you would stop her,' Shepherd said. 'What did you mean by that?'

'I was going to contact the publisher she'd secured and tell them to drop her contract. She knows nothing about the subject.'

'And you do?'

'Yes, I'm an expert in that period.'

'Did you contact the publisher?'

Randall scowled. 'No, I couldn't find out which one it was. In fact, I doubt she even had a contract,' he snapped.

'And yet you still threatened her?'

'It wasn't a threat,' Randall blustered, 'more of a warning.'

Burton dismissed the answer with a wave of a hand. 'I'd like to know if you've seen Dr Winter recently?'

Randall shook his head. 'I haven't seen her since last year.'

'You didn't know she was back in town?'

Randall said nothing.

'See, I don't believe you,' Burton said, feeling her frustration mounting. 'I think you went looking for her.'

'How would I know she was back?' Randall snapped. 'She hadn't responded to my emails.'

'Had you tried calling her?' Burton asked. She glanced at Shepherd. 'I wonder what we'll find on Dr Winter's phone when our tech team has a look.' They both turned to stare at Randall.

The man met their gaze stonily. 'I know nothing about her being in town.'

'Do you know why she went to Old Manor Hall?' Burton asked.

Randall stared at her. 'What?'

'Do you know why she would go to Old Manor? It's an easy-enough question.'

Randall shrugged. 'I've no idea. I certainly wouldn't have gone there. The building should be condemned. It's almost on its last legs. I'm not surprised the ceiling fell in on her.'

'Who said anything about the ceiling?' Shepherd said.

Burton could almost see Randall catch his breath. 'What do you mean?'

'I don't think anyone mentioned a ceiling falling in,' Shepherd said, leaning forward.

'The newspaper – they reported—'

'That Dr Winter was murdered,' Shepherd said. 'She was beaten over the head and left to die.'

'I wouldn't have ... I would never...' Randall blustered.

'Oh, come on, Professor Randall...' Burton leaned forward and slapped her hand on the desk, 'enough of this messing about. Where were you on Tuesday at about four thirty in the afternoon?'

'You're asking me for an alibi?' Randall demanded, swelling indignantly.

'Yes,' Burton snapped.

'I was at home, alone.'

Burton snorted. 'That's not very convincing,' she added.

'It's the truth,' Randall snapped. 'I certainly wasn't at Old Manor murdering Jayne. I didn't even know she was—'

Burton got to her feet and held up a hand.

'That's all for now, Professor Randall, but I'm sure we'll have more questions soon.'

***

In the corridor, Shepherd glanced at Burton.

'Interesting that he knew the ceiling had fallen in,' he said, quietly.

Burton nodded grimly. 'Either he was there himself or he knows someone who was.'

'We'd need evidence of that: fingerprints or a sighting of his car.'

Burton chewed her lip. 'Gaz hasn't had anything back from any CCTV cameras near Old Manor, so we've got nothing there. We know there was a second person there because of those footprints. See if you can corroborate his alibi that he was at home alone.'

'Do you think he knew she was back?' Shepherd asked as he

pushed open the door and they walked out into the chilly morning air.

'Given the animosity, I don't know why she would tell him she was here without a very good reason,' Burton said, tightening her scarf and buttoning up her coat. 'But did you see his reaction when I mentioned her phone? I think he might have called or texted her, and I'm guessing it's quite incriminating.'

'Threatening messages?'

'If his emails are anything to go by.' Burton pulled the end of her long, blonde ponytail. 'I just wish we knew why she was back in town.'

'Something to do with *The Curse of Simeon Burns*?' Shepherd asked.

'It could be, but I keep wondering, would someone really kill over a book?'

'Jayne was looking into Simeon Burns' murder. Maybe she was doing a true crime tell-all and someone didn't want her to tell,' Shepherd suggested.

'Randall, you mean?' Burton asked. They arrived at the car, and she leaned her forearms on the door frame. 'I'm just not convinced this is about a book. She was up to something, and we need to find out what it was and why someone – probably Randall – would want to stop her from doing it.'

Chapter Twenty-Two

As they walked to work on Monday morning, speedily because of a steady drizzle, Dan and Ed were still discussing the events of the weekend. Dan felt like they'd spoken of nothing else.

'So, what do we do now?' Ed asked.

'Stay as far away from Stewart Randall as we possibly can,' Dan said, knowing that the flickering in his stomach was, for once, not excitement.

Ed glanced sideways at him. 'You're worried?'

Dan nodded. 'You saw how he reacted to the notebook. A thousand pounds? There's definitely something in it he wants.'

'He's not going to act on it though, is he?' Ed asked, sounding scornful.

Dan sighed. 'I wish I was that confident. I thought we were consulting an expert on Simeon Burns, not the person who could have killed Jayne.'

Dan walked on a few paces before realising Ed had stopped and he was alone.

'You think he killed Jayne?' Ed asked, eyes widening.

Dan shrugged. 'I think it's possible. He's clearly desperate to get his hands on something. What if Jayne got in his way? What if she found it – whatever it is – what would he have done?'

Ed frowned and Dan could almost hear the cogs of his brain whirring.

'You think he followed her to Old Manor?' he asked. When Dan nodded, Ed continued, 'But he can't have done because otherwise he would know whether she found it. His reaction seemed genuine that he didn't know where it was.'

Dan thought for a moment and then waved for Ed to catch him up. 'He still wants the notebook, which suggests to me that neither of them has found what they were looking for. Hurry up, I'm getting soaked.'

'It was that doctor's letter that got his attention,' Ed said, puffing slightly as he hurried up the hill to catch Dan, 'so maybe that explains what actually killed Simeon Burns.'

Dan jammed his hands into his coat pockets, wishing he'd brought his gloves. 'That's why Jayne was convinced it was murder and not natural causes,' he said, his stomach starting to flicker in the right way.

'But why is Jayne researching Simeon Burns in the first place?' Ed asked, tugging at his scarf to tighten it slightly. 'How did she find out something that an expert didn't know?'

Dan frowned. 'Search me. Maybe she read something that got her interested?' His brain was racing ahead. Had Jayne found something valuable, or something that was hidden for years, and someone wanted it to stay that way?

'Maybe it was something explosive that would throw academic circles into disarray,' Ed said, miming an explosion with his hands.

When Dan was silent, Ed looked at him. 'I was joking,' he said. When Dan didn't respond, he added, 'What are you thinking?'

'Remember what happened to Harry when he stuck his nose in where it didn't belong?' Dan said. He couldn't forget how much Harry's life had been danger when he got involved in a research project that didn't belong to him.

'But this is different, surely,' Ed said. 'I mean, it's some dusty old documents, not science and chemicals. It wouldn't be valuable financially, would it?'

But the more Dan thought about it, the more clenched his stomach felt. Why the hell had Jayne sent him something that could be so dangerous? She'd put his life, and Ed's, at risk. 'People are passionate about their stuff. What if it's a cover-up? Jayne found something, threatened to publish it and someone stopped her. Permanently.'

'And now someone knows that we know?' Ed asked, looking anxious.

Dan nodded. 'We need to solve this thing quickly, before anyone else gets hurt.'

Chapter Twenty-Three

Dan felt nervous as he stood on the Winters' doorstep. Suzy had phoned almost as soon as he'd sat down at his desk, saying the family were interested in doing a tribute piece. He'd dropped everything and said he'd go round straight away. Now he felt anxious. It was going to be strange to write about someone he sort of knew.

The door was opened by a young man in his late twenties, who looked at him quizzically.

'Are you from the paper?' he asked.

Dan introduced himself.

'I'm Jordan, Jayne's brother. Come on in.' He stepped back and held the door, closing it behind Dan. The smell of freshly cut flowers hung in the air and it seemed that every flat surface held a floral arrangement.

'We had to borrow some vases from the neighbours,' Jordan said, seeing Dan eyeing the flowers.

'Friends and relatives paying tribute to Jayne,' Dan said. A slight eye-roll from Jordan surprised him as he turned to lead the way into the sitting room.

'Mum,' he said to a woman in a wheelchair, 'it's the guy from the newspaper.' Jordan showed Dan to an armchair and perched on the edge of the sofa. 'Sorry, we're not really sure how this tribute piece thing works,' he said.

Dan smiled. 'It's just a chance to chat about Jayne, her life, her work and that kind of thing.'

He got a conversation started, scribbling frantically as Della and Jordan talked about Jayne growing up.

When they got to school days, Jordan said: 'You sound like you know Jayne.'

'I sat next to her in A Level history,' Dan said. He paused and then decided to test the waters. 'I hadn't spoken to Jayne in years and I heard she'd moved away. Was she actually living here?'

Della shook her head. 'No, she doesn't live in Allensbury. She only came back to stay with me last Friday. I don't know how long she was planning on staying.' She paused and then said, 'But she was working at Allensbury University for a while last year, so maybe that's what you'd heard.'

'Did she mention why she was back? Was she working on something specific?' he asked.

'Why?' asked Jordan, looking suspiciously at Dan.

Dan took a chance. 'Well, she sent me a notebook through the post with some research into Simeon Burns. Did she mention it to you at all?'

Jordan frowned. 'She hadn't told us anything. She never did.'

Della nodded. 'Like I said, she just turned up on the doorstep last weekend, wanting somewhere to stay. She went straight to the spare room, shut herself away and wouldn't come out until dinner time. It was like the old days.' She smiled fondly.

Dan felt his chest tighten. Jayne had only returned to Allensbury the weekend before she died. She'd come back, sent him the notebook and then died within a few days.

'Did she have a laptop with her?' he asked.

Della nodded. 'She had her laptop and some old books in a holdall with some clothes and suchlike.'

Dan's stomach flickered. 'Do you still have the laptop? Would I be able to have a look at it?'

'The police have got it,' Jordan said. He looked at Dan suspiciously. 'Why do you want it?'

Dan decided that a little white lie wouldn't hurt. 'I was wondering if she was working on a book or something. I thought that might be on her laptop.'

'A book?' Della looked at Jordan. 'Did she say anything to you about writing a book?'

Jordan shook his head. 'But then we'd not spoken for a few months. I'd been busy with work and Jayne never called me, always me doing the calling.'

Dan detected a note of irritation rather than sadness, that he'd never be able to call Jayne again. Feeling like he was outstaying his welcome, he got to his feet. 'I'd better go. I'm so sorry again about Jayne.'

Suddenly Della grabbed Jordan's arm. 'I've just remembered. Where did I leave my handbag?' she demanded.

Jordan looked surprised and stood up. 'It's in the kitchen. I'll get it.' He disappeared out of the door.

'She left something with me,' Della said breathlessly, 'and it might be useful to you.'

When Jordan returned, she almost snatched the bag from him, digging inside and pulling out the contents one by one. 'Where is it?' she muttered to herself. Then she tipped the bag upside down and something fell to the floor.

Jordan stooped and picked up a memory stick. 'Is this it?' he asked, handing it to her. 'Mum, what's going on?'

'Do you think there could be something on here?' Della asked, holding it out to Dan. 'Something that could show you what she was up to?'

Dan took the stick, feeling his stomach flicker as he turned it in his fingers. 'Very possibly. Do you mind if I take it?'

Della waved a hand. 'Yes. You're going to investigate, aren't you? You'll find out what happened to her?'

'That's exactly what I'm going to do,' he replied.

Jordan led Dan to the door and thanked him for coming. As he stepped outside, Dan turned back.

'When you make funeral arrangements, will you let me know? I'd like to say goodbye.'

Jordan nodded. 'And you keep us posted on what you find,' he said. Dan nodded and held out a hand. The men shook hands in farewell and Dan walked down the garden path.

He got into the car and sat for a moment, staring at the memory stick in his hand, his brain buzzing. The plot was thickening. Why had Jayne left the memory stick with her mum but sent him the notebook? Would the two together be the pieces that would help him solve the puzzle? Or would it just bring more trouble now that he had both?

He started the engine. One thing was for sure: he wasn't going to tell anyone other than Ed that he had the memory stick. Randall's reaction had made it clear there was something significant at stake. Now he just had to find out what it was.

Chapter Twenty-Four

That evening, Dan spent a freezing two hours on the touchline of a local school five-a-side tournament, standing in for the chief sports reporter who'd been called away by a family emergency.

'Ironically, my son's broken his arm playing football in the school playground,' the man had said.

Dan was now regretting his own generosity because he hadn't had a chance to change and was underdressed for the weather. At the full-time whistle, he completed his interviews, pen slipping in numb fingers and walked back to his car. As he pulled his car keys from his trouser pocket, his fingers brushed Jayne's memory stick. Immediately he got a shot of adrenaline that blew away his tiredness and shivering. He got into the car and texted Ed to say he was on his way home. Before he'd even turned on the ignition, his phone beeped.

I have leftovers for you. Shepherd's pie, OK? came the response.

Excellent. On way. I've got something to show you. And turn up the heating, I'm freezing.

***

When he opened the door of the flat, Dan sniffed the warm air appreciatively.

'Something smells good,' he shouted as he pulled off his shoes and hung up his coat.

'This may be my best shepherd's pie yet,' Ed called from the kitchen.

Dan padded into the living room as Ed appeared in the doorway.

'How was the football?' Ed asked.

'Too cold for me to enjoy it properly,' Dan said, flexing his fingers. 'I've still not got the feeling back in them.'

'How was Jayne's mum?' Ed asked. 'Did she know any more about what she was up to?'

Dan recounted the story as he stepped past Ed and filled a glass of water. Then he pulled the memory stick from his trouser pocket and held it up.

'What's that?' Ed asked, stepping forward and taking it from his hand.

'It's Jayne's. She gave it to her mum for safekeeping.' Ed's eyes widened and Dan grinned. 'Whatever she was up to, I think it could be on here.'

Ed turned the memory stick over in his hands. 'Let's make sure no one knows we've got this,' he said, holding it up. 'Grab your dinner and I'll get my laptop. Let's see what she's got on here.'

While Dan balanced a plate of shepherd's pie on his lap and started shovelling it into his mouth, Ed sat on the floor and put his laptop on the coffee table. Dan watched over his shoulder as Ed logged in, plugged in the memory stick and waited. The computer whirred and then a box opened on the screen.

'Right, there's five files in here,' Ed said, pointing at the folder symbols on the screen.

Dan blew on a forkful of mashed potato and minced lamb and shoved it into his mouth. He knew he was eating too quickly, but he couldn't wait.

'Anything?' he asked, wincing as the food burned his mouth.

Ed was scanning down the list of documents. Then he stopped and went very still.

'What is it?' Dan asked, finishing his pie in two forkfuls and almost dropping the plate on the floor in his haste to put it down.

'A file called "The Curse of Simeon Burns".'

Dan leaned forward and read over Ed's shoulder. 'That's a good book title,' he said.

Ed double-clicked on the document icon and they waited. After a couple of seconds, a white page appeared on the screen. The book title was written in thick black letters and Ed scrolled down to the next page, which said 'Introduction'.

'Bingo,' Dan said triumphantly. 'This is it. She *is* writing a book.'

They skim-read the introduction, which gave the background of the Burns family, from Oliver Burns, Simeon's grandfather, down to Simeon's children.

Then Ed read aloud, '"It's my belief that in fact Simeon Burns was murdered by someone who wanted to punish him and settle a score, to right a wrong that was done by him."'

Dan frowned. 'That's probably quite a long list.'

'But, remember Franklin Tudham. He had an excellent motive to want Simeon out of the way. He blamed him for the ruin of his family.'

Dan pulled a face. 'But how would Tudham have killed Simeon? How did anyone kill Simeon?' Then he paused. 'Hang on a minute. In that doctor's letter, he wrote to his mentor that Simeon was sicker than anyone else he's seen who had cholera. He said Simeon had sickness and diarrhoea, which you'd expect, but also muscle cramps and swears that he is losing movement in his feet. I did a bit of online research and I couldn't find any reference to feet in anything to do with cholera.'

'We need to narrow down what diseases could do that to you,' Ed said.

Dan grinned. 'And who do we know who's curating an exhibition on diseases at the moment?'

Ed groaned and reached for his phone.

'I'm taking her for one coffee. And you owe me. Big time.'

Chapter Twenty-Five

At the *Allensbury Post* office on Tuesday morning, Dan was hammering out Jayne's tribute piece.

'How's it going?' Daisy asked, coming to stand behind him.

Dan puffed out his cheeks. 'It's difficult when practically the only person to say something nice about you is your mum.'

Daisy winced. 'Ouch. That bad?'

Dan nodded. 'To be honest, I don't remember her being particularly nice at school, so clearly she hadn't mellowed. But I've got the last comment I needed so I can file it this morning.'

Daisy sat in the chair next to him. 'Have the police said anything new?'

'I've not had an update yet.' Dan glanced at his watch. 'I'll finish this and then call them.'

There was a discreet cough and Daisy and Dan looked up. One of the junior reporters stood behind them, clutching a tray.

'I'm doing a tea run. Do you, y'know, want a cuppa?'

Daisy declined the offer and went back to her desk.

Dan sighed. 'That would be great. It's—'

'Milk, no sugar,' the man replied. Then he glanced at Dan's

screen. 'Is that the woman who was killed at Old Manor? She was a friend of yours, wasn't she?'

Dan nodded. 'Well, I knew her a long time ago at college.'

The man shook his head. 'It was only a matter of time before someone got hurt,' he said, picking up Dan's mug and turning away.

'Er, Neil,' Dan asked, leaning forward to stop him. 'What does that mean?'

'Well, the treasure hunt. It was only a matter of time, I mean—'

'What treasure hunt?'

Neil looked surprised. 'The Allensbury Historical Society anniversary treasure hunt. I'm surprised you didn't see my article on it.'

'Sorry, I must have missed that. So what's it all about?'

Neil put the tray of mugs down on Emma's desk, next to Dan's, and sat down. 'They've set up this thing to hunt for Simeon Burns' lost treasure. It's celebrating the bicentenary of the museum opening.'

'I don't remember any lost treasure,' Dan said, 'and I studied him at school.'

Neil laughed. 'I don't think the treasure actually exists, but they've set up clues and puzzles for people to solve. Entrants submit their answers and then announce the winner at the big fundraising event.'

Ed arrived at that moment, shaking water off his jacket. '*Il pleut*,' he said.

'You don't say,' Dan replied. He gestured to Neil. 'He's just been telling me about the Simeon Burns' treasure hunt that the historical society has set up for the anniversary.'

Ed raised his eyebrows. 'Treasure hunt?'

Neil sighed. 'Do neither of you read the paper? It was a two-page spread. With pictures and everything.' When Dan and Ed both shrugged, he rolled his eyes. 'You don't deserve a cuppa.'

'Ah, don't sulk. I'll read it now,' Dan said with a grin.

The man picked up the tray, collected Ed's mug as well, and walked away.

'Who's in charge of the historical society?' Dan called after him. Seeing the doubtful look on the man's face, Dan laughed. 'I'm not trying to steal your story. I just need to ask him something about Simeon Burns.'

'It's Donald Bloom. I'll get his number for you when I get back.'

Ed leaned over and spoke to Dan down the side of their computers. 'A Simeon Burns' treasure hunt,' he said. 'Do you think that's why Jayne was really back? She was going to take part?'

Dan wrinkled his nose. 'Would an academic be interested in a charity treasure hunt?'

'If she believed there was actually treasure, she might.'

'I don't remember anything in her notes, but it would probably be a more interesting reason for her to get killed, rather than just the theory that Simeon Burns was murdered.'

'Follow the money, you mean?'

'Exactly.'

Ed paused to switch on his monitor. 'So, we're now looking for treasure hunt clues in Jayne's notes?'

'And hopefully, as a bit of an expert on Simeon Burns, she would have had a bit of a head start in solving them.'

Chapter Twenty-Six

Burton, Shepherd and Madison were updating Jayne Winter's timeline when Gary Topping arrived in the office on Tuesday lunchtime.

'Nice of you to join us,' Burton said, glancing at her watch.

'Sorry, boss, but you'll like what I've got for you.'

Burton raised an eyebrow and folded her arms. 'This better be good.'

Topping joined the group with a thick sheaf of A4 pages in his hands. 'The uniforms who initially interviewed Jayne Winter's colleagues were very thorough,' he said, 'but I had to follow up on a couple of them.

'Anything new?' Shepherd asked.

Burton braced herself as Topping flicked through the pages and then pulled one out.

'This one. The head of archaeology, Dr Lula Blackthorn, said she saw Jayne in the library on campus on the Thursday before she died,' he said, handing the sheet to Burton. She took it and scan-read.

'An academic being seen in a library isn't much of a lead, Gaz,' she said, disappointed.

'But she said what stood out was that Jayne isn't a member of their library anymore. Her entry card would have expired when she left last year.'

'How did she get in?' Shepherd asked, frowning.

'That's why Lula Blackthorn said it stuck out for her, because Jayne shouldn't have been able to get access. Lula hasn't seen Jayne at all since last year and she shouldn't have been there.'

Burton watched as Shepherd stepped to the whiteboard and added *Thursday* and *uni library* to the start of the timeline.

'So, she came to Allensbury on Thursday and went to the university library, but didn't go to see her mum until Friday,' Burton said, pointing at the board. 'Where was she on Thursday night? We know she didn't have any friends to stay with.'

'That's the thing,' Topping said, grinning. 'The library is open twenty-four seven at the moment. Some exam thing that's going on. Not the usual time of year they do it. It's usually summer, but I reckon she slept at the library.'

'In the absence of anywhere else, it would make sense. Can't have been comfortable,' Burton said, staring at the timeline.

Topping laughed. 'It's a modern library, boss. They have sofas and bean bags. She'd have been OK.'

Burton exhaled heavily. 'What the hell was she up to? This is making less sense the more information we get in.'

'And another colleague said they saw her in the town centre on Saturday morning,' Topping continued.

'Did she say what she was doing?' Shepherd asked, as he made a note of Saturday on the timeline.

Topping shook his head. 'He said hello to her and asked what she was doing in town because he was surprised to see her, but she fobbed him off and he made his escape as soon as he could.'

'Did he see where she went?' Burton asked.

Topping grinned. 'Allensbury Museum, which just so happens to have a special exhibition running. And the star of the show is?'

Burton grinned back at him. 'Our good friend, Simeon Burns. Right, get yourself over there and—'

But Topping held up a hand. 'That's why I'm late. I popped in there on my way back from the university.'

Burton felt her chest tighten. This could be it, the lead they were waiting for.

'I spoke to the curator,' Topping said, 'and Jayne spent some time in there on the Saturday morning.'

'The curator remembered her? It must have been a quiet day. That place is usually rammed.'

'They went to school together at Old Manor, apparently. That's how she remembered her,' Topping added. He handed the sheaf of papers to Shepherd and pulled out his notebook. 'She said Jayne was in the exhibition for about two hours and was sitting on the floor scribbling in a notebook.' He grinned. 'A notebook that she now believes is in the possession of Dan Sullivan from the *Allensbury Post*.'

Burton glared towards Shepherd. 'He didn't bloody tell us that, did he?' she snapped. 'How did he get it?'

Topping shook his head. 'The curator doesn't know. In fact, she said he lied and said it was one of his own notebooks, but she didn't believe him.'

'Right, I want to speak to Dan Sullivan now and find out exactly what is in this notebook.' Burton turned and strode away across the office, with Shepherd following. 'And if I find he's been with-holding information, he's in serious trouble.'

Chapter Twenty-Seven

Dan had just filed Jayne Winter's tribute piece when his desk phone rang with an internal call. He groaned.

'Oh, what now?'

It was the receptionist. 'There's someone here to see you.'

'I'm busy. Can you take a message?' Dan pleaded.

There was a pause. 'Erm, no, I can't. It's the police. They need to talk to you.'

Dan hung up the receiver and stood up.

Ed looked at him, surprised. 'Where are you going?'

'Reception. The police are here.'

Ed's eyes widened. 'Why? Surely Suzy would just ring with an update.'

Dan shrugged. 'I've no idea, but usually a personal visit means I'm in trouble.'

When he arrived in the front office, he found Burton almost breathing fire, Shepherd standing at her side. Dan waved them into the small meeting room that led from the reception area. They all sat down at the table and Dan looked at Burton expectantly.

'Why are you here?'

'Let's start with Jayne Winter's notebook,' Burton snapped, leaning forward on the table.

Dan stared at her. 'How do you know about that?'

'So you have her notebook?'

'Well, yes, but—'

'So you lied to me when you said you hadn't seen her?' Burton asked.

Dan frowned. 'No, I didn't. I haven't seen her. She posted it to me.'

'And you didn't think I needed to know about that?' Burton demanded.

'It had only arrived that afternoon and I hadn't opened the parcel, so I didn't know it was from her,' Dan insisted, feeling his irritation rise.

'But when you found out who it was from, you still didn't think to tell us about it?' Burton gestured to herself and Shepherd.

Dan looked at her, frowning. 'I didn't think it had anything to do with your case,' he said, 'but...'

When he trailed off, Shepherd also now leaned in towards him. 'Now you think it is?' he asked.

Dan exhaled heavily. 'She posted it on the Monday and then the next day she got killed. That seems a bit too much of a coincidence to me.'

'What's in it?' Shepherd asked, scribbling in his notebook.

'She's been doing research into Simeon Burns and has this theory that he was murdered, rather than dying of cholera.'

'We know that,' said Burton. 'We've seen her laptop and she's writing a book.'

Dan nodded. 'But then we talked to Professor Sir Stewart Randall at the university—'

'How did you find him?' Burton asked sharply.

'Through a friend. He's an expert on Simeon Burns, so we thought he might shed some light on Jayne's research.' He shook his head. 'That was a bit of a mistake.'

'Why?' Shepherd asked.

'We showed him a letter in the book, and he got all weird and tried to buy it. Offered a thousand pounds, which is just ridiculous. But I was a bit worried. It sounded like they were both looking for something.'

'Why do you think that?' Burton asked.

'He asked if she'd found it at Old Manor. I said I didn't know what he was talking about, but he got a bit agitated and I didn't like that, so Ed and I skedaddled.'

'You hadn't seen Jayne Winter for twenty years, but she sends you her notebook. Why?'

Dan shrugged. 'I have no idea. Maybe she saw my name in the paper.'

'Can we see this notebook?' Burton asked.

'Why do you want it? It's only got some research in it.'

Burton glared at him. 'You just said it yourself that Stewart Randall tried to buy it from you. That suggests there's something important in it.'

'Randall reacted when we mentioned Simeon Burns being murdered, but he kept asking if Jayne had found it and was that why she was at Old Manor,' Dan said.

Shepherd frowned at him. 'Found what?'

Dan shrugged. 'Search me. But I wondered if it's something to do with the treasure hunt.'

Burton sighed. 'What treasure hunt?'

Dan explained the historical society's competition and she

groaned. 'So there's going to be hundreds of people digging into this?'

Dan nodded. 'Probably.'

Burton rested her forehead on her hand. 'Where is the notebook now?'

'It's safely tucked up at home.'

'We need to see it and make sure there's nothing pertinent to the investigation.'

Dan promised to bring it to the police station the following day for assessment. 'But I want it back,' he said. 'I want to know what Jayne found, and if it is the treasure, where it might be.'

When Burton and Shepherd left, Dan remained in the meeting room, collecting his thoughts. He didn't want the police to decide that they needed to keep the notebook, but he couldn't hide anything that could lead to Jayne's killer. He'd promised Jordan Winter that he'd find out who'd done it and that's exactly what he was going to do.

****

When Dan got back upstairs to the office, Neil had been true to his word and, with slightly bad grace, gave Dan the phone number of the chair of the Allensbury Historical Society.

'Bloom,' announced a voice loudly in Dan's ear when he called, making him jump. Ed peered down the side of his computer screen, clearly having heard the proclamation as if Donald Bloom were present. Dan introduced himself.

'What can I do for you?' Bloom asked.

'I wanted to ask if you knew a Jayne Winter? She was doing some research on Simeon Burns.'

There was a brief silence. 'Why would I know her?'

'Well, you've got the treasure hunt going, so I wondered whether she'd contacted you.'

Bloom sighed. 'She emailed me through the historical society website wanting help with her research.'

'Did she say what she was looking for?' Dan asked, tapping his pen against his notebook. He wondered how much of her work Jayne would have shared with an outsider.

'I don't think so. I doubt there's anything new left to study about him.'

'Whose idea was it to have the treasure hunt?'

'It was mine,' Donald Bloom said, sounding proud. 'I wanted something to celebrate the museum's anniversary and, as Benjamin Burns opened it, I thought a search for the treasure might be fun.'

Dan felt his stomach start to flicker. 'So, the Burns family treasure is real?' he asked.

Bloom made a slight snorting noise. 'Well, it's more of an urban legend but some members of the society believe in it. People have spent a lot of time over the years searching, with no success.'

'If the treasure doesn't exist, where do your clues lead, then?' Dan asked, feeling confused.

'They lead to various historical places around the town. You go to the place and answer a question about it. We're expecting a lot of people to get the right answers, so we'll pick a winner out of a hat at the benefit event.'

'Is there still time to join in?'

'Aha, fancy yourself as a bit of a treasure hunter?' Donald Bloom guffawed. 'Of course. If you sign up on the website, you'll get an email with the clues, but there's only a week or so left to work out the answers.'

'And you don't know if Jayne Winter was taking part?'

'I wouldn't be able to tell you, data protection and all that, but we set up a forum on our website for people to chat about it and suggest ideas for where they think it is.'

'Oh great, I'll have a look.'

Dan thanked Bloom and said goodbye. Ed stood up and looked at him, hands on hips and eyebrows raised.

'What was that all about?'

'We're going on a treasure hunt,' Dan said. 'And hopefully we can glean some insights before I have to hand it over to the police tomorrow. It's going to be a busy evening.'

'I can pick Gracie's brains a bit tomorrow morning when we go for coffee,' Ed said.

'The priority has to be finding out what else Simeon Burns could have died of,' Dan said, pointing at Ed with his pen, 'so don't forget that. We need to work out if Jayne was really onto something.'

Chapter Twenty-Eight

Gracie Lincoln was waiting for Ed in the Italian cafe on Wednesday morning when he arrived.

'I wish this rain would stop,' she said, observing his wet coat and hair.

Ed laughed. 'You think I'd be able to remember an umbrella by now, wouldn't you?' He took Gracie's order and while he waited for it to be prepared, he tried to think of how to broach the subject.

When he joined her at the table, an Americano for him and a large pumpkin-spiced latte for her, Gracie said, 'It was good to hear from you again so soon. I was hoping you would call.'

'Well, it only seemed fair to buy you a coffee to say thanks for your help at the museum.' He cast around for a start to the conversation, but Gracie got there before him.

'When you called, I had another look at the exhibition. I know you were interested in cholera, but I thought these pictures might give some context.' Gracie dug in the handbag on the chair beside her and pulled out her mobile phone. She brought up a picture gallery and moved her chair closer to Ed to show him.

'This is one of someone dying of cholera,' she said. The skinny body of a man lay in a hospital bed, unmoving, clearly too weak.

'He's not in pain,' Ed said. 'I thought cholera was painful.'

Gracie gave him a sideways look. 'Apparently it can be painful because low blood salts mean the muscles cramp, but I don't know how painful that would be.'

'What else did you find?'

Gracie swiped to the next photograph. 'This is someone suffering from typhus.'

Ed looked down at the picture. 'No, that's not quite right either. Simeon Burns' doctor said he was sicker than any other cholera patient he'd ever seen.' He explained the additional symptoms the doctor had described.

Gracie frowned. 'I think this might be what you're looking for,' she said, flipping to the next photo. The patient was writhing in agony, sweating profusely and drooling.

'What's he got?' Ed asked, staring at the picture.

'Arsenic poisoning,' said Gracie, casually clearing the pictures from the screen and slipping her phone back into her bag. She reached for her coffee and took a somewhat victorious swig. Ed took a thoughtful sip from his Americano and sat back.

'So Simeon Burns could have died of arsenic poisoning?' he asked.

Gracie nodded.

'Would it have been a quick death? The doctor's letter didn't say how long he was ill for.'

Gracie pulled out her phone again and tapped the screen twice. She opened a note-taking app and looked at the words. 'It depends on the dose,' she said. 'If it's small doses repeatedly, then it can take a while. A big dose shows symptoms within a couple of hours and you can die quite quickly. It's not a nice way to go.' She took another sip and put her cup back on its saucer. 'Did the doctor's letter say anything else?'

Ed frowned. 'I don't think so, but the writing was almost illegible.'

'This is from Jayne Winter's research, isn't it? From her notebook?' Gracie asked.

Ed took a fake sip from his cup, playing for time while he tried to think of an excuse. But nothing came to mind. Dan would be disappointed in him.

'Jayne thought Simeon Burns might have been poisoned, then?' Gracie asked. 'What's the theory? Someone in the house decided he needed to go?'

Ed shrugged. 'We're not sure what happened. But it would change things if he didn't die of natural causes.'

'It wouldn't be a surprise if he was killed,' Gracie said. She downed the last of her latte and started pulling on her coat. 'He was a nasty man.' She stood up. 'Thanks for the coffee. Hope we can do it again soon.' With a little wave, she left the café. Ed watched her go, feeling like he'd given away more than he'd learned.

Chapter Twenty-Nine

Dan was crossing the high street on his way back from the police station when he heard someone calling his name. He turned to see Ed waving for him to wait.

'Hey, good timing,' Ed said, grinning. 'I've just finished with Gracie.' He recounted the conversation.

'Arsenic?' Dan asked, surprised. 'So Simeon Burns was probably poisoned?'

'And most likely by someone in his own household,' Ed put in as they walked across the pedestrian crossing, 'because you'd need access to him to give him the stuff.' He looked at Dan. 'How did you get on at the cop shop?'

'I handed over the book,' Dan said. They had walked down the hill and were almost at the *Post*'s office. 'I was told we'd get it back as soon as possible, once they've made sure it's not relevant to the case, but I don't see how it can't be relevant.'

Ed opened his mouth to respond, but before he could, a voice called, 'Are you Dan Sullivan?'

They looked up to see a squat man in a knee-length black leather jacket hurrying up the hill towards them. The top of his head was bald and what remained of his hair was long and tied in a ponytail. Chunky black leather boots completed the look.

'Yes,' Dan said warily as the man stopped in front of him, slightly out of breath.

'I've been looking for you. I saw your photo in the paper.'

Dan looked sideways at Ed, who looked like he was about to make a run for it.

'You wrote about Jayne Winter's murder,' the man said.

Dan looked the man up and down. 'Yes, I did. Do you know her?'

The man snorted. 'After a fashion.'

Dan and Ed waited for him to continue, but he just stared at them.

'How did you know her?' Dan asked, wondering how this man could have known an academic.

'Let's just say we had shared interests.'

'Simeon Burns' treasure?' Ed asked.

The man bristled. 'What do you know about that?' he demanded. 'Do you know her?'

'We went to college with her years ago,' Ed said, with a sideways glance at Dan.

'We'd not spoken to her since—' Dan began, but halted when the man took a half step forward.

'She told you, didn't she? She's found something out about the treasure and she's told you where it is.'

Dan backed away slightly, hands raised as if in surrender. 'No, look, she hasn't told us anything. Ed's talking about the Allensbury Historical Society treasure hunt, but I don't think Jayne was even taking part in that.'

The man growled. 'That treasure is mine by right. You know

where it is, and you will give it to me.'

'Donald Bloom, the guy from the historical society, said the clues are just a game. Who are you anyway?' Dan demanded.

'My name is Tobias Tudham. That treasure was stolen from my great-great-grandfather – and I want it back.'

'Why do you think Jayne had it?' Dan asked.

But before Tudham could say more, the door to the office building opened and Emma appeared at the top of the steps. She looked taken aback and stared at them.

Tudham turned his face away and hissed, 'We can't talk here. Meet me in the park behind the museum at six o'clock tonight.'

He strode away before Dan or Ed could say anything else.

'Another person with an interest in the treasure,' Ed said, looking after the black-clad figure.

'A crazy bod who thinks it's real,' Dan replied. Then he turned to Emma, who had joined them on the pavement.

'When did you get back?' he asked, realising he sounded more snappy than he intended.

Emma smiled nervously. 'Last night. The secondment finished early. It was really late or I'd have texted you.'

There was an awkward silence. Dan was conflicted. He was pleased to see Emma despite their arguing, but was resentful she hadn't let him know she was coming home early.

Ed stepped in. 'How was the secondment?' he asked brightly. 'Was it fun?'

'It was fine,' Emma said. She looked up the hill where Tudham was rapidly disappearing. 'Who was that guy and why are you meeting him later?'

Ed opened his mouth to speak, but Dan cut him off.

'Just someone for a story,' he said. 'We're late,' he added, gesturing towards the office building. 'We can explain later.'

'You've been missing out on some fun,' Ed said, grinning.

Emma smiled. 'I've got to pop out now, but catch you later?' Dan gave a short nod and, with a little wave, Emma turned and headed up the hill.

'Well, that was awkward,' Ed said, as he followed Dan into the building. 'You really didn't know she was coming back early?'

Dan shook his head. He didn't trust himself to speak. It had really hurt that Emma hadn't let him know she was home safely, as she usually did.

'I'm sure she didn't mean to upset you,' Ed said, clearly correctly reading Dan's silence.

'What does it say that she *didn't* tell me?' Dan asked, as they crossed the reception area.

'You weren't exactly getting along before she went away. Perhaps she didn't want to do it by text.'

Dan sighed. 'Maybe you're right.'

But he had no idea how he was going to share desk space with Emma all day when he felt so let down.

Chapter Thirty

It was five minutes to six when Dan and Ed arrived at Castle Park for their meeting with Tobias Tudham. Now that they were here, Dan was feeling uncomfortable. What if he was walking himself and Ed into danger? How crazy was Tudham if he believed in the treasure?

As they walked through the park gates, Ed asked, 'Do you really think the treasure is his? He sounds a bit crackers, doesn't he?' His eyes were scanning the area in front of them.

'I'm more worried that he thought Jayne had the treasure and that she's given it to us. What might he do to get it back?' Dan asked, glancing over his shoulder.

Ed stared at him. 'You think he might have killed her?'

But before Dan could reply, Tudham appeared from behind a nearby tree, making them jump. 'Were you followed?' he demanded with an aggressive step forward.

Dan and Ed instinctively took a step back and looked at each other.

'Erm, no, I don't think so,' Dan said, looking over his shoulder. 'Does it matter?'

Tudham glared at him. 'I don't want anyone to overhear us.'

'OK,' Dan said, gesturing around, 'we're here, there's no one else around. What do you want?'

'I want to know what Jayne Winter told you about the treasure. She said she was close to finding it. Did she tell you where it is?'

Dan raised his hands in surrender. 'Hey, no, she didn't tell us anything about the treasure. Why do you think she did?'

'You're friends with her and you've got her notebook.'

Dan felt a chill run down his spine and he could see Ed tense up.

'Why do you think we've got her notebook?' he asked, trying to keep his voice level and calm.

'I know you have it and it tells you where the treasure is,' Tudham snapped.

'What makes you say that?' Dan asked, wracking his brains for how to get out of this situation.

Tudham paced in front of them. 'I've been researching my family tree and I came across some online message boards from the Allensbury Historical Society. People were talking about the upcoming exhibition and what was in it. I was following the conversation when a message popped up from Jayne Winter.'

'What did she say?'

'She said she knew where the treasure is. She just needed one more bit of proof and she'd have it. But it's mine and I wanted her to give it to me.'

'What else did Jayne say?' Dan asked.

'She said that she was coming to town to do more research at the exhibition, so I staked out the museum until the day I saw her going in. I followed her inside and watched her. She was walking around looking at the exhibition pieces and scribbling in that notebook. I thought if I could just sneak a look at it, then I'd be able to find out where the treasure is.' Tudham took a deep breath. 'When she left the museum, I followed her.'

'Straight to Old Manor?' Dan asked.

'I didn't know where she was going and I lost her at a set of traffic lights,' he said, not meeting Dan's eye.

Dan glanced at Ed, not sure whether he believed Tudham.

'Now,' Tudham said, 'I want that notebook.' A small pistol appeared in the man's hand. 'And you're going to give it to me.'

'What are you doing?' Dan asked, hoping his voice didn't sound as shaky as he thought it did. 'We don't know anything about the treasure.' Out of the corner of his eye, he saw Ed raise his hands in surrender.

'I want that notebook.' The hand holding the gun was as steady as a surgeon's.

'I don't have it, I gave it to the police,' Dan said, suddenly wishing he had the notebook to hand.

Tobias Tudham was glaring at him.

'They think it's relevant to Jayne's murder, that she was killed because of what was in there,' Dan said.

Tudham stared stonily at Dan. 'Who else is looking for the notebook?' he demanded.

'Professor Sir Stewart Randall. He offered us money for it and—' Ed paused, seeing a look flash across Tudham's face. 'You know him, don't you?'

Tudham lowered the gun slightly and shook his head. 'Never heard of him.'

'He's the one who told you we've got the notebook, isn't he?' Ed continued, moving slightly backwards, away from Tudham. Dan, seeing him, did the same.

Tudham shifted from one foot to the other. 'No, I – well—'

'He knows about the treasure too, doesn't he?' Ed asked. He glanced at Dan, who was unsure where Ed was going with this. 'I'd be surprised if he doesn't already know where it is, wouldn't you?' he asked, eyeing Dan.

Tudham was taking the bait. 'He knows where the treasure is?' he demanded.

Ed nodded. 'I think he's probably got the evidence hidden in his office at the university.'

But Tudham was clearly making another decision and the gun was again levelled at them.

Suddenly a voice yelled, 'Stop right there.'

Dan and Ed spun around to see Emma standing a short distance away, her phone trained on the trio. Tudham lowered the gun in surprise.

'Emma?' Dan and Ed said in unison.

'I've got it all recorded,' Emma said, 'that entire conversation, and I think the police will be very interested in it.'

Tudham's gun turned on her.

Emma's phone stayed on him. 'There's no point in killing me. It backs up into the cloud straight away. Someone else can access it from there.'

Taking advantage of the distraction, Dan yanked a folded-up copy of that day's *Allensbury Post* from his bag and flung it into Tudham's face. The man cried out, took several steps backwards and fell over a tree root. It sent him sprawling to the ground.

'Run!' Dan yelled.

Ed didn't need telling twice and they both sprinted towards the park gates. Dan grabbed Emma's hand as he passed and yanked her along behind him. They dashed onto the High Street and, as they passed the museum, Ed noticed the front door was still open.

He grabbed Dan's arm, dragging him and Emma inside. As they peered out of the door, Tudham raced past, the gun apparently now stowed away in his pocket.

After a few minutes, Ed looked out of the doorway and down the High Street.

'I think he's gone,' he said, sagging against the wall and trying to get his breath back. He coughed heavily several times. 'Need to give up the ciggies,' he gasped.

Dan was trying to recover his own breath. 'Thank God today's edition is one of the heavier ones. I never thought I'd be grateful for the property section.' He dragged a hand through his hair. 'What the hell just happened?' he asked.

'I think we were just threatened by a treasure hunter with a pistol,' Ed replied, coughing again. 'That's one for the memoir.'

'And what the hell were you doing?' Dan turned on Emma. 'You could have been killed.'

'I was saving your backside, in case you hadn't noticed,' she snapped, hands on hips.

'How did you know where we were going?'

'After I saw you with that man earlier, I assumed you were probably going to do something incredibly stupid. So I thought I'd better come along and see what was going on. And aren't you glad I did?'

'Definitely,' said Ed, pushing Dan aside and flinging his arms around Emma. 'I've never been so pleased to see anyone in my life.'

She grinned and Dan had to agree that he was glad she'd turned up unexpectedly for the second time in one day.

'Did you really get a video?' he asked.

Emma nodded. 'I got there just after you did. I thought we might need some evidence.'

Dan rubbed his forehead. 'This whole treasure thing is getting more bizarre every minute. Donald Bloom says it's a myth; Tudham says it's real and belongs to him. I mean, what could Simeon Burns have that really belonged to Franklin Tudham?'

Ed took a deep breath and coughed again. 'Maybe there's more in Jayne's notebook.' He jerked a thumb at the museum. 'I didn't see anything about treasure in there.'

Dan took a deep breath and puffed out his cheeks. 'But Tudham definitely knows Randall, or at least knows who he is.'

'Have they teamed up to find the treasure?' Emma suggested.

Dan shook his head. 'My guess is that neither would want to share. But you're right that they both have a motive for killing Jayne.'

Ed coughed heavily and then said, 'What do we do now?'

Dan glanced over his shoulder into the museum. 'Firstly, we need to get out of here before Gracie sees us and wants to know what we're doing.'

'Who's Gracie?' Emma asked, looking puzzled.

'I'll explain later,' Dan said, ducking out of the doorway. 'We need to call the police and report him. If we can convince them that Tudham is involved, then it'll get him off our backs for a while. I'd rather not get a gun pointed at me again.'

Chapter Thirty-One

Burton was standing in her office doorway on Thursday morning, squinting at a sticky note she'd removed from her desk. *What the hell does that say?* she thought, looking down at the tightly packed scribble.

Gary Topping appeared at her elbow, clutching two takeaway coffees. 'I heard you chatting to the DCI, so I thought you might need this.'

Burton took a coffee, grateful for his thought. 'Thanks, that makes a better start to my Thursday than a chat with the boss. However,' she dangled the note in front of his face, 'I have no idea what that even says.' She handed him the note and turned back into her office.

'It's an update on the notebook,' he said, looking downcast as he followed her. 'I thought that was obvious.'

Burton took back the note and looked at it again. 'That doesn't look like it says anything about a notebook.' She sat in her desk chair and indicated to Topping to sit down as well. 'Scruffy hand-writing aside, what have you got?'

'Well, I'm not sure how much use it'll be,' he said, putting his coffee down on Burton's desk. 'Sullivan was right. It's basically all the research she's done on Simeon Burns and his murder. Her handwriting is worse than mine.'

Burton laughed. 'She *is* a doctor. They always have rubbish handwriting.' Then she frowned. 'So you don't think this got her killed?'

Topping leaned back in his chair. 'I dunno, boss. I mean, you said Randall tried to buy the notebook from Sullivan. Why do that if the notebook isn't relevant?'

'It may be relevant to him, but not to our investigation,' Burton said, stroking her chin. 'He might have nothing to do with her murder.'

'Oh, I wouldn't say that,' said a voice from the doorway.

Burton looked up to see Shepherd grinning, with a document in his hand.

She sat up straighter. 'You've got something good?' she asked, feeling adrenaline kick in. Topping looked like he was holding his breath.

'Jayne Winter's car had only her fingerprints, and hairs on the seat headrest were hers too.' He continued scanning the document. 'So it looks like she didn't have anyone in the car with her.'

'Stands to reason,' Burton said, 'if she didn't know anyone locally, and she doesn't sound the type to just offer someone a lift.'

'But,' Shepherd said, pausing for dramatic effect, 'remember those prints that they found on the door frame at Old Manor?' When Burton nodded, he continued, 'They had some technical issues, but they've now managed to ID one set of prints. They were in our system after a speeding arrest.'

'Get on with it,' Burton snapped. 'I can't bear the suspense. Whose are they?'

'Professor Sir Stewart Randall.'

Burton stared at him. 'Professor Randall? He was at Old Manor Hall?'

Shepherd nodded. 'He lied when he said he'd never been to the place. The question is, was he there before or after Jayne Winter, or was he there at the same time and he's our killer?'

'Let's go and find out, shall we?' Burton got to her feet and swung on her suit jacket. She glanced at her watch. 'I think a trip to the university is in order.'

Chapter Thirty-Two

At the *Allensbury Post* office, Dan and Emma sat side by side at their desks in a slightly uncomfortable silence. Out of the corner of his eye, Dan could see her watching him as he tapped quickly at the keyboard, desperately trying to write up his latest copy for the news editor's deadline. He clicked send and spun his chair to face her.

'What's the matter?' he asked.

'I'm sorry,' she whispered.

Dan stared at her. 'About what?' he asked in his normal voice.

Emma flapped a hand. 'Shhh. I mean, I'm sorry I didn't tell you I was back early. You're cross at me, aren't you?'

Dan sighed and shook his head. 'I was surprised because normally you would text but, to be honest, I don't blame you at the moment,' he said, matching her speaking volume. 'We've not exactly been in each other's good books lately.'

'That's an understatement, but I did save your life,' Emma said, 'so I must get some brownie points for that.'

Dan couldn't help himself. Emma could always make him smile. He laughed. 'That's exploitation, you know, using that kind of scenario to—' But before he got any further, he was interrupted by Ed's desk phone ringing. He picked up his receiver and tapped a few buttons to take the call.

The voice on the other end was shaky and tear-filled. 'Ed? Ed, is that you?'

'No, it's Dan,' he said. 'Who is this?'

'It's Gracie. Gracie Lincoln.' Her voice was wobbling on the verge of tears. 'Is Ed there? I tried his mobile, but he's not answering.'

'He's at court. His phone will be off. What's the matter? Has something happened?'

Gracie's voice cracked. 'Can you come now? I found a dead body in the museum. I'm scared.'

Dan stood up, suddenly making a passing sub-editor jump several feet and drop the page he'd just taken from the printer.

'What? Who is it?' He paused. 'Have you called the police?'

'Yes, they're coming now.' Gracie was breaking into sobs. 'I don't know what to do.'

Dan cradled the phone under his chin as he grabbed his coat from his chair and started shoving his arms into the sleeves. 'OK, don't worry. I'm on my way.'

'Don't worry?' Gracie squeaked. 'How can I not worry? He's dead, on the floor, in the exhibition. And there's blood everywhere. I think he's been stabbed.'

Dan's hand shook slightly. 'Do you know who it is?'

Gracie sniffed hard. 'Yes. His name is Professor Sir Stewart Randall.'

Chapter Thirty-Three

Dan dropped the handset back onto the phone with a loud clatter.

Emma got to her feet. 'What is it?' she demanded as Dan dragged on his coat and stuffed his notebook into his pocket. 'Where are you going?' she asked as he rooted around on his desk for a pen.

'The curator at the museum just found a dead body in the Simeon Burns exhibition,' he said, lowering his voice. 'It's Professor Sir Stewart Randall.'

Emma gaped at him. 'The guy who tried to buy Jayne's notebook?'

Dan nodded. 'And now he's dead.'

Emma pulled on her jacket and grabbed her handbag.

'What are you doing?' Dan asked.

'Coming with you. It could be dangerous.'

Dan laughed as he started to walk away down the office. 'The guy's dead. He can't do anything to me now.'

Emma fell into step beside him. 'No, I just meant that—' She caught sight of his grin and elbowed him. 'Hey, I was being nice and trying to help.'

Dan laughed more. 'Much appreciated,' he said, holding the

door for her.

They hurried down the stairs and out into the street.

'You know what this means,' Emma said as they headed up the hill to the high street. 'This is the second person with a connection to this case – to that notebook – who's been killed. That crazy Tudham guy knows you've got it. He knew about Stewart Randall as well. What if he—'

Dan looked at her as they dodged through shoppers on the high street, her words sinking in. 'You think he killed Randall and he's going to come after me again?'

Emma eyed him. 'What if he does?' she asked in a small voice.

'Look, I'll be fine,' he said, hoping his voice sounded more confident to her than it did in his head. 'If you give that video to the police, Burton will get him in no time. You know what she's like.'

'Jayne's really put you in the firing line,' Emma said, slightly out of breath as they hurried along the high street.

Dan thought for a moment. 'She sounded scared in that letter.'

'And now we know why,' Emma snapped.

When they arrived at the museum, both slightly out of breath, they stared at the front door. Shards of wood protruded from the wooden outer door where someone had ripped the lock from its frame. Glass from the smashed inside door littered the floor in the reception area.

'Wow, someone really wanted to get in here,' Emma said, peering at the scratches around the lock. 'A crowbar?' she asked, looking at him over her shoulder.

Dan shrugged. 'Possibly.' He stepped into the entrance hall, glass crunching under his feet.

Gracie was huddled behind the reception desk, tears running down her face. He called her name and she crossed the room, throwing herself into his arms. He patted her awkwardly on the back and led her back inside. Emma followed them, bristling slightly at Gracie's reaction.

'What happened?' he asked.

Gracie sniffed and stepped away from him, pulling a tissue from her jeans pocket. 'When I came in this morning, I found the doors like that. I was worried about the exhibits, so I went through there.' She pointed towards the door into the Georgian exhibition. 'That's when I found him.' She turned as if to lead the way to the other room. Dan desperately wanted to see the scene, but his conscience got the better of him.

'We'd better stay out of there,' he said. 'It's a crime scene.'

Gracie nodded miserably. 'I've never seen anyone dead before,' she said.

Dan patted her arm, not sure what else to do. He'd encountered dead bodies before and he remembered the feeling of shock and queasiness it brought on. 'You said it's Professor Sir Stewart Randall in there,' he said, pointing.

Gracie nodded and sniffed. 'I don't know why he'd break in. He just had to come round when we're open.'

Dan puffed out his cheeks. 'Why would someone want to stab him?' he asked, looking round at Emma.

Gracie suddenly clapped a hand to her mouth. 'I think I'm going to be sick.' She charged through a door marked 'staff only' and it slammed behind her.

Dan looked at Emma, stomach flickering. 'It's too much of a coincidence that two people with an interest in Simeon Burns have been murdered within days of each other,' he said.

Emma nodded. 'Two people who knew each other, and both were somewhere that they shouldn't be.' She looked towards the exhibition doorway. 'Reckon we can have a peek?'

Before they could move, the 'staff only' door where Gracie had gone reopened and she came out, looking pale and sweaty.

Dan turned to offer comfort, but his brain was buzzing. He'd suspected Randall of being involved in Jayne's death, but now he was dead too, murdered. Could this really be about research into Simeon Burns and the treasure hunt? Either way, he knew which name he'd be offering to the police as soon as they arrived.

***

It wasn't long before uniformed officers arrived on the scene and forced Dan, Emma and Gracie outside. The latter was still shaking like a leaf and fainted, which meant an ambulance was called. By the time Emma had made a trip to the nearest café for a sugary tea for Gracie, Burton and Shepherd had arrived at the scene.

'How do you do it?' Burton demanded, hands on hips. 'How are you at the scene before us?'

Dan opened his mouth to defend himself, but Gracie interrupted.

'I called Dan,' she said. 'I didn't know what else to do.'

Leaving Shepherd to speak to Gracie, Burton led Dan and Emma to a safe distance. 'Why did she call you?'

'Ed and I saw her on Saturday when we went to the museum.' Dan shook his head, running a hand through his hair. 'God, this is crazy.'

'You know who it is?' Burton asked, pointing over her shoulder.

Dan nodded. 'Gracie said it's Professor Sir Stewart Randall.' He paused and then said, 'It's suspicious, isn't it, that he and Jayne were both killed so close together, while they were both investigating Simeon Burns?'

Burton puffed out her cheeks. 'I definitely don't think it's a coincidence.'

'There's something else,' Dan said.

'Isn't there always with you guys?' Burton asked. When Dan told her about Tobias Tudham, she gave a low whistle. 'And you have this incident on video?' she asked.

Emma nodded. 'We were going to give it to you today.'

'Do that. We need to get this guy ASAP. And you say he was talking about treasure, not about Simeon Burns being murdered?' Burton asked, pulling out a notebook and scribbling on a clean page.

Dan nodded. 'He was talking about it like the treasure is real and belongs to his family.'

Burton looked confused. 'He thinks the treasure is real?'

'Yes, and he thinks the treasure hunt will actually lead to it.'

'But it won't?'

Dan shook his head. 'The chair of the historical society says no one knows if it really exists, so they just made up some clues.'

Burton checked her watch. 'Right, I need you two to leave now. You'll get an update later today,' she said, holding up a hand to stem Emma's protestations. 'And send me that video. I don't suppose you know where to find this Tudham fella?'

'He found us,' Dan said, 'which is more than slightly worrying.'

'If he comes near you again, you call nine nine nine.'

Dan and Emma agreed and reluctantly left the scene.

'Do you think Tobias Tudham killed Jayne and Randall?' Emma asked as they walked down the high street.

'Maybe, if he thought it would stop them from finding the treasure first,' Dan said. 'Tudham definitely knew Randall, so maybe he got him to agree to meet. But would you meet someone at the museum at night?'

'Depends how desperate I was for information,' Emma said.

They were passing the Italian café when Dan stopped dead. 'I've not had enough caffeine today. Do you want one?'

Emma nodded. 'Then we need to find out more about the Burns family and whether Jayne and Randall knew something that might be a reason to kill them.' She took a deep breath. 'And before the killer decides to come after anyone else who's seen that notebook.'

Chapter Thirty-Four

Burton walked across to the ambulance to see a paramedic helping Gracie Lincoln down the steps from inside. She was shivering and wrapped in a foil blanket. Having left her coat in the car, Burton considered asking for one herself.

'How are you feeling?' she asked Gracie as the other woman perched on the back step of the vehicle. 'Are you up to a few questions?'

Gracie nodded and Shepherd sat down beside her. The ambulance dipped under his weight, making her sway.

'Ugh, that doesn't help the queasiness,' she said, giving Shepherd a pale smile.

'Sorry,' he replied, smiling back at her. 'We just need to talk to you quickly to check what you saw when you came into work this morning,' he said.

Gracie described seeing the doors smashed.

'And you went inside?' Burton asked, shoving her hands into her trouser pockets to stop them shaking. 'You didn't think someone might be in there?'

'I was more worried about the exhibits,' Gracie said.

'The burglar alarm didn't trigger. Why would that be?' Shepherd asked.

Gracie frowned. 'I don't know. I definitely set it last night.'

Burton, who was now shivering herself, asked, 'What did you see next?'

Gracie took a deep breath. 'I went straight into the exhibition space and then I found Professor Randall just lying there.'

'You know him?' Burton asked.

Gracie nodded. 'He's around the museum quite a lot. He did a lecture here about four months ago.'

'Had he been to the museum more recently, to see the Georgian exhibition, for instance?'

After a moment's thought, Gracie said, 'I'm sure he'll have been here at least once. Cath, she's my boss, might have seen him. He was certainly around a lot when we were planning the exhibition, trying to tell me what I should put in it. But I'd already agreed the content with the Allensbury Historical Society.'

'It's the museum's anniversary, isn't it?' Shepherd asked.

Gracie nodded. 'It's been two hundred years since Benjamin Burns established the museum. He was Simeon Burns' dad.'

Burton sighed. 'We've heard a lot about Simeon Burns already this week.'

'Because of Jayne Winter's death?' Gracie asked. 'I told your officer about her being here.'

'Do you know why Professor Randall would be here outside of opening hours? Was he a key holder?'

Gracie shook her head. 'No, he's a "Friend" of the museum, and that brings some perks like cheap exhibition tickets and things like that, but not keys or the burglar alarm code.' She wiped her eye on her sleeve. 'It's crazy that he broke in.'

Shepherd was frowning. 'Was Professor Randall involved in the treasure hunt?'

Gracie wrinkled her nose. 'He was very scathing when Donald said that they were going to do it.' Then she frowned. 'He mentioned the treasure once, when I was sorting out pieces for the exhibition. I was sorting through some papers and he came in and started trying to look through them. I shooed him away because he didn't have gloves on and he might damage the documents. He got really cross and then said if I found anything about the Burns' treasure, I had to tell him.'

'And did you find anything?'

Gracie snorted. 'It's a game to raise some money for the museum and the historical society. It doesn't exist.'

'Does the name Tobias Tudham mean anything to you?' Burton asked, earning herself a surprised look from Shepherd.

Gracie frowned for a few moments and then said, 'Well, I know of Franklin Tudham, who was a mill owner like Simeon Burns. Why?'

'Just a name that came up in our investigation.' Burton glanced at Shepherd, who had finished scribbling. 'I think that's all we need for now, Miss Lincoln, but we may have questions later. We'll also need a list of people with the alarm code for the museum.'

'No problem.' Gracie got to her feet, swayed slightly and then righted herself. 'I can get that for you.'

Before she took a step, a small woman with tightly curled grey hair and a padded anorak rushed to Gracie's side and enveloped her in a hug.

'This is Cath,' Gracie said, sounding slightly muffled by Cath's shoulder.

'Why are you questioning Gracie?' the older woman demanded.

'She's a witness,' said Shepherd gently. 'We need to find out what she saw and heard when she found Professor Randall, that's all.'

'The alarm didn't go off, Cath,' Gracie said, interrupting Cath revving up to argue, 'so they think whoever did this had the alarm code.'

Cath bristled and glared at Burton. 'Are you suggesting that someone from the museum would—'

But Burton held up a hand. 'We're not accusing anyone, but we need to know who could have had access.'

Cath swept an arm towards the front of the museum. 'None of our staff would do this.'

'We just need to rule people out of the investigation,' Shepherd said, trying for a reassuring smile, but the older woman didn't look convinced.

'When can we go back inside?' she asked.

'The museum will have to stay closed until our forensic team finishes its investigation,' Shepherd said. 'We'll let you know when you can reopen.'

Cath pursed her lips, and Burton reflected that Shepherd's charm was cutting no ice here. She tucked an arm around Gracie, who was still shaking. 'We'll get you somewhere warm for a nice cup of tea,' she said to Gracie, 'while I inform the museum board what's happened. Then I'll get you home.'

Burton nodded. 'That's a great idea.' She pulled a business card from her suit jacket pocket and handed it to Gracie. 'Take care, and if you think of anything else, call me. An officer will be along later today to take a formal statement.'

Gracie nodded, but before she could say anything else, she was tucked firmly under Cath Middlebury's arm and led away towards the nearby café.

'So, who is Tobias Tudham?' Shepherd asked, tucking his note-book into his pocket.

'You won't believe me when I tell you,' Burton said, leading the way towards the museum door.

***

'Stilettos are not compatible with broken glass,' Burton said, as she paused in the museum doorway to pull on crime scene booties.

Shepherd grinned. 'They've thought of that already,' he said with a grin, pointing to the thick foam pads that created a pathway across the reception area.

Burton laughed. 'All about my safety and comfort,' she said, as she stepped delicately from pad to pad.

'Who is this Tobias Tudham, then?' Shepherd asked as he carefully followed her. His eyes widened as Burton explained. 'Blimey, he threatened them with a gun?'

'What worries me more,' Burton said, chewing the inside of her mouth, 'is that he did it in the middle of a public area in broad daylight. He chased them onto the high street as well before they lost him.'

'He found them easily in the first place,' Shepherd said. 'So he could do it again.'

'Hopefully now he knows they got him on video, he'll leave them alone. But finding him is a priority.'

Shepherd nodded and pulled out his phone. 'I'll call Madison now. Do we know anything about him?'

Burton sighed in frustration. 'So far, just his name and what he looks like, courtesy of that video.' She stepped inside the darkened exhibition room, taking a couple of seconds for her eyes to adjust to the lower ambient lights.

Eleanor Brody looked up from the floor. 'This lighting is not making my job any easier,' she grumbled.

'Can they not put more light on?' Burton asked, looking around.

Brody shook her head. 'Bad for the exhibits, apparently.'

Burton tutted. More respect for ancient artifacts than a human life, she thought.

'First impressions?' she asked Brody.

'As your witness thought, he has stab wounds to the abdomen. Two, and they're pretty forceful ones.'

'A man or a woman?'

Brody sighed. 'Could be either. A sharp weapon wouldn't need much weight behind it.'

When Shepherd appeared, Burton asked, 'Did Gracie Lincoln say if she touched anything?'

He nodded. 'Before you came over, she said she turned him over, thought he'd collapsed or something. Then saw the blood and ran to phone an ambulance.'

Burton looked around the room, hands on hips. 'But phoned Dan Sullivan first,' she said. 'What was he doing breaking in here?' she asked, pointing at Randall. 'What couldn't wait until opening hours?'

'We've also just lost our prime suspect for Jayne Winter's murder,' Shepherd said. When Brody gave him a quizzical look, he added, 'Those fingerprints the crime scene team found on the door frame at Old Manor belonged to him.'

Burton rubbed her nose. 'So now we're looking for someone who wanted to kill Jayne Winter and Stewart Randall,' she said, looking at Shepherd.

'It sounds like Tobias Tudham had a reason if he thought they were trying to get the treasure first. It also sounds like he knew both of them,' Shepherd said.

Burton screwed up her forehead. 'Do you think he lured Randall here or the other way around?' she asked. 'Neither of them would have keys, which would explain the broken doors, but not the burglar alarm.'

'And why the museum?' Shepherd asked.

'Exactly. They could have met anywhere, anytime, so why here? What were they hoping to find?'

'A clue to the treasure?' Shepherd suggested.

'Maybe, but why not come during the day? What was so important that they had to break in?' She sighed. 'Has Randall's family been informed?'

Shepherd nodded. 'I sent a couple of uniforms round to his daughter. She seems to be the only family.'

'Right,' Burton said, as they turned to leave the museum, 'maybe she can shed some light on what he might have been doing.'

Chapter Thirty-Five

When Helen Randall opened the door to Burton and Shepherd, she looked drained. Behind a closed door at the end of the hall, they could hear what sounded like fifteen children shouting and arguing.

She rolled her eyes. 'There are only three of them,' she said, 'despite the amount of noise they're making.'

Burton smiled, recognising the sound. 'My two are exactly the same, especially when they're tired after school.'

Helen led the way into the sitting room and perched on a leather recliner. Burton and Shepherd took the sofa and an armchair, respectively.

'They're my kids and I love them, but right now I just need some peace and quiet.'

Shepherd nodded. 'We're sorry about your father,' he said.

Helen's shoulders drooped. 'I can't believe someone killed him,' she said. 'He could be difficult at times, but...' She trailed off and raised a hand to wipe away a tear with her cardigan sleeve.

Shepherd leaned forward in his chair. 'We were hoping to ask you a few questions about your dad,' he said. When Helen nodded, he continued, 'Given the injuries he suffered, can you think of anyone who may have wanted to hurt him?'

Helen sighed. 'That's just it ... I can't. He was single-minded, which could sometimes rub people up the wrong way, but surely that's not enough to make them kill him?'

'You can't think of anyone specifically?' Shepherd pressed.

The woman shook her head, her mouth pulling down at the corners. Then she frowned. 'Actually, now you mention it, there was a man who came knocking a couple of days ago looking for Dad.'

'Does your father live here?' Burton asked, surprised.

Helen shook her head. 'He used to. When Mum was alive, this was their house, our family home. I grew up here. When she died, he said he didn't need such a big house, so my husband and I bought it from him and he bought a bungalow.' She sniffed. 'He never minded downsizing, although we had to be sure to find one with a room big enough for all his books.'

'But the man came here?' Burton asked, keen to know who the visitor was.

'I thought maybe he had Dad's address from a few years ago. He's only been in the new bungalow for about two years.'

'Did you give him your father's address?'

'God, no,' Helen said, looking shocked. 'He seemed a bit crazy and not the kind of man my dad would be friends with.'

Burton leaned forward in her chair, pretty sure she already knew what Helen was going to say next. 'What did he look like?' she asked.

Helen thought for a moment. 'He looked a bit like an aging rocker. Long grey hair in a ponytail, dressed all in black with massive chunky boots.'

'Did he say what he wanted?'

'He started off really calm and polite, asking to speak to Dad. When I asked what about, he said that Dad would know what it was about, that it was urgent.'

'Then when you refused to tell him?'

'He got angry, shouting and saying that he had to find Dad, that it was a matter of life and death.' She sighed. 'I tried to shut the door on him, but he wouldn't leave. In the end, I told him to try the university. I figured he would have to go to the reception area, and the tigers in the office would never let him through.' She smiled. 'They're very protective.'

Burton smiled back. 'We met them when we went to see your father last week.'

Helen looked surprised. 'Why did you need to speak to Dad?'

'He didn't tell you?' Burton asked, taking her turn to look surprised.

The other woman shook her head.

'A former colleague of his died last week and...' Burton began.

Then, to her surprise, Helen asked, 'Jayne Winter?' When Burton nodded, Helen added, 'She was a bit of a menace.'

'Menace?' Shepherd asked. 'What makes you say that?'

Helen sighed. 'She made Dad's life incredibly difficult. Only stayed at the university for a year, but caused him all kinds of headaches.'

'How do you mean?'

'Dad was very competitive about his work, I suppose all academics are, but he used to drive Mum mad because every holiday they went on turned into a research trip.'

Shepherd smiled. 'We've heard that Jayne Winter was cut from the same cloth,' he said.

Helen nodded. 'She drove Dad crazy. He didn't take any holiday for the whole time she was there. He was obsessive about locking his office door and bringing important material home with him, but she still broke in and stole a really important document.'

'What did she steal?' Burton asked.

'It was a letter about Simeon Burns, something about a doctor asking for help with Simeon's illness. Dad thought no one knew he had it, but she found out, took it and wouldn't give it back.'

Suddenly, the living room door flew open and a wailing child rushed in.

'She's broke my dolly,' sobbed the little girl, the doll's body in one hand and a leg in the other.

Helen looked entirely non-plussed, clearly not expecting mothering duties at such short notice.

'Let me have a look,' said Burton, holding out a hand to the little girl. She looked unsure. 'I have special skills in doll healing,' Burton said seriously. 'Maybe I can help?'

Reluctantly, the child approached and held out the body and limb.

Burton carefully examined the patient and said, 'This won't hurt a bit.' Then she quickly pushed the leg into the hip socket with a satisfying click. She moved the leg back and forwards a few times and then beamed at the child. 'All fixed.' She held up the doll to her ear. 'And she says she's perfectly fine and can you both go and play, please?'

The child was all smiles, took the toy and gave Burton's arm a quick hug before dashing back out of the room and slamming the door.

Burton rubbed her hands together and smiled at Helen. 'My daughters have the same doll, and arms and legs are always coming off.'

Helen smiled back and drew her cardigan sleeve across her eyes again. 'Thank you,' she said, tiredly. 'Their dad will be home soon and he's usually the doll surgeon.' Then she shook herself. 'Sorry, where was I?'

'Jayne Winter and the stolen source material,' Shepherd said.

Helen nodded. 'She was always nipping at his heels and messing up her teaching so he'd have to step in and take classes, creating more research time for her and less for him.'

'We found some angry emails from your father on Jayne's computer,' Shepherd said. 'Saying that she should stop writing the book she was working on or he would stop her.'

Helen sighed. 'The bloody book,' she said. 'He was working on a new Simeon Burns angle, something he said no one else knew about. He had a publishing contract all lined up and then she came along, saying she was writing the same thing and would publish hers before him.' She shook her head. 'I thought it would be the death of him. He was so stressed.'

'She was back in town for a few days before she died,' Burton said. 'Did your father mention if he'd seen her?'

Helen shook her head. 'Until I saw her death in the paper, he hadn't mentioned her at all.'

'We found his fingerprints in Old Manor Hall, where Jayne was killed. Do you know why he would have gone there?'

Helen gasped. 'No, he would never ... He said it wasn't safe, that he—' She broke off. When Burton raised an eyebrow, she added, 'He said he didn't need to go there, but what if he...' She trailed off, clearly imagining what could have happened. 'You don't think he hurt her, do you?'

'We're looking at all possibilities at the moment,' Shepherd said.

'Was there anyone else you can think of who was causing him problems?'

Helen thought for a moment. 'He was upset with the Allensbury Historical Society about the treasure hunt. He hadn't told me officially what his book was about, but I had a feeling it was about the Burns family treasure, because he overreacted when Donald Bloom told him about the competition.'

'Was your dad a member of the society?' Shepherd asked.

Helen shook her head. 'I think he thought it was beneath him,' she said awkwardly. 'Amateurs playing at being historians was how he described them.'

'We understand he'd tried to get involved in setting up the exhibition at the museum.'

'Another bugbear for him. He felt he was the most qualified, but the curator wouldn't let him near it. I remember Dad having a row with Donald Bloom about it. We'd taken the kids to the museum and we bumped into him. They didn't quite have a shouting match, but Donald told Dad to keep his nose out, that he'd catalogued all the papers and if anything went missing, he'd know where to look.'

'What papers?' Burton asked, sensing a new lead.

'I don't know. But Dad said if Donald went ahead with the treasure hunt, he'd sabotage it because no one else should be looking for it.' She sniffed. 'Donald said if Dad spoilt their fundraising efforts, then he wouldn't be responsible for his actions. I didn't think he really meant it, but now...' She trailed off, clearly not liking her own train of thought.

***

As they settled themselves in the car, Shepherd asked, 'Do you think this Donald Bloom would really have hurt Randall to prevent a charity treasure hunt being ruined?'

Burton puffed out her cheeks, not sure what she believed. 'It sounds so childish to say that you're going to sabotage a charity event. Unless he really believed there's treasure and he wanted to find it first.'

Shepherd dropped the car key into the cup holder between the front seats and pressed the button to start the engine. Then he looked at Burton. 'Was the society expecting to make a lot of money from the treasure hunt? If they desperately need money, would that be enough to make someone kill?'

'I'm more interested in what appears to be Tobias Tudham knocking on the door, claiming he needs to speak to Randall urgently and it's a matter of life and death. Was he exaggerating to get Randall's attention or was he threatening him?'

Shepherd shook his head. 'Either way, that's the second time he's threatened people in the last few days. I'll get Topping to team up with Madison and track him down.'

'Meanwhile,' Burton said, holding up a set of keys, 'we go to Randall's house and have a look around.'

Shepherd checked over his shoulder and pulled out of the parking space. 'Let's find out if he was hiding anything at home that his family doesn't know about,' he added. 'Something that put his life – and possibly Jayne Winter's – at risk.'

Chapter Thirty-Six

Stewart Randall's home was an exceptionally neat bungalow in a cul-de-sac of exceptionally neat bungalows. Front gardens were uniform with closely clipped lawns and flowerbeds without weeds. Inside, its hallway was a plain shade of beige with a slightly darker beige carpet.

'This is clearly the book room,' Shepherd said with a grin, pushing open the door with his elbow. Floor-to-ceiling shelves lined the room, and each shelf was full of books. A much-sat-on wingback leather armchair and matching footstool occupied one corner.

Burton wrinkled her nose. 'Smells very dusty,' she said.

'Well, you can't clean them all every week, can you? It would take hours.'

'Fair point.' Burton walked into the hall. Then she stopped. 'Can you feel a draught?' she asked.

Shepherd stepped out of the room. 'Now you mention it,' he said. He walked past her and into the kitchen, following the cold air. 'Boss,' he called, 'you need to see this.'

Burton followed him and groaned when she saw the broken window in the back door.

'Oh, for God's sake,' she said, pulling out her mobile phone. 'I'll get the CSIs. Don't touch anything else. We'll wait outside.'

They had been standing outside Stewart Randall's house for half an hour before the crime scene manager came to give a report.

'His study is the definition of an untidy search,' he said. 'The place is a right mess. Doesn't look like they've touched any other rooms, apart from the broken glass in the kitchen.'

'Any idea when it might have happened?' Burton asked, not holding her breath. It was a long shot at best.

The man shook his head. 'No, it's impossible to tell. We're hoping to get some fingerprints, but it'll be tricky if the person wore gloves. You never know, we might get lucky,' he said with a grin.

Burton thanked him and watched as he turned back into the house. She groaned again.

'Now his house has been broken into,' she said, rubbing a hand over her face. 'Someone thought there was something in that study, but what? And who?'

Shepherd jammed his hands into his trouser pockets. 'And we don't know if they got what they came for.'

He turned as Sophie Madison joined them, notebook in hand. 'What have you got?' he asked.

Madison's eyes scanned down the page. 'The neighbour next door didn't see or hear anything, but they work long hours and so aren't in the house much. Two doors down, they saw a man in black come to the house on Friday evening. She can't remember exactly what time. After dark, but at this time of the year that could be any time. Thought it was weird because he didn't knock or ring the bell. He just went straight round the back.'

'Did she report it?'

Madison shook her head. 'She thought it must have been Randall, but she's kicking herself now for not saying something.'

Burton sighed. 'Can't be helped, but when Brody gives us a time of death, it might suggest whether someone already knew he wasn't at home.'

Shepherd nodded. 'And the description of a man in black—'

'Sounds exactly like Tobias Tudham,' Madison said, scoring a heavy line under the witnesses' details with her ballpoint pen and tearing the page.

'We need Tudham and we need him now,' Burton said, jabbing a finger at Madison. 'I want to know exactly where he was last night and whether he knew Randall was dead.'

Chapter Thirty-Seven

It was Dan's turn to cook that evening, which meant pasta with a jar of ready-made sauce. He carefully measured out dried pasta onto three plates.

'D'you reckon that's enough?' he asked, looking up at Ed who stood in the doorway.

Ed laughed. 'Enough for a small army, but I'm hungry, so go for it.' Then he frowned. 'Three plates?'

Dan opened the pan lid and looked down at the small bubbles in the big pan of water. 'Emma's on her way over,' he said, hoping Ed wouldn't read too much into it. But it was too late.

Ed's eyes widened. 'You guys have patched things up? That's great news, that's—' He stopped, seeing Dan's expression. 'You haven't patched things up.'

Dan shook his head and took a sip from the pint glass of orange squash on the kitchen worktop. 'Let's call it a temporary ceasefire. She did save our lives last night.'

'It's a start.' Ed grinned. 'You know we need her brain, though, don't you? She's cleverer than both of us. Put together.'

Dan glared at him. 'Speak for yourself.' Turning to look into the pan, he saw it was boiling and poured in the pasta. He stirred it, put on the lid and turned back to Ed.

'Poor Gracie,' Ed said.

Dan nodded. 'What I don't understand,' he said, pointing at Ed with a wooden spoon, 'is why Randall was there during the night?'

'He was looking for something that he couldn't get at when other people were around?' Ed asked.

Dan turned to remove the lid and give the pasta a stir. 'It can't have been something that was already on display. Maybe Gracie would know if they have anything in storage.' He scratched his head. 'But can you really see that guy crowbarring a door? I'd more have believed that of Jayne, if I'm honest. She was pretty determined.'

Ed laughed. 'She probably wouldn't have bothered with a crowbar and just chewed through it.'

Dan laughed and turned to stir the pasta. 'Do you think he had help?' he asked, looking over his shoulder at Ed.

'An accomplice, do you mean?'

'And who do we know who is looking for Simeon Burns' treasure?' Dan asked, pointing with the wooden spoon.

Ed stared at him, eyes widening. 'Oh my God, Tobias Tudham. And I told him that Randall had—'

Dan shook his head. 'He already knows Randall. That's the only way he could have known we had the notebook.'

The doorbell rang and Ed turned to go. Then he looked back. 'Your water's boiling over,' he said.

'Oh crap,' Dan said, spinning back to the hob to stir the pasta. It was sticking a bit, but an attack with the spoon soon freed the penne.

'Great, it's pasta night,' Emma said, appearing in the kitchen doorway. 'Good job I'm starving.'

'Why does pasta night mean you need to be starving?' Dan demanded.

'Because you always make way too much,' she said, as if explaining to a small child, 'then I scoff it all, put weight on and moan about it. I just wish you'd make less and save my waistline.'

'Drink, Emma?' Ed asked, quickly squeezing past her to break up what could become a fight.

She nodded and soon had a glass of water in her hand.

'So, where does this museum bloke fit in?' she asked.

Ed gave her the update on their interaction with Professor Sir Stewart Randall.

Emma's eyes widened. 'He offered you a thousand pounds for the notebook?'

Ed nodded, watching as Dan again battled to stop the pasta sticking to the pan. 'He seemed pretty desperate to get his hands on it.'

'Why would anyone pay that much money for a notebook?'

Dan turned away from the pasta. 'Jayne said she'd found something no one else had,' he said. 'It must be in the notebook and that's why he wanted it.'

'It was that doctor's letter that he reacted to,' Ed put in. 'His hands were shaking.'

'What did the letter say?' Emma asked. Dan recounted the contents, and Emma raised her eyebrows. 'And you think that shows that someone murdered Simeon Burns?' she asked.

'According to Gracie, the symptoms he described could be arsenic poisoning,' Ed put in.

Emma stared at him. 'Someone poisoned him with arsenic? Who?'

'That's what we don't know,' Dan said, turning round to stir the pasta again.

Emma picked up the sauce jar and smiled at the label. 'Mmmm, carbonara, my favourite.'

Dan didn't need to look at Ed to know he was grinning. He felt his cheeks flush and he hoped the steamy pan would cover it. So what if he'd chosen her favourite sauce? It didn't mean anything, he told himself.

Emma stood for a moment, head tilted to one side. Dan looked round at her, knowing what that silence meant. The cogs were turning.

'We now have two people,' Emma said, 'both interested in Simeon Burns, who knew each other, who were murdered just a few days apart. That's not a coincidence.'

'But what's the motive?' Dan asked. 'The treasure or the murder?'

Emma shrugged. 'I'd be inclined to say the treasure. Money is a much better motive than a 160-year-old murder. How does that affect anyone?'

'Maybe there's a link between the treasure and the murder?' Ed asked. 'Simeon Burns cursed his family when he was dying and said they'd never find it.'

'Someone killed him to get the treasure?' Emma asked, frowning. 'So he was only really cursing one person?'

'If that's the case,' Dan said, 'that doctor's letter could be the key. Maybe that's why Randall was so desperate to get the notebook. He reacted when he saw that letter.' He turned back to the pan and gave the pasta a quick stir. Then he turned back to look at Emma and Ed. 'If you're right' – he pointed at Ed with the wooden spoon – 'then the notebook just became more important and we need to get it back from the police.'

'Even if it puts us in danger?' Emma demanded. 'Tudham knows you've got it.'

'No,' Dan reminded her, his stomach flickering. 'He thinks the police have it. If we can get it back, then we can work out who killed Simeon Burns and where the treasure is.'

***

Once they'd eaten, washed up and put everything away – under Emma's stern eye – they sat back at the table and looked at each other.

'So,' Dan said, looking at Ed, 'what was Gracie's theory about the arsenic?'

Ed took a sip of his drink. 'She said that the symptoms he had were the same as arsenic poisoning, which can happen over time with small doses or rapidly with large doses.'

'But how would they give it to him?' Emma asked.

'I looked it up,' Ed said, 'and there were a lot of products that had arsenic in them which no one worried about. The Victorians used face cream that had arsenic in it.'

Dan pulled a sceptical face. 'Do you really think that Simeon Burns used face cream?'

'Who knows but that was just one example,' Ed said, glaring at him. 'Lots of women poisoned themselves using that kind of thing.'

Dan thought for a moment and suddenly had a flash of inspiration. He jumped to his feet and dashed into his bedroom.

'Where are you going?' Emma called. She frowned when he

165

returned, clutching his laptop and Jayne's memory stick. 'What's that?'

Dan explained how he got the memory stick and what was on it.

'I just remembered,' he said. He sat back down at the table and Emma pulled her chair closer to his to look over his shoulder. The scent of coconut wafted in his direction. He opened up the image of the letter and turned the screen towards her, trying to ignore the fragrance.

'I saw this letter from his daughter to a friend of hers, but I didn't take it in. She says that he took ill suddenly and "suffered a vast deal".'

'Hmmm, she doesn't sound too sympathetic, does she?' Emma asked, reading down the screen. 'She sounds like she's wishing he was already gone, and not to ease his suffering.' She read a few more lines and then said, 'Ah, so, she wants to get married but Simeon won't let her.'

Dan nodded. 'She makes it sound as if he's stopping her out of spite. What if she poisoned him so she could get married?'

'She would need to know she had money coming once he was gone,' Emma said. 'Which would mean she knew what was in his will, if he had one.'

'Or maybe if her brother is in line for the inheritance, he could have killed Simeon. Or they could be in it together and he'd promised her money,' Dan said, feeling more confused than when they'd started.

'So, our suspects for Simeon's murder are his son and daughter,' she began counting on her fingers, 'the Tudhams...'

'The families of the other people who died in the fire at Tudham's silk mill,' Ed said, 'but I don't know how they would have got to him.'

'It has to have been someone who was in the house,' Emma said, 'given how quickly the arsenic acted.'

Dan ran a hand through his hair, making it stick up in several places. 'Maybe there's something about that in Jayne's notebook. We need to get that back ASAP.'

'I have a briefing with them tomorrow,' Emma said, 'so I'll ask if I can collect it then.'

'Just be careful when you're carrying it around,' Dan said. 'We don't know where Tudham is and he might try to grab it again.'

'I'll be fine. What are you going to be doing while I'm working hard?' Emma asked, patting his arm.

'My diary is stacked for tomorrow,' Dan said. 'Nothing interesting, I hasten to add, so I can't do anything on this 'til the weekend, but I'm going to do some research on wills. If Simeon Burns left one, we can see who benefits and how much was in the kitty. See if it was worth bumping him off before his time.'

'I'm going to the library,' Ed said. 'I'll see if there's anything else useful in there. It's unlikely they'll have what Jayne was looking for, but you never know.' He grinned and rubbed his hands together. 'Who knows, by Saturday night we might have some nice juicy leads to follow up.'

Chapter Thirty-Eight

For once, Brody agreed to meet Burton and Shepherd in her office on Friday morning, rather than in the morgue. When they got there, they found she'd even put on a pot of tea.

'We're honoured,' Burton said, grinning, as they sat down.

'Don't get too used to it,' Brody said sternly. 'This is the first time I've sat down since five o'clock this morning.'

'Early call-out?' Shepherd asked, wincing.

Brody nodded. 'A young lad on an electric scooter hit by a drunk driver.'

Burton and Shepherd were both silent, and she could tell they were as saddened as she was. There was only one way that had gone.

'Did they get the driver?' Shepherd asked.

Brody's hand shook slightly as she poured from the teapot. 'Yes, but I haven't been told the circumstances, apart from him being three times over the legal limit for alcohol,' she said.

Burton shook her head, feeling the doctor's pain. 'No wonder you're tired,' she said, watching as Brody heaped sugar into her own cup. The pathologist stared into her cup as she stirred it, and both Burton and Shepherd took a sip of their tea to give her the time she needed.

Brody took a sip and then put the cup down on the saucer. 'Right, Professor Sir Stewart Randall,' she said, picking up a cardboard folder. 'I did the post-mortem late last night, so we're waiting on toxicology results, etcetera, but I'm not expecting them to show anything that will affect my initial findings. He's going a bit tubby around the middle – not surprising in a man of his age – but he's been battling against it. Lungs in good condition and good muscle tone.' She paused and read the next few lines. 'The cause of death is, as expected, two stab wounds in the abdomen. One hit an artery and he bled out quickly, so he wouldn't have suffered, which is a small mercy for his family.'

'What time of death are we looking at?' Burton asked, thinking of their timeline.

Brody sighed. 'Unfortunately, not as precise as you'd like. The museum is quite warm, even overnight, so it's difficult to say, but any time between seven o'clock and about midnight would be my best guess.'

'OK,' Burton said, 'that's helpful. We know it was definitely after the museum closed.'

'What about the angle of the wounds?' Shepherd asked, scribbling in his notebook.

'Right-handed person, so that's not much help,' Brody said, 'but not an expert in stabbing. The blows are angry rather than accurate.'

'Male or female?' Burton asked, thinking of Tobias Tudham.

Brody pursed her lips and looked down at the folder in front of her. 'It could be either. The knife was very sharp and had a long, thick blade. It didn't take much force to do it.'

'Did he have any cuts on him that don't relate to the stabbing?'

Shepherd asked. Burton gave him a sideways look. 'He supposedly smashed the front door, so is there any evidence of that?'

Brody shook her head. 'No, no damage to his hands.'

'Meaning?' Burton asked, as Shepherd nodded along with Brody.

'He most likely didn't crowbar the other door, either,' Brody said. 'His hands were perfectly smooth, so no way had he used any tools recently or ever, judging by how soft they were.'

'Was he killed where they found him?' Shepherd asked.

Brody nodded. 'There was no blood trail.'

'Any fingerprints other than his? I know it's a long shot,' Burton said.

'Thousands of fingerprints,' Brody said. 'It's a public space and people seem to touch anything and everything. There was a mix-up with the cleaners and they thought they were due there in the morning, not the night as usual, so it's all a bit of a mess.'

Burton sighed heavily. 'Not much to go on,' she said. 'The killer could be male or female, armed with a sharp knife and right-handed.' Then she frowned. 'Do you know what type of weapon it is?'

Brody shook her head. 'I'll make a cast of the wound and see what it looks like.'

'And it wasn't found at the scene?' Burton asked.

Brody shook her head. 'Nothing so far. My guess is the killer took it with them, but the team will keep looking.'

As they left the morgue building, Shepherd looked at Burton. 'Why would someone choose to kill him in the museum? There must have been umpteen opportunities that didn't involve break-ing in somewhere.'

'I agree it seems an odd place to meet.' Burton paused. 'Unless they *had* to meet there.'

'How do you mean?' Shepherd asked.

'What if someone lured Randall to the museum with the promise of something that would help him find the treasure?'

'Tobias Tudham, you mean?'

'He's my prime suspect, but I keep coming back to the burglar alarm code.' She frowned. 'I want to know everyone who has access to this museum and where they were on Wednesday night. Someone helped him and I want to know who and why.'

***

Burton was standing with Sophie Madison updating the timeline board with one for Stewart Randall. Shepherd appeared behind them, grinning, and gave a slight cough to attract their attention.

'I know that look,' Burton said, smiling back and narrowing her eyes. 'You've got something.'

Shepherd held up a plastic evidence bag containing a mobile phone.

'It's a phone,' Burton said, raising her eyebrows, slightly underwhelmed.

'It's Jayne Winter's phone,' said Shepherd, dangling the bag between his thumb and forefinger.

Burton stared at him. 'Have forensics had it all this time and not told us? I'll have a go at the boss if they've—'

But Shepherd held up a hand. 'It was handed in this afternoon by a member of the public who found it in the park.'

'The park?' Burton and Madison asked in unison.

'Apparently so,' Shepherd said. 'They picked it up this morning. The battery was flat so they charged it enough to see if they could switch it on and see whose it was.' He pressed the sides of the phone and the screen lit up. He held it out to Burton, who peered at the screen.

'Jayne Winter,' she said, slowly, taking the phone from him, 'in her graduation outfit.'

Shepherd nodded. 'They recognised her from the photo in the paper, so they brought it in.'

'So did she lose it or was it stolen?' Burton asked.

'And did it happen before or after she was killed?' Madison put in.

'You think the killer took it?' Shepherd asked.

Madison shrugged. 'Given that she didn't have it on her and it wasn't at home or in her car, then I'd say it's a fair shout.'

Burton nodded. 'Her brother did say that she would never have left it behind.' She thought for a moment. 'She told Dan Sullivan that she had proof of something and that someone wanted to steal it from her.'

'And you think it's on the phone?' Shepherd asked.

Burton shrugged. 'Maybe, maybe not, but someone took it *thinking* that it was on there.'

'They killed her for the phone?' Madison asked.

'If they thought the proof was on there and she wouldn't give it up, I can see someone attacking her for it, whether they intended to kill her or not.'

Burton rubbed her hands together, the tiredness that had been plaguing her suddenly lifting. 'Right, get that over to tech. I want a full rundown of what's on it and I want it fingerprinted. I want to know who's had their hands on it.'

Chapter Thirty-Nine

Suzy was sitting with Burton in the interview room when Emma arrived.

'I wasn't expecting to see both of you,' she said, smiling.

'We need your formal witness statement for the Tobias Tudham incident,' Burton said. 'You said you have a video for us.'

Emma nodded and got out her phone. She tapped the screen to find the video and then passed the phone to Burton and Suzy. The two women put their heads together, looking at the small screen and the latter gasped when the gun appeared in Tudham's hand. She jumped when Emma's voice shouted close to the microphone.

'He sounds unhinged,' Suzy said, 'ranting on about this treasure.'

'Which everyone else swears to me doesn't exist,' Burton said, pushing the phone back to Emma. 'Can you email that to us?'

Emma nodded and, after a few clicks on her phone, Suzy and Burton's phones beeped.

'So, what else do you know about this guy?' Burton asked, pulling out her notebook.

Emma shrugged. 'All I know is that he approached Dan in the

street outside the office. He'd seen the articles Dan wrote about Jayne. He wanted to know whether Dan knew anything about the treasure.'

'And they've never met before?' Burton asked, scribbling in her notebook.

Emma shook her head. 'Dan doesn't know him at all. He just popped up out of nowhere.' She paused. 'Tudham said he doesn't know Professor Randall, but Tudham knew Dan had the notebook, and the only other person Dan and Ed told was Randall.'

Burton glanced up from her notebook. 'You think Tudham was working with Randall?'

'I don't know,' Emma said. 'He doesn't sound like he'd want to share the treasure, but maybe he was prepared to work with someone to find it and then keep it for himself.'

'He also said he was stalking Jayne Winter,' Burton said.

'Yes, but he swears he didn't follow her to Old Manor. I don't know whether I believe him.'

Burton snorted. 'That's definitely something we'll be asking him when we catch up with him,' she said. 'And speaking of the notebook,' she added, reaching into a pocket and pulling out the battered leather-covered object. 'As requested, we finished with it and we don't see a reason not to return it.'

Emma took the notebook and turned it over in her hands. 'So long as Tudham thinks you've got it, I think we will be safe.'

'How are you finding working on such a cold case?' Burton asked with a grin.

'Well, historical research isn't our usual ball game,' Emma said, 'but it's getting quite interesting. We now think that Simeon Burns' murder has a connection to the treasure hunt. Dan thinks the treasure is the Burns' family inheritance.'

Burton tapped a pen against the notebook. 'This is the inheritance that he cursed?'

Emma nodded. 'And apparently that's why no one has found it.' She rolled her eyes. 'Honestly, the things people make up.'

Suzy laughed. 'And now, back in the present day, we have an update on Professor Sir Stewart Randall's murder case,' Suzy said. 'The post-mortem was done late last night, so this is hot off the press, to use your terminology.'

Emma put pen to paper and looked up at Suzy expectantly.

Suzy took a deep breath and then switched to her giving-a-statement voice. 'Police in Allensbury have launched a second murder enquiry following the death of an Allensbury University academic. Professor Sir Stuart Randall, fifty-five, was found dead in Allensbury Museum on Wednesday morning. A post-mortem examination showed that he died from stab wounds to the abdomen. The front door of the museum was smashed open, and officers will examine CCTV footage from the building and surrounding area. We would ask anyone who was near the museum between seven o'clock in the evening and midnight to come forward and speak to us. We are also seeking dashcam footage from anyone who may have been driving past. Detective Inspector Jude Burton, leading the investigation ...'

Suzy gestured to Burton, who leaned forward on the table and said: '...this attack was vicious and left a much-loved father and grandfather dead. We don't know why this attack took place, but our investigation is ongoing to piece together what happened. It goes without saying that we are keen to catch the culprit as soon as possible to get a violent criminal off the streets. If you know anything, please come forward and speak to our officers in confidence.' She waited for Emma to stop scribbling. 'Is that OK?'

Emma nodded. 'That will give me enough for now. You don't know why he was there?'

Burton shook her head. 'No one seems to have a clue. There seems to be no reason for him to be at the museum outside of opening hours.'

'What about Jayne Winter?' Emma asked. 'Is there any update there?'

Suzy shook her head. 'Apart from an ongoing appeal for witnesses, there's nothing for you. We're looking at CCTV and automated number plate recognition in the Old Manor area, but no luck so far.'

'Are you linking the two deaths?' Emma asked.

'Off the record,' Burton said, 'I think we can assume that they are linked, but so far we're not issuing that publicly.'

Emma nodded. 'Fair enough. But if that changes, let me know.'

***

When Emma got back to the office, it was quiet, with most of the reporting team having gone home for the evening. She briefed the evening news editor on the update from the police and then sat down to type up the story. Her mobile rang before she had even written ten words, showing a video call from Dan. She sighed and put on her Bluetooth headset before answering.

'What did Burton give you?' he asked immediately.

'Good afternoon to you too,' Emma said, slightly frostily.

'Oh, yeah, sorry.' Dan looked contrite. 'How are you?'

'Not great, given that Tudham is still out and about. Burton said that they're going all out to find him and that we should stay away.'

Dan laughed. 'I think that's a given, don't you?'

'I don't know. Usually, you'd be all up for doing something dangerous, like chasing him down and trying to get a story out of him.'

Dan snorted. 'Even I'm not stupid enough to go after a guy who threatened to shoot me.' When Emma gave him a questioning look, he insisted, 'I'm not.'

Emma tried to keep the smirk off her face and failed. 'Anyway, I've given Burton the video of Tudham, so hopefully it'll help somewhere along the line, but they've got to find him first. I didn't really have anything to tell them apart from the little he told you and Ed. But' – she smiled – 'I got the notebook back and it's safe in my bag.'

'Do you want to bring it round later?' Dan asked. 'I'd like to keep it here.'

'Sure, I'll come by when I've finished here.'

There was a slightly awkward silence, and Emma desperately tried to think of something to say.

Dan rumpled his already untidy hair. 'This is driving me nuts,' he said. 'We don't even know where to start. Oh, by the way, I got us set up as a team for the treasure hunt.'

Emma paused. 'Us as in you and me?'

'And Ed,' Dan said. 'He'd never forgive me if he got left out and we found the treasure.'

Emma rolled her eyes. 'But is there any treasure?' she asked. 'And what are they counting as treasure?'

Dan's eyes focused off into the distance. 'Now that would be interesting,' he said slowly.

'What do you mean?'

'Different people have different ideas about what's valuable, don't they?'

Emma wrinkled her nose. 'Are you saying you believe there *is* treasure?'

'Not as such, but what if it's not gold and jewels, but something like old papers and stuff. They would be highly valuable to a historian.'

'Hmmm. Tobias Tudham is going to be very disappointed when he finds no family silver, just some books.'

'I wouldn't mind seeing his face, actually,' Dan said, laughing.

A loud cough made Emma look up. The news editor was glaring and tapping his watch.

'I've got to go – copy to file,' Emma said.

There was a slightly awkward pause and then Dan said, 'Right, catch you later,' and hung up.

She sighed. Clearly, she still wasn't forgiven. She didn't think she had anything to apologise for, but maybe it was time to make amends even so.

Chapter Forty

The library was not usually one of Ed's Saturday haunts, but he hoped that he might find some inspiration.

'It's very strange having so many people in here looking for this information so late in the year,' the librarian told him. 'Usually, it's only Old Manor Sixth Form College students doing the annual essay in April because it's around the time of Simeon Burns' birthday.'

'The historical society's treasure hunt is causing something of a stir?' Ed asked, with a laugh.

The woman nodded. 'We've had to make all these books reference only,' she waved an arm at the shelf, 'so that we can make sure that they're available for everyone, but we still caught someone trying to walk off with one.'

'Who was that?' Ed asked.

The woman shook her head. 'I didn't recognise her. A blonde woman, about your age, rather rude.' Jayne Winter, thought Ed, and if Jayne was here, does that mean she found something?

He tried to keep up as the woman wove left and right between the bookcases and then stopped so suddenly he collided with her.

She gestured to the shelves. 'These are all the papers and books that we have,' she said.

'Which book did that woman try to take away?' Ed asked, stepping forward to look at the spines.

The librarian stepped forward and pulled out a volume. She handed it to Ed. 'It's quite a useful volume if you're looking for Kent relatives.' She smiled and moved away through the bookcases.

Ed looked down at the book in his hand, his brain whirring. What was in this book that was so important that Jayne tried to steal it?

Pulling a selection of books from the shelves, he sat down to read. Half an hour later, his eyes were bleary from staring at the printed text. *Maybe I need glasses,* he thought. *Too much time on the computer at work.* His thumbs ached from taking notes into his phone. So far, he'd not discovered anything that made sense to him. He still had no idea what Jayne had been looking for or whether she'd found it. He made a note of the title of the book, meaning to check it against Jayne's memory stick and notebook.

The rattle of coffee cups and saucers in the library's café was calling to him and he was ready to pack up, but as he was about to shut one book, a news article caught his eye.

'Benjamin Burns' obituary,' he said under his breath, scanning the article. 'Hmmm, he sounds a lot nicer than Simeon.'

But as he read on, a shiver ran down his spine. The report described the symptoms Benjamin had experienced: headache, dizziness, delirium...

Exactly the same symptoms as Simeon.

Ed's chest tightened and suddenly a cheeky cappuccino was the last thing on his mind. Burns senior just became his new priority and he realised why Jayne had been looking at that book.

***

After Ed had left for the library, Dan made himself his third cuppa of the day and sat down at his laptop. He was a morning person and had already been out for a run, but it hadn't helped his foggy brain. He'd not slept well. Being around Emma and trying to pretend everything was fine was taking its toll. For now, though, he had to put it aside and focus on the task at hand.

Neither Jayne's notebook, which sat next to him on the table, nor the memory stick, gave them any clues as to the beneficiary of Simeon's will, if one even existed.

'Maybe that's what she was looking for at Old Manor?' Ed had suggested earlier that morning. He'd arrived home very late the previous evening and had required a very large coffee to get him going, while fighting to keep the smug grin off his face at the same time. At least someone's love life was working out.

'I doubt it. Someone would have found it before now.' He sighed. 'I'm not even sure we're barking up the right tree.'

Ed had peered at him. 'Are you feeling OK? You were all excited about it the other day.'

Dan looked down at the notebook. 'I just keep thinking about Jayne, about what she's missing out on.'

'And that someone killed her for it?' Ed asked.

Dan sighed. 'I'm trying not to think about that bit, but we still don't know what she was looking for. In fact, I feel like the solution is getting further away.'

Desk research was not his forte and he longed to be out actually doing something. The problem was that he didn't know what it was.

After Ed left for the library, he logged into his laptop and opened an internet browser. A few searches found him the National Probate Index, which held details of wills that were submitted after eighteen fifty-eight.

'Just in time to find Simeon's,' Dan said to himself.

The website asked for the date of Simeon Burns' death, which Dan quickly typed in. Another source had told him to search up to three years after that date. Sometimes wills could take some time to be approved, it said.

With a feeling of triumph, Dan grinned as he found exactly what he was looking for.

BURNS, Simeon – effects £600; 18 June 1858. The will of Simeon Burns, silk mill owner, of the town of Allensbury, Kent, died 18 June 1858 at Allensbury aforesaid.

Blah, blah, thought Dan as he read through the legal jargon. Then he beamed. The document continued, *The whole estate, including mill and Old Manor Hall, are left to my brother Nathanial Burns for services rendered.*

The will was approved by two executors whose names Dan didn't recognise, but they were unimportant. His stomach was already flickering. Simeon Burns had left everything to his brother, with no provision for his wife or his children. And what did he mean by services rendered? Could it be that Nathaniel had helped him to set fire to Franklin Tudham's mill?

But what was most important was who knew about the will? If his wife or children thought they were in it, then they had a financial motive, but now Nathaniel also had a reason for his brother to die prematurely. They needed to know more about Nathaniel and what had happened to him after Simeon's death.

Suddenly, his phone pinged. Ed on the WhatsApp group with him and Emma.

I've got something.

Another ping as Emma responded: *What have you got?*

Ed's response came quickly. *Ah now that would be telling. Our place, 6 p.m., and I'll explain everything.*

Dan tapped quickly at the screen. *I've got news for you too.*

Another ping. Emma. *Am I the only one with nothing to share?*

It would appear so and therefore you pay a forfeit. The takeaway is on you, Ed responded with two smiley faces. *You won't want to miss out on this.*

Chapter Forty-One

When Burton returned from updating her boss on progress in the investigation, she found Topping glued to his computer screen. As she approached, he suddenly leapt to his feet and shouted, 'Bingo!'

'Bingo?' asked Burton, stopping in her tracks. She narrowed her eyes. 'You're not playing online, are you?'

Topping rolled his eyes. 'Of course not. I think I've got something on Tobias Tudham,' he said, grinning.

'What?' Burton asked, striding over to his desk.

'Well, I started thinking about this treasure hunt malarky,' he said, sitting down and swinging back and forth on his swivel chair. 'I figured there must be somewhere for the people taking part to chat to each other.'

'And?'

'There is. My nan pointed me to the historical society's website and—'

'Your nan?' Burton asked, surprised.

Topping nodded. 'She's a member of the historical society,' he said, 'and she said they've set up a forum for people to chat about the treasure hunt. There are loads of discussions on here.'

He turned his screen so that Burton could look at it.

'Wow, that's a lot of people taking part,' she said, staring at the screen.

'I've got a call in to that Donald Bloom guy to find out exactly how many people registered or have submitted answers so far, but the forums are really busy,' Topping said. He scrolled down and pointed to the screen. 'Look at this message here.'

'The username is TobiasT56,' Burton said slowly.

Topping beamed. 'And look, he's getting really narked with someone who's saying that the treasure isn't real, that the society has just made it up.'

Burton was silent as she read down the page. 'No sign of Randall or Winter?' she asked.

Topping shook his head. 'Not yet, but here Tudham says he's prepared to do anything to find the treasure. It looks like he worries everyone because they try to calm him down, but it doesn't work because he types in capital letters. That's the online equivalent of shouting in someone's face.'

'The conversation gets shut down by the moderator at that point,' Burton said, pointing to the screen. 'I'm surprised they haven't suspended him from the forum.' She folded her arms. 'Keep looking and see if you can find any angry exchanges between him and Jayne Winter or Randall.'

'Do you think he's involved in both murders?' Topping asked.

'He had a beef with both Jayne Winter and Stewart Randall, according to that video Emma Fletcher gave us, so I want him in custody. He also seems a bit separated from reality and I don't like him on the loose.'

'If they find the treasure at the end of this hunt, we might re-evaluate the idea that he's crazy,' Topping said, laughing.

'But it's not real,' Burton said, exasperated.

'Not according to my nan,' Topping said. 'She reckons Donald Bloom from the historical society knows where it is.'

Burton raised her eyebrows. 'Why does she think that?'

'He keeps telling everyone it's a myth. She's convinced it's reverse psychology,' Topping said, laughing.

'Was the treasure hunt his idea?'

'She thinks it was.'

'Hmm, something that we can ask him about, I'm sure. He's on the list after rowing with Stewart Randall.'

'Nan said Randall could be a bit of an arse. My word, not hers. He did a couple of talks and things for them, but he clearly didn't value their knowledge. He was really rude to one woman, Maisie Barratt, and Nan said if looks could kill, Randall would have dropped on the spot.'

Burton raised an eyebrow. 'Fortunately for Maisie, we know he wasn't actually killed by a death glare,' she said. 'Does your nan know anything about Tudham?'

Topping wrinkled his forehead. 'I don't think he's a member of the society, but I can ask her. If he's into local history, she might have come across him at some point.'

'Great, thanks. If you find anything out, let me know as soon as possible.'

Burton and Topping both turned as Sophie Madison slammed down her phone, leapt to her feet and jogged over to them.

'Finally,' she said, 'I got through to someone at the DVLA. They're not a speedy crew.'

'And?' Burton asked.

Madison grinned. 'We now have his address, right here in Allensbury.'

Burton snatched the note and said, 'Let's go and have a chat with Mr Tudham, shall we?'

Chapter Forty-Two

Shepherd parked the car neatly two doors down from Tudham's three-storey Georgian town house. The street lamp above them created a pool of light around the car.

'Not surprised that it's Georgian,' he said.

'Given his obsession, it probably belonged to his great-great-grandfather,' Burton said. She unbuckled her seatbelt and stepped out. 'OK, let's see if he's in.'

Light spilled from an un-curtained living room, illuminating the front path ahead of them. A man crossing the room stopped and looked out when he saw Burton and Shepherd.

'Someone's home,' Shepherd stated.

Burton pressed the bell and, after a minute or two, a man in his fifties with a long-grey ponytail growing from a bald head answered it. He cocked his head enquiringly. Burton had just presented her warrant card when he turned and bolted back inside, attempting to slam the door in her face. She prevented it from closing, although it cost her a broken fingernail.

'Mark!' she yelled, but Shepherd had already vanished, and she heard clattering and scrabbling as he climbed over what she assumed was a side gate. Dashing through the house, she reached the kitchen window just in time to see Shepherd take Tudham to the ground in a perfect tackle, lit up by the outside security light.

Hands on hips, she waited in the kitchen doorway as Shepherd marched Tudham up the garden in handcuffs.

'I love it when they run,' he said as she stood back to allow them inside.

'You can't do this … You've no right…' Tudham was spluttering as Shepherd deposited him none-too-gently into a chair at the kitchen table.

'We've got every right,' Burton said, 'when you run from the police.'

'I didn't know that you—' Tudham began to protest but stopped when Burton thrust her warrant card in his face.

'As I was about to say before you rudely slammed the door in my face, I'm Detective Inspector Jude Burton, Allensbury CID. You've already met Detective Sergeant Mark Shepherd.'

'What's this about?' Tudham demanded, trying to regain some control over the situation.

'Two things really,' Burton said. 'It's now six o'clock on Saturday evening and, one, I'm arresting you on suspicion of threatening behaviour and possession of what I assume is an unlicensed firearm. But more importantly, two, you're also under arrest on suspicion of the murders of Dr Jayne Winter and Professor Sir Stewart Randall.'

Chapter Forty-Three

Ed refused to speak until Emma ordered the takeaway, sitting at the wooden dining table with a smug grin on his face. Only when they had beers in front of them would he begin.

'Well? Out with it,' Dan said, rolling a hand for him to get started. Ed was infuriating when he knew something you didn't.

'The plot has thickened,' Ed said, grinning smugly.

'OK, what have you got?' Emma asked.

Dan felt a flicker when Ed told them about the attempted book theft.

'Stealing a library book is a bit low,' he said. 'Do you know why she did it?'

Ed grinned and took a sip of beer.

'Oh, for God's sake, get on with it,' Dan snapped.

'Well,' Ed continued, clearly enjoying the limelight, 'I started with that book, but at first, I couldn't make head nor tail of why Jayne wanted it so badly. It's really old, so I couldn't work out why she thought it would tell her about the murder – if that's the new angle she was working on.'

'And?' Emma asked. 'What did you find?'

'Like I said, it didn't make sense until I saw this.' Ed pulled out his phone and tapped a few times. He turned it to show Dan and Emma a photo of Benjamin Burns' obituary. Dan bent his head to look at the picture. Then he looked back up at Ed.

'Someone killed him too,' he said.

Ed nodded. 'Looks like it. That's why she wanted that book.' He took his phone back and switched to the next image. 'Read that.'

Dan scanned the screen, Emma looking over his shoulder.

'He's got his own section in the book,' Emma said, 'and he sounds like a totally different bloke to Simeon.'

Ed nodded. 'Described as "the poor man's friend" because he used to give medical care, education and clothing to people who couldn't afford it.'

'Gave charitably of coal for cooking, basic schooling for children and medical care,' Dan read aloud. 'So he was just giving stuff away?'

Ed nodded. 'He was making money from the mill and giving it to anyone who needed it. The "deserving poor", according to the obit.'

Dan frowned, feeling some puzzle pieces slot into place. 'You're wondering why someone murdered such a good guy,' he said.

Ed nodded. 'Exactly, and he had the same symptoms as Simeon, except Benjamin died first.'

'Someone got away with poisoning him, so they did it again to Simeon,' Emma said. Then she spotted the look on Dan's face. 'What?' she asked.

Dan ruffled his hair. 'That makes sense of something I found in his will.'

Ed and Emma both leaned forward on the table. 'Go on,' Ed said.

Dan showed them the printout he'd made of Simeon Burns' will.

'Six hundred pounds?' Ed asked. 'Is that all?'

Dan laughed. 'Allowing for inflation, apparently that's worth nearly ninety-two grand in today's money.'

'Definitely worth killing for,' Emma said, 'but it says here it was going to his brother, Nathaniel.'

'For services rendered,' Ed finished.

Dan nodded. 'What if,' he said with a dramatic pause, 'the service was killing Benjamin?'

Ed and Emma stared at him, eyes widening.

'You think they killed their father?' Emma demanded. 'That's bonkers.'

'Is it? Maybe Simeon was worried that his dad was giving away all their money to the poor, establishing museums and who knows what else.'

'So he got his brother to kill Benjamin?' Ed asked, staring at Dan with a doubtful expression on his face.

'As the eldest son, Simeon would get the entire estate, unless Benjamin's will said otherwise. So Simeon promised Nathaniel that it would pass it all on to him.'

'You think Nathaniel decided not to wait for the money and killed Simeon?' Emma asked.

Dan shrugged. 'He'd already killed his dad, so why not his brother as well? Imagine how Simeon felt when he realised he had the same symptoms as his dad had when he died.' He rubbed the back of his neck. 'So, do we think Jayne came across the doctor's letter, realised what it meant, and that's what started her researching?'

'That Simeon was poisoned,' Emma put in.

'Exactly,' Dan said, pointing at her. 'Maybe that's what put her onto writing the book. She figured out that the curse related to his being murdered and most likely by someone in his family. She looks into it, goes to the library and finds that book. Putting two and two together, she works out that Benjamin was also murdered.'

'Now someone is trying to cover up the murders of Simeon and Benjamin?' Emma said. 'They were about two hundred years ago. Why do they matter now?'

Dan thought for a moment. 'Who would benefit from both their deaths? It has to be someone in the family.'

'I'm still coming back to why it matters now,' Emma said.

The doorbell rang and Ed leapt to his feet.

'Hurray, dinner. Let's shelve this for now and come up with a plan of attack for tomorrow after we've eaten.'

Reluctantly, Dan put the notebook away and helped to set the table. His stomach was flickering again and not just because he was hungry. He'd been sure that Tobias Tudham was involved, but why would he be trying to cover up the murders? Unless Simeon had promised money to Franklin Tudham, a share in the treasure maybe, and then failed to deliver. That would explain why he thought the treasure was his. And if Jayne and Randall were going to get the treasure first, how far would he go to stop them?

Chapter Forty-Four

Tobias Tudham's mouth was set in a thin, hard line when Burton and Shepherd entered the interview room. He sat at the wooden table, arms tightly folded.

'You nearly broke my ribs,' he almost snarled at Shepherd.

'You shouldn't have tried to run,' Shepherd replied mildly, sitting down opposite him. 'DI Burton identified herself as a police officer and you should have stayed put.'

Tudham glared at him, but then lowered his eyes against Shepherd's hard stare.

Burton sat down next to Shepherd and placed a cardboard folder in front of her. Deciding to intervene, she said, 'The list of charges is growing, Mr Tudham.' She flipped open the folder and looked at the top page. 'First, we'd like to deal with your threatening three *Allensbury Post* reporters with a gun in broad daylight in Castle Park.'

Tudham glared at her and said nothing.

'I hope he's not going to deny it,' Shepherd said to Burton, eyes fixed on Tudham. 'That would be a mistake, especially when we've got video evidence.'

Tudham's eyes snapped up to Shepherd's face. 'What?'

Shepherd nodded. 'The reporter who said she was recording the incident wasn't bluffing and she's provided us with a copy. So, you'll be charged with threatening behaviour and an unlicensed firearm because there's no licence on record.'

'I didn't mean—'

'Didn't mean what? Didn't mean to threaten them?' Shepherd interrupted, 'because I think you failed in that.'

'No, I mean I wouldn't have shot them. It was just for show. It's not even a real gun.'

'What?' Shepherd asked.

'It's a replica, made of plastic,' said Tudham.

'Not to worry, the officers searching your home will find that for us,' Burton said.

Tudham's face reddened. 'You've no right to—'

'I've every right,' Burton snapped back. 'Don't worry, we got a warrant.'

Tudham folded his arms and slumped back in his seat.

'So, why did you threaten the journalists?' Burton asked. 'Didn't like a story they'd written?' When Tudham refused to speak, she continued, 'It was about Jayne Winter, wasn't it? I understand you were stalking her.'

'I wasn't stalking her,' Tudham snapped. 'I was just following her to see what she knew.'

'I'd call that stalking,' Shepherd said, looking at Burton. 'Did she know you were following her?'

Tudham shrugged. 'I don't know.'

'Do you know Professor Sir Stewart Randall?' Burton asked.

'No.'

'So why did you go to his daughter's house and demand to see him? A matter of life or death, you told her.'

Tudham glared at Burton, but said nothing.

Burton exhaled heavily. 'This is getting tiresome, Mr Tudham. We have two people murdered. You were stalking one of them, and then we find that you've been harassing the other one as well.'

'I wasn't harassing,' Tudham snarled. 'I was—' He halted.

'You were what?' Burton asked, leaning forward with her forearms on the table.

But Tudham's mouth had become a thin, hard line again. 'I'm not saying anything else until I've got a solicitor.'

Chapter Forty-Five

In the *Allensbury Post* lunchroom on Monday, Dan pored over Jayne's notebook, trying to keep his cheese-and-pickle sandwiches from leaking over it. Multi-tasking was not his strong point. Then he spotted something and put down his sandwich, wiping his hands on his trousers without thinking. Thank God they were black and Emma wasn't here to see him.

Squinting down at the page, he said aloud to himself, 'Does that say "county records"? I wish her handwriting wasn't so totally crap.'

He flipped back a page, stared at it and then returned to the page. Based on how Jayne had written those other words, it seemed to be the name Lynda Philby and a phone number.

Grabbing his phone, he dialled it immediately.

'County records office, Lynda speaking. How can I help?' said a low female voice.

'Hi, my name's Dan Sullivan. I'm hoping you can help me.'

'I can try,' Dan could hear the smile in her voice. But when he explained what he was looking for, her tone became cagey.

'Sorry, we can't give out anyone's details,' she said. 'It's against data protection.'

'Jayne was a friend of mine,' Dan said quickly, 'and she left her notebook with me for safekeeping. I'm trying to work out what she was researching. I don't suppose you remember when she came in.'

Lynda was silent for a moment, clearly thinking about whether she should give away the information. 'It was just last week,' she said eventually. Well, that was her most recent visit.'

'When was she there before?'

He heard a voice in the background and Lynda spoke away from the mouthpiece. 'I can't really talk now,' she said, quietly into the phone, 'my manager is here. Listen, if you want me to help, you'll have to book an appointment and come to the records office. Do you know what you're looking for?'

'That's just it. Jayne's handwriting is so messy that we're struggling to work out what's in the notebook.'

'It was Simeon Burns, wasn't it?'

'Yes, did she tell you what she was doing?'

'No, but I have a record of what we put aside for her. When would you be able to come in?'

'I could do Wednesday,' Dan said, his stomach flickering.

'Come to the front desk at about ten thirty and ask for me,' Lynda said. 'I'll book an appointment so I can speak to you and I can show you what your friend was looking at.'

A quick message on their WhatsApp group updated Ed and Emma on his progress.

Nice catch, Ed wrote. *Reckon Daisy will give you time off?*

Dan replied: *She owes me for swapping call shift with Neil last week at short notice.*

Well played, Ed replied. *Count me in for coming too. I've got lieu time saved.*

What are you going to do in the meantime? Emma responded.

Dan chose a 'thinking' emoji. *Go back to see Gracie Lincoln later on and see whether she's learned anything new.*

And if she's OK after finding a dead body? Emma asked, adding her own thinking emoji.

Of course. You coming?

Emma responded quickly. *I'm in. Shall I meet you there? When can you get away?*

Dan glanced at his watch. *I've got a job up that way shortly, but I should be done in about an hour.*

You're on. See you then.

You can update me later, Ed typed.

Dan texted a general thumbs up and then pocketed his phone. He hoped Gracie had recovered enough to tell them more about Stewart Randall and why he was at the museum so late in the day.

***

Gracie Lincoln looked as surprised as Emma felt to find themselves alone in the museum foyer.

'Oh, I was expecting Dan to be here,' Emma said, suddenly feeling awkward.

'Really? Why? I didn't think museums were his thing,' Gracie replied.

Emma smiled. 'They definitely aren't, but he said he was going to pop by to see how you were.' She felt herself do a sympathetic head-tilt. 'How have you been?'

Gracie held out a hand and wobbled it from side to side. 'So-so,' she said. 'It still feels weird that someone died in there.' She gestured towards the exhibition room door, which was still decorated with crime scene tape. 'I've been struggling to sleep, but at least work has been keeping me busy.'

'It must have been such a shock,' Emma said. She knew from personal experience how it felt to discover a dead body and she shook her head to push away the image that flooded to mind. 'The police aren't finished yet?' she asked, gesturing to the crime scene tape.

Gracie shook her head. 'They seem to have checked every inch of the gallery.' She puffed out her cheeks. 'The powers-that-be seem more worried about reopening than that someone died.'

Emma raised an eyebrow. 'Are they worrying about the treasure hunt if people can't come and look around?'

Gracie winced. 'I think that's it, although no one is actually saying it. The police have allowed us to open the other areas of the museum, just not that exhibition. We've had some people coming in, but I think they just wanted to see what the police are doing rather than actually look at stuff.' She sighed. 'At least those detectives weren't too scary.'

Emma tried not to laugh. That wasn't her impression of Burton.

'Did you know Professor Randall well?' Emma asked, leaning against the counter that stood between her and Gracie.

'Sort of. I mean, not very well. He was sticking his nose in when I was setting up the exhibition, but he wasn't really a bad bloke. A bit full of himself, but all academics are like that, I suppose.'

'And you don't know why he was here after hours?' Emma asked.

Gracie shook her head. 'I've no idea, but the police were interested in why the burglar alarm didn't go off.'

Emma straightened up slightly. That was an excellent point and not something that she'd considered previously.

'So why didn't it go off?' Emma asked.

Gracie shrugged, straightening some booklets on the reception counter. 'I definitely set it before I left, so I don't know.'

Looking up at the corners of the room, Emma asked, 'Did the CCTV catch him coming in?'

'I don't know. Mrs Middlebury was looking at that for the police. I'll ask her when she comes back later.' She glanced at her watch. 'She probably won't be long.'

Emma stared at the exhibition room door. 'What was he looking for?' she asked, almost to herself. 'What did he need to see so badly that he couldn't wait 'til the next morning?'

'He was by the maps of the Old Manor estate,' Gracie said.

Emma looked back at her. 'Why would he be looking at those? Surely he's seen them dozens of times.'

Gracie shook her head. 'I've no idea but—'

Just then, two older women, jackets buttoned to the neck and woolly hats balanced on well-set curls, pushed open the door to the museum. Emma moved away from the reception desk, and Gracie greeted them with a beaming smile.

Emma wandered away to look at the visitors' book on one side of the foyer. She flipped over to the previous week and scanned down the list of names, noting a somewhat scathing review from Jayne Winter. She snapped a picture on her phone, thinking it would give Dan and Ed a giggle. She took pictures of the previous two pages as well.

'Did you need something else?' Gracie asked, making Emma jump.

'Sorry, just checking out your reviews,' Emma said, laughing. 'I see Jayne didn't think much of it.'

Gracie wrinkled her nose. 'Like her opinions matter,' she said.

The strength of Gracie's comment surprised Emma, and she was about to ask another question when the door flew open and Dan appeared.

'Sorry I'm late,' he said to Emma, moving towards her and leaning in as if to kiss her. But he seemed to recollect himself and stepped away to greet Gracie. Emma took a deep breath, trying to slow her heart down. It was the closest they'd been for weeks and it made her sad.

She listened as Dan chatted to Gracie, asking all the same questions about her welfare. Then he asked, 'Do you know anything about Nathanial Burns?'

'Simeon's brother?' Gracie asked, but then to Emma's trained eye looked as if she wished she could take back the words. 'What about him?' She sounded casual but Emma noted definite tension in her shoulders.

'I read something about him recently being Simeon's sole beneficiary in his will,' Dan said.

Emma knew she wasn't wrong; Gracie was looking uncomfortable.

'Look, I'm sorry,' Gracie said, looking at her watch. 'It's almost time for my break and Cath will be back soon, so I can't stand around chatting.'

Emma saw Dan look surprised at the sudden dismissal, but he hid it well.

When they were outside, Emma asked, 'What was that all about?'

'I thought it might be a good shortcut to having to send Ed back to the library to read loads of books.'

Emma laughed. 'I knew you'd delegate something like that,' she said. 'Here, I thought you'd like this. Check out Jayne's museum review.' She held out her phone and Dan took it to look at the picture.

'Ouch,' he said. 'She doesn't pull her punches. Did Gracie have much to say before I got there?'

'She said that she found Stewart Randall's body in front of the map of the Burns' family estate.' When Dan opened his mouth to speak, she held up a hand. 'Yes, I was wondering why he broke into a museum to look at something he's probably seen a gazillion times or could have looked at as soon as the doors opened in the morning.'

Dan sighed. 'We need to get another look at the map, but it'll have to wait until the police have finished with it.' He groaned. 'How frustrating.'

'I'd also love to know why the burglar alarm didn't go off,' Emma said, 'when someone put the door in with a crowbar.'

'Clearly they had the code, but who could it be?' Dan asked. 'It has to be someone with a connection to the museum who knew what Randall and Jayne were researching, but I'm damned if I can think who it might be.'

Chapter Forty-Six

Burton's fingers were rattling against the keys of her computer keyboard as she typed up a request for further time to question Tudham. A knock on the door made her look up. Shepherd lounged in the doorway, grinning.

'OK, out with it,' she said, clicking *save* on the document. 'I need to get this away to the boss ASAP.'

Shepherd pushed himself away from the door frame and crossed the room to hold out a piece of paper.

'Update from tech on Jayne Winter's phone.'

'Can you just give me the abridged version?' Burton asked, worrying about her deadline.

Shepherd beamed. 'They haven't done a full assessment of the phone, but they found some fingerprints on it.'

Burton tipped her head on one side. 'Yes, and?' she said again, indicating for Shepherd to get on with it.

'Two sets of prints. One is Jayne Winter's, obviously. The other...' he paused dramatically, 'is Tobias Tudham.'

'What?' Burton demanded.

Shepherd nodded, grinning smugly. 'Yup. He was stalking

Jayne, but says he'd never spoken to her. So, how did his finger-prints get on her phone?'

'Let's find out, shall we?'

***

In the interview room, Tudham still looked sullen, but beside him sat a young woman in a smart black suit, her hair pulled back into a neat French plait. She had a spiral-bound notebook open in front of her, with a pen resting on top of a full page of detailed notes.

'Detective Inspector,' she said, getting to her feet and offering a hand to Burton, who shook it. The woman shook hands with Shepherd as well and then returned to her seat.

'Good to see you, Jamilia,' Burton said. 'What have you got for us?'

'My client would like to make a statement before we go any further,' Jamilia said, gesturing towards Tudham.

Burton nodded. 'Go ahead.'

Tudham cleared his throat and read from a piece of paper on the table in front of him. 'I approached the *Allensbury Post* reporters because they had been writing about Jayne Winter and I thought they might know more about what she'd found. I shouldn't have behaved how I did and I apologise to them.'

'Good of you,' Burton said, looking from Tudham to Jamilia and back again. 'Is that it?'

Tudham shoved the paper across the table and Burton passed it to Shepherd.

'We found the gun at your house and it is a replica. However, that isn't enough to get you off a charge of threatening behaviour.

Although I'm sure the journalists will really appreciate your apology,' Burton said, controlling her temper with effort.

'There's no need to be sarcastic,' Tudham muttered.

The solicitor opened her mouth, but Burton held up a hand.

'Moving on from that, we have more questions for Mr Tudham based on evidence we've gathered since we last spoke,' Burton said. She eyeballed Tudham. 'Last time we spoke, you admitted that you'd been stalking Dr Winter, correct?'

'It wasn't stalking—' Tudham began, but Burton interrupted.

'I actually think you got a lot closer to her than just following her around as you claim,' Burton asked. 'You met up with her, didn't you, and I'm guessing you argued?'

Tudham didn't speak but just stared down at the table.

'Oh, for God's sake,' Burton snapped, banging a hand on the table, 'do not play games with me.'

Shepherd stepped in, placing the mobile phone in a plastic bag on the table. 'If you never met Jayne Winter, why are your fingerprints on her mobile phone?'

Tudham stared down at the table refusing to meet Shepherd's eye. Jamilia shifted in her seat and nudged him.

'In case you were wondering, a kind member of the public found it in the park and handed it in,' Shepherd said. 'Presumably it fell out of your pocket when you chased the reporters. The question is, where did you get it?'

Tudham gave a sideways glance at his solicitor, who nodded. He mumbled something.

'What was that?' Burton demanded.

'I found it.'

'Found it where?'

When Tudham said nothing, Shepherd leaned forward. 'You

followed her to Old Manor Hall, didn't you? I'm guessing you thought she was going for the treasure and—'

'She said she knew where it is,' Tudham said quickly.

'Right, now we're getting somewhere,' Shepherd said to Burton. 'This is the treasure you say belongs to your family?'

'Yes,' Tudham snapped, 'it belongs to the Tudhams, not the Burns family. They took it from us.'

'This is the fictional treasure the historical society is using to raise money for charity?' Burton asked.

Tudham growled. 'People say it doesn't exist, but it does. I'm going to find it.'

'And Jayne said she knew where it was?'

Tudham nodded. 'A few people were putting forward theories, saying they knew where it was, but she said she had proof. She was already close to finding it.'

'So how did you come to find her phone and get your finger-prints on it?' Shepherd asked.

'She was already dead,' Tudham mumbled, without making eye contact.

Shepherd stared at him. 'What?'

'My client would like to clarify that—' the solicitor began, but Shepherd held up a hand, silencing her.

'Jayne Winter was already dead?' he demanded, leaning forward on the table.

Tudham nodded, eyes fixed on the table. 'I found her at Old Manor, but I didn't kill her.' He looked up, meeting Shepherd's eye. 'I found her phone on the floor. She must have dropped it and I picked it up.'

'Wait a second, let me check if I've got this right. You found her, but you didn't call for help?' Shepherd asked, looking disgusted.

'Instead, you robbed her?'

'I didn't rob her. It was on the floor. I picked it up thinking that—' He broke off.

'Thinking what? That it might contain information on where the treasure is?' Burton said, stepping in to diffuse Shepherd's rising temper.

Tudham nodded. 'I knew from what she was saying on the forums that she was close. I followed her to Old Manor and saw her going into the building. I waited a while to see if she'd come out, but when she didn't, I was sure she'd found something.'

'And you wanted to take it from her?' Burton said.

'It's my family's treasure.' Tudham's mouth pulled down slightly at the corners. 'I went inside and I could see from the footprints in the dust which way she'd gone. When I got to the room, she was lying on the floor. Then I heard voices, so I grabbed the phone and ran.'

'Could you open it?'

Tudham shook his head. 'There was a passcode, but I didn't know what it was, so it wasn't any use to me.'

'It's a good job you didn't wipe off your fingerprints, or we'd never have been able to track it back to you.' Burton paused. 'Did you hear anything else while you were at Old Manor?'

Tudham screwed up his forehead with the effort of remembering. 'I heard a car as I was walking towards the building. The engine revved really loudly, so it caught my attention.'

Burton sighed. 'So, given that you lied about your connection to Jayne Winter, would you care to revise your comments about whether you were harassing Professor Sir Stewart Randall?'

Tudham exchanged a look with his solicitor, and she nodded.

'I went to his house and the woman said he doesn't live there anymore,' Tudham said, 'but I knew she was lying.'

'She wasn't,' Burton said shortly. 'He's now living somewhere else.' She leaned forward, resting her elbows on the table. 'How long did it take you to find his new address?'

Tudham glared at her. 'I never found it. I've never been there.'

Burton raised her eyebrows. 'That's funny because we have a neighbour of Professor Randall who says they saw a man in black going round to the back of his house on Wednesday night. We later found a broken pane of glass in his back door. Someone has been in and rifled through his study.'

When Tudham was silent, Shepherd asked, 'Was that you? Because whoever it was knew that Professor Randall wouldn't be at home when they called. They didn't even ring the doorbell.' Tudham said nothing and Shepherd tapped on the table with his forefinger. 'Mr Tudham, answer the question, please.'

The solicitor put a hand on Tudham's arm. 'Detectives, we're not getting anywhere on this. My client says he's never been to Professor Randall's home and you have no evidence to the contrary.' She glanced at her watch. 'Time is marching and my client has answered everything you've asked him. I think we're done here, aren't we?'

Burton got to her feet, chair legs scraping. 'OK, that's all for now. You'll be going to court on the threatening behaviour charge, but I'm bailing you in relation to the murders of Jayne Winter and Professor Randall while our investigation continues. Don't go anywhere, will you? I'm sure there will be more questions as we proceed.'

***

As they watched Tudham and his solicitor leave through the reception area, Shepherd said, 'The voices he heard were probably our trio of ghostbusters. Brody's time of death suggests that she was already dead, if he got there when he says he did.'

Burton pursed her lips. 'I'm inclined to believe him when he said he heard voices. It's too much of a coincidence that he made that up when there were actually other people there.'

Shepherd frowned and folded his arms. 'What about the revving car engine? Also coincidence?'

'Randall's fingerprints were also at the scene. So, was he the one who went to the scene first, killed Jayne and then fled?'

'And Tudham heard him leaving?' Shepherd asked, holding open the door for Burton to walk into the corridor. 'If he wasn't dead himself, then I'd agree.'

Burton exhaled heavily. 'If Tudham is involved, then I'd say the motive was the treasure. It seems like a better motive than Simeon Burns' murder, which Dan Sullivan and friends are chasing.'

'Maybe they're connected,' Shepherd suggested. 'Someone killed Simeon Burns trying to find the treasure.'

Burton rolled her eyes and groaned. 'I need a drink,' she said. 'This is making my head hurt.'

Shepherd laughed. 'Beers on me when we clock off,' he said, and Burton grinned.

'You're on. The girls are sleeping over at my mum's and my husband is out, so a couple of beers sounds great.' She frowned. 'Tudham still feels like our best suspect, but we need evidence tying him to Randall's murder. Get back onto the crime scene manager and have them go through Randall's home and office like a dose of salts. I want fingerprints or DNA that match Tudham. I also want to know if there are any calls or texts between him and

Randall or him and Jayne Winter. We need something to prove he's involved.'

Chapter Forty-Seven

On Tuesday morning, Gary Topping limped down the office and flopped into his chair. Shepherd turned and grinned at him.

'What happened to you?' he asked.

'Five-a-side football last night,' said Topping with a wince.

Sophie Madison looked over her shoulder and grinned. 'You boys and your blood sports,' she said, shaking her head.

'Hey, you're enjoying my pain, aren't you?' Topping said, picking up a mini football stress toy from his desk and throwing it at her. It missed and hit the partition between hers and the next desk. Laughing, she scooped it up and threw it back. When Topping caught it one-handed, she applauded and then turned back to her computer.

'Were you at least doing something flashy when you did that?' Shepherd asked, feeling sure there was a heroic story behind the injury.

'I was heading for the goal, preparing a Messi-style finish,' Topping said, fidgeting in his chair, 'when this massive defender came charging at me and wiped me out.'

Shepherd winced. 'Ouch. It's lucky you weren't seriously hurt.'

Topping shrugged. 'Not sure what's most bruised: my ankle or my pride. At least we scored the penalty.'

Shepherd nodded. 'Worth the injury, I suppose. Let's hope you don't have to run anywhere today.'

Topping groaned. 'Fortunately, I'm on CCTV-viewing duty today, so I can keep my feet up, metaphorically speaking.' He turned to his computer but then turned back. 'What did Tudham have to say for himself?'

Shepherd updated him on the interview with Tudham.

Topping looked disgusted. 'He found her there and took her phone rather than help her? What a tool.'

'He thought there might be proof of the treasure's location on it,' Shepherd said, rolling his eyes.

Topping shook his head. 'This treasure stuff is just getting stupid. I've tried to get my nan not to play it anymore, but she's adamant. If there's treasure out there, she wants to be the one to find it.'

'Will she spend it on you?' Shepherd asked.

'Nah, she wants it to go to the museum. Says that's where it belongs.' He watched as the CCTV video opened on his screen. 'At least we've finally got this through from the museum this morning. It's a good job we've got a relatively tight timescale from Dr Brody, so there aren't hours to watch.'

He pressed *play* on the screen.

'OK, there's Gracie Lincoln locking up at six o'clock,' said Topping, 'just like she said she did.'

'Having set the alarm,' Shepherd replied, glancing at Madison's timeline on the wall to confirm it.

Topping nodded. 'That's the camera that covers the doorway and a little bit of the outside area. She walks out of shot here.'

He stopped that recording and clicked on another. 'Then all goes quiet on the other CCTV camera as well.' The recording ran on as they watched. Then a figure walked on the screen. Topping pointed. 'And here comes Professor Randall.'

'He's looking at his watch,' Shepherd said, 'so he must have been there to meet someone.' He got up and walked to the timeline, making a note of Randall's arrival.

Topping nodded. 'Now we just have to hope they're on camera, too.'

They watched as Randall checked the time again and then looked up and down the street. He appeared to recognise someone off camera and smiled slightly. But the person who approached him stayed outside the range of the camera.

'Oh, damn it,' Topping said. 'Just half a step forward and we'd have them.'

'They know where the cameras are,' Shepherd said, sitting down and leaning closer to the screen, willing the person to appear. 'They know not to come any further forward.'

Topping flipped back to the front door camera, but Randall and his companion had already gone inside.

'Hang on,' Shepherd said, feeling a mini lurch of adrenaline. 'They've just let themselves in with a key. Why did they need to smash the door?'

Topping stared at him. 'The damage was done when the killer left?'

'Yeah, to cover for the fact they had a key.'

'We might see the killer coming back out,' Topping said. But Shepherd had a feeling they were going to be out of luck. He sat back at his desk and picked up a report that was filed the previous day. Then he heard Topping say, 'Are you kidding me?'

Shepherd turned to face him. 'What?'

Topping ran the video back a few minutes and set it to play. After about two minutes, the screen went black.

Shepherd groaned. 'Tell me that's not a power cut.'

Topping wrinkled his nose. 'If it is, it's the most convenient power cut I've ever seen. Just after the victim and potential killer go inside and before the killer comes back out?'

Shepherd stroked his chin. 'Plus, if the power had cut out, it would have triggered the alarm, wouldn't it?' he asked. 'Meaning that our killer had a key and the alarm code. Have we got a list of the people who are key holders?'

Topping seized a printout from his desk and waved it. 'Not had a chance to check it yet. It's all yours if you want it.'

Shepherd took the page and turned back to his desk, scrutinising the list of names. 'Oh, hello,' he said, turning back to Topping.

'What's that?' Topping asked.

'Look who we've got on the list of people who have the alarm code.' Shepherd pointed to a name on the list with a meaty finger.

'Donald Bloom,' Topping said.

'Exactly. Someone who threatened Randall about the treasure hunt.'

'Why would he have the keys and alarm code? He doesn't work there.'

'That's just what I intend to ask him,' Shepherd said, getting to his feet and walking across to Burton's room to give her an update.

Chapter Forty-Eight

Donald Bloom looked very much at home in the museum as he fussed around Gracie Lincoln.

'I'm sure you shouldn't be working after such a shock,' he said, wagging a finger at her. The woman smiled patiently, and the eye-roll she gave Burton and Shepherd behind his back had some affection in it.

'It's OK, Donald,' she said, 'Cath is keeping a close eye on me. It was a horrible shock, but I'm fine now.' She sent a pleading look at Burton and Shepherd. 'Can I help you?' she asked, angling her body away from Bloom. 'Did you get the information you asked for?'

Burton recognised the need for a rescue and opened her mouth to speak, but Bloom interrupted.

'What did you ask for?'

'CCTV footage from when Professor Randall was killed and a list of people with out-of-hours access to the museum,' Gracie told him, causing Burton to groan inwardly.

'Oh, really?' Bloom asked in a light tone, but Burton could feel the tension come over him.

'Thanks, yes, we did,' Shepherd said to Gracie, 'but one of the external videos goes dark after a couple of minutes. Do you know if there's any other footage we could look at?'

Gracie frowned. 'Not that I'm aware of. Everything was so upside down after I found poor Professor Randall that I didn't even think about anything else.' Her eyes glistened with tears and Bloom interrupted again.

'Do you have to interrogate poor Gracie when she's still in shock? It's most unfair.' He cleared his throat a few times when Burton turned to face him.

'We haven't come to speak to Miss Lincoln,' she said, smiling sweetly and enjoying Bloom's discomfort when she added, 'We want to speak to you.'

Donald Bloom stiffened. 'Me? Why ... why would you want to speak to me?'

'As Miss Lincoln pointed out, we've been looking at the list of people who have keys and access to the alarm code and your name is right at the top.'

'Well, it *is* alphabetical,' Bloom said, defensively. He shrank back under Burton's steely gaze.

'That's not what I was getting at,' she snapped. 'Is there somewhere we can speak to Mr Bloom privately?' she asked, glancing at Gracie.

'Oh, erm, yes, of course.' Gracie looked flustered. 'The auditorium is closed to the public today, so you could use that? We don't have any meeting rooms available.'

Bloom turned to lead the way and, as Burton passed, Gracie touched her arm.

'He's a bit of a fusspot,' she said affectionately, 'but he means well. I'm sure he has nothing to do with all this.' She gestured towards the exhibition. Burton recognised the subtle dig for information but simply smiled.

'Just a few questions,' she said, turning to follow Shepherd and Donald Bloom.

***

Bloom took a seat in the back row of the auditorium. Burton sat beside him, her body angled in his direction, while Shepherd stood in the row in front.

'So, how can I help?' Donald asked.

'As you know, we're investigating the deaths of Dr Jayne Winter and Professor Sir Stewart Randall,' Burton began.

Bloom nodded. 'Such a shocking affair,' he said. 'I can't believe Professor Randall died here in the museum.'

'Do you know why he would be here so late at night?' Burton asked.

Bloom's eyes widened. 'I've no idea. Why would I?'

'How well do you know him?' Shepherd asked, writing in his ever-present notebook.

Bloom puffed out his cheeks. 'Not very well, to be honest. The historical society tried to avoid him as much as possible. He was rather scornful about us and the members weren't happy.'

'When did you last see Professor Randall?' Burton asked.

'It was a couple of weeks ago, I think,' Bloom said.

Burton tilted her head on one side. 'Was he involved in the exhibition?'

Bloom sighed. 'He was pushing to be part of things since he's an "expert" in Georgian Allensbury, but as he's not a member of the historical society, he couldn't.'

'He called you a bunch of amateurs, didn't he?' Shepherd asked. 'But you are amateurs, aren't you? In the sense that this isn't your day job.'

'Technically, we're amateurs, but I like to think we approach everything we do with professionalism.'

'Is shouting at him in the middle of the museum professional?' Burton asked.

Bloom froze. 'What do you mean? I've never—'

'We heard from his daughter that you had a shouting match with him while he was visiting the museum with his grandchildren,' Shepherd put in. 'She said you threatened him.'

Bloom sighed. 'It wasn't a threat.'

Shepherd flipped back a few pages in his notebook. 'You said you wouldn't be responsible for your actions.'

'I didn't mean I would murder him,' Bloom snapped.

Shepherd eyed him. 'What did you mean?'

Bloom sighed and rubbed a hand across his face. 'He was trying to steal from us.'

Burton raised her eyebrows. 'Steal what exactly?' she asked, puzzled.

'Our secretary received some new papers, diaries and letters, that kind of thing. We were trying to decide whether to include them in the exhibition. Official authentication is required before you can show that kind of thing. Randall tried to take some of them, saying he'd get them authenticated, but I didn't trust him.'

Burton frowned. 'You didn't trust an expert to authenticate the papers?'

Bloom shook his head. 'Not that. I didn't think he'd give them back.'

'Why?' Burton asked, eyes widening.

'He was being very cagey and wouldn't give me a straight answer when I asked what was going on. He started shouting at me. I tried to calm him down, but I'm ashamed to admit that I lost my temper too.' Donald looked down at his hands. 'I told him I had catalogued the papers, so I'd know if anything went missing and exactly who to come to.' He sighed. 'It wasn't a threat so much as a warning that I was onto him.'

'Is he the only person who'd approached you about getting access to those papers? Jayne Winter hadn't been in touch?' Burton asked.

Bloom frowned. 'Only a few society members knew about the papers, and none of them would tell anyone about what we had.'

'So how did Professor Randall find out?' Burton asked.

Bloom shrugged. 'No idea.'

'Where did the papers come from?' Shepherd asked.

Bloom smiled. 'Like I said, our secretary, Maisie Barratt, received them anonymously in a brown envelope. It was very exciting.'

'Did you not think it was odd to receive something anonymously?' Shepherd asked.

'Of course. That's why we needed them authenticating.'

'What papers were they?'

'One was a diary of Simeon Burns' wife. Absolutely priceless if it's real. Also some letters from Franklin Tudham to his wife after the mill was destroyed and he had to move away for work.'

'Tudham?' Burton asked. 'Do you know a Tobias Tudham?'

Donald rolled his eyes. 'Oh yes, ever since we set up the exhibition, he's been sniffing around. But it was the treasure hunt that really got him fired up.'

'In what way?'

'He was livid that we were encouraging people to find it. He's adamant that the treasure belongs to the Tudhams.'

'And does it?' Burton asked, her brow wrinkling.

'There's been no proof of that, until now.'

'But that's what those letters show?'

Bloom shrugged. 'Until we know if they're genuine, we can't say publicly what's in them, but there is certainly an implication that Simeon Burns tricked Franklin Tudham out of money. That could be the treasure, I suppose.'

'But you say the treasure isn't real?' Shepherd asked, looking up from his notebook.

Bloom rolled his eyes. 'There's been a lot of research done over the years and there's no sign of it anywhere.'

'If the treasure isn't real, why did you set up the treasure hunt?' Burton asked.

'It's just a game,' Bloom insisted. 'It's a fun thing to do to raise money for the museum and the society.'

'But now it appears people are taking it too seriously,' Burton said.

Bloom's eyes widened. 'You think they were murdered for the treasure?' When Burton and Shepherd didn't respond, he leaned forward. 'You're joking, surely? Why would anyone—'

'You said that diary was priceless,' Shepherd said. 'Does that mean it has no monetary value?'

Bloom looked surprised at the change of angle. 'I'm saying I couldn't put a price on it. Something is only worth what someone will pay for it, isn't that what they say? It's valuable to me because it'll build on our town's history. I've been planning to do a little book of my own on the social history of Allensbury, but so far I've not had time.' He beamed. 'Maybe this new material will spur me on, eh?'

'When did you last see Tobias Tudham?' Burton asked.

Bloom scratched his chin. 'I've not spoken to him for a month or so, thank God. But now you mention it, I did see him lurking around in here last week. Or was it the week before?'

'Do you remember what day?' Shepherd asked.

'It was a Saturday, I think. I'd only popped in for a moment to speak to Gracie about ticket sales for the fundraising event and she said there were a couple of people looking around the exhibition then. I peeped through the door. There was a woman sitting on the floor writing in a notebook. She looked familiar, but I couldn't place her.'

'Jayne Winter,' Burton said shortly.

Bloom tilted his head to one side. 'Was that her? Well, then I saw someone hiding at the end of the cabinets, watching her. I think it was Tudham.'

'Were you around the museum on the night Stewart Randall was killed?' Burton asked.

'You think I killed him?' Bloom swelled indignantly. 'How could you ... I would never...'

'Just answer the question,' Burton said, leaning in towards him. 'Where were you?'

'Well, it was a society committee meeting night, and we met here, but we packed up at about eight o'clock and then decamped to The Tavern for a few cheeky drinks.' Then he frowned. 'Actually, now you've mentioned it, Maisie had to dash off straight after the meeting. She usually stays for a drink, but she made her excuses and left.'

'Did she say where she was going?'

'No, she just said she had to go and disappeared.'

'What time did she leave?'

Bloom frowned. 'Actually, I don't know exactly. I just know she didn't come to the pub.'

'What about you? When did you leave the pub?'

'It was about nine o'clock, or thereabouts.'

'Why do you have keys to the museum?' Burton asked. 'You don't work here.'

Bloom blustered. 'Well, I, erm, I help out from time to time so they gave me keys. I mean, I live fairly close, so if there are any issues, I can get here quickly.'

'That's another thing,' Burton said. 'The alarm didn't go off the night Professor Randall was killed, so his assailant must have had access to the alarm code.'

Bloom stared at her. 'And you think that I—'

'You clearly had a problem with him,' she said. 'How big a problem I've yet to establish.'

'I didn't ... You can't...' Bloom stuttered.

Burton got to her feet and Shepherd followed, clicking away the nib of his pen. 'We'll be speaking to your colleagues in the society and the pub staff, so we can verify that you were where you say you were. We'll be in touch.'

As she turned away, Burton got a sense of satisfaction from the worried look on Bloom's face.

Chapter Forty-Nine

It had taken some negotiation with Daisy to get a simultaneous day off, but on Wednesday morning, it was Ed who piled into the car with Dan. Once again, he was looking tired, but also very smug.

'She must be worth it for you to be out so late on a school night,' Dan said with a sly sideways grin. He was glad that Ed was finally back in a solid relationship, even though he had yet to meet or vet the new woman. Ed was being surprisingly cagey.

Ed laughed. 'No comment. But getting up early on a day off shows genuine commitment to our relationship,' he said. 'I bet Emma's gutted she's missing this.'

'She thinks I'm punishing her by doing this when she can't come,' Dan said, indicating to turn out of the car park onto the main road.

'Is that what you're doing?'

'No,' Dan snapped, feeling a bit fed up with the allegation that he was pushing Emma out. 'It wasn't my choice when to do it, it was Lynda Philby's. Plus, Daisy would never have let her out in a week when the crime beat is so busy. I said—'

'All right, all right,' Ed said, holding up his hands in surrender.

'I only asked. Clearly you've still not let it go.'

'I can't just switch off being mad at her, but I wouldn't deliberately shut her out.'

He fell silent and he knew Ed wouldn't push any further. For now, at least.

'So, what are we expecting to find?' Ed asked, swiftly changing the subject and rubbing his hands together.

'Lynda's promised to get us whatever Jayne was looking at so we should know what leads she was working on,' Dan said, manoeuvring the car around a roundabout and accelerating onto the bypass. 'Can you check my tablet is in my bag?' He indicated his satchel, which lay on the floor at Ed's feet.

'Oooh, you've gone all high tech,' Ed said, opening the bag and peering inside. 'Yup, it's here. I thought you were a notebook and pen lover.'

'They have some weird rule about only being able to use a particular type of pencil rather than pen and I thought no to that. Plus, the tablet syncs to my computer, so it's backed up.'

'I do love this,' Ed said, stroking the tablet's notebook-style cover.

Dan laughed. 'Mum got me that for Christmas last year.'

Ed slid the tablet back into the bag. 'You've got Jayne's notebook as well.'

Dan nodded. 'I wanted to show Lynda and see if she can help translate.'

'Jayne might have shown her, I suppose,' Ed said.

Dan indicated to pull off the bypass and headed towards Tildon. 'We just have to hope that whatever Jayne was looking at in the records office will give us another lead to follow. I'm at a total dead end otherwise. I really thought Stewart Randall was involved, but now he's dead, we can't ask him about it.'

'And we definitely don't want to ask Tobias Tudham anything,' Ed said, shuddering.

'He's unhinged,' Dan said, shaking his head.

'Do you really think Jayne had found out about the treasure?' Ed asked, looking out of the car window.

Dan wrinkled his nose. 'I've no idea. If she had, she's not written it down anywhere. I got the treasure hunt clues through yesterday and I've sent them straight to Emma. She's good at puzzles, so I reckon she'll make a good start on it.'

Ed pointed out of the car window. 'The car park is the next left,' he said, pointing. 'I wonder if Lynda will help us with the treasure hunt clues.'

Dan laughed. 'It might be against the rules to ask an expert.' He indicated and turned into the road Ed was pointing at. 'Anyway, let's focus on finding out what Jayne was researching.' He parked in a space and got out of the car. 'I'm sure if we can work out what she was doing, what she was looking for at Old Manor, we'll be able to work out who killed her. And I, for one, am not letting go of that.'

***

Lynda Philby was tall and elegant, with perfectly set blonde hair. She also appeared to be a lot younger than the other women working there.

Dan and Ed followed her as she wove her way through the metal-framed bookcases. Wooden-sided cubicle tables among the bookcases gave people privacy to work and most were occupied.

Dan was glad when Lynda led them to a small meeting room at the back. On the circular table in the middle of the room was a stack of three box files. She gestured for Dan and Ed to sit down and closed the door before joining them at the table.

'Because your friend booked these, I found exactly what she'd looked at,' Lynda said, patting the box on top of the pile. 'I wanted to offer my condolences. You must be so upset at her passing away, and I understand from your newspaper that she was murdered.'

Dan nodded. 'We think it had something to do with the research she was doing,' he said, pulling Jayne's notebook from his bag. He pushed it across the table to Lynda, who opened it.

'Yes, I remember her having the notebook,' she said. Then she smiled. 'One of the few people who already knew that using a pen is a no-no and came prepared.' She turned a few pages and stopped when she found notes in pencil. 'Here's what she would have found here.' She pushed the book back to Dan and Ed, who both looked down at the page.

Dan squinted at the page and then looked at Ed. 'She wasn't looking for treasure at all,' he said, his stomach starting to flicker. 'We were right. She was looking into Simeon being murdered. That's why the book is called curse and not treasure.' He looked up to see Lynda with her eyebrows raised. 'Jayne thought someone poisoned him with arsenic, rather than him dying of cholera,' he added.

Lynda sat back in her chair, eyebrows raised. 'I don't think she found that out here,' she said. 'I've not seen anything that would suggest that.'

'We think she got it from this letter,' Ed said, turning to the page with the doctor's letter.

Lynda's blonde head bent forward to peer at the writing. Then her eyes widened. 'That's interesting,' she said. 'It certainly sounds like he was very ill. He was a nasty man, nothing like his father.'

'Benjamin Burns?' Ed asked.

Lynda nodded and placed the book back on the table. 'He was a friend to all, if the history books are to be believed.'

'I found an obituary of Benjamin in a book in the library,' Ed said. 'It looked like he died of the same symptoms at Simeon.'

Now Lynda's eyes really widened. 'You think he was murdered too? Who would do that?'

'That's what we're hoping to find out,' Dan said.

Lynda looked over her shoulder and they could see an older woman with grey hair watching them from a distance, arms folded. 'Ooops,' she said, 'Edith will be on the warpath. I have filing to do and she thinks I'm shirking. Will you be OK in here?'

Dan and Ed nodded.

'Just shout if you need anything else,' she said, getting to her feet. 'I'll be around.' She left the room and Dan and Ed took a box file each.

'Right,' said Dan, 'let's see what we can find out about the Burns family.'

***

After almost an hour of silent reading, Dan got to his feet and stretched his arms over his head.

'I don't know how Jayne sat and did all this research,' he said, rubbing his eyes. 'Her back must have been ruined.'

'A pattern is emerging though,' Ed said, looking down at the papers arranged in neat lines on the table. He got to his feet and leaned down to touch his toes. He groaned as his fingers barely got past his shins.

'You need to do some regular stretches,' Dan said, grinning. 'You're about as flexible as a block of wood.'

'Even less flexible than that, I think,' Ed said, 'without having Lydia forcing me to practice yoga with her.'

Dan waited a moment and then asked, 'Did you hear from her after you guys split up?'

Ed shrugged. 'At first. She kept phoning me all the time, usually late at night, crying and begging me to take her back, but how could I? She'd been going behind my back with yoga-boy and—' He broke off, voice choking a bit.

'You're better off without,' Dan said. 'Emma never liked her.'

'Least said soonest mended, as my gran would say,' Ed added, trying unsuccessfully to touch his toes again. 'Right, enough of that nonsense,' he said, returning to the table and staring down at the papers. 'What have we got here?'

Dan flopped into his chair, making the papers shift on the table. 'Ooops,' he said, returning them to their rightful places, keen to not mess up their system. 'We still don't have a response to the doctor's letter, so I'm guessing that's lost.'

Ed pointed. 'There's another letter from Simeon's daughter, Millicent. She's talking to a friend about how she can soon get married.' He frowned at the document. 'I thought she needed money to do that.'

Dan leaned over to read the letter. 'She does. This suggests she thought she was due to come into money.'

'You think she killed him, thinking she'd be provided for in the will?' Ed asked.

Dan nodded. 'She would have probably had beauty treatments

and stuff with arsenic in it. She could have dosed him with that. They say poison is a woman's weapon.'

'Don't let Emma hear you say that,' Ed laughed.

'It's a well-known fact. Other people say it, not just me.'

Ed looked back down at the document, squinting a bit. 'Millicent would have been living at Old Manor, so she would have access to him all the time.'

'Imagine the atmosphere if they're in the same house and she's barely speaking to him,' Dan said. 'Talk about awkward, especially at mealtimes.'

'So where is Simeon's wife in this? Does Jayne have anything in her notebook about her?'

Dan flicked through the pages with pencilled notes and shook his head. 'No, which suggests there's nothing here about her, either. Add her to the list of other people to investigate.' He gestured towards the box files. 'There might be something in here.' He flipped open a lid and pulled out a stack of pages in plastic wallets. 'I'm so glad they have this stuff in protective covers. I'd hate to damage anything.' Then he frowned. 'Hang on. Here's a letter from Simeon to Nathaniel.'

'Did he live locally?'

'You're thinking why write to him if you can just go to speak to him?' Dan asked. When Ed nodded, Dan continued, 'I've no idea. Anyway, in the letter Simeon mentions some guy called Elias Hannigan and tells Nathaniel that they need to "do something about him".'

'Business rival?' Ed asked.

'Like Franklin Tudham? And we know what happened to him.'

'Electoral roll?' Ed asked. 'Did they have one in those days? We can see if he's local.' He pulled Dan's tablet in front of him and tapped in some notes on the screen's keypad. He peered at the other notes Dan had made and then looked up to see Dan scratching his head.

'What?'

'That name, Elias Hannigan. It's ringing a bell somewhere in my head, but I can't for the life of me work out where I know it from.'

He flicked through the rest of the papers in the box file, but couldn't come up with anything new. His stomach rumbled loudly, making Ed laugh.

'Was that a hint?' he asked.

Dan grimaced and glanced at his watch. 'Have you seen the time? We've been here for four hours. No wonder I'm hungry.'

Ed rubbed his eyes. 'Interesting stuff, though. I can see how people get sucked into doing this all the time.'

Dan sighed. 'Right, let's pack this up and head out for something to eat. I need a coffee too.'

'You always need coffee,' Ed remarked.

'At least we've got some leads. We need to find out who this Elias guy is and why the Burns brothers weren't fans.'

Chapter Fifty

Dan was packing up his tablet and Jayne's notebook, when he heard a chorus of 'Hello, Donald' from five different directions. Dan looked around the side of the bookcase and saw Donald Bloom speaking to the woman on the reception desk.

'He's like a rock star round here,' Dan said to Ed, laughing.

'Well, he *is* an important man in local history circles,' said Ed, mimicking Bloom's plummy voice.

As they approached the counter to say goodbye to Lynda, Donald Bloom spotted them.

'The intrepid *Allensbury Post* reporters,' he boomed.

'Hi, Donald,' Dan said, grinning. 'How's the treasure hunt going?' He saw the woman behind the counter roll her eyes.

Bloom laughed nervously. 'Well received so far,' he said, side-eyeing the woman, 'by most people.'

'We've had the world and his wife and his kids trying to get in here, Donald, thanks to your clever treasure hunt idea,' she snapped. 'Simeon Burns has never been so popular.'

'He certainly wasn't popular during his life from what we've read,' Dan said, grinning at her.

The woman nodded. 'A horrible man. I don't see why people make such a fuss about him?'

'He's an important part of Allensbury history, Maureen,' Bloom said. 'Without the Burns family, there would have been no silk mill, no migration into the town, no museum,' he added, counting off the options on his fingers.

'I understand all that,' Maureen said, with the attitude of someone who'd had the conversation many times before, 'but making up this treasure nonsense is beyond me. That man would never have given anything to anyone.'

'It's a game to raise money for charity,' Bloom said, beginning to sound frustrated.

Maureen's response was to turn away and viciously straighten a stack of magazines on the counter.

Bloom suddenly seemed to remember Dan and Ed. 'What brings you two here on the first sunny November day we've had so far?' he said, in a slightly false cheerful voice. 'Shouldn't you be outside making the most of it?'

'Research,' Dan said with a grin. 'Not for the treasure hunt,' he said, giving Maureen a wink.

'Someone with sense,' she said, not smiling back. 'Did Lynda get everything you needed?'

Dan nodded. 'I think so. A lot of food for thought.'

'We need a coffee,' Ed said, turning to Bloom. 'Fancy joining us?'

Bloom looked flattered and agreed. 'Lead on,' he said, pointing towards the door.

'What are you doing?' Dan muttered to Ed as they led the way outside.

'The man is an expert on Allensbury history,' Ed hissed back.

'There might be something that we – and maybe Jayne – have missed. Let's see what we can get out of him.'

***

Dan smiled inwardly as Donald Bloom was welcomed warmly by the waitress at the doily-strewn chintzy café he'd chosen. Another woman who treated him like a rock star, he thought, as she ushered them to a table in a cosy corner.

'I much prefer this to one of those ghastly chain cafés,' Donald said, looking around and smiling. Dan could tell Ed was as relieved as him when the woman reappeared almost immediately to take their order.

'So,' Donald asked, leaning forward with his elbows on the table, 'how can I help you?'

'We're still following up on Jayne's research, and we wondered whether we can pick your brains,' Dan said.

Donald nodded. 'Of course, whatever I can do to help.'

Now they were here, Dan wasn't sure how to start. So many questions were bouncing around in his brain. He decided to open the conversation with, 'How much do you know about Benjamin Burns?'

Bloom raised his eyebrows. 'A good man, by all accounts, and funded the museum in honour of his father, Oliver.'

'His father?' Dan asked. 'Do you mind if I write this down?' he added, pulling out his phone.

'By all means,' Bloom waved an airy hand as if he was used to being interviewed. 'I can't remember the exact dates but Oliver came to Allensbury, bought Old Manor and set up the silk mill.

He left Benjamin well set up financially when he died, so Benjamin used his good fortune to support the town's poor and establish the museum.'

Just then, the waitress delivered their coffees, with accompanying milk jugs and sugar bowl. Donald added both to his cup and then, after biting into one of the biscuits that arrived as well, looked up at Dan and Ed expectantly.

'Why do you want to know about Benjamin Burns?' he asked. 'I can't help with the treasure hunt clues, you know.'

Dan glanced at Ed and the latter gave a slight nod. 'We think someone murdered Benjamin and Simeon Burns,' he said, somewhat entertained when Donald Bloom's mouth fell open.

'How ... how do you know that?' he gasped.

But something about his reaction suggested to Dan that the information was not totally new to him.

'We found a letter from Simeon's doctor describing his symptoms and they tie in with arsenic poisoning,' Dan said, taking a sip of his coffee and then deciding it was still too hot.

'Then we found Benjamin's obituary,' Ed put in, 'and he died of the same symptoms.'

Donald Bloom was staring at them in shock. 'You think the same person killed both of them?' he demanded.

Dan shrugged. 'We're not sure yet,' he said, stirring his coffee to cool it. 'But we think that's what Jayne was really investigating. The treasure hunting was just a smokescreen.'

Donald sat back in his chair, looking stumped. 'And do you think that her discovery had something to do with her death?'

'We're not sure,' Dan said, glancing at Ed.

'But we think Stewart Randall knew about the murders, or at least suspected them,' Ed added. He paused. 'Now he's dead too.'

Donald Bloom took a sip of his coffee, seemingly in a daze, and winced. 'Not enough sugar,' he said, seizing another packet and adding it to his cup. He stirred for several more minutes than were necessary. Dan and Ed waited in silence. Eventually, their technique for encouraging reluctant interviewees worked.

'Do you have any ideas about who might have committed the murders?' Bloom asked, shifting in his chair.

Dan shook his head, not wanting to give away any clues. 'How well did you know Randall?' he asked.

Donald took a sip of coffee. 'He was well known in local history circles, even though he wasn't one of us.'

Dan raised his eyebrows. 'One of us?'

'By that, I mean he wasn't born and bred in Allensbury. Most members of the historical society have a personal connection to the town. He refused, quite rudely I might add, to join the society. He thought it beneath him as an academic, which put a few backs up, I can tell you.'

'Like who?'

'Maisie Barratt, for one. Now, *she* could help you with anything related to the Burns family. She's a bit of an expert.' Dan and Ed glanced at each other and Dan made a note on his phone. 'She also had a bundle of papers, letters and suchlike, sent anonymously to her through the post. Randall was desperate for a look at those, but Maisie was having none of it.'

'Why did she not want Professor Randall to see them?' Dan asked, taking a sip from his cup.

'She said she didn't like the way he acted about them, and I have to say I agreed with her. I didn't trust him either.'

'Didn't trust him? What did she mean by that?' Ed asked.

Donald shrugged. 'You'd have to ask her.'

'Was he involved in the treasure hunt?' Dan asked.

Bloom snorted. 'He tried to stop us from hosting it, saying people shouldn't be looking for it. I think he wanted to find it himself, but I told him it was just a game. It was Maisie's idea to use the treasure.' He took a sip of his coffee. 'Like I say, she's a bit of a Burns family expert. She made up all the clues, but she won't tell anyone where they end up.'

Dan glanced at Ed. Did this Maisie Barratt know where the treasure was, or were the clues genuinely made up? Would Jayne have been in touch with her as an expert on Simeon Burns?

'Do you know Tobias Tudham?' Ed asked.

Donald Bloom smiled. 'The police asked me the same question. I don't know why they're so interested in him.'

Dan and Ed exchanged a look.

'He told us he's a descendant of Franklin Tudham, the guy whose mill got burned down,' Ed said. 'He said Simeon was to blame for it.'

Donald gave a slight roll of the eyes. 'The fire was a significant event, but there was never any proof that Simeon or his family had anything to do with it.'

'Tudham also said the treasure belonged to his family? That it was his by right.'

'I don't know anything about that,' said Donald, 'but if he really believes in the treasure, I'd question his sanity.'

'Do you know much about the Tudhams?' Dan asked.

Bloom shook his head. 'Very little, to be honest. Maisie would probably know more than me.'

'Do you know the name Elias Hannigan?' Dan asked.

Bloom looked surprised and scratched his head. 'It rings a bell, but again Maisie is probably the woman to ask. I'll get her to call you.'

Dan could feel his stomach start to flicker and a quick look at Ed's widening eyes suggested he was feeling the same. Clearly Maisie Barratt needed to be on their list if they were going to track down the mysterious Elias Hannigan.

Chapter Fifty-One

The report on Jayne Winter's phone landed on Shepherd's desk late in the afternoon, and Burton perched on his desk, desperate to hear the results.

'So, what have we got?' she asked, rubbing her hands together to warm them.

'Pretty standard stuff. Given what we know about her, there aren't many texts to friends. Her mum pops up on here, and her brother: they're saved contacts. This number here' – he pushed the paper across the desk to her and pointed – 'is the *Allensbury Post*'s switchboard.'

Burton took the pages and looked down at them. 'Presumably she couldn't get Dan Sullivan on the phone so she sent the notebook instead.' She continued to scan the page. 'Anyone else stick out?'

Shepherd took the pages back. 'There's one here from Stewart Randall's mobile and his office. I called to check, and the manager was about to call us because she'd just found his room has been broken into and tossed. The crime scene team is down there now.'

Burton huffed and folded her arms. 'Someone is getting desperate. They didn't find what they were looking for at his house so they've tried his work. How did they get in there?' she demanded.

'They took a crowbar to the door of the department office and took the spare key that's kept in there. I've got someone looking at the CCTV footage they sent us,' Shepherd said, still reading from the page. 'The staff reckon it must have happened late in the evening because no one saw anyone suspicious hanging around during the day. However—'

'I love a good "however",' Burton said, smiling.

Shepherd grinned. 'However, our burglar dropped the keys outside. They're being tested for fingerprints, although there's no guarantee they'll get anything.'

'Whoever this is really isn't afraid to get their hands dirty, are they?' Burton said, getting to her feet and frowning at the timeline on the wall. 'OK, so someone must think Stewart Randall knows what Jayne Winter was looking for. He might even have been looking for the same thing.'

'And lied when he said he didn't know what it was,' Shepherd said, leaning back in his chair, making it creak ominously. 'They suspect he does know or that he's got it himself.'

'Exactly,' Burton said, pointing at him. 'They lure him to the museum, maybe saying they've got the information he needs. He goes along, won't give them what they want and so they kill him.' She frowned. 'Tudham knew Jayne didn't have it because he looked when he found her at Old Manor.'

Shepherd nodded and held up the phone records. 'This is Randall's number here, calling her, and the calls are a couple of minutes each time so you could surmise that they've spoken.'

'Or he was leaving voicemails. Has she called him?'

Shepherd shook his head. 'Not since she left Allensbury University, but there are a lot of text messages since she left. A lot of them from him to her go unanswered.'

'Anything recent?'

'Asking her to meet at Old Manor, you mean?' Shepherd asked with a slight smile.

Burton chewed the inside of her mouth. 'Too much to ask, I suppose. Any sign of Tudham's number on there?'

Shepherd shook his head. 'No, sorry. But tech are looking at Randall's phone and computer, so we may get lucky on there, especially if Emma Fletcher was right and they knew each other.'

'Could it be someone who is on the treasure hunt forum, do you think?' Burton asked, fiddling with the end of her long, blonde hair.

Shepherd nodded. 'It's possible. We know she was posting that she knew where the clues led and she was going to get there first. That's how Tudham found her.'

Burton groaned. 'This bloody treasure. I'm sure it's just muddying the waters, but while we've got both victims involved in it, I can't totally discount it.'

'But there is more,' Shepherd said, pulling out his mobile and tapping the screen. 'The CSIs at Randall's house sent me this.'

Burton took the phone and looked at the picture on the screen. 'A sticky note with a phone number on it?'

Shepherd nodded and held up the tech report. 'Yup, and here on Jayne's phone, we have the same number. It doesn't say whose number it is, but it suggests both our victims have been in contact with this person. There are about ten outgoing calls from Jayne's phone and only one or two incoming. I'd be prepared to hazard a guess that we'll find calls on Randall's phone as well.'

'Is it Donald Bloom?'

Shepherd shook his head. 'No, completely different.' He grinned. 'This one is his number here.'

Burton stared at him. 'He acted like he didn't know her, but he's been phoning her?'

Shepherd grinned. 'Exactly. Incoming and outgoing, so it was going both ways.'

'So whose number is that?'

'It's a mystery. I tried calling and no answer.' He paused. 'Topper has gone round to his nan's tonight for dinner. She's in the historical society, so hopefully she'll know something or know someone else who does.'

Burton glanced at her watch. 'Right, I think we call it a day for now. Bright and early tomorrow, hopefully to hear from Gaz's nan.'

Chapter Fifty-Two

'So our next priority is to find Elias Hannigan?' Emma asked, peering at the screen of Dan's tablet. Dan had summoned her to meet him and Ed in the back corner of The Old Tavern.

Dan nodded. 'I've seen the name somewhere else recently. I just can't think of where.'

'If we find out who he is, we'll know why the Burns brothers wanted him dealt with,' Ed said, slurping his pint.

Dan was staring down at the table and turning his phone over and over. Then he slapped a hand to his forehead. 'Oh, for God's sake, I'm so stupid. Where's your phone?' he asked Emma.

Looking surprised, she took her phone from her bag and held it up. 'Here.'

'Can you find that picture you took of the museum guest book?' he said.

Emma did as she was asked and handed it over. Dan zoomed into the photograph and groaned.

'Bloody look at this.' He turned the phone towards Ed and Emma. When they looked nonplussed, he said, 'Read the names on the list.'

Ed and Emma stared at the screen and then sat back at the same time and stared at him.

'Elias Hannigan,' Ed said, eyes widening.

Dan jabbed a finger at the screen, feeling his stomach flicker again. 'And if he was a mate – or not – of Simeon Burns, he must be long dead. So how come he's leaving reviews of the Allensbury Museum, saying how much he enjoyed his visit?'

'Jayne's name is right next to it,' Ed said. 'Do you reckon she knows who he is?'

Dan dragged the notebook out of his bag and rapidly flipped through some pages. 'Here,' he said, smoothing it open.

'EH connected to BB,' Ed read aloud.

Emma frowned. 'BB?'

'I think she means Benjamin Burns, Simeon's dad,' Dan said. 'I reckon she was very surprised to see Elias Hannigan's name in the guest book.'

'Well, this clearly isn't the real one,' Emma said, pointing to the phone.

Ed snorted into his pint. 'Yeah, I think we'd have noticed if there was a zombie loose in Allensbury.'

Emma paused with her glass of wine halfway to her lips and laughed. 'I'm sure it would have been front page news,' she said.

'Gracie would have probably spotted a member of the undead when he went into the museum,' Ed chuckled.

Dan tapped on the table. 'Normally, I'd join in this merriment, but we need to find out who this is. He was important enough to the Burns family that they wanted to get rid of him.'

Emma frowned. 'Do you think Gracie might know who he is? She put together the exhibition so she might have seen something in their papers.'

Dan shrugged. 'I think what we really need to do is track down Maisie Barratt, the woman from the society. I think if anyone can tell us something, it'll be her.'

'Donald Bloom made it sound like she's the fount of all knowledge, didn't he?' Ed said.

Dan took a sip from his pint and then looked at Emma. 'Did you make any progress on the clues I sent you on email?'

Emma nodded and pulled some printed pages from her handbag. 'I managed the first one easily. It took me to the doll museum, which is super creepy, by the way, all those eyes staring at you. When I went inside, I found the plaque and the name you need for the next bit.' She sighed. 'That one is tougher, so it may take a bit more thinking time. I started by making a list of all the historic places in Allensbury that I know of – museums, that Roman excavation just outside town, and suchlike – to see whether that makes it easier to work out the answers.' She handed the list to Dan, who scanned his eyes down the page, hoping something would spring to his mind.

'That's a pretty long list.'

'We can divide it up between us,' Ed said, 'if you print us a copy. We need to know where this treasure hunt is sending people. Any chance Jayne could have made a mistake with one of the clues and that's why she ended up at Old Manor?'

Emma shrugged. 'It's possible, I suppose. Maybe look out for something that could have more than one possible answer.'

'OK,' Dan said, 'division of labour. I'll look for Maisie Barratt and go to see her. Ed, can you go on the treasure hunt forum and see if there's anything in there?'

Ed saluted.

'Emma, you continue with the clues and see what you can find.'

Emma nodded.

Dan rubbed his hands together. 'We're definitely onto something. I can feel it. Hopefully, the next couple of leads will help us sort it out.'

Chapter Fifty-Three

Gary Topping was pulling open the lid on a plastic food box, when Burton and Shepherd entered the office on Thursday morning. The scent of curry powder and cumin filled the air. The latter's eyes widened.

'Are they leftovers?' he asked, pointing at the container.

Topping grinned and held out the box. 'Yup, Nan's special meat samosas. Want one?'

Shepherd didn't need asking twice and dipped a meaty hand into the tub. Burton watched as he bit into the pastry and moaned with delight. 'They're delicious,' he said through a mouthful of food.

'They are the best,' Topping said, holding out the samosas to Burton. 'It's a recipe she learned when she went on a tour to India a couple of years ago.'

Burton selected a small one and delicately bit into it. She chewed and then her eyes widened.

'Wow, they're amazing,' she said, pulling a tissue from a cardboard cube on a nearby desk to wipe her fingers and mouth.

'She'd made tons, as well as a curry,' Topping said, 'so I couldn't eat them all last night. She said I had to share them with you guys, or I'd get fat.' He patted his trim waist. 'Not sure why she thinks that. She's been overfeeding me for years and it's never changed anything.'

Burton laughed and demolished the last of her samosa. Shepherd was already hungrily eyeing the leftovers again, but Topping clicked the lid back in place. 'Sorry, big man,' he said. 'Have to save some for Madison or she'll kill me. You can have a second if there's any left later.'

Shepherd stuck out his bottom lip, but then laughed. 'I do *not* want a hangry Madison after me, so I'll let you off.'

Burton pulled out a desk chair and sat down. 'Apart from amazing food, did your nan have any pearls of wisdom for us about the case?'

Topping nodded and sat down on his own chair. 'First off, she thinks that there definitely is treasure, and she suspects that Maisie Barratt knows where it is but she's deliberately written clues so that no one else can find it.'

Shepherd laughed. 'Your nan thinks there really is treasure?'

Topping nodded. 'She's been doing her own research into it, even before the treasure hunt started, looking for places where Simeon Burns might have hidden it. She's solved four of the clues in the treasure hunt already.'

'What did she know about Jayne Winter and Randall?' Shepherd asked, perching on the corner of his desk.

Topping winced. 'She did *not* like Randall. Said he was an arrogant s-h-i-t and that's a direct quote – because he wouldn't share what he knew with the society.'

'What about Jayne Winter?'

'Nan's never met her. Said Jayne's never been to any of their meetings, but she overheard Donald Bloom and Maisie Barratt talking about her.'

'Saying what?' Shepherd asked.

'Saying that she was getting in the way of the treasure hunt, that she'd been on the message boards saying she was close to finding the treasure for real and that the competition was a load of rubbish.'

'Did they say anything about trying to stop her?' Burton asked, still trying to wipe her fingers clean.

'Nan wasn't sure. She thought Donald said something about having a word with her, asking her to stop what she was doing. Maisie seemed quite angry, said Jayne might put people off taking part. I think Maisie's quite invested in it.'

'Did she say anything about that phone number, the one that Jayne and Randall were calling?' Shepherd asked.

Topping grinned. 'I was getting to that. Nan recognised it straight away. It's Maisie Barratt's number.'

Chapter Fifty-Four

When Maisie Barratt opened the door, she was wearing a sling on her right arm and a purple bruise blossomed on her cheek.

'Have you been in an accident?' Burton asked, almost feeling the need to wince at the other woman's discomfort.

'You might say that. I was mugged,' Maisie said, leading the way into an extremely neat living room.

'Mugged?' Burton asked, as they all sat down on sofas.

'Yes. Is that not why you're here?' Maisie asked, frowning.

Burton shook her head. 'No, but tell me what happened.'

Maisie sighed and shifted her arm awkwardly. 'I was walking along Harman Street in town yesterday when someone ran up behind me and grabbed my shoulder bag. I tried to fight back, but before I knew it, I was in a heap on the floor. There was a shooting pain in my arm and I screamed. A man rushed over to help me and the mugger ran away with my bag.'

'Were you able to give a description?' Burton asked.

Maisie shook her head. 'All I saw was someone in a black coat running away. I couldn't tell you if it was a man or a woman because I was in so much pain.'

'Not to worry,' Shepherd said, looking sympathetic as he scribbled down the information. 'There's CCTV in that street so it might have caught the incident. Officers will already have that.' He pointed to her arm with his pen. 'Is it broken?'

Maisie nodded. 'Apparently, I was lucky that it was a simple break, so they could patch it up and send me home.' She looked down at the cast on her arm. 'I don't feel particularly lucky at the moment.'

'Was there anything important in your bag?' Shepherd asked, nodding sympathetically.

'Just the usual – purse, keys, mobile phone. Fortunately, we could stop all my cards and block my phone.' She paused. 'But if you didn't come to see me because of the mugging, why are you here?'

Burton sat forward, glad that they were getting back on track. 'We need to talk to you about the murders of Dr Jayne Winter and Professor Sir Stewart Randall.'

Maisie's eyes widened. 'Why do you want to talk to me?'

'You spoke to both of them in the days before they died. What was that about?'

Maisie frowned and said nothing.

'Mrs Barratt, we have your mobile number on both of their phone records. They each called you numerous times, and several calls lasted for more than a couple of minutes, so you must have spoken to them. What did you talk about?'

Maisie rolled her eyes. 'Neither of them believed we should encourage people to look for Simeon Burns' treasure.'

'Why did they think that?' Shepherd asked.

'I've no idea. Maybe they both believe the treasure is a myth and so not worth looking for, but to be honest, I thought at first they were fishing for answers to the clues.'

'But you don't think that now?' Shepherd looked up from his notebook.

Maisie frowned. 'As you've seen, Jayne contacted me a few times over a week or so, but our last conversation was strange.'

'How do you mean?'

'Well, I nearly didn't pick up the call. I was busy in the kitchen and I recognised her number. I was fed up with her, and Stewart Randall if I'm honest, both calling. It was becoming very tiresome.'

'But you answered?' Burton asked, frowning.

'I was planning to tell her to leave me alone, but she sounded – well – odd.'

'Odd in what way?' Shepherd asked.

'She sounded scared. She said she'd found out something that would definitely be interesting for me. That the treasure could be real, but there was a lot more at stake than we'd previously thought.'

Burton felt her chest tighten slightly. 'What did she mean by that?'

'I don't know. She just said she'd found proof that the treasure didn't belong to who we thought it belonged.'

'Not to Simeon Burns, you mean?' Shepherd asked.

Maisie nodded. 'But she wouldn't say who. She said there was one bit of proof she needed to get. When she had it, she'd bring it all to me because it was information I should have.'

'You particularly?' Shepherd sounded puzzled. When Maisie nodded, he asked, 'What did she mean by that?'

'I have absolutely no idea. Next thing I heard, she was dead.'

Burton leaned forward in her seat. 'She didn't say where she was going to look for it?'

'No, but I don't know why she would go to Old Manor. If she'd told me where she was going, I'd have tried to stop her. It's not safe.'

'Did you mention her call to Donald Bloom?' Shepherd asked.

'No, I didn't tell anyone about our conversations.'

Burton frowned. 'But you have spoken to Donald Bloom about her previously, haven't you?' When Maisie said nothing, Burton continued, 'We have a witness who says they overheard the two of you talking, and Donald said he was going to speak to Jayne about what she'd been writing on the forums and you seemed angry about her.'

Maisie sighed. 'There's always someone spying, isn't there?' she said. 'It was Donald who had seen what she'd been writing. He was worried that she was going to spoil the treasure hunt, so he said he'd call her.'

'Where did he get her number? He implied to us he didn't know her.'

Maisie shrugged. 'I don't know. He just said he'd phone her.'

Burton glanced at Shepherd. Clearly Donald Bloom knew Jayne Winter better than he'd admitted.

'Where were you on the night she died?' Shepherd asked.

Maisie stared at him. 'You're asking me for an alibi?'

'I'm sure you can understand why. You'd been in contact with the victim right before her murder.'

'Well, I know but—'

'Just answer the question,' Shepherd said.

Maisie sighed. 'I was here alone. My husband had gone to see his mother. She's had pneumonia and we've been taking turns to pop in and make sure she has everything she needs.'

'On the night of Stewart Randall's murder, where were you?'

Burton could see that Maisie was no longer keen to answer questions. 'What are you talking about? Why do I need to account for my movements that night?'

'It's the same as with Jayne Winter, Mrs Barratt. You'd been in contact with Professor Randall regularly in the last couple of weeks.'

Maisie frowned. 'I was at a historical society meeting.'

'We've been told the entire group went out for a drink afterwards, as usual, but that you didn't go with them. Where did you go?'

Maisie sighed. 'I had a headache so I went home early. It had been a long day.'

'Did anyone see you arrive?'

'No, my husband was out playing snooker with some friends.'

'So you have no alibi for the time Professor Randall was killed?' Burton asked.

'I didn't think I'd need an alibi. I don't have access to the museum after hours and I certainly wouldn't have smashed down the door.'

'We have CCTV that shows the door wasn't smashed to let Professor Randall into the building. Someone with a key accompanied him.'

'Well, I don't have one,' Maisie snapped. She shifted her arm awkwardly and winced.

'Have you had any new sign-ups to the treasure hunt in the last week or so?' Burton asked.

Maisie frowned. 'I don't know. Bear with me.' She left the room, returning with a slim laptop computer. She settled back in her chair and logged in. 'Here we go,' she said. Then she froze.

'What's the matter?' Burton asked.

'N-nothing. Here's the list.' She turned the computer to face them.

Burton and Shepherd leaned forward and peered at the screen. 'Can we take a copy?' Burton asked.

Maisie was staring off into the distance. She came out of her reverie. 'Sorry, what?'

'Can we take a copy of the list?'

'I'm not sure, with all the data protection stuff. I don't think we can pass that on to you. What do you need it for?'

Burton sighed. 'I thought it would be obvious why. I have two murder victims and there may be people on this list who can help us in solving those murders,' she snapped.

Maisie thought for a moment. 'Let me check with Donald and make sure I have his agreement as chair.' She put her laptop on the coffee table, got to her feet and left the room, taking the landline handset with her. They could hear her speaking quietly in the hall.

'One of those names freaked her out,' Shepherd whispered.

Burton nodded. 'I didn't see which one. Could you tell?' she asked in a low voice.

Shepherd shook his head as Maisie returned to the room. She smiled.

'Donald is happy for me to share the details so I can print out a copy or email it?'

'Email would be fine,' Shepherd said, handing her his business card. Maisie took it and lifted the laptop onto her lap as carefully as she could with one hand. She tapped at the keyboard for a few minutes. Shepherd's phone beeped and he checked the screen.

'Brilliant, thanks.'

'Is there anything else?' Maisie asked. Burton thought she

looked very relieved when the answer was that there wasn't. For now.

***

When they got outside, Burton said, 'She was alone at the time of both murders, which seems very convenient when both people had been harassing her for the past two weeks.'

'And she said both were asking about the treasure. No mention of Simeon Burns being murdered.'

Burton chewed the inside of her cheek. 'We know that Jayne Winter was playing that card close to her chest, so maybe she was holding back until she had proof. But she said that the treasure didn't belong to who we thought it was.'

'So not Simeon Burns?'

'Exactly. Is Tobias Tudham right and it belongs to his family?'

Shepherd grimaced. 'Let's hope there's someone more knowledgeable who can answer that for us. Shall I go to Donald Bloom?'

Burton nodded. 'It's worth a try. Send Gaz. He knows the guy, so maybe he can get him to be honest.' They arrived at their car and Burton spoke over the roof. 'Let's allow Mrs Barratt to stew a bit. Without alibis, even though she didn't have museum keys, she's got to stay high on the list. Why would Jayne say that what she'd found was so important to her specifically? It just seems odd.'

Shepherd pressed the key to unlock the car door. 'I'll have a look at the treasure hunter list and see if Jayne Winter and Randall are both on there.' He pulled open the door. 'I also want to know who is on that list that upset her so much.'

Chapter Fifty-Five

With Thursday's afternoon court session cancelled, Ed headed straight home. He made himself a coffee and sat down in front of his laptop. Clicking through to the historical society's website, he accessed the forum and scanned down a series of discussions posted by Simeon Burns' treasure hunters.

'Wow, people are having great fun with this,' he said to himself. Across most of the chat threads, the messages were full of smiley emojis and light-hearted teasing about whether someone was clever enough to solve it. Someone boasted they'd solved all five in about twenty minutes, which led to some derision from others as being untrue.

Ed was laughing to himself as he read, trying to imagine those people in real life. He thought if you put them in an actual room together, they would have a good evening.

But as his eye ran down the screen, a particular thread jumped out at him.

WillTaylorAuthor: *I'm loving this treasure hunt. It's really stretching my cryptic crossword brain. So disappointed that it's not real. I'm hoping for, at least, some gold chocolate coins at the end!*

(smiley face).

JayWin9: *This treasure hunt is made up, but the treasure is real. I know this for a fact.*

WillTaylorAuthor: *Are you serious? How do you know? What evidence have you got?*

JayWin91: *I'm not saying in an open forum. Suffice to say the historical society clearly knows nothing. The last clue tells you everything you need to know.*

ProfSRan: *You don't know what you're talking about, Jayne. There's no way you have found proof.*

JayWin91: *And why not? You know I'm a better researcher.*

ProfSRandall: *Not a chance.*

WillTaylorAuthor: *Woah, guys, this is supposed to be a fun thing for charity. No need to get so aggro about it. Have you really found it JayWin91?*

ProfSRan: *No, she hasn't. She's lying. There's no evidence of the treasure. If there was, I would find it.*

JayWin91: *I have found it. If you were cleverer, you'd have worked it out too.*

ProfSRan: *Stop talking such nonsense. You can't have found it – there's no evidence.*

JayWin91: *Shut up, Stewart.*

WillTaylorAuthor: *Do you guys know each other?*

TobiasT56 has joined the conversation

TobiasT56: *JayWin91 is right. There is treasure and I will find it first. It belongs to the Tudham family.*

WillTaylorAuthor: *Wow, I thought I knew Allensbury history well. Who is the Tudham family?*

JayWin91: *They're nobodies. Franklin Tudham was stupid enough to overplay his hand, literally. A man like Simeon Burns isn't the sort of person you bet against.*

WillTaylorAuthor: *Sounds like a great story. Any chance you'd talk to me about it, TobiasT56? I'd love to hear more.*

TobiasT56: *I don't want to talk about it. Simeon Burns tried to destroy my ancestors and they suffered hardship for years.*

WillTaylorAuthor: *He was nothing like his father, was he? If only Benjamin hadn't died so early.*

JayWin91: *Died? Try murdered.*

WillTaylorAuthor: *Woah, what do you mean by that?*

JayWin91: *Murdered, just like Simeon.*

WillTaylorAuthor: *Simeon was murdered too???? What are you talking about?*

JayWin91: *I have proof.*

ProfSRan: *No you don't. Simeon Burns died of cholera, as did Benjamin.*

JayWin91: *Don't be so stupid. Of course they were murdered. Why do you think they were so ill?*

EliasHannigan has joined the conversation.

EliasHannigan: *The treasure was never Simeon Burns' to begin with. It belonged to someone else and his family stole it.*

WillTaylorAuthor: *Hi Elias! Who did the treasure belong to?*

EliasHannigan: *Don't worry, you'll find out soon*

EliasHannigan has left the conversation.

WillTaylorAuthor: *Well, that was a bit weird.*

Will Taylor had a point, Ed thought. Yet another appearance from the long-dead Elias Hannigan and he seemed adept at technology. But who was he? The conversation seemed to have ended there. His appearance had been something of a showstopper. There was a bit more discussion about Elias's revelation, but Jayne logged off shortly afterwards as well.

But now there was another new lead to follow, Ed thought to himself. Jayne agreed with their theory that Benjamin Burns was murdered in the same way as Simeon, but who would have killed a philanthropist?

He walked across to the coffee table and picked up Jayne's notebook before returning to his seat. Flicking through the pages, he came to Jayne's note: *EH connected to BB*. So, what was the connection?

He peered down at Jayne's untidy handwriting. Two lines down, she'd written: *It goes back to OH*. But who was OH? There were no other notes about him. Ed sighed and rubbed the back of his head, stretching his neck. If EH and BB were connected, did that mean either or both had a connection to this OH? Was this the proof that Jayne was looking for when she went to Old Manor? Had she found it and had the killer taken it away with them? If only they knew what they were looking for and they could ask the police. He needed to find that connection, but he didn't know where to start. Unless...

Ed returned to the table and pulled his laptop towards him. There was one place he hadn't looked so far.

***

Gracie Lincoln eyed Ed suspiciously when he walked through the door of the museum an hour later.

'Shouldn't you be at work?' she asked.

Ed grinned. 'Afternoon off,' he said.

'So you thought you'd come and see me?' she asked, her face lighting up. 'To what do I owe the pleasure?'

'I need some help,' Ed said. 'Do you know the name Elias Hannigan?'

Gracie looked disappointed, but then suspicion returned.

'Why do you want to know about him?'

'You know who he is?' Ed asked, feeling his heart quickening.

'Well, no, I mean, I might have read the name somewhere.' Gracie seemed to backpedal quickly. 'Did Jayne tell you about him?'

Ed frowned. 'Sort of. We found a letter in the county records office from Simeon to his brother Nathaniel that mentioned him. Then we found Jayne had written EH connected to BB in her notebook.'

Gracie raised her eyebrows. 'What did the letter say?'

'I can't remember exactly, but something along the lines of they needed to "do something" about this Elias bloke.'

'Not someone that I'm familiar with,' Gracie said, straightening the pile of guidebooks on the counter in front of her.

The books were already straight, Ed noted.

'Do you know if there's a Burns' family tree anywhere?' Ed asked. 'There isn't one in the exhibition, is there?'

Gracie shook her head. 'We don't have one here. The county records office might? Or Maisie Barratt from the historical society? She's a bit of a Burns expert. Do you think Elias Hannigan will be on it?'

Ed frowned, thinking quickly. 'I don't know. I mean, there's no suggestion that he's related to the Burns' crew, but it was just a thought.' He looked around the foyer hoping for some inspiration, but nothing suggested itself.

'You know what you could try,' Gracie said casually.

Ed turned to find her unpinning and repinning a poster on the notice board. 'What?'

'Buying me another drink.' She grinned at him.

Ed opened his mouth to reply, but was saved from it by the beeping of his mobile phone.

Where are you? Dan's message said.

Investigating, Ed typed, adding an emoji face with a magnifying glass.

Dan responded with a laughing face. *All right, Sherlock, take-away at our place tonight? My treat?*

Sounds good. Emma coming too?

There was a slight delay.

Of course, Dan replied.

Brilliant. See you both then. I have news...

Ed pocketed his phone. He could only hope that Dan and Emma would sort out their living arrangements. At least they were talking now, but—

His train of thought came to a grinding halt and he slapped a hand to his forehead.

'What's the matter?' asked Gracie.

Ed jumped, having forgotten she was there. 'I've just had a brainwave. Thanks Gracie, that was really helpful.'

He dashed out of the door, almost missing Gracie's farewell and happiness at being able to help.

Chapter Fifty-Six

'OK, clearly you have got news as you promised,' Dan laughed, as Ed yanked open the door to let him and Emma into the flat. He paused to take off his coat and shoes and then bundled Ed down the corridor to give Emma space to do the same.

'Oh yes, I think you're going to like this one.'

Dan sat down at the dining table and pointed to Ed's laptop. 'I assume there's something on here?'

Emma sat down beside him and leaned her elbows on the table. The scent of coconuts momentarily distracted him but he shook himself internally. No time for that now.

'Right then, out with it,' Emma demanded.

'Look at this.' Ed turned his laptop to face Dan and Emma with the forum open on the screen. He watched as their eyes scanned down the page and widened in unison.

'So Elias Hannigan has popped up again,' Emma said. 'He's good at technology for a dead bloke.'

Ed nodded. 'But what's weird is that no one reacts to the name.'

Dan frowned. 'They don't know who he is, do they?' he asked, looking up at Ed. 'No one recognises the name, or at least they don't say they do.'

'Correct,' Ed said, holding up a finger. 'Even Jayne, who has his initials in her notebook, doesn't question why a man who's been dead for hundreds of years is joining a treasure hunt discussion.'

Dan exchanged a look with Emma.

'Is there anything more in Jayne's notebook about him?' Emma asked.

Ed shook his head, grinning. 'Nope, but I've found a connection myself.'

Dan and Emma looked at him expectantly. When Ed continued to grin at him, Dan snapped, 'Come on, out with it.'

'Well, I went to the museum because I thought Gracie might know who he is—'

'And does she?' Dan asked, unable to help interrupting.

'She says not, but I'm not sure I believe her. Anyway, I got to thinking about family trees, y'know. What if he's related to them, or something like that?'

Dan nodded, wondering where Ed was going with this. 'Because Jayne had written he's connected to Benjamin?'

'Exactly. I couldn't find a family tree but' – Ed held up a finger – 'then I had a flash of inspiration. The census.' He pulled out his phone and opened the note-taking app. He held it out to the others, still grinning.

Dan took it, looked down at the screen and then up at Ed, eyes widening.

'He was living with the Burns family?' he asked.

Ed nodded. 'Well, the census shows he was there in eighteen forty-one when they collected the data, but he's noted down as "visitor", which according to my research, means he wasn't a permanent resident of the house, just in the house on the day the survey was taken.'

'So what was he doing there?' Dan asked, frowning as Ed shrugged.

'Whatever it was, Simeon and Nathaniel weren't happy about it,' Emma said.

Dan stared at the bookcase at the end of the room. What was Elias Hannigan's connection to the Burns family? He felt sure this related back to Jayne's murder, but he felt like they were no further forward than they were when they'd started.

'Earth to Dan,' Emma said, waving a hand in front of his face and making him jump. 'You're miles away.'

He frowned. 'I was just thinking that this is all well and good, solving a one hundred and seventy-year-old murder, but what about Jayne? Is this really enough to get her killed?'

'You think there's something else?' Emma asked.

'I just keep thinking, why does it matter now that Simeon Burns was poisoned? Who would care if he died of natural causes or not?'

Emma and Ed looked at each other and then back at him.

'I think,' Dan continued, tapping a finger on the table, 'someone has an interest in keeping the murder a secret. But it's not necessarily him being murdered that's the story. It's the who.'

'Whodunnit?' Ed asked.

'Exactly. The treasure is a smokescreen, but someone is determined that no one will find out who really killed Simeon Burns. They thought that Jayne and Randall had worked it out and killed them to keep them quiet. Someone is tying up the loose ends of people who know about the murder.'

He could see from Ed and Emma's faces that they'd just had the same cold shudder go down their back as he had.

'Far too many people now know that we've got the notebook,'

Ed said. 'That puts us in the firing line, doesn't it?'

'Exactly. We need to work out who has a motive to want to protect the murderer of Simeon Burns before he or she works out how much we know. And I think I know the place to start.'

Chapter Fifty-Seven

Maisie Barratt looked apprehensive when she opened her front door on Friday morning and found Dan on the doorstep.

'Can I help you?' she asked.

Dan turned on his most charming smile. 'I was a friend of Jayne Winter. You might have met her? I'm following up on some research she was doing, and Donald Bloom suggested you might help.'

Maisie frowned as she stepped back to allow him into the house. 'I was sorry to hear about Jayne,' she said, 'but if you're after the Burns' treasure, I can't give you any hints, you know.' She spoke lightly, but Dan sensed an edge to her voice.

He laughed. 'No, I already have a top brain working on that.' He followed Maisie down the hall, which was heavily scented with an expensive vanilla room fragrance, making him want to sneeze. 'Did you know Jayne?'

'We've spoken,' Maisie said, 'just on the phone.'

'And she was asking you about Simeon Burns?' Dan asked.

Maisie pushed open a door and they stepped into a large room where books lined one wall and a large wooden table sat in the centre. A small wooden easel on the table held an expensive-looking tablet and a corkboard covered in with sticky notes and index cards took up a second wall. A large hand-drawn family tree hung on a third. Maisie swept her arm around the room.

'My research headquarters,' she said.

Dan looked around, mouth slightly open. 'Wow, this is impressive,' he said. 'You must have spent hours on this.'

Maisie chuckled. 'Try years,' she said.

Dan moved towards the family tree, but Maisie spoke and he turned back to face her.

'You were asking about Jayne. I don't know how much help I can be, because we mostly spoke about the treasure.' When Dan paused, Maisie asked, 'What is it?'

'I don't think Jayne was really interested in the treasure,' he said. 'She was actually investigating Simeon Burns' murder.'

'Murder?' Maisie gasped. 'Where did she get that idea?'

Dan was slightly puzzled. If Maisie was the authority on Simeon Burns, had Jayne really not confided in her? He suddenly had a feeling that he needed to proceed with caution.

'She'd found out that he didn't die of cholera,' Dan said, pulling Jayne's notebook out of his bag. 'She sent me this. In it, there's a letter from a doctor suggesting that Simeon is more ill than any other cholera patients. The symptoms he describes could result from arsenic poisoning.'

Maisie stared at him. 'What?'

'We're not sure why someone would poison him. My friend Ed found an obituary for Benjamin Burns, Simeon's dad, and it sounds like the same thing happened to him.'

Maisie wrinkled her nose. 'What makes you say that?'

'His symptoms are the same as Simeon's,' Dan said with a slight shrug. 'It was kind of obvious when you put the two together.'

Maisie was staring off into the distance, a hand to her mouth.

'What's the matter?' Dan asked, surprised by her reaction.

Maisie shook herself. 'Nothing. Why did you think I would know something?'

Dan had the feeling that Maisie was concealing something, but couldn't work out what or why.

'Donald Bloom said you're the authority on the Burns family. He said if there was anything to know, you'd know it.' He knew it was blatant flattery and wasn't surprised that it didn't work on Maisie.

'Benjamin Burns was a philanthropist from what we heard, a friend to the poor,' he said. 'Can you think of any reason why someone would want to poison him?'

Maisie shook her head. 'He was a very popular man. Of course, he had the money to do charitable works and still have the high life of a gentleman.' There was a sudden tightness in her voice.

Dan's highly attuned journalist sense – almost as powerful as his sight or hearing – told him he was getting into borrowed time territory.

'Do you know the name Elias Hannigan?' he asked.

Maisie's cheeks flushed. 'I ... er ... I don't think I've heard that name before. Who is he?'

'He's got a connection to the Burns family.'

Maisie shrugged. 'Not a name I've ever come across.' She glanced at her watch. 'I'm sorry, I forgot I have an appointment and I'll be late if I don't get moving now.'

Dan thanked her and headed out into the corridor.

On the doorstep, Maisie said, 'I think you'd be wasting your time if you go chasing this Elias Hannigan. It sounds like a made-up name.'

Dan turned to look at her. 'Oh no, he *is* real. We found him in a letter at the county records office, and he was living with the Burns family around the time Benjamin Burns died,' he said, enjoying the look of surprise on Maisie's face before turning and heading back to his car.

As he opened the driver's door, he could see Maisie watching him from the window with her mobile phone to her ear.

Chapter Fifty-Eight

Donald Bloom beamed when he saw Gary Topping on his doorstep.

'Gary!' he said. 'How are you? I've not seen you for ages. Maggie didn't tell me you'd be dropping round.' His face fell as Topping held out his warrant card.

'This isn't a social call, is it?' asked the older man.

Topping shook his head. 'Sorry, Donald, but no.' Bloom stepped back and waved for Topping to follow him into the house. He led the way into the kitchen and gestured for Topping to sit at the scrubbed wooden table.

'I spoke to your colleagues a couple of days ago. What else do you need?'

'You lied to them,' Topping said. 'You told them you didn't know Jayne Winter.'

'Well, I don't. I mean—' Bloom broke off when Topping held up a hand. He hoped his nan would forgive him for being tough on a friend of hers.

'You're making this worse for yourself,' he said, reaching into his pocket and pulling out a folded sheet of paper. He spread it out on the table in front of Bloom and pointed to a phone number.

'That's your number on Jayne Winter's phone record, isn't it?'

Bloom put his face in his hands. 'Yes, it is.'

'How did you get her number?'

'She contacted me through the society's website because she was interested in the social history project I'm working on.'

Topping winced. 'Is that the history of Allensbury you've been promising to write for the last three years at least?'

Donald nodded, shoulders slumping. 'She said she could help me, so I shared some source material with her. I didn't realise then that she was researching for her own book.'

Topping looked up from his notebook. 'She was writing a history of Allensbury?'

Donald shook his head. 'No, it was something different. About a month ago, another historian I know and follow on social media contacted me, asking how the Simeon Burns project was coming along because he hadn't had an update from Jayne.' Donald snorted. 'That's when I realised she'd used my name to get him to share information with her. Something he wouldn't have otherwise given away.'

'Were you angry?'

'Of course. He was mortified when he realised he'd been duped. I called Jayne and shouted at her, but she didn't care. She laughed and said a real academic does everything they can to get the materials they need.'

'And she kept posting on the forum?'

Bloom nodded. 'Maisie was furious. I called Jayne again, but she just said I was jealous that she was going to shake up the academic world with what she'd found.'

Topping stared at him. 'Did she mean the treasure?'

Bloom shrugged. 'I don't know what she meant.'

'Did you try to find her in person?'

Bloom shrugged. 'I wouldn't know where to start.'

Topping eyed him steadily and tapped his pen rapidly against his notebook. 'Donald, stop lying. You told my colleagues that you saw her in the museum two days before she died. Did you speak to her?'

Donald shook his head, looking slightly shamefaced. 'I was going to give her a piece of my mind, but then Gracie called me away. By the time I got free of her, Jayne had gone, as had Tobias Tudham.'

'You didn't look for her anywhere else?' When Bloom shook his head, Topping added, 'Did you tell anyone else that you'd seen her?'

Bloom looked uncomfortable. 'I may have mentioned it to Stewart Randall. When we argued about the treasure hunt, I said I'd been having trouble with Jayne Winter.'

'Was he surprised by that?' Topping asked, pen scratching on his notebook page.

'He got really agitated and asked what I meant. I mentioned the research she was doing and how I thought the treasure hunting was a smokescreen.'

Topping frowned. 'Why do you think that?'

'She'd asked the other historian for some resources on arsenic poisoning and how it could be done. He'd also given her some guidance on tracing name changes.' Bloom scratched his head. 'I don't know what that meant to Stewart, but he stormed out in a rage. If he wasn't dead himself, I'd have said he'd make a good murder suspect.'

'That's the thing, Donald. We've got a few suspects on the list and you're one of them. We've still not confirmed your alibis, and you knew and disliked both victims.' Topping got to his feet and clicked away his pen nib. 'I wouldn't go anywhere just now. I'm sure we'll have more questions.' He paused on his way to the door. 'If you want to get off the suspect list, tell the truth in the future. It makes life much easier.'

Chapter Fifty-Nine

'You're back,' Burton said, as Topping arrived in the office and joined her and Shepherd at the timeline on the wall. 'Anything useful from Donald?'

Topping recounted the conversation and Burton felt her irritation rise as his story continued.

'So that confirms that he knew her and had spoken to her on the phone several times?' she said, frowning.

Topping nodded. 'He freely admitted that he yelled at her. Not surprisingly, she didn't care. But for what it's worth, I don't think he killed her.'

Burton frowned, wondering where Topping was going. 'Why not?'

'For one thing, he wasn't angry about the forum messages, just frustrated. For another, he doesn't think she was really interested in the treasure. He thinks she was onto something else entirely.'

'Which she was: Simeon Burns' murder,' Shepherd said.

Topping tapped his pen against his notebook. 'But he doesn't know that, which I think is very good for him right now. I don't understand why some one hundred and sixty-year-old murder is enough to start people getting killed *now*.'

Burton turned to face the timeline, brow furrowing. She was finding this case increasingly frustrating.

'OK, so, we know Jayne was investigating Simeon Burns, as did Stewart Randall and Dan Sullivan.'

'Although Sullivan didn't know until after she was dead,' Shepherd put in.

'Right,' Burton said, turning to face him. 'What's new from Donald is that we know she was looking into arsenic poisoning and that clearly meant something to Stewart Randall.'

Topping frowned. 'Tobias Tudham didn't know about that. He believed she was looking for the treasure.'

'So who else?' Burton asked. 'Her brother says she was insanely private, so how did anyone find out what she was working on? She must have told them.'

The door clattered open, and Sophie Madison came trotting down the office.

'Good of you to join us,' Burton said, casting a glance at her watch.

'Sorry, boss, but I was just waiting for an update from the CSIs at Stewart Randall's home,' she said.

Burton folded her arms and nodded for Madison to continue, praying for some useful information.

'There are several sets of fingerprints at the house. Randall's, obviously, but there's another set that, based on the size, they think belongs to a woman. On a hunch, I asked them to check against Jayne Winter's fingerprints.'

'And?' Shepherd asked.

'Not a match,' said Madison.

'His daughter?' Shepherd asked.

Madison shook her head. 'I went to see her and she gave me her prints to compare. Not a match.'

Burton frowned. 'So, we have a mystery woman's fingerprints at his house.'

'It gets better,' said Madison, grinning. 'We found the same ones in his university office and on the keys that were used to break in.'

Burton felt her heart quicken. 'Finally,' she said, 'finally we have something concrete. The same woman broke into his home and office and presumably both instances were after he was murdered.'

'One snag,' Madison said, 'is that we don't have an ID. No match in our system.'

'If they're women's fingerprints, does that put Donald Bloom in the clear?' Topping asked, dropping his notebook and pen onto his desk and shoving his hands into his trouser pockets.

Burton thought for a moment. 'That doesn't mean he's not involved. Maybe he teamed up with a woman to do this?'

'Maisie Barratt?' Shepherd asked.

Burton shook her head. 'I don't know. Can you really see Maisie Barratt armed with a crowbar?' She sighed heavily. 'OK, so we have some forward movement.' Looking at the clock on the wall, she said, 'Right, let's call it a day and head home. Tomorrow, we need another word with Maisie Barratt and a set of her fingerprints. I also want another review of everything we've got so far. We're missing something and we need to find it ASAP.'

Chapter Sixty

Emma yawned as she left the *Allensbury Post's* office at about six forty-five on Friday evening. The day had felt endless, having to fill pages left empty by several adverts being withdrawn late in the day. But she felt virtuous, having stayed late to help the on-call junior reporter finish tomorrow's edition. All she wanted now was a long, hot bath. She felt drained and wished she didn't have to walk home in the dark and cold. The beep of her phone gave her a boost. Dan, asking if she wanted to grab some food with him and Ed.

Sounds great, she texted back. *Where?*

Come here first and we'll make a plan once you get here.

She texted back a thumbs up and changed course to cross at the traffic lights to head towards Dan and Ed's. It was much closer than hers and she thought about how warm and cosy it would be. Plus, there might be a takeaway. Although that was even less good for her waistline than Dan's pasta mountains. Lost in thought, she started walking across the car park of the flats. One streetlight was off and Emma tutted. She'd get Dan to report that to the council. How were people supposed to protect their cars when—

Halfway through the thought, something slammed into her

from behind and she crashed to the ground. She landed face first and screamed as her chin collided with the tarmac, making her eyes fill with tears. She tried to turn to see her attacker, but a gloved hand shoved her face away, banging her head into the ground again. Emma whimpered as a knee in the small of her back pinned her down. Hands felt her pockets and she tried to struggle. Her bag was up-ended and its contents, including her laptop, crashed to the floor.

'Where is it?' a harsh voice demanded.

'What? I don't—'

'The notebook. I know you've got it.'

'I haven't got—'

'You don't want to end up like Jayne Winter just because—'

A man's voice yelled 'Oi!' and the attacker leapt to their feet, dropping Emma's phone on the floor and stamping on it, shattering the screen. Emma tried to turn, but a boot lashed out. She screamed again as it caught her a glancing blow to the head. The attacker turned and fled. Emma sat up, dabbing at her bleeding chin with a gloved hand, tears running down her face.

'Emma!' a familiar voice shouted and she saw Dan running towards her, with Ed in hot pursuit. Dan dropped to his knees beside her and folded her in his arms. 'Em, what the hell...?'

'Went that way,' Emma mumbled, trying to point in the direction the mugger had gone.

'What just happened?' Ed demanded, following her finger. 'I was on the balcony having a ciggie when I saw them jump you. I didn't see where they came from. What did they want?'

Emma shrugged, unable to stop the tears from coming. 'My laptop ... it's—' she gestured weakly.

'Never mind that now,' Dan said. 'We need to get you inside.'

He gently pulled her to her feet. 'Ed, get the phone.'

'On it,' Ed said, stooping to pick up the phone and Emma's bag.

Dan led Emma into the building, not letting go of her until they were safely inside the flat. 'Christ, Em, look at the state of your face.'

He helped her out of her coat and shoes and guided her into the bathroom to find something to stem the bleeding from her chin. He peered at the wound and then dabbed it with a wet flannel. 'I don't think it needs stitches but keep pressure on and if it doesn't stop, we'll go to the hospital.' She tried to protest, but he held up a hand. 'You don't know what damage that could have done. Ed said you hit the deck pretty hard. He didn't realise what was happening at first.'

'They came out of nowhere,' Emma mumbled, her whole body aching.

Ed reappeared with a large ice cube in a plastic bag. 'Try putting that on your cheek,' he said. 'That should take some of the swelling down.'

'Did they say anything?' Dan asked as Emma perched on the side of the bath, trying to control her shaking hands.

'Wanted the notebook,' Emma mumbled. She heard Dan's sharp intake of breath.

'What did they say?'

'Said I'd end up like Jayne.' A fresh wave of sobs came over her and Dan pulled her into a tight hug.

Ed left the bathroom and they heard him moving around. Dan led Emma into the living room and sat her on the sofa. Ed was looking down at Emma's smashed laptop and phone.

'They wanted the notebook,' Dan said, and Emma saw a look pass between him and Ed.

She drooped forward and Dan grabbed hold of her.

'Are you OK?' he asked.

'I feel a bit woozy,' Emma said. Then everything went black.

***

Vague images flashed through Emma's mind as she floated in and out of consciousness. Faces looked down at her. Someone prodded the wounds on her face, making tears leak down her cheeks and fluorescent lights hurt her eyes.

When she was finally aware of her surroundings, she could hear two voices murmuring.

'I feel so bad about this,' Dan was saying.

'Mate, it's not your fault,' Ed replied. 'You couldn't know someone would do this to Em.'

'But if I hadn't started poking about in Jayne's research and trying to find out who would kill her, Em wouldn't be in this mess.'

'Does it really look that bad?' Emma asked, trying to move her head and regretting it.

Dan and Ed both leapt to their feet and peered at her.

'Welcome back to the land of the living,' Ed said with a grin. 'You had us worried then, keeling over on the living room carpet.'

Emma winced. 'I hope I didn't get blood everywhere.'

Dan snorted. 'I don't think that should be the prime concern right now.' He looked pale. 'How are you feeling?' He squeezed her hand and Emma squeezed back.

'I feel like shit,' she said, trying to smile and wishing she hadn't. 'Does it look as bad as it feels?' Dan and Ed glanced at each other. 'Oh my God, I must look terrible.'

'Let's just say there's a lot of bruising and about ten stitches in your chin,' Dan said. 'I think it's going to hurt a lot once the local anaesthetic wears off.'

'Ah, I am not looking forward to that,' Emma said, trying to pull herself into a better sitting position.

Dan rushed to straighten the pillows behind her. 'Be careful,' he admonished. Then he sat back down on the chair by her bed. 'I'm so sorry, Em. I shouldn't have let that happen.'

'Hey, it's not your fault,' Emma said. 'You couldn't have stopped a mugging.' The lads exchanged a look. 'What?' she asked.

Dan paused, then said, 'Don't you remember? You said the person asked you for the notebook?'

Emma paused, and the harsh voice came back to her.

'Oh God, you're right. They did. They said I'd end up like Jayne.' She gulped.

'Thank God we came running when we did,' Ed put in.

Emma gestured towards her face. 'Is this related to Simeon Burns' murder?'

Dan nodded. 'Well, I think someone is trying to cover up his murder, for whatever reason, and we've found out something they didn't want us to know.'

'The same thing Jayne and Randall found out?' Emma asked, feeling her bottom lip wobble. Dan and Ed nodded. 'But we don't know what that is,' Emma said, trying to marshal thoughts to remember what they'd done recently. 'We were looking into some bloke, weren't we? What was his name?'

'Elias Hannigan,' Dan said. 'I went and spoke to Maisie Barratt about him this morning.' He recounted the interview. 'She said she doesn't know who he is, but I think she's lying.'

'What makes you say that?' Emma asked, trying to frown and

finding it too painful.

'She blushed and got all awkward when I asked and then came up with a reason for me to leave. Also, who was she phoning the minute I was out of the way?'

Ed tilted his head to one side. 'When you said that Jayne was actually investigating Simeon's murder, it sounds like Maisie kind of glossed over it.'

Dan nodded. 'But there was definite tension when I asked about Benjamin. She made some snarky comment about him being wealthy, which was odd. Her reaction when I mentioned the doctor's letter and how the symptoms were the same as arsenic poisoning was interesting.'

Ed shrugged. 'Maybe she was annoyed that there was something Burns-related that she didn't know about?'

'We know that there's a connection between Elias and Benjamin Burns because they were living in the same house on the eighteen forty-one census,' Emma said, feeling her eyelids droop.

'You're tired. Let me get the doctor,' Ed said. 'They said they want to admit you overnight, so I'll let them know you're awake and they can get you sorted.'

He pushed his way out through the curtain.

'The police want a word as well,' Dan said, standing up and coming to the bedside. When Emma tried to pull a face, he said, 'Not my fault. Well, not directly. When the doctor asked what happened, I told them it was a mugging, he insisted on calling the police. Ed and I have given a statement, but they'll want to speak to you too.' He reached for her hand. 'Em, I'm—'

'Don't say you're sorry,' Emma interrupted. 'This is not your fault.' She thought for a moment. 'No way could we have predicted this might happen. It's frustrating that I didn't get any kind of look at them.'

Dan nodded. 'And I can't imagine any of our suspects doing this. Which means there's another player in the game and, at the moment, I have no idea who it could be.'

Chapter Sixty-One

Sophie Madison had thought Saturday was going to be a good day, with a short coffee shop queue and her bus on time. But the apologetic expression on Shepherd's face when she arrived at the office told her the day was about to plummet.

'Sorry, but I need you to take on some of the admin today,' he said, as she put down her coffee cup and took off her coat. 'We've got a couple of people off sick and they,' he pointed to a stack of reports on his desk, 'need adding onto the investigation log. Would you be able to...'

Madison groaned inwardly but smiled and picked up the stack of paperwork.

'Sure, not a problem,' she said. 'Always happy to help.'

Shepherd patted her arm. 'Brilliant. Thanks, Soph, much appreciated.'

She watched as he sat down at his desk and sighed under her breath. She'd been working for about twenty minutes when Shepherd's phone rang and he grabbed the receiver.

After a brief conversation, he replaced the receiver and looked at Madison. 'Maisie Barratt is downstairs. I'll see you later.'

Sophie nodded and watched as Shepherd walked away, collecting Burton from her office on his way out. Then she dug a hand into her bag and pulled out her glasses case. It was definitely a day for those if she was going to be staring at the screen for hours.

Twenty minutes later, just as her right hand was going into cramp from moving the mouse around, Madison clicked open the treasure hunt clues document. She read through it and wrinkled her nose. Riddles and cryptic clues were not her forte. But as she dragged and dropped the next file, her hand twitched and she added it to the wrong on-screen folder. Madison flexed her fingers. Time for a break and a coffee, once she'd put the file in the right place. As she corrected her mistake, she noticed a Jayne Winter email that was also out of place. Opening the email to check where it should be, she read the contents and her eyes widened. She inhaled and exhaled slowly, trying to control her excitement.

Hitting the print icon, she scuttled across to the printer and scanned her ID pass to start it. The pages seemed to emerge far too slowly. She snatched them as soon as they hit the out-tray and scanned her eyes down the page. Heart beating faster, she returned to her desk, locked the screen and headed for the office door. She grinned to herself as she hurried down the stairs. This was going to be needed in the interview.

***

Maisie Barratt didn't look happy to see Burton and Shepherd when they arrived. She was perched on a sofa in the interview room, a glass of water on the low table in front of her.

'How's your arm?' Burton asked, as they sat down on the sofa opposite.

Maisie bristled. 'Painful, since you ask. Has there been any progress in my case?'

Shepherd smiled at her. 'The CCTV is on its way and I'll make sure one of the team reviews it as soon as it arrives.'

Maisie frowned, as if she was trying to work out how to ask something without saying the wrong thing.

'Have you made any progress with the murder cases?' she asked.

Burton glanced at Shepherd and then looked back at Maisie. 'We're following several lines of enquiry at the moment,' she said blandly.

'One of those being me?' Maisie asked.

Burton said nothing but stared back at her.

'I don't understand why you need my fingerprints,' she said. 'Am I being arrested?'

Burton sat down on the sofa opposite. 'No, but we found a woman's fingerprints in Stewart Randall's home and office, and we need yours for comparison.'

'I've never been to his house or office,' Maisie insisted, voice wobbling slightly.

'Then there's nothing to worry about,' Burton said, smiling.

'Because I haven't done anything. I would never ... I hardly knew...'

Just then, there was a knock on the door and Sophie Madison stuck her head into the room. She gestured to Shepherd and he disappeared into the corridor. Burton was happy to let the silence run while they waited. Maisie was fidgeting and shifting her arm into a more comfortable position when Shepherd reappeared with some printed pages in his hand.

'Mrs Barratt,' he said, sitting down, 'I've just had a really interesting discussion with my colleague. Can you tell me why Jayne Winter received different clues from those sent to other participants?'

Chapter Sixty-Two

Maisie Barratt's mouth fell open. 'What?' she gasped. 'What do you mean?'

'It's quite simple,' Shepherd said, putting the pages on the table and pushing them towards Maisie. 'My colleague has compared the clues sent to participants in the treasure hunt competition to the clues that were sent to Jayne Winter. The last one is different; does it direct the finder to go to Old Manor Hall?' He pointed a stubby finger at the page.

Burton watched as Maisie looked down at the page and then back at them, wide eyed.

'I ... I don't understand. This isn't the clue I wrote.'

'Really?' Burton asked, feeling satisfaction that Maisie was rattled.

'I swear to you I didn't write a separate clue for her. It's too dangerous to go anywhere near Old Manor Hall. My husband helped me to write them. He's very good at puzzles, but he would never have come up with something like that.'

'So where did the clue come from?' Burton demanded.

'How should I know?' Maisie snapped back, her voice rising for the first time. 'I told you I didn't write it.'

'Can you think of anyone who would do that?' Shepherd asked.

Maisie shrugged. 'No. I mean, the treasure hunt is just a bit of fun to raise money for the historical society.'

'You believe in the treasure, don't you?' Burton asked, trying to capitalise on Maisie's unsettled appearance.

'Yes, but why is that important?' Maisie asked, eyes narrowing.

'Jayne Winter was harassing you, asking questions about the treasure,' Burton said, leaning forward with her elbows on the table. 'Did you think she'd found it? Were you trying to put her off the scent?'

Maisie was looking panicked. 'I have no idea what you're talking about. Please, you have to believe me. I wouldn't hurt anyone, especially not over a silly game.'

'But it's not really a game, is it, Mrs Barratt?' asked Shepherd. 'You believe that the treasure is real, and you want to be the one to find it first.'

Maisie's eyes had filled with tears. 'Yes, I believe there's treasure, but I would never hurt someone to get it. Besides, like I told you, I got the impression that Jayne wasn't really after the treasure.'

'So what was she after?' Burton asked, feeling as if they were going in circles.

'She just said it was something I would be interested in. So you see, I wouldn't have had a reason to stop her. I wanted to know what that was.'

'Something you'd be interested in? What could that be?'

Maisie shrugged. 'I've no idea.'

Shepherd leaned forward. 'When we last spoke, you reacted to a name on the list of sign-ups for the treasure hunt. Who was that?'

Maisie looked puzzled. 'I don't know what you're talking

about.'

Shepherd looked about to speak again, but Burton held up a hand. 'We're not getting anywhere here. So, Mrs Barratt, you can go for now. But at the moment, you have a strong link to both victims. Don't go anywhere, will you? I'm sure there'll be more questions to answer.'

With that threat hanging in the air, she collected the papers from the table and swept from the room.

She was waiting in the corridor when Shepherd returned after showing Maisie out. He raised his eyebrows.

'No alibi for either murder and a motive for both,' she snapped, 'so why can't I see her doing it?'

Shepherd smiled. 'She's a cool customer.'

'But would a cool customer not have alibis sorted out?' She exhaled heavily and turned towards the stairs to the first floor. 'We're getting nowhere fast. Right, get Madison to look at the clues that were sent to Randall and also Tudham. They were both at Old Manor Hall recently and I want to know whether they went of their own accord or were led there.'

Her mobile phone beeped and she looked at the screen. 'Madison. Talk about speak of the devil.' She tapped the screen and read the message, her eyes widening.

'What?' Shepherd asked, holding the door open for her to pass through.

'She's been trawling Stewart Randall's emails to see if he's been sent treasure hunt clues as well.'

'Any luck?'

'Not treasure hunting, but she's pulled together a list of his recent contacts and she says there's something we need to see.'

'I love it when people say that,' Shepherd said with a grin as he followed her out of the door.

Chapter Sixty-Three

Having spent a weekend trying to get Emma to rest, Dan felt exhausted when Monday came around. Now he was ignoring multiple messages from her, asking what was happening.

'I wondered who'd be covering for Emma,' Suzy, the police press officer, said when she sat down opposite Dan in the small meeting room off the police station reception area. 'How is she? The report sounded awful.'

Dan shrugged. 'She looks terrible, but is insisting she's fine, as ever.'

'Can't keep a good reporter down,' Suzy said with a smile. 'But seriously, we've got an appeal out for witnesses and we're looking at CCTV. Hopefully, we'll get the mugger on camera.'

'It wasn't just a random mugging,' Dan said. When Suzy's eyes widened, he added, 'They asked her for the notebook and said she'd end up like Jayne if they didn't get it.'

Suzy gasped. 'Oh my God. You think this is all about your cold case?' Dan nodded, and Suzy added, 'Well, we're doing everything we can to catch them. If you think of anything else that might help, just let us know.'

Dan tried not to sigh too heavily. He knew what that platitude meant.

Suzy flipped open the folder she had placed on the table and looked down at the first page.

'There's not much else to update you on for either of the murders,' she said. 'We've got CCTV from outside the museum and we're examining it. Still appealing for witnesses, traffic cam footage, etc.'

Deploying his reading-upside-down skills, Dan looked at the folder as Suzy turned the page and spotted a familiar name on a printed email.

'Elias Hannigan?' he asked. 'Why are you looking at him?'

Suzy raised an eyebrow. 'What do you know about him?'

'Well, he's dead, for a start,' Dan said, sitting back in his chair.

Suzy sat forward, staring at him. 'What?'

'He's dead. He has some connection with Benjamin Burns, Simeon Burns' dad.'

Grabbing a pen, Suzy dragged a piece of paper in front of her. 'Elias Hannigan was part of your mate Jayne's research?' she demanded.

Dan nodded. 'Yeah, we don't know where he fits into the picture yet because Jayne's notes are really sketchy.'

'But he's definitely dead?'

Dan shrugged. 'If he was a contemporary of Benjamin Burns, then yes. Why?'

Suzy grabbed her mobile and started dialling. 'Because he recently sent Professor Sir Stewart Randall an email.'

***

Burton appeared in the interview room so quickly Dan thought she must be on roller-skates.

'Elias Hannigan,' she said, without preamble. 'What do you know about him?'

'He's been a busy boy for someone who's dead,' Dan said with a grin. 'He's been chatting on this forum' – he pulled out a printout from Ed's forum hunting and handed it to Burton – 'and he's visited the museum and signed the guest book.'

'As well as learning how to use email,' Burton said, eyes scanning down the forum. She raised her eyebrows. 'He's certainly got a good sense of timing – pops in, drops a bombshell and disappears again.'

'I feel sorry for Will Taylor,' Dan said, 'getting in the firing line of those nutters.'

'I thought Jayne Winter was a friend,' Burton said, laughing.

'She wasn't behaving in the sanest manner in all this,' Dan replied.

'What have you found so far?' Burton asked, looking up from the forum printout. 'Had this Elias Hannigan been in touch with Jayne?'

Dan fiddled with his pen. 'Apart from that forum, I don't know. All we've found so far is that he has a connection to the Burns family. He was staying in the house at the time of the eighteen forty-one census.'

'So why is someone pretending to be him now?' Burton asked.

Dan shrugged. 'We're struggling to find anyone who will admit to knowing who he is.' He recounted his conversation with Maisie Barratt.

Burton raised her eyebrows. 'You think she should know him?'

'Well, she's done a lot of research into Simeon Burns. We found

Elias quite easily in the county records office, so it stands to reason she should have been able to find him too.' Then he frowned. 'Hang on, you just said that he emailed Stewart Randall?'

Burton sighed. 'Off the record,' she said, glaring at Suzy who Dan assumed had overstepped the mark, 'he emailed Professor Randall inviting him to meet to discuss how they could work together to find the treasure.'

'So Stewart Randall may have recognised his name,' Dan said. 'Was the meeting place the museum?'

Burton nodded.

Dan sat back in his chair, staring into space.

Burton glanced at Suzy and then back to Dan. 'What's that look for?'

'I'm just trying to think who would want to lure Randall to the museum, and who would have the strength to kill him. Tudham would be my bet, but we don't know if he knows about Elias Hannigan. He seems to be all about the treasure.'

'Do you think he attacked Emma?' Suzy asked.

Dan shook his head. 'Looking at his boots, she'd be in a much worse condition if it was him.' He exhaled heavily. 'I just wish me and Ed had got downstairs quicker. We might have caught whoever it was.'

'Or you might both be in hospital as well,' Suzy said. 'Maybe it's time to step aside from your investigation.'

Burton nodded. 'Clearly someone has a secret and they're not afraid to hurt someone to protect it. We'll find out what happened to Jayne, so leave this to us.'

Chapter Sixty-Four

Gary Topping sat at his desk, staring at the screen with his elbow on the desk and his chin resting in his hand. It took a thrown pen from Shepherd to break his concentration. He started as the plastic object clattered across his desk. He turned towards Shepherd, rubbing his eyes.

'What?' he asked.

'How are you getting on with the Maisie Barratt CCTV?'

'I don't think it was a random attack,' he said, enjoying Shepherd's surprised expression.

'What?' Shepherd asked, scooting his swivel chair to Topping's desk.

'She was being followed. Look.' He scrolled back through the footage and pointed to the screen. 'This is her in the high street. See there, that figure just ducking into the doorway when she looks around? Then, when she walks into the bookshop, that person waits outside as if they're looking in the window.'

'Do you know how long they were following?'

Topping shook his head. 'I'm not sure. I'm working backwards from the attack, and this seems to be the first time the camera picks up the tail. But then when you go to the Oscar Terrace camera, Mrs Barratt is walking along and the person is still there. She's got no idea she's got company because' – he rolled the recording forward and pointed again – 'here she turns into Taylor Court and this happens.' They watched as the figure started running, barging into Maisie Barratt and grabbing the strap of her handbag. A tussle ensued, which ended with Maisie in a heap on the floor clutching her arm, passers-by rushing to her aid and the mugger running away clutching the shoulder bag.

Topping paused the recording and turned to look at Shepherd.

'Someone targeted her,' he said.

'Is there a better angle on the mugger's face?' Shepherd continued.

Topping shook his head. 'They always have that hood up, so it could be anyone.'

Shepherd scratched the back of his head. 'I wonder what was in her bag that the mugger wanted so badly. She said it was the usual – phone, purse, keys etc. – but there must have been something else for them to target her.' He frowned. 'Right, speak to Suzy and let's get an appeal for information out with the photo. It's crap quality, but you never know, it might trigger someone's memory.'

'It wasn't wet or particularly cold that day,' Topping said, 'so hopefully someone noticed the hood and paid attention.'

'Good point. Let's see if there are any witnesses prior to the incident. Also, given that it's clearly a targeted attack, we need to know from Mrs Barratt what was in the bag and why someone else would want it enough to jump her in the street.'

***

Topping and Shepherd both turned as Sophie Madison arrived at her desk, dumping her coat and bag on it and taking a swig from the takeaway coffee she was holding. She put the cup down and looked at Topping's computer.

'Oooh, CCTV. I know how much you love that.'

Topping laughed and mimed going cross-eyed.

'How did you get on with the forums?' Shepherd asked, stretching his arms over his head. Sitting watching CCTV for any amount of time was not his idea of fun.

'Well, I spent about an hour going through a few of those the *Post* had told Burton about. The main one is people joking around about the treasure hunt, sharing clues and that kind of thing.'

'Sounds fairly innocuous,' Shepherd said, slightly disappointed.

Madison nodded. 'That forum was, but then I went down a bit of a rabbit hole. I searched for Simeon Burns' name and, after adding a couple of other words, I hit gold.'

'OK, you've got me,' Shepherd said, sitting forward and leaning his elbows on the desk. 'And that led to?'

Sophie grinned. 'A forum, not historical society related, in which Jayne Winter also says that she has proof, that she needs one more piece of information and that she's coming to town to get it.'

'Get the treasure?' Topping asked, brow furrowed.

'That's just it,' Madison said, shoving her hands into her trouser pockets. 'She doesn't specify the treasure.'

Shepherd frowned at her. 'What do you mean?'

'Well, in all the previous conversations it's been clear they're talking about treasure, but this one is more opaque.'

Shepherd's eyes widened. 'Did she say when she was coming?'

Sophie nodded. 'She said she'd be in town from last weekend and then she would have everything she needed.'

'Basically, she's told all those people where she would be,' Shepherd said, getting to his feet and crossing the room to the timeline. He added to the start of the line to show the new information.

Sophie nodded. 'And it gets better.' She sat down in her chair, logged into her computer and showed Shepherd the screen. 'Look who is also in that chat.'

'TobiasT56 again,' said Shepherd slowly.

'Yup, he knew exactly when she was coming to town and I'm guessing that's how he found her at the museum. Plus, there's this bit where she says that the treasure should go to a museum and—'

'He says it belongs to his family and he'll take it by any means necessary,' Shepherd read aloud from the screen. He sat back and puffed out his cheeks. 'That sounds like a threat if ever I heard one. Does the boss know?'

'Yes. I told her before I went out. She's gone upstairs to speak to the DCI.' Madison paused. 'But, like I said, I don't think Jayne's talking about the type of treasure Tudham thinks it is.'

'What makes you say that?'

Madison shrugged. 'I'm not sure. There's just...' She trailed off. 'If I can put my finger on it, I'll let you know.'

'Great, thanks,' Shepherd said. He looked round as a phone rang, and Topping spun to pick it up. They waited while he spoke into the receiver, hung up and turned back.

'Someone has handed in Maisie Barratt's handbag to reception – intact, purse, keys, phone, etcetera.'

'Nothing taken?' Shepherd asked, frowning.

'So I've been told.' Topping looked at Shepherd. 'You're wondering why.'

'Exactly. You don't follow someone around for the best part of half an hour, mug them in the middle of the street and then not take anything. She must have had something else in there.'

'But what?' Topping asked.

'Get your coat,' Shepherd said, getting to his feet. 'Let's tell her the good news about the bag and see how she reacts.'

Chapter Sixty-Five

Maisie Barratt sighed when she opened her front door and found Shepherd and Topping standing on the doorstep.

'More questions?' she asked as she led them into a comfortable living room, holding her arm stiffly as she sat down and gestured them to a sofa.

Shepherd smiled. 'We have good news and, yes, more questions,' he said, settling himself on the squishy cushions.

Maisie raised an eyebrow and Shepherd could see she was uncertain about their visit.

'Good news?' she asked, sounding cautious.

'Your handbag was found,' Shepherd told her. 'It's with our forensics team for fingerprints and then we'll be able to give it back to you.' He paused. 'Everything was inside – purse, keys, mobile phone, all safe and sound.'

An expression he couldn't quite place flitted across Maisie's face.

'Is there something missing from the list?' he asked, feeling alert.

'No, I told you what was in there. Where did you find it?' she asked, her grateful smile now looking a little forced.

'Dumped in a flower bed in the next street,' Topping said, with a glance at Shepherd. The latter nodded to Topping to go ahead. 'We're surprised that the mugger assaulted you only to dump the bag minutes later with the contents intact,' he said.

Maisie nodded. 'Me too. I mean, why do that?'

Topping raised his eyebrows. 'Mrs Barratt, there must have been something important in your bag for the mugger to take a chance of grabbing it.'

She stared at him. 'Nothing.'

Shepherd frowned. 'Or maybe the right question is, what did the mugger think you had in your bag?'

'I've told you. It sounds like everything is still in the bag.' But she wouldn't quite meet Shepherd's eye.

'Mrs Barratt,' Topping began, 'we have the mugger on CCTV following you for about half an hour before they attacked you.' Shepherd was pleased to see a look of shock on Maisie's face. Maybe this would shake her into being honest. 'It just seems odd that someone would clearly target you, steal your bag and then just throw it away,' Topping continued. 'What else was in there?'

'I'm telling you, nothing. Otherwise I'd have asked you where it was.' She shook her head and tears started in her eyes. She blinked them away. 'Sorry, it's just all been such a shock, particularly that they were following me and I didn't notice.'

'Can you think of a reason why someone would follow you?' Topping asked.

Maisie shook her head again. 'No, I mean, it's not like I'm any-one important. How would they know where I would be?'

'How would who know?' Shepherd asked, pouncing on her words.

'What do you mean?' Maisie asked, looking confused.

'You said why would they even know. Who is they?'

'The mugger. Who else?'

Shepherd continued to stare at her for a moment, and she seemed to find holding his gaze difficult. 'Mrs Barratt, if you know who the mugger is, then it's better that you tell us now and we can make sure they don't come looking again.' When Maisie said nothing, he asked, 'Do you know the name Elias Hannigan?'

A look flitted across Maisie's face, but the self-possessed mask soon slipped back into place.

'No, it's not a name I'm familiar with,' she said.

'That's funny, because he's been posting on your treasure hunting website. He's clearly taking part and claims that the treasure really belonged to someone else and the Burns' family stole it.'

Maisie shifted in her seat and refused to meet his eye.

Suddenly, something slotted into place in his head.

'That's the name on the treasure hunters' list that shocked you, isn't it?' he said. 'It caught you off-guard. Who is he?'

Maisie shook her head. 'Someone's idea of a joke, signing up with a Georgian-sounding name. I don't recognise it at all. Why not ask Donald? Maybe he knows who it is.'

Chapter Sixty-Six

'Do you think she's the killer?' Topping asked as they returned to the car. 'I just can't see it.'

Shepherd beeped the car alarm and opened the door. He stared at Maisie's house for a moment, brain whirring. 'Neither murder suggested a loss of control and, in Jayne Winter's case, Maisie would know where she would go because of that clue.'

'But she wouldn't know when,' Topping put in. 'Unless she was following Jayne as well.'

Shepherd pulled a face. 'Unlikely that there was more than one stalker, but she's definitely lying about something. I think there was more in that handbag than she's told us.'

Topping climbed into the car. 'But what? What could she have been carrying that the mugger knew about and wanted?'

'My thoughts exactly,' Shepherd said as he swung himself into the car and started the engine. He glanced over his shoulder and pulled away from the kerb. 'And what about Elias Hannigan?'

Topping shook his head. 'She knows more about him than she's letting on.' He sighed. 'But whether we can get it out of her, I don't know. She's a pretty cool customer.'

'She believes in the treasure,' Shepherd said, indicating to turn left at a T-junction. He glanced at Topping when the other man was silent. 'You don't believe in it, do you?' he asked, eyes narrowing.

Topping shook his head. 'Nah, but if anyone could convince me, it would be her. She's so calm and rational, she could tell me the moon was cheese and I'd be straight up there with some crackers.'

Shepherd laughed.

Topping's phone beeped and he looked down at the screen. 'The boss,' he said. Shepherd kept his eyes fixed on the road while Topping read the message.

'Well?' he asked. He couldn't see Topping's face, but he was clearly reading the message more than once. 'Come on, out with it.'

'Well, this is a turn-up. She got called into a press briefing because the journos have found Elias Hannigan.'

Shepherd's eyes widened. 'Wow, they don't do things by half. Does the boss want us to pick him up?'

'That's just it.' Topping glanced at Shepherd. 'He's dead. He was a mate of Simeon Burns' dad.'

Shepherd laughed. 'Pull the other one.'

'I'm serious. She says he's a dead guy.'

Shepherd shook his head in disbelief. 'What does she want us to do?' He thought for a moment. 'We could go back to Mrs Barratt and ask her. Maybe that'll shake her. Actually, no, tell Burton we'll swing by Donald Bloom's house. Maisie said he would know who Elias is – whether that's past or present, who knows. Let's see what he knows.

'You think he could be present-day Elias?' Topping asked, thumbs typing quickly.

'It's possible. Let's go and ask him.'

A minute later, Topping's phone beeped again. He read the screen and laughed.

'She says "feel free to use any Georgian torture methods you know of" to get information.' He frowned. 'I might need to Google that, or call my nan. She'd know.'

Shepherd grinned and prepared to head off at a different exit at the approaching roundabout.

'We should ask him about the clue that was sent to Jayne Winter, see if he knows anything about that,' Topping remarked, looking out of the car window.

Shepherd frowned. 'What I don't get is that he doesn't believe the treasure is real, so why would he be trying to find out where it is? It feels a bit much that he would kill two people to stop them spoiling a charity game.'

'There's more to it, you mean?'

'Exactly. Remember what Madison said. She doesn't think Jayne Winter was talking about finding treasure. Maybe Donald knows more about what she'd found than he's letting on. And, would it be worth killing her for?'

***

It was Donald Bloom's wife Margery who opened the door to Shepherd and Topping. She beamed at the latter, immediately asking after his family. Topping assured her they were all fine and she led them through to Donald's 'den'. When they declined tea or coffee, she left the room beaming.

The room was square and relatively small, with a stuffed bookcase covering one wall. A brand-new laptop sat on a sturdy wooden desk, and piles of paper littered every other part of the surface. A metal filing cabinet stood by the door, drawers open with papers spilling out.

'I do wish she wouldn't call it a den,' Bloom said with a roll of his eyes. 'It makes me sound like a wild beast.'

Shepherd smiled, hoping to put Bloom at ease.

'You look busy,' he said, gesturing towards Bloom's desk.

Bloom sighed and ran a hand over his sparse hair. 'It's my monthly tidy-up,' he said, 'but somehow it never really gets any tidier.'

Shepherd sat in the armchair indicated by Bloom and Topping leaned against the filing cabinet. Bloom perched on the edge of his computer chair, looking from one to the other.

'I'm guessing you haven't come to discuss my tidiness,' he said, smiling awkwardly.

'Do you recognise the name Elias Hannigan?' Shepherd asked.

Bloom raised his eyebrows. 'Hannigan? Possibly, I mean, in what context?'

'We believe he had a connection to Simeon Burns,' Shepherd said.

'Oh, I see.' Donald Bloom's gaze moved around the room. 'Erm, well, no, I don't think I do.'

'He's also joined the treasure hunt, which is impressive given that he's been dead for over a century,' Shepherd said, feeling irritated that Bloom was clearly lying.

Bloom stared at him. 'What?'

'Someone is pretending to be Elias Hannigan, and we need to find out who and why,' Shepherd said, trying to appear calm. 'We believe they're also involved in Stewart Randall's murder and probably Jayne Winter's as well.'

Bloom stared at him. 'What? Why?'

Topping leaned forward. 'Donald, he or she emailed Randall asking him to meet at the museum on the night he was killed. They also had the keys and the alarm code to get into the museum.'

Donald sat up straight. 'What are you implying?'

Shepherd almost held his breath as Topping asked, 'Is it you, Donald? Are you Elias Hannigan?'

Bloom leapt to his feet. 'No, I'm not. How dare you ... How dare you ask such a thing?'

Shepherd sat forward in his chair. 'You have a motive to kill both Jayne Winter and Stewart Randall. They were both threatening your treasure hunt. Your alibi for Randall's murder isn't great and you have access to the museum keys. I'm sure you can understand why we're asking.'

'But I wouldn't – I could never—' Bloom blustered, but he sank back into his chair, sighed and rubbed his hands across his face. 'The treasure hunt was supposed to be a bit of fun and now two people are dead.'

Topping glanced at Shepherd and the latter nodded, wondering where Topping was going.

'You told me before that Jayne had asked your colleague about arsenic poisoning and historic name changes. Do you know why that was?'

Bloom shook his head. 'No, she wouldn't tell me.'

Shepherd sat up in his chair. 'You told us before about some papers sent to Maisie Barratt. Do you know if they would have contained anything about the murder of Elias Hannigan?'

Bloom looked uncomfortable and Shepherd felt he'd hit the right nerve. 'Mr Bloom?'

'I don't know,' Bloom said. 'We weren't able to look closely at them before they went to the authenticator. It would be easy to damage such old material. But old diaries can be so fruitful. Of course, you have to do due diligence – who wrote it, why, were they expecting someone else to read them, etcetera.'

'Did you tell Jayne Winter about the diary?' Shepherd asked. 'We know you've been in contact since she came back to Allensbury.'

Bloom shifted in his seat. 'I might have done.'

'Is there any chance she could have seen it?'

Bloom shook his head. 'The authenticator works out of the records office,' he said, 'but even she asked to see them – he wouldn't allow it without my permission.'

Topping raised an eyebrow. 'But previously she has managed to get information that she wasn't supposed to have. Could she have persuaded him?'

Bloom's shoulders drooped. 'It's possible, I suppose.'

Shepherd felt another connection click into place. 'Could Jayne have sent the diary to Mrs Barratt? So she saw it before you did?'

'It's possible,' Bloom said, 'but not likely. There was a note with the papers saying that they were a gift from a Burns' descendant. Was Jayne related to the Burns family, do you know?'

Shepherd shrugged. 'She could have been, but it's more likely that she's interviewed someone for her research.'

'Who would want to hide such an important piece of historical evidence?' Bloom asked.

'Anyone who wants to hide the fact that Simeon Burns was murdered,' Topping said.

'Well, the reporters from the *Allensbury Post* told me they think someone also murdered Benjamin Burns. He was Simeon Burns' father, you know.'

Shepherd exchanged a glance with Topping and saw his confusion mirrored in the other man's face.

'Two murders in the same family?' he asked.

Bloom nodded. 'If they're right, then someone killed father and son, both with arsenic from the sounds of it.' He paused. 'That must have been why Jayne Winter asked for the evidence from the other historian. Although why she wanted name changes is a mystery to me.'

It's a total mystery to me too, Shepherd thought.

Aloud, he said, 'Someone is clearly trying to cover up those murders, so until we know who, don't tell anyone else about those papers or where they are. We need to find Elias Hannigan and, until we do, I don't want anyone else getting hurt.'

Chapter Sixty-Seven

After work, Dan and Ed headed round to Emma's cottage.

'Reckon she's following Dr Dan's advice and resting?' Ed asked.

Dan laughed. 'Not a chance. I'm surprised she wasn't in the office this afternoon.'

Ed grinned as he pressed the doorbell. As suspected, a fully dressed Emma answered the door. 'I'm so glad you're here. I've been cleaning just in case you came round,' she said, leading the way into the living room. She pottered into the kitchen and they heard the sounds of the kettle and tea being made. When she returned with three steaming mugs, Dan pulled a pack of cookies from his bag with a flourish.

'Ah, what a man,' Emma said, grabbing them and ripping open the packet, without offering one to Ed who stood beside her. 'Thank you.' She took a big bite of one cookie and sighed happily.

Dan watched her, suppressing an eye-roll. 'Have you eaten at all today?' he asked, dropping into an armchair.

Emma frowned. 'I think I had breakfast. After that, I'm not sure.' Seeing Dan's face, she tried to smile charmingly, but the stitches prevented it.

'That's more of a grimace than anything else,' Ed said, laughing and pulling a face back at her.

Emma elbowed him in the ribs, making him laugh more. 'So what's been happening?' she asked, sitting down on the sofa opposite Dan, demolishing her cookie and quickly changing the subject.

'We'll talk more later about looking after yourself,' Dan said, genuinely concerned about how pale and edgy Emma looked. He recounted his conversation with Burton and Suzy.

Emma, in the act of scoffing another biscuit, stopped with it halfway to her mouth.

'It must be important,' Ed said, joining Emma on the sofa. 'You've distracted Emma from a chocolate chip cookie.'

Emma glared at him. 'I'm not that much of a pig. You said Elias had emailed Randall, inviting him to the museum to discuss the treasure?'

Dan nodded, reaching for a cookie himself before Emma had the opportunity to polish off the whole packet. 'Which suggests that Elias is someone with access to the museum after hours.'

'Someone with the strength to stab Randall to death,' Emma said.

Dan finished his cookie and wiped his fingers on his trousers. 'Not necessarily. I know Randall was a big bloke, but if it was someone he knew, he might have let them get close. If the weapon was sharp enough, it might not need much strength to do it.'

'But we know Elias died years ago, so someone is impersonating him, meaning they know the original Elias and the fact he's connected to the treasure.'

Dan nodded. 'Who do we know who might know that?'

Emma counted on her fingers. 'Maisie Barratt?'

Dan pulled a face. 'I can't see her wielding a weapon. Plus, we don't know how well she knew Randall. Would he let her up close and personal?'

'Gracie?' asked Emma. Then she shook her head. 'She said she didn't recognise the name, plus I don't see her stabbing someone.'

'Donald Bloom?' Ed put in, taking a swig of tea.

'We know he didn't think much of Stewart Randall, and if the prof was threatening the treasure hunt, that would give him motive,' Dan said, 'plus he has access. But my money is on Tobias Tudham.' When Emma and Ed gave him a questioning look, he added, 'First off, he's clearly a bit unhinged. Second, he knew that Jayne and Randall were both researching the treasure. He has a cast-iron motive for stopping them.' Dan paused, feeling a flicker in his stomach. 'Third, he's the kind of person who would attack you to stop you digging,' Dan said, pointing at Emma. Then he frowned. 'Although I did say to Burton that I thought you've have been more hurt if it was him.'

'But he was in that forum at the same time as Elias Hannigan,' Ed said, grabbing another cookie.

Dan gave him a patient look. 'And no one can have more than one profile on a website?' he asked.

Ed took a bite and chewed before saying, 'So he uses the Elias Hannigan account to bait Jayne.'

Dan nodded. 'Maybe they corresponded through private messages and he arranged to meet her at Old Manor.' He sighed. 'If only it wasn't such a risk to approach him.'

Emma laughed. 'When has a bit of danger ever stopped you?'

Dan glared at her. 'Even I'm not stupid enough to go looking for a guy who tried to shoot me.'

Ed frowned. 'We just need to find the connection between Elias and Benjamin Burns. That might give us a reason why someone is using that as an alias.'

Dan peered at Emma. She was looking pale. 'First things first. We need to feed Em properly before she pegs out.' Emma opened her mouth to protest, but closed it again at the determined expression on Dan's face. Dan got to his feet. 'If I'm OK to make use of your kitchen, shall I put some pasta on?'

Emma and Ed both nodded.

'Make your usual mountain. I'm starving,' Emma said, and Dan laughed as he headed into the kitchen.

***

Dinner eaten, and washing-up dried and put away, they reconvened at the dining table. Dan had fetched Jayne's notebook from his bag, and it sat in the middle of the table. They all looked at it.

'I don't understand why you're carrying this around after what happened to me,' Emma said, pointing to the cuts and bruises on her face.

'I haven't had it with me all day. We fetched it from the flat before we came over. Plus, I had a bodyguard,' Dan said, pointing to Ed, who flexed his arm muscles.

Emma reached for the notebook and flipped through it until she found the page she wanted. 'Here she says EH is connected to BB,' Emma said.

Dan nodded. 'But I've been through it umpteen times and I can't remember anything else about him.'

'But we weren't looking for Elias before, were we?' Emma said, pointing to the notebook.

Dan took back the book and started to leaf through the pages.

Two had caught together and he gently prised them apart. He felt his breath catch in his chest. 'Oh my God, I can't believe I missed this before,' he said, eyes scanning a photocopy of a letter that was stuck to a page.

'What is it?' Emma and Ed demanded in unison. Dan turned the notebook so they could both read it. He enjoyed the dawning of realisation on their faces.

'I didn't take much notice of this when we were looking at Jayne's stuff earlier,' he said, 'but this is from a solicitor to Benjamin Burns.'

The letter said: *I have done as you asked and with splendid success. I have found Elias. If you wish me to proceed, then I will contact him directly. My source says he seems to be a respectable fellow, a widower with no children, and lives frugally, which may mean he will welcome your overtures.*

Ed looked up at Dan. 'Benjamin Burns asked his solicitor to find Elias,' he said, eyes wide.

Dan nodded. 'But look at the date. He's only found him in eighteen forty, which is the year before Benjamin died, if I'm remembering correctly.'

Ed peered at the screen. 'Do you think they actually met?'

Dan shrugged. 'The census says he was a visitor in the house in eighteen forty-one, but we don't know exactly when he actually arrived there. They may well have spent time together. But why was Benjamin making overtures to him?'

'This is exciting, isn't it?' Emma asked, re-reading the letter. She turned the laptop back to Dan. Then she frowned. 'Remember that letter you found at the records office?'

'Simeon and Nathaniel talking about "dealing with" Elias?' Dan asked.

'Can you remember the date on it?'

'Hang on, we made some notes.' Dan pulled his phone from his pocket.

'We used your tablet,' Ed said.

Dan sighed. 'All mod cons, Eddie boy. The tablet syncs to the cloud, so it's all on here as well.'

Ed glared at him but said nothing.

'Damn it,' Dan said. 'The date isn't in the notes.' He sat back and scratched his nose. 'We'll have to go back and look at it again.'

'But at least we know from that letter that Simeon and Nathaniel knew about Elias, whether or not he was in the house at the time of the letter, and that they didn't want him around,' Emma said. 'That's a start.'

'We need to go back to the records office,' Dan said.

'Shotgun,' Emma said immediately.

Dan and Ed stared at her.

'Shotgun?' Ed asked. 'You know you can only call that when you can see the car, don't you?'

'Don't care. It's my turn to go to the records office.'

Dan laughed. 'There's no need to fight about it,' he said, as Ed opened his mouth to protest. 'I'll call Lynda in the morning and see when she can get the document for us. I'll ask if there's anything else specific about Elias as well.' He beamed. 'I finally feel like we're making progress.'

Chapter Sixty-Eight

Burton fixed her gaze on each of the team as they gave their updates on Tuesday morning. When Topping recounted his and Shepherd's conversation with Donald Bloom, she smiled with satisfaction to see the junior officer's new train of thought.

'So, you think Jayne Winter might have got her hands on the diary and sent it to Maisie Barratt?' she asked, folding her arms.

'She's an experienced researcher and we know she's good at getting information out of people,' Topping said, clicking his ballpoint pen repeatedly, 'so I wouldn't be surprised if she did get her hands on it.'

'But what I can't get,' Shepherd said, 'is how she found it? How did she know it existed?'

Burton eyed Topping, who immediately stopped the irritating pen clicking.

'She could have found a Burns' descendant in her research?' she suggested. 'Through one of those forums, maybe?' She almost felt Madison and Topping give a collective wince, knowing that aspect of the investigation would come their way.

'But it doesn't explain why, if it was her, she would send the documents to Maisie Barratt,' Topping said. 'How would she know Maisie was the right person to contact?'

Burton shrugged. 'The historical society website, perhaps? Got her name and contact details through that?' She paused and pointed at the timeline on the wall. 'That's how she contacted Donald Bloom, wasn't it? Did he recommend Maisie?'

Topping shook his head. 'Donald hadn't thought of that until I mentioned it.'

'Although it wouldn't surprise me if he was lying,' Shepherd said. When Topping opened his mouth to object, he added, 'I know he's your nan's mate, but he's been dodging the truth from the start. If he knew Jayne had seen that diary, and had made the Burns' murder connection, that could be a motive.'

'But he didn't know about the murder,' Topping insisted.

'So he says.'

Burton raised a hand to interrupt, keen to get the conversation back on track. 'So, we still think Donald Bloom could be in the frame for this one. What about Maisie Barratt?'

Shepherd sighed and Burton could see he was reluctant to start an argument with Topping again. 'Jayne could have told her about the diary during one of their conversations. She says they only talked about the treasure, but we have no proof of that. And there's the fake clue, which she denies all knowledge of.'

Burton continued to stare at the timeline on the wall. She had a feeling they were missing something, something important, but she couldn't put her finger on it. Somewhere in the back of her consciousness, she heard Shepherd's phone ring. When she came out of her reverie, he was grinning.

'You're going to love this,' he said. 'The CSI team has found the murder weapon, and you will not believe where.'

Burton waved a hand for him to get on with it.

'You were right. It's a sword and it's been hiding in plain sight in a display of Roman weapons.'

***

Cath Middlebury was almost wringing her hands when Shepherd and Topping arrived at the museum. A 'closed for the afternoon' sign was propped up outside the main door.

'What is going on, Detective?' she asked anxiously. 'We're trying to host an exhibition for charity and we can't do that with the museum closed.'

'I'm sorry, Mrs Middlebury, but as I'm sure you've been told, our team found the murder weapon in a museum display,' Shepherd said, trying to sound soothing.

The woman sighed and put a hand to her forehead. 'I can't believe this. I can't believe that someone would use an exhibit to stab Professor Randall.' She caught the half smile on Topping's face. 'I know that's what it was originally for,' she snapped, 'but to have it used now is shocking.'

'And you had no idea there was blood on it?' Shepherd asked quickly, trying to cover for Topping's faux pas.

Mrs Middlebury shook her head. 'We don't clean the exhibits on a daily basis so it could have stayed there for months if your team hadn't found it.' She rubbed her hands together as if washing them. 'I just can't believe all of this,' she said again, looking around the room.

'Why don't we find somewhere quiet to chat?' Topping suggested, taking her by the elbow.

She looked at first like she was going to object, but relented. 'Let's go to the staff room. We should have peace and quiet there.'

Topping and Shepherd followed her into a tiny room that held two low wood-framed armchairs, a small dining table with two upright wooden chairs and a small kitchen area, including a kettle and a toaster. A woman seated at the table looked up in surprise.

'Oh, Julie, could you cover the front desk for me?' Mrs Middlebury asked. 'I need to speak to these gentlemen in private.'

Julie nodded and left after putting her mug in the sink. She eyed Topping and Shepherd, clearly desperate to know what was happening.

Once they were all seated, Shepherd began. 'We need to speak to you about the people who had out-of-hours access to the museum,' he said. 'Someone let Professor Randall in.'

He indicated to Topping, who pulled out his phone and brought up the CCTV footage of Randall in the street. 'Here,' he said, holding out the mobile to Mrs Middlebury, 'you can see that he's waiting and then someone comes up to him.'

'You can't see who it is,' Mrs Middlebury said, taking the phone and sliding her glasses down her nose to peer at the screen. 'Don't you have a better shot? There must be other footage.'

Topping shook his head as she handed back the phone. 'Unfortunately, that's the only angle we've got.'

She frowned. 'What about the other cameras?'

'What other cameras?'

'There's another camera outside and one in the lobby. Did you not get that footage?'

Shepherd looked at Topping, who shook his head.

Mrs Middlebury exhaled heavily. 'Gracie was supposed to send all that over to you,' she said. 'That poor girl, her head's been all over the place since she, you know...' She trailed off, gesturing vaguely toward the exhibition room.

'Understandable,' Shepherd said, not feeling like he meant it. Did these people not realise how important their evidence was? he wondered. 'Do you think you'd be able to get that for us?'

Mrs Middlebury nodded. 'I'm not the most technical minded, but I'm sure I can get someone to help. Donald is supposed to be in later, he might—'

'We'd rather you kept it quiet that you're doing it,' Shepherd said, raising a hand to stop her. 'We like to keep things under wraps during an investigation.'

Topping side-eyed him, but Shepherd kept his gaze on Mrs Middlebury.

She smiled and leaned forward to pat his hand. 'Don't worry, I'll call my husband instead.' Then she frowned. 'Why don't you want Donald to know?' she asked. Before Shepherd could reply, he could see the truth dawn on her face. She pointed at the screen, 'that person lets Professor Randall in with a key.'

Shepherd nodded. 'And the burglar alarm didn't go off, which means we have to investigate everyone who has keys to the museum and access to the alarm code,' Shepherd said.

Mrs Middlebury looked shocked. 'That would include me,' she said, eyes wide.

Shepherd smiled. 'We've already checked your alibi,' he said, 'so don't worry, but we'd prefer other people not to know what we're doing just yet.'

'But the door was broken,' Mrs Middlebury said. 'Why do that if they had a key?'

'We believe they broke the door on the way out to make it look like Professor Randall broke in.'

Mrs Middlebury shook her head. 'I can't understand why any-one would do that,' Mrs Middlebury said, her shoulders slump-ing. Then she sat up straight, clearly regaining her stiff upper lip, Shepherd thought. 'Is there anything else you need?' she asked.

'Do you have CCTV inside as well?' Topping asked.

'Oh, for goodness' sake, did she not send that either?' Mrs Middlebury sighed in frustration and clicked her tongue. 'I'll make sure you get everything this time.'

'One other thing,' Shepherd asked as Mrs Middlebury started to stand up, 'we know that someone pretending to be a man called Elias Hannigan emailed Professor Randall and asked to meet here. Can you think of anyone who would do that?'

'Elias Hannigan?' Mrs Middlebury asked.

'Yes. Do you know who he is?'

The woman frowned. 'No, but the name does sound familiar. Related to the Burns family, I suppose?'

'We're not sure. His name has come up in our enquiry.'

'Everything seems to relate to the Burns family at the moment,' said Mrs Middlebury with a shake of the head. 'It's the treasure hunt and the exhibition. And with what's happened to Professor Randall, it seems to have brought out the worst in people.'

'Do you know of anyone who would ask him to come here after hours?' Shepherd asked.

Mrs Middlebury shook her head. 'It's not just whether someone would let him in. I have to ask what could there be in here that he hasn't seen before?'

'Do you know what Professor Randall was looking at?' Shepherd asked.

Mrs Middlebury winced. 'I can't say I looked that closely myself, but Gracie said it was a map of the Old Manor estate. Why he'd be studying that, I don't know.'

'Could we have a look?' Topping asked.

Mrs Middlebury got to her feet and led the way to the exhibition. She walked across to a glass display case in which a map was hanging. 'This is it.'

Standing side by side, Shepherd and Topping peered at it.

'So that's what it would have looked like,' Shepherd said.

Mrs Middlebury smiled. 'It's all in rack and ruin now, of course, but it would have been a very fine and valuable estate in its day. All those gardens and farmland and suchlike. Very grand.'

Topping nodded. 'Take a turn in the shrubbery?' he said, grinning over his shoulder at Mrs Middlebury, who tittered. 'That's what they always do in those period drama things on the telly,' he said, answering a questioning look from Shepherd.

'But why would Randall be looking at this?' Shepherd said to Topping in a low voice. 'He's a subject expert. Surely he'd have seen it before. He wouldn't need to sneak in after hours to look at it.'

Topping nodded. 'My thoughts exactly,' he muttered back.

'So what was he really looking for?' Shepherd asked. 'And why did he need to come when there was no one else around?' Then he turned to Mrs Middlebury, who was watching the muttered exchange. 'Is there anything in here related to the treasure?'

Mrs Middlebury shook her head. 'Nothing really, given that the treasure is only a myth. One of the historical society clues leads to this exhibit here,' she said, leading the way to another display case and pointing out a portrait of a stern-looking man and a pretty young woman with ringlets arranged down each side of her face. 'That's Benjamin Burns and his wife Adelia,' she said. 'Very sad story that she died in childbirth after her fourth child. Simeon was the second child in the family.'

'But he inherited everything, didn't he?' Topping asked.

Mrs Middlebury nodded. 'The money passed straight to him and missed his elder sister out completely. She married a rich man, though, so it wasn't too bad for her.'

They said goodbye to Mrs Middlebury and stepped out into the blinding sunshine outside the museum.

'I hadn't realised how gloomy it was in there,' Topping said, squinting. He sighed. 'A bit of a wasted visit,' he said. 'We didn't learn much.'

'We learned that Gracie Lincoln didn't send us all the CCTV,' Shepherd said.

'That could be a mistake. She was a bit of a mess after finding the body.'

Shepherd nodded. 'I suppose so.' He shoved his hands in his pockets as they headed back to their car. 'It's still a mystery why Randall was in the museum after hours and looking at something he's probably seen in numerous books.'

Topping sighed. 'And now I've got some more footage to watch,' he said gloomily.

'Don't worry, you'll get your reward in heaven. Or in the pub later. I'm buying,' said Shepherd, nudging him with an elbow.

Topping beamed. 'Definitely a suitable reward.'

Chapter Sixty-Nine

Topping and Shepherd hadn't even taken their jackets off in the office before the former's mobile phone rang. Topping took the call and Shepherd heard him say, 'What? Don't worry, that's not your fault. Thanks for letting me know.' He hung up and groaned loudly.

'What?' Shepherd asked, a feeling of foreboding sweeping over him. He took off his suit jacket and hung it on the back of his chair.

'The boss is not going to like this.' Topping indicated for Shepherd to follow him as he headed to Burton's office. He knocked on the frame of the open door, and Burton looked up from the papers she was reading on her desk.

'Come in,' she said, rubbing her eyes. 'You're a very welcome distraction from overtime claims.'

'You might not say that when I tell you what I've just heard,' Topping said, moving across and sitting on the edge of the round table at the side of Burton's office. Shepherd leaned his bulky frame in the doorway.

She sighed. 'Out with it.'

'That was Cath Middlebury from the museum on the phone,'

Topping said.

Shepherd raised his eyebrows. 'We've just left her.'

Topping nodded. 'And she was looking for the rest of the CCTV footage from the night Stewart Randall died.'

'Did we not get it all at the time?' Burton demanded.

Topping shook his head. 'Apparently, Gracie Lincoln, the other curator, had forgotten to send it. Anyway, Mrs Middlebury went to look for it this afternoon and lo-and-behold it's disappeared.'

Shepherd gave a sharp intake of breath. 'What?'

Burton put her head down on the desk. 'Oh, for God's sake, why didn't she send it all when we first asked for it?' she asked, sounding pained.

'Mrs Middlebury asked her and Gracie said that what she sent us was all the footage she could see on the system,' Topping said, almost apologetically.

Shepherd sighed. 'So the person who killed Randall could have deleted it,' he said, 'meaning they also had access to the computers, as well as the keys and the alarm system code.' He thought for a moment. 'Would Donald Bloom have access to the computers? Mrs Middlebury offered to get him to help her.'

Topping sighed. 'I doubt he'd have been able to log in on his own. She probably would have used hers.'

Burton rested her elbows on the desk and cradled her chin. 'I feel like it's one step forward, two steps back yet again.' She rubbed her face with both hands. 'Right, no sense crying over spilt milk, so let's look at what else we have.'

'We need to find out who Jayne Winter interviewed for her research,' Topping said.

Shepherd watched as Burton nodded. 'Yes. Can you go back through her laptop and see what notes she has on there? She's bound to have kept records.'

Topping saluted and headed out of the office. Shepherd watched as he unlocked the cabinet where they stored the laptop and took it back to his desk.

Shepherd looked at Burton, who was staring off into the distance.

'What are you thinking?' he asked.

'Our intrepid journalists have Jayne Winter's notebook, so they may have more insight. Tomorrow, can you track them down and find out what they know? So far, we don't have anything but theories, and I want something concrete. This feels like one big tangle at the moment, and we need to work out which strand to pull to make it make sense.'

Chapter Seventy

Dan and Emma were lucky, and a quick call to Lynda Philby ensured they could head down to the records office on Tuesday lunchtime.

'I've pulled out the letter you were asking about,' Lynda said, resting a hand on top of the box, 'but I also found a couple of other things that I think might be handy for you.'

'About Elias Hannigan?' Emma asked.

Lynda grimaced slightly. 'Not quite, at least not openly. I suspect that's who it refers to, though.'

Dan thanked her, and they moved away to a desk to examine the documents. Although the atmosphere between them had thawed somewhat after Emma's attack, he still felt awkward near her. He sensed she felt the same because she stiffened when their chairs were pulled closer together. But now was not the time to examine those feelings. There was work to do.

'Look at the date,' Emma said, breaking into his thoughts. She was pointing to the letter from Simeon to Nathaniel. 'It's from before Benjamin died, so that suggests they knew about Elias, regardless of whether they'd met him.' She scanned down the letter.

'Ouch.'

'What?' Dan said, looking up.

'Well, look at the wording. Simeon says they have to "prevent this travesty from happening". That doesn't bode well for Elias.' She frowned. 'Although this is only a couple of weeks before Benjamin died.'

Dan turned and looked at her. 'Are you saying that you think Simeon and Nathanial killed Benjamin?'

Emma shrugged. 'I don't know. Maybe I'm creating issues where there are none. I'd love to know what the travesty was, though.'

'Your instincts are usually good,' Dan said. 'I wouldn't discount it.'

They divided up the remaining pile of documents Lynda had given them and started reading. After a silent fifteen minutes, Dan felt his stomach flicker. 'Oh my God,' he said, a little louder than he'd intended to, earning him a loud shush from the woman two desks away.

'What? What have you got?' Emma whispered, leaning forward as he pushed the page towards her.

'Oh my God,' she echoed.

'Exactly,' Dan said in a hushed tone. 'Elias Hannigan is Benjamin Burns' half-brother.'

***

They sat back in their chairs and looked at each other.

'Well, Jayne was right about a connection,' Dan said, still staring at the letter.

'Something of an understatement,' Emma replied. She picked up Dan's tablet, which sat on the table in front of them. She typed in the passcode and then winced.

'What?' Dan asked.

'Sorry, I should have asked before I did that.'

Dan smiled. 'I trust you not to nick anything,' he said.

Emma tapped the screen and opened the camera app, snapping a picture of the letter.

Dan looked down at the page. 'So, in eighteen thirty-nine, Benjamin writes to his solicitor, asking him to look for Elias. The letter says, "I am sorry for how my father treated Elias. I feel like he is owed some of my good fortune".'

Emma frowned. 'Benjamin was going to find his half-brother and do what? Give him half his money?'

Dan took a deep breath. 'We know Benjamin was a good fellow, generous with his cash. It seems perfectly natural that he would want to help someone.'

'But why had he waited so long to look for him? That's what doesn't make sense.'

'He might have only just found out that Elias existed,' Dan said.

'But how? Who would have told him? Clearly his dad kept it a secret. Do you think Benjamin's dad had an affair?'

'It could have been a second marriage?' Dan suggested. 'I think women tended to die younger than men.' He looked at Emma. 'Why are you frowning?'

'I feel like if it was a second marriage, Elias would have been living with his dad, with the family. This suggests that they were estranged.'

'Hence the reason Benjamin needed the lawyer to find him.'

'And the letter suggests Benjamin was going to give his

step-brother what he deserved, presumably financially speaking, and he must have invited Elias to stay; that's how he was in the house.' Emma stared into space for a moment and then said, 'If I were Simeon and Nathanial, I would not be happy to have Uncle Elias appear out of the woodwork.'

Dan nodded. 'Any money given to Elias would mean less inheritance for them.'

Emma leaned her chin on her hand. 'So Simeon and Nathaniel "dealing with" Elias could mean they killed him,' Emma said.

'Or,' Dan said, 'they killed Benjamin before he could make any financial arrangements in favour of Elias. Protecting their own interests. It's an excellent motive.'

Emma nodded. 'And we know from Benjamin's obit that his symptoms were like Simeon's, which we think was arsenic poisoning.'

Dan wrinkled his nose. 'Would people not notice if Simeon died of the same thing as his dad?'

'They all thought it was cholera, remember?' Emma said. 'If someone killed Benjamin, they got away with it, so maybe they thought they could get away with it a second time.'

'And they did,' Dan said, 'until Jayne started sticking her nose in.'

'But that wouldn't matter to Simeon or Nathaniel Burns,' Emma said. 'They're long dead.'

Dan shrugged. 'I know, but I reckon this might be what got Jayne killed.' He tapped a finger on the document. 'She found out about Elias Hannigan and what that would have meant for the Burns' family succession.'

'Is EH being connected to BB enough for someone to murder her?' Emma asked, forehead wrinkling.

Dan could feel his breath catching in his chest. 'We need to know who she spoke to when she found out about this,' he said, tapping on the letter.

'But anyone could have seen this at any time,' Emma said. 'It's in the archive.'

Dan shook his head. 'Even if that's the case, whoever it was covered it up. Jayne was going to tell all in her book, Simeon's murder, maybe even Benjamin's and I bet the existence of Elias Hannigan was part of it.'

'But why? Why does that all matter now?'

'No idea, but it matters enough to someone that they've killed twice and attacked you to protect the secret. We need to find out who, and fast. That's why they were putting Elias' name out there, in the museum book and on the forums. They were trying to lure Jayne out into the open. I bet they were messaging privately on the forum website and arranged to meet her at Old Manor.'

Emma took a deep breath and exhaled. 'Would she really be that stupid?'

'Maybe. She seemed desperate to find out what was happening.'

Emma wound a strand of curly, red hair around her finger. 'But how did Elias Hannigan find out what she was doing?'

Dan gave her a patient look. 'She was posting on the forums about what she was working on. I think she got onto Simeon's murder and it snowballed.'

Emma dug a tissue from her pocket and sneezed. A nearby woman started at the sudden noise and broke the tip of her pencil. She turned to glare at Emma, making Dan snigger.

'Come on,' he said in a low voice. 'Let's get out of here before you get lynched by the ssshhhh brigade.'

He packed his belongings into his bag, and they returned the documents to the counter.

Lynda Philby asked, 'Did you find everything you wanted?'

Dan nodded. 'Although we're now left with more questions.'

She grinned. 'Let me know how you get on.'

Dan turned away, then had a flash of inspiration. 'Do you have a plan for the whole Old Manor site? I seem to remember it being bigger than the one in the museum.'

'I'll have a look around and see what I can find.'

Dan and Emma waved as they headed outside.

'Right,' he said. 'Back to base. I know what we need to do next.'

Chapter Seventy-One

Back at Emma's cottage, they sat side by side at the dining table, Emma on her laptop and Dan working on his tablet. The only sound was the tapping of their fingers.

'Gotcha,' Dan said,

'Ditto,' Emma replied.

'What have you got?' he asked, not sure whether he was more excited about his discovery or what Emma might have found.

'I had to sign up for a free trial on this family research website to get it, but I've found a Hannigan family tree.'

'Excellent,' Dan said, leaning over to look at her screen.

'We've got the usual structure going back years, but here we have Elias' – she pointed to the name – 'and we have his dad, Oliver.'

Dan thought quickly, his stomach flickering more. 'What if Oliver Hannigan became Oliver Burns?' he asked.

Emma stared at him. 'What?'

'OK, so' – Dan got to his feet and started pacing – 'Elias and Benjamin are half-brothers. They share a father, so what if – for whatever reason – Oliver abandoned Elias and his mum, changed his name and then had another family?'

Emma nodded. 'With you so far, although sceptical.'

Dan frowned at her, irritated. 'Look at my tablet.'

Emma bent her head and read the screen. 'Oliver's will.'

'In which he leaves his fortune to "his eldest son".' When Emma looked puzzled, he said, 'Elias was born well before Benjamin. So he's the eldest son.'

Emma stared at him. 'But because no one knew about him, with the name change and everything, they assumed he meant Benjamin.'

Dan started pacing again. 'When Benjamin found out about Elias, he felt he'd been wronged. So he asked his lawyer to find him so he could "share his good fortune".'

'That also gives Simeon and Nathaniel an excellent reason to deal with Elias when he turned up,' Emma said. 'If Benjamin was going to cut their inheritance by making provision for Elias, they wouldn't be happy about that.'

Dan rubbed his nose. 'Do you think they killed Benjamin before he could do anything about it?'

'Either that or they killed Elias, meaning there'd be no reason to change. Hang on.' Emma was peering at her screen.

'Do you need glasses?' Dan asked, grinning.

She glared at him. 'No, this screen is just too small.' He watched as her eyes scanned the page. 'Ah, here we go.' She consulted Dan's screen. 'No, Elias died after Benjamin. So they must have targeted Benjamin before he could change his will.'

Dan sat back at the table and looked at Emma's screen. 'Now we need to find someone who has more information about Oliver Hannigan and why he left his family. His first family.' He gave a sharp intake of breath and pointed to a name at the bottom. 'And I know just who to ask.'

Chapter Seventy-Two

Maisie Barratt looked nervous when she opened the door and found Dan and Emma on the doorstep the following morning.

'You're a Hannigan,' Dan said, before she could speak. He could see from her facial expression that he was right.

Maisie's shoulders sagged. 'You'd better come in,' she said.

'That looks nasty,' Emma said, nodding towards the bruise on Maisie's face. 'Did you have a fall?'

'I was mugged,' Maisie said, leading the way through to the study where she'd taken Dan before. 'You don't look much better.'

'Similar experience,' Emma said, touching her chin wound and wincing.

Meanwhile, Dan had walked straight to the family tree on the wall and pointed to it.

'You distracted me from this last time,' he said. 'You knew I'd realise the connection.'

She nodded. 'Few people know about the Hannigans or their connection to the Burns family. We're not a local family but I assume you know that given you're here.'

Dan knew it was time to be blunt. 'We think Jayne found out

something about the Hannigans and Burns families that a member of the family would want to conceal.'

Maisie looked uncomfortable. 'Why would someone kill over a two hundred-year-old secret?'

'That's an excellent question,' Dan said. 'Only someone who knows about the Hannigans would know that.'

Maisie stepped towards him. 'Are you accusing me of murder?' When Dan stared back at her, she turned to Emma. 'Is he really accusing me?'

Emma looked from Dan to Maisie. 'He is, and with good reason. Jayne came to you, didn't she? She'd found out who your family is and wanted to share what she'd found out. That Elias was Benjamin's half-brother.'

'That your family should have had the inheritance, not Benjamin or Simeon Burns,' Dan added. 'Did it make you angry that she'd found out?'

Maisie sighed. 'You've done better than she did. She first approached me because Donald had told her I was an expert on Simeon Burns and she wanted to know if I knew anything about the murders.'

'What did you tell her?' Dan asked.

'Nothing. I had my suspicions that Simeon's death wasn't natural because he'd allegedly cursed everyone, but I could never prove it. Then Jayne turns up, saying she has proof that he was killed.'

Dan nodded. 'She had a doctor's letter where he talks about Simeon's symptoms. They match arsenic poisoning.'

Maisie nodded. 'She was going to write a true crime tell-all about the murders. I told her I didn't think it would be worth anything. Then she told me she'd found Elias Hannigan on the census and a newspaper article saying he was the killer.'

'She was going to ruin your family name,' Emma said. 'That must have made you angry.'

Maisie shrugged. 'No one knows of my Hannigan connection,' she said, then smiled. 'Apart from you two. How did you find out?'

Emma recounted the story of finding the family tree, and Maisie shook her head.

'I never should have agreed to be part of that,' she said. 'Jayne looked him up and found me the same way. At first I thought she was going to blackmail me or something, about my ancestor being a murderer, but then she called saying she had something that would be of great importance to me.'

Emma fiddled with a piece of paper on the table. 'Did she say what?' she asked.

'No, but then I got some old papers through the post. I couldn't believe my eyes when I opened it.' Maisie crossed the room to the pinboard and removed two pieces of paper fastened with a drawing pin. She placed them on the table.

As they studied them, Maisie said, 'Marriage certificates for Oliver Hannigan and Oliver Burns. I have his birth certificate and the ages match for them to be the same person.'

Dan looked up at her, thinking quickly. 'So Oliver Burns was Elias's father; that means Benjamin was illegitimate.'

Maisie nodded. 'All the Burns' money should have gone to the Hannigans. Jayne said it was an injustice and she was going to use the book to put that right.'

'Did you want her to do that?' Dan asked.

Maisie laughed. 'You think I killed her to stop her publishing?' she asked. 'It wasn't my family who would be ruined by that information.'

Dan stared at the family tree on the wall. He was missing something, he could tell. The pieces just wouldn't fall into place. Then he realised Maisie was speaking.

'And of course there's the fake treasure hunt clue,' she was saying.

Dan stared at her, frowning. 'Fake clue?'

'Yes. The police said someone sent Jayne a fake treasure hunt clue that would have led her to Old Manor, but it didn't come from me,' Maisie said, quickly. 'They don't know where it came from.'

'Elias Hannigan,' Dan said, slowly. 'They met on a forum, and we think they've been corresponding. He must have sent her the clue. Someone using that name must have seemed legitimate.' He could feel his heart racing. 'That's why he signed the guest book at the museum. He knew she would go there. It was a taunt, implying that he'd been there first and found out what she needed. That's why she spent so long there, trying to work it out.'

'She went straight to Old Manor after she'd been in the museum,' Emma said. 'We know that from Tobias Tudham.'

Dan nodded. Maisie looked bewildered as she tried to follow the conversation.

Dan jumped to his feet. 'We need that clue. Do you have it?' he asked Maisie.

She shook her head. 'The police have it. Apparently, it was emailed to her.'

Dan looked at Emma. 'Reckon we can persuade Burton to let us have a look?'

Emma grinned. 'If we use a quid pro quo, I bet we can give it a try.'

Chapter Seventy-Three

After a quick phone call on Wednesday morning, Shepherd was pleased to find Dan and Emma waiting for him in the reception area when he came back from lunch.

'I'm surprised you could get away so easily,' he said, directing them to a small meeting room. He'd been a little suspicious about why they were both so quick to agree to come in.

'We have a slight ulterior motive,' Emma said, 'in that we'd like a small favour in return.'

Shepherd shrugged. 'Let's see what you give me first,' he said, grinning at Emma.

She nodded. 'No worries. What do you need to know?'

Shepherd flipped open his notebook. 'Donald Bloom told us you think Benjamin Burns was murdered as well as his son,' he said.

Dan and Emma nodded.

'They had the same arsenic poisoning symptoms,' Dan began. 'Actually, we were just talking to—' He halted with a wince, and glared at Emma.

Shepherd looked at her and she smiled back sweetly. He had a feeling there had been a sly kick under the table.

'Why do you need to know about that?' she asked.

'Did you tell Donald anything else?' Shepherd asked, feeling irritated.

Emma glanced at Dan.

'We asked him about Elias Hannigan,' Dan said. 'He said he didn't know the name, but I got the feeling he wasn't being entirely truthful about that.'

Shepherd made a note in his book. 'We thought the same about Maisie Barratt.' He glanced up from his notebook in time to see a look that he did not like pass between Dan and Emma. He took a deep breath. *Talk about a pair of slippery fish*, he thought.

'OK, out with it,' he said. 'If you know something and you withhold it, then I can charge you with—'

'All right, all right,' Emma said, holding up her hands in surrender. 'Jayne had been talking to Maisie about Elias Hannigan.' She looked at Dan and then back at Shepherd. 'Maisie is a descendant, and Jayne found out that he was accused of killing Benjamin Burns.'

Shepherd frowned. 'Did Jayne come across this while investigating the murder, or was that her starting point?'

'We think she found out about the murders first,' Dan said, 'and then found a news report about Elias being accused.'

Shepherd sat back in his chair. Maisie Barratt was now squarely back in the frame. 'Does she know who the present-day Elias is?' he asked. 'Did you get the impression it's her?'

'For what it's worth,' Dan said, 'I don't think it is. She did tell us something interesting, though. Jayne had found out that Oliver Burns, Benjamin's dad, was a bigamist, which means the whole Burns' line is illegitimate.' He grinned. 'I can imagine Burns' descendants wouldn't want that coming out.'

Shepherd tapped his pen rapidly against his notebook. 'Do you know if Jayne spoke to any descendants as part of her research?' he asked.

Dan shook his head. 'I wouldn't know who they were anyway.'

'We're trying to compile a list of people who Jayne Winter interviewed in her research,' Shepherd said. 'We need to find out who she spoke to.'

Emma looked at Dan and frowned. 'But you've got Jayne's computer. Isn't it all on there?'

Shepherd wrinkled his nose. 'We've got some people, but I want to make sure we're not missing anyone. Is there anyone she mentions in the notebook?'

He waited as Dan and Emma looked at each other, as if they were trying to concoct a story without actually speaking aloud. When the time stretched on, he tapped his pen on the desk. 'Come on, out with it.'

Then Emma said, 'You could try Lynda Philby at the county records office. I don't know if Jayne interviewed her as such, but she knows about what Jayne was looking at.'

'Maisie Barratt,' Dan said. 'Jayne's spoken to her.'

'We have Maisie already,' Shepherd said. 'Anyone else you can think of?'

Dan shook his head. 'Nothing that we've seen in her notebook. Do you think someone she interviewed killed her? Did she speak to Tobias Tudham, do you know?'

Shepherd shook his head. 'There's no sign that they interacted offline, but you stay away from him,' he added, not liking the light that had sprung into Dan's eyes.

'No worries,' Dan said, holding up his hands in surrender.

Shepherd sighed. 'So, what did you want from me?'

'Maisie also told us that someone sent Jayne a false treasure hunt clue that might have led her to Old Manor.'

Shepherd tried not to roll his eyes. These two were far too good at getting people to talk to them.

'And if they did?'

'Do you know who it was from? Was there an email address?'

Shepherd eyed Emma. 'No, it looked like it came from the historical society, but it was fake. I'm surprised Jayne didn't notice.'

'Probably too blinded by wanting to get on with it,' Dan said.

Emma was staring into space. Then she said, 'Have there been any messages from any other dead people – Simeon Burns or his brother Nathaniel, for instance?'

Shepherd sat back in surprise. 'What do you mean?'

'Well, Elias has come back, but actually it's Simeon and Nathaniel who have the most to lose if their illegitimacy becomes widely known. It's their descendants' reputation that would be ruined.'

Dan leaned forward with his elbows on the table. 'But Jayne wouldn't have gone to meet them. If another Burns' family member popped up, it would have put her on her guard. It was Elias specifically that got her attention.'

Shepherd was looking from one to the other. Was he in a parallel universe where dead people came to life and learned how to use email?

'You think it's a Burns' descendant who killed Jayne and Stewart Randall?' he asked.

Emma shrugged. 'It's as good a theory as any, but I've no idea if any still exist.'

'Well, it's best that you don't go looking,' Shepherd said. He clicked his pen away and stood up. Dan and Emma got to their feet too. As he showed them out, Shepherd said, 'Thanks for coming in. Keep all of this to yourselves. Clearly Jayne tipped someone off about what she was researching, and they killed her to stop her revealing what she'd found out. Please be careful who you interview.'

Chapter Seventy-Four

When Shepherd returned to the office, he updated Burton on the interview with Dan and Emma.

Burton stared at him. 'They think there are more dead people wandering around town?'

Shepherd nodded, not liking the fact he sounded crazy in his own head. 'Although it did sound like Emma had *just* come up with the idea.'

'Hmmm, sending us on a wild goose chase?' Burton asked, tilting her head on one side.

Shepherd thought for a moment. 'No, more like a flash of inspiration while we were talking.'

'And they think the Burns boys might be involved?'

Shepherd laughed. 'I think Elias Hannigan is more where they're focused. I'm going to go back through Jayne Winter's emails again,' he said. When Burton raised her eyebrows, he added, 'Jayne is a research expert. She might have found out who this Elias Hannigan is. The modern-day version, I mean.'

'And if she did?'

'He might have messaged her as well as Randall. There might be some clues there.'

'Good plan,' Burton said, and he sensed she was mentally crossing her fingers for a solid lead.

He crossed the room to the evidence cupboard and took out Jayne's computer and mobile phone, returning to his desk with them.

Tapping at the keyboard, his eyes scanned down the screen, chin resting on his hand. Then he stopped and reached for his phone.

'Tech team,' a cheery voice said.

'Is that Aiden?'

'Speaking.'

Shepherd identified himself and, after a couple of minutes of football chat, he got Aiden onto the subject he wanted. It required Aiden to access Jayne's computer remotely and dig for five minutes before Shepherd let out a long breath and grinned.

'Hmmm, she's done a good job hiding that,' Aiden said. 'I'm actually quite impressed.'

Shepherd thanked Aiden and rang off. He grabbed Jayne's phone and accessed her messaging app. Then he grinned, grabbed the phone and laptop and headed back to Burton's office.

She was already looking at him before he entered.

'That looked like a useful conversation,' she said, pushing her keyboard to one side to allow him to put the laptop in front of her.

Shepherd could feel excitement bubbling in his stomach. 'Tech missed it last time because she's done a pretty thorough job of deleting it, but look at this.'

EliasHannigan: *I know what you're looking for.*

JayWin91: *Who are you?*

EliasHannigan: *You know.*

JayWin91: *The real Elias Hannigan is dead.*

EliasHannigan: *I know what you're looking for.*

JayWin91: *You don't. I'm not after treasure like those idiots.*

EliasHannigan: *You're looking for my treasure, aren't you? You know what should have been mine.*

JayWin91: *What if I do?*

EliasHannigan: *You need proof and I want to help you get it.*

JayWin91: *You don't know where it is. You can't. But I know where to look.*

EliasHannigan: *Sadly you don't and I'm going to get there first. But I may be prepared to share – if the price is right. You know what I mean.*

'Is that all?' Burton asked.

Shepherd shook his head. 'Nope, at this point they took it off the public forum and into a private chat.'

EliasHannigan: *I knew you couldn't resist.*

JayWin91: *OK, let's hear it then. What do you know?*

EliasHannigan: *What's in it for me if I tell you?*

JayWin91: *A twenty-five per cent cut when we find it.*

EliasHannigan: *Oh, I think you can do better than that, given it was mine to start with. When you know what I know, you'll give me everything.*

'So what's his treasure?' Burton asked, looking totally baffled.

'I think the Burns family owed Elias Hannigan something and that's what this person is talking about,' Shepherd said, pointing to the screen.

'But what?'

Shepherd shrugged. 'Gold, jewels ... who knows? But what's important is that Jayne's taken the bait that this person can help her find it.'

Burton tapped her fingers rapidly on the desk. 'So she was after treasure, just not the one we thought it was?'

Shepherd pulled Jayne's mobile phone from his pocket as if doing a magic trick. 'From there, they went onto WhatsApp,' he said, handing her the phone.

Burton read the screen and gave a low whistle. 'So, Jayne demands more information, and Elias Hannigan says, "If you're smart enough to solve the last clue to the treasure hunt, then you'll know where to go. You just have to be master of your head over your heart."' Burton rolled her eyes. 'Head ... master? Not the hardest code to crack,' she said.

'Maybe that's because we already know where she went,' Shepherd said. 'Either way, it means Elias Hannigan knew she'd been sent the fake clue.'

'He knew where she was going to go, but not when,' Burton said.

'The message dates back to the day before Jayne died,' Shepherd said, 'so he must have known she'd want to get after it quickly and suspected she was going to double-cross him and keep it for herself.'

'We presumably can't trace his phone because the messages are encrypted, so get onto the historical society and their website hosting. See if there's any way we can trace his IP address. Well done, Mark. Finally, there's a chink of daylight.'

Chapter Seventy-Five

Dan and Emma were sitting on the sofa at his and Ed's flat, staring at the TV, which wasn't switched on.

'So, whoever is pretending to be Elias Hannigan knows Jayne,' Dan said.

He could feel Emma look sideways at him and then she bounced on the cushion to turn her body towards him. 'What do you mean?'

Dan turned so he was facing her. 'He knows her, I'm sure of it.'

'Why do you say that?' Emma asked. She was looking at him like he was crazy.

Dan felt like he was just putting the thoughts together as he was speaking. 'Someone sent her a fake clue for the treasure hunt, and she went running off to Old Manor. It's someone who knows her and knew exactly what she would do with the information.'

Emma's head tilted to one side as she stared at him. 'You think Elias was deliberately going after Jayne in the forum?'

Dan nodded. 'I think they were waiting for her to pop up, and then they've said just enough to get her interested. Remember the chat that Ed found? I bet Jayne contacted Elias as soon as they left that chat.'

Emma perched on the armchair. 'So, like Shepherd said, it must be someone she's spoken to while she was researching Simeon Burns.'

'Exactly. And unfortunately, there's quite a list.'

'It can't be Maisie Hannigan,' Emma said. 'She's been too helpful to us.'

'That could be a front,' Dan said, sitting forward and resting his elbows on his knees. 'It could be Donald Bloom.'

'Not Lynda Philby,' Emma said with a grin.

'If it was Lynda, she'd have made sure we didn't find what Jayne was looking at,' Dan said, laughing. Then he frowned.

'I was kidding,' Emma said. She peered at Dan. 'You're actually considering it now, aren't you?'

Dan shrugged. 'Not necessarily Lynda Philby, although that would be an ace twist.'

Emma opened her mouth to speak, but Dan's mobile interrupted. He answered and switched it onto the speakerphone.

'Hi, Dan, it's Lynda Philby.'

Emma clamped a hand over her mouth and Dan's eyes widened.

'Is the flat bugged?' he mouthed, hoping that he wouldn't set Emma off laughing.

'Hi, Lynda. How are you?' he asked into the phone.

'I'm well, thank you. The reason I'm calling is that I have what you're looking for. I found a blueprint for the Old Manor Hall building.'

Dan felt his heart sink. 'But that's what they already have in the museum. Apparently, that's what Professor Randall was looking at when he was attacked.'

'But that's not the whole site,' Lynda said.

Dan's stomach flickered. 'What do you mean?'

'I've seen that map, and this one is bigger.'

Dan looked at Emma and suspected she looked as shocked as he felt. 'What?' he asked, his voice coming out almost hoarse.

'This is bigger. Like I said, it covers the whole site, the gardens and everything.'

Dan stared into space for a moment.

'Hello? Are you still there?' Lynda asked, sounding confused.

'Yes, sorry. Do you think you can send me a copy?' Dan asked.

'Sure, I'll scan it and email it to you tomorrow morning. Is that OK?'

Dan gave her his email address, said thank you, and hung up.

Emma stared at him. 'Well, that was freaky,' she said. 'Talk about speak of the devil.'

Dan's chest felt tight, as if he'd been running in cold air. Hopefully, the blueprint would help him to connect the dots.

'What's so important about an Old Manor site map?' Emma asked.

Dan grinned. 'If I'm right, I think it will answer some questions to help us find the treasure.'

Chapter Seventy-Six

Dan was in the post-lunch slump the following day when he got a call from the newspaper's reception desk.

'There's a Maisie Barratt here to see you,' the receptionist said.

Dan grabbed his notebook and pen and strode along the office towards the main doors.

When Dan greeted Maisie and led her to the small interview room in the reception area, he could almost sense the receptionist's disappointment at missing out on whatever was happening.

'How are you?' Dan asked, pointing at Maisie's arm.

She sighed. 'A bit fed up. It's still painful but more frustrating that I can't do more for myself. I had to get my husband to bring me into town rather than driving myself.'

'How can I help you? Have you thought of something else?'

Balancing her handbag on her lap, Maisie dug her free hand inside. 'After you left the other day, I had a flash of inspiration. Donald has been on at me for years to collaborate on a social history of Allensbury.'

Dan nodded. 'He mentioned to me he wanted to write one.'

Maisie rolled her eyes. 'I suspect the collaboration will be a very broad term. I'll do all the work and he'll add his name at the end. He's easily distracted by new ideas.'

Dan laughed. 'And there was me thinking he was the steady, dependable type.' He reached over and steadied the handbag when it almost fell to the floor.

She grimaced and said, 'Thanks. You see what I mean about frustrating?' She pulled out a small, stapled A5-sized booklet, crudely put together from folded sheets of A4 and a thick card cover. Maisie smiled down at it. 'I have no idea where this came from, probably via Donald, but I found it in my study after you left yesterday.'

Dan took the booklet and noted the slightly childlike handwriting and design on the front. He flicked through it and then looked up at Maisie, eyebrows raised. 'It looks like someone has given you a good starting point on the treasure of the Burns' family,' he said.

Maisie nodded, putting her handbag onto the floor. 'Whoever made it hasn't added their name, but there *is* a date.' She glanced at her watch. 'I'd better get home. I need to dust off my party frock.'

Dan grinned. 'It's the benefit event tonight, isn't it?'

Maisie got to her feet and puffed out her cheeks. 'Yes, and all the treasure hunt nonsense will be out of the way by tomorrow morning.' She sighed. 'I'll be glad when it's all over. I wish we'd never started it.'

'Why do you say that?'

'Well, this isn't the first time searching for the treasure has led to a death.'

Dan stared at her, stomach flickering. 'What do you mean?'

'I'd forgotten until a couple of days ago. There was a girl years ago, well, a teenager. She came to Donald, convinced she'd found out where the treasure was. He humoured her and told her to come back and tell him when she found it.'

'When did that happen?' Dan asked, scribbling details in his notebook.

Maisie pursed her lips. 'About twenty years ago. Actually, that might be her pamphlet. I seem to remember she wrote something. It's ironic that Jayne Winter died at Old Manor because that's where the young girl died, too.'

***

After getting Dan's text message, Emma left the house, rattling the door three times as usual, and set off on the short walk to the office. When she arrived, the receptionist looked up with her ready-for-the-customer smile. She saw Emma, and her smile lessened a bit.

'Hey, mate,' she said, glancing at her watch. 'You're a bit late, aren't you?'

Emma grinned. 'On a lieu day,' she said.

'Why are you here on your day off?' the receptionist asked, looking at her as if she was mad.

'Dan texted me. Something about the archive? It was so badly spelled, I almost couldn't work out what he was on about.'

'Oh, it may have something to do with a woman who came in to see him earlier. Maisie someone? Anyway, after she left, he went belting off upstairs.'

Almost forgetting to say goodbye to the receptionist, Emma took the stairs to the top floor of the building at a run. When she arrived, gasping, at the door of the archive, she pushed it open, breathing in the scent of old dried paper. She sighed. One of her favourite smells.

Bookcases lined the room, each stuffed with box files labelled with dates and subjects. The oldest computer in the world stood on a table in the middle of the room, with Dan sitting at it.

'What's going on?' Emma asked, taking off her coat and hanging it on the back of his chair.

'Maisie Barratt came in.'

'The receptionist told me. What did she say?'

'Someone else died trying to find the treasure. A girl at Old Manor. She couldn't remember anything else, but I'm hoping to find it in here.'

'What?' Emma demanded. 'Someone else died and the police didn't tell us?'

Dan shook his head. 'This was twenty-odd years ago.' He stopped tapping at the keyboard. 'I can't believe I don't remember it, although I think I was away at uni then, so probably had other things on my mind.'

'What have you tried in search terms?' Emma asked.

Dan held out the piece of paper where he'd written all the combinations he'd tried. 'If you can think of anything else, that would be marvellous.'

Emma scanned down the list and groaned as she handed it back.

'You've done everything that I would have done,' she said, running a hand through her long curls.

'Where do we go from here?' Dan asked, getting to his feet and stretching.

Emma walked around the room, running a finger along the files on the shelves. 'I've got no idea,' she said. Then Dan's phone beeped and he pulled it out of his pocket.

'Aha, it's Mum,' he said.

'You asked your mum?' Emma said.

'Mum was still here after I went to uni. I thought she might know.' He read the text message and then gasped.

'What? What does she say?' Emma demanded.

'She's given me the name of the girl who died, and you'll never believe who it is.'

***

The receptionist looked up as Dan and Emma dashed past her desk.

'Where are you going?' she called, but they didn't stop to answer.

Dan almost collided with the door on his way out, eyes on his phone as he dialled. 'Damn it, he's not answering,' he said.

'Who are you calling?' Emma asked, panting along behind him.

'Donald Bloom. We need to find him immediately.' Then he slapped a hand to his forehead. 'It's the benefit event tonight, so he's bound to be at the museum already. Right, hurry up. We need to get there now.' He dialled again. When Ed answered in a low voice, Dan asked, 'Mate, where are you?'

'I'm in court. Well, in the court building. Why?'

'You need to get to the museum and find Donald Bloom. Emma and I are on our way, but you're closer.'

He could hear a rustling, and realised Ed was putting on his coat.

'I'm on my way,' Ed said. 'What's going on?'

'I know who the killer is and they're about to strike again.'

Chapter Seventy-Seven

Burton smiled when she heard Suzy's cheery voice on the other end of the phone.

'You sound like you have something for me,' she said.

'Oh I do, and you're going to love it.'

Burton waited for the press officer to continue, but there was silence on the line. 'Well, out with it.'

Suzy laughed. 'That was a dramatic pause.'

'You know I hate those, right?'

'OK, here goes,' Suzy said, recognising Burton's impatience. 'I have a witness to Maisie Barratt's mugging.'

Burton sat up straight in her chair. 'Really? What did they say?'

'It was weird because it's the guy who helped her and called the ambulance.'

'Did he not speak to anyone at the scene?'

'He helped her and then went off about his business. It was only when he saw the appeal in the paper that he realised he should have given a statement.'

Burton sighed. 'Usually people who watch TV crime dramas drive me mad, but just this once I wish he was a fan and knew the procedure. What did he say?'

'Well, he said he'd already seen Maisie Barratt twice that afternoon. In fact, he said he thought she was following him because she kept popping up everywhere.'

'How does he know her?'

'He doesn't know her, per se, but he's seen her a few times at museum events or something like that.'

'Did he see the mugger following Maisie?' Burton demanded, wishing Suzy would get on with it.

'He did, and he said he noticed because she had her hood up when they were inside the bookshop on the high street. We thought she's stayed outside, but she actually went inside, lurking by the local history section and watching Maisie while she was paying for what she'd picked up.'

'She? It was a woman.'

'And you'll never believe who it is.'

***

Dan flung open the door to the museum with Emma in hot pursuit. An older woman standing behind the reception desk jumped as they entered.

'Hello, can I help? The museum is closed to prepare for the formal event,' she said.

'Is Donald Bloom here? We need to speak to him,' Emma gasped.

'He's just in the auditorium with—'

Dan and Emma ignored her and sprinted through the exhibition space toward the auditorium. They could hear voices. One male, one female. They burst through the door and were halfway down the aisle before they took in the scene on the stage.

Donald Bloom stood centre stage, hands raised. Facing him, holding a very long blade, stood Gracie Lincoln.

Chapter Seventy-Eight

Burton drove out of the police station car park far too fast, throwing Shepherd against the passenger door.

'Woah, careful,' he said, almost dropping his phone.

'Sorry.' She glanced at him as he tapped at the phone screen. 'What are you doing?'

'Just searching for Gracie Lincoln to see what comes up.'

Burton took the next roundabout at speed, almost cutting up another car. Shepherd glared at her.

'Remember that old speeding campaign "Arrive alive"?' he asked.

'Sorry,' said Burton, slowing down. She kept her eyes on the road, but watched Shepherd in her peripheral vision. He was staring at the screen and scrolling a page. Then he stiffened in his seat.

'Did we check Gracie's alibi for the night of Jayne Winter and Stewart Randall's deaths?' he asked.

Burton nodded. 'Gaz got them, well, for Stewart Randall. She doesn't have a connection to Jayne Winter.'

'She does,' Shepherd said, frowning. 'They were in the same year at Old Manor, remember. So why didn't we ask for an alibi?'

Burton frowned. Adrenaline was coursing through her. 'At the time, we didn't need to. Why?'

'Look what she's put on Facebook today: "It's twenty years since my sister died because others lied to her. It ends here."'

'What does that mean?'

'Reading the comments on the post, apart from the usual "U OK hun?" stuff, there's one saying, "I know you're hurting, babes, but Claire would want you to get on with life and be happy." Gracie has replied saying, "He made her write that stupid booklet, made her do the research and he's got to pay for what happened. He's going to regret the stupid treasure hunt."'

Burton froze. 'Shit, she means Donald Bloom, doesn't she?'

Shepherd was already dialling a number and speaking briefly into the phone. When he hung up, he grabbed the handle above the passenger's door. 'Step on it. She's there and in a private meeting with Donald Bloom.'

Burton didn't need telling twice.

Chapter Seventy-Nine

Dan and Emma froze halfway down the aisle, unsure what to do next.

'Gracie, love, what are you doing?' Donald was asking.

'Don't love me,' Gracie snapped. 'You killed my sister!'

Donald's jaw dropped. 'What? I don't even know your sister.'

'See, you don't even remember her. You killed her, and you don't even have the courtesy to remember her name,' Gracie snarled.

'Claire, Claire Lincoln,' Dan called, advancing down the aisle, having avoided Emma's restraining hand. He just needed to keep Gracie distracted until Ed could call the police. He would have done that by now, surely.

Gracie and Donald both turned sharply.

'Who's that?' Gracie demanded, momentarily blinded by the footlights. When Dan came closer, she recognised him. 'What are you doing here?'

'Saving you from making a huge mistake,' Dan said, inching closer. 'You don't want to do this.'

'Oh, but I do. He caused Claire's death and now he's going to pay for it.' She took a step forward, and Donald backed a few steps away.

'No, Gracie, stop. He didn't cause Claire's death. It wasn't him who sent her up to the attic.' Dan was now climbing the stairs onto the stage, and he could sense that Emma had started following him.

Gracie turned to face him. 'How do you know that?'

'Donald doesn't believe in the treasure. He wouldn't have sent Claire anywhere other than Allensbury library, isn't that right, Donald?'

The society chair read Dan's expression and nodded rapidly. 'I had no—'

But Gracie raised a hand to silence him. 'Go on,' she said to Dan, who was inching across the stage.

'It was Jayne who suggested Claire try the attic at school, wasn't it? She'd been looking for the treasure herself and wanted to throw Claire off the trail.'

Gracie nodded, her mouth pulling down at the corners.

'When did you find out?' Dan asked, side-eyeing Donald Bloom to move further away, but Gracie turned on him with the blade. 'Don't move,' she snapped. Then she turned back to Dan. 'She admitted it when she was here last year. She laughed about how she'd tricked Claire into going to the attic when it wasn't safe.' A tear ran down her cheek. 'She was laughing about my sister's death.'

'What about Stewart Randall? He didn't have anything to do with Claire,' Dan said. He could feel Emma edging up behind him and glanced over his shoulder.

Gracie was now facing Dan and Emma. 'Oh, I see you've brought your little girlfriend with you? Where's Ed? You guys seem to be joined at the hip.'

'He doesn't know we're here,' Dan said, hoping that Ed was

actually in the corridor ringing the police. They were going to need reinforcements very soon.

Gracie sighed. 'That's a shame. I was hoping he'd be here.'

'You got Jayne's attention by pretending to be Elias Hannigan, didn't you?' Dan asked.

'You asked me about him before. Who is he?' Donald Bloom demanded.

'Benjamin Burns' half-brother,' Dan replied, eyes still fixed on Gracie. He heard Donald gasp. 'You found that out, didn't you, Gracie? And you know Jayne would know, too.'

'You faked that treasure-hunt clue to get Jayne to go to Old Manor,' Emma put in.

'Quite inspired, don't you think? I knew she wouldn't be able to resist that one. I signed the guest book once I knew she was back in town, knowing she'd come to the museum to see what was in the exhibition.' Gracie gave a disdainful laugh. 'If you'd seen her face when she spotted that. Then Elias Hannigan found her online, helped her to solve the clue, and off she rushed to Old Manor. Such an easy mark.'

Ed appeared in the wings of the stage behind Gracie, but Dan kept his eyes fixed on her. He reached behind him and indicated to Emma not to react to the sight of Ed. He felt her hand squeeze his and keep hold of it.

'But she wasn't really looking for the treasure, was she? You thought she was, but she was trying to prove that Elias Hannigan should have got the Burns' inheritance.'

'What?' Donald Bloom demanded, but Dan's glare silenced him.

Gracie snorted. 'Like that even matters. She killed my sister, and she had to pay.'

'What about Stewart Randall?' Dan repeated. 'Why did you kill him?'

'He was stupid, following Jayne when she went to Old Manor. He saw me kill her and tried to blackmail me for more information about the treasure.'

'But rather than give him the information yourself, you sent him emails as Elias Hannigan. I bet he was surprised when you turned up to let him in.'

Gracie nodded. 'He was such an idiot to not realise that dead people don't send emails. I stabbed him with one of these.' She waved the blade and turned to Donald. 'You probably recognise it from the permanent collection. We have several of them. It's Roman, but it's still very sharp.'

Ed was edging through the wings and was almost on the stage just behind Gracie. He froze as a floorboard creaked slightly. But Gracie was focused on Dan and didn't seem to hear the sound.

'So all this time Jayne's research and the treasure hunt had nothing to do with it,' Dan said, 'except giving you the opportunity to kill Jayne. You finally got one over her after all these years.'

Gracie's grip slackened on the knife as she took in Dan's words. Seeing her distracted, Ed leapt forward, knocking her to the floor. The blade flew away across the stage as he grappled with her. Dan bounded across the stage and helped him to pin her down. Donald Bloom staggered away and fell to the ground with a resounding thud.

'We need something to tie her hands,' Ed panted, pinning Gracie's arms behind her back as she fought against him.

Emma dragged the elastic hair bobble from her ponytail and wound it around Gracie's hands.

'Stop struggling and it won't hurt so much,' she said.

Suddenly the doors at the back of the theatre flew open and Burton and Shepherd came running down the aisle, followed by five or six uniformed officers. They saw the scene on the stage and rushed up the steps. Shepherd pulled out a pair of handcuffs and secured Gracie's hands. Sensing a professional, she went limp, and he could pull her to her feet.

'Makeshift zip ties?' he asked Emma with a grin, pointing to the hair bobble.

'I didn't know what else to use,' she said, 'but you should get them off now because they do cut off the circulation.' Shepherd dug a hand into his pocket and pulled out a Swiss Army knife. In seconds, the hair bobble was in two pieces.

'Sorry,' he said to Emma as the destroyed hair bobble fell to the floor.

'Don't worry,' she said with a grin. 'There's plenty more where that came from.'

***

Emma turned to help a trembling Donald Bloom to his feet and down the steps. He collapsed into a front-row seat and put his face in his hands. Dan and Ed got up too, brushing stage dirt from their trousers.

'Oh damn, I've torn them,' Ed said, looking down at his knee. 'I'll never be able to repair them.'

'You'll just have to buy one of those woven patches from the museum shop,' Dan said. 'Maybe they have one of Simeon Burns.' They both laughed.

Emma was looking at Donald. 'Are you OK?' she asked.

He was shaking his head. 'I don't know what just happened,' he said. 'Why would she think I'd killed her sister?'

'You didn't,' Dan said, sitting down beside him. 'Her sister, Claire, was into history and started researching Simeon Burns after doing the essay the school sets every year. She asked you for some advice and you told her to write it all down. Maisie still has the pamphlet she wrote.'

Donald put a hand to his chest. 'Oh, good Lord. So it *is* my fault. I remember now, she wanted to write a history of the Burns family. We don't have one in our archives, so I said that would be a great idea.'

'She was only fifteen,' said Dan. 'Why would you want something in the archive from a child?'

Donald sighed. 'I suppose I thought it would encourage her in her love of history. It would be a good starting point for the society to create something.' He looked down at the floor and his shoulders slumped.

'Jayne Winter told her there was a secret room in the attic at school and that the treasure was in there, so Claire went looking and tried to move a bookcase.' Dan paused. 'It fell and crushed her.'

'She died looking for the treasure?' Donald asked, shaking his head. 'I remember saying to her it wasn't real, only a myth, but she couldn't be deterred so I let her go with it. I should have done more to persuade her to stop.'

Burton and Shepherd appeared beside them at that point.

'Mr Bloom, are you OK?' Burton asked.

Donald shook his head. 'I'm not sure I'll ever be OK ever again. I caused a child's death.'

'No, Mr Bloom, you didn't. Jayne Winter gave Claire the information that sent her up to the attic,' Shepherd said.

'But why did Gracie do this now?' asked Donald.

'I can answer that,' Emma said. 'The treasure hunt started it, and it's the anniversary of Claire's death today, according to the newspaper archives. I think it added insult to injury and set her off.'

Ed sighed and leaned back against the stage, crossing his arms. 'I can't believe this has all happened because of a treasure that doesn't exist.'

Dan grinned. 'Oh, I wouldn't say that.'

Ed stared at him. 'What do you mean? You know what it is?'

'Not exactly,' Dan said, grinning smugly, 'but I think I know where to find it.'

Chapter Eighty

A crowd of six gathered around the dining table in Dan and Ed's flat. Burton, Shepherd and Topping had arrived for Dan's denouement.

'My nan is gutted that you've found it before she did,' Topping said, grinning as he looked down at the map.

'OK, detective,' Burton said to Dan, hands on her hips. 'Let's have it.'

Dan grinned, enjoying himself. He pointed to an image on his tablet, which was propped up on the table. 'So, this is the map that's in the museum. That's what Randall was looking at when he was killed because Elias Hannigan, or should I say Gracie had told him it shows where the treasure is.'

Ed and Emma, both standing, arms folded, said, 'And?' in unison, making everyone laugh.

'And this one,' Dan said, pointing to the A3 printout on the table, 'is the version that Lynda found in the records office. If you look closely, you'll find the second one is much bigger.'

Topping sighed heavily. 'Yes, we can see that, but what does it mean?'

'You can see more of the site for a start,' Dan said. 'You can see all the grounds, gardens etc.'

'I don't see why that's important,' Burton snapped, clearly impatient to get on.

'Well, I looked at the clue that Gracie sent to Jayne. Once I worked it out, it directs you to look for a secret room at Old Manor.'

'A secret room?' Ed asked.

Burton sighed. 'The one in the headteacher's study,' she said, 'where we found Jayne's body.'

But Dan raised a finger. 'That's what Jayne thought, and what I thought initially. We all suspected back in the day that there was something behind that wall, but we never found out.' He paused and cleared his throat. 'So, it wasn't that room—'

'Did Stewart Randall know about it?' Burton asked. 'We found his fingerprints at Old Manor.'

'I thought that as well,' Dan said, 'but what confused me was that he didn't have Jayne's clue. But Gracie told us he had followed Jayne to Old Manor. I think Gracie got him to the museum after hours by saying she had more evidence about the secret room at the house.'

'Which was why he was looking at the map?' Burton asked.

Dan nodded. 'Exactly, but the secret room that Jayne and Claire found out about isn't on that map. It's not even in the house.' He looked up to see a row of puzzled faces and grinned smugly.

'So where is it?' Ed asked.

Dan pointed to the map on the table.

'I don't follow,' Ed said.

'Look here.' Dan pointed to a mark on the plan of the grounds of the Old Manor site.

The others all crowded forward to look.

'What is that?' Topping asked.

'It's the secret room,' Dan said, grinning. 'I asked the head of archaeology at Allensbury Uni, and she said that it could be an ice house.'

'An ice house?' Emma said.

'Yup. Obviously they bricked it up or something to stop naughty school kids from finding it and doing themselves an injury by exploring. You know we'd have been there having a look, don't you?' he said to Ed, who laughed.

'Very true. What happens now?'

Dan grinned. 'The head of archaeology said they're going to do a survey of the site and then decide whether they can dig there. Who knows, we might find the treasure after all.'

***

Later in the evening, Dan and Emma sat on a bench in Castle Park by the boating lake, having felt the need to speak privately.

'What are you thinking?' Emma asked, wishing they'd thought of somewhere warmer. But neutral territory felt like the right thing to do.

'About what?'

Emma groaned. 'Oh, for God's sake, Dan. About us moving in together. That's the only mystery we need to solve now.'

Dan took a deep breath. 'I'd still prefer if we had our house, rather than me moving into yours. So—'

'Are you saying you want us to break up?' Emma interrupted, feeling a lump building in her throat.

'Of course not. I've really missed you.' Dan took her hand and kissed it. 'But if you let me finish my sentence.'

'Sorry,' Emma mumbled, wincing as a chilly breeze threatened to defeat her woolly scarf.

'How about we have a trial period? Say I move in for six months and we see how we feel after that?'

'What about Ed?'

'I'm not bringing him.'

Emma laughed. 'I'm so glad to hear that. No, I mean what about your flat?'

'Well, I'll keep paying rent on this flat to keep Ed from going bankrupt, and then if in six months we've not killed each other, he can start looking for a new flatmate. I reckon this new girlfriend will be in by then.'

Emma stared at him. 'Really? They've only been together a couple of months. He never suggested moving in with Lydia.'

Dan nodded. 'He's really smug and happy with this one, not how he was with Lydia. I can't put my finger on it exactly, but she seems to have won him over quickly.'

'We'll need to start the vetting process,' Emma said.

Dan laughed. 'I think it might be too late for that. Just don't accuse this one of murder, eh? It ruins the dinner table atmosphere.'

Emma laughed. 'I promise. I'll be nice.'

Dan put his arm around her, and she snuggled into him.

'I suppose we'd better tell Ed about this and start making plans.'

Emma grinned. 'Perfect,' she said.

Chapter Eighty-One

MUSEUM KILLER CONVICTED

By Ed Walker, Court Reporter

A woman has been convicted of killing two people in revenge for her sister's death.

Gracie Lincoln, 35, of Elton Terrace, Allensbury, murdered Dr Jayne Winter and Professor Sir Stewart Randall and used a charity treasure hunt to cover her crimes.

Tildon Crown Court heard how Lincoln sent a fake treasure hunt clue to Dr Winter to lure her to Old Manor Hall in Allensbury. Lincoln lay in wait and then killed Dr Winter with a blow to the head.

John Evesham KC, prosecuting, told the court: 'Miss Lincoln's actions were cold-blooded and in response to learning of the role Dr Winter played in her sister's death.

'She preyed on Dr Winter's desire to find the treasure and further her academic research to perpetrate her crimes.'

The court also heard how Lincoln killed Professor Sir Stewart Randall after he witnessed her murdering Dr Winter.

'Again, Miss Lincoln lured someone to their death. Professor

Randall had tried to blackmail her into helping him to find the treasure,' Mr Evesham said. 'She led him to believe that she would show him evidence at the museum after hours but, when he arrived, she stabbed him in the stomach.'

Mary Cusack KC, mitigating, said Lincoln had been driven to act in finding out why her younger sister had died. Claire Lincoln was just 15 years old when she died in 2005 in an accident at Old Manor Hall. The teenager had been searching in the school's attic for the Burns' family treasure when a solid wood bookcase fell on her.

Miss Cusack said: 'My client has never really recovered from the death of her younger sister and recently found that Claire had gone to the attic on advice from Dr Winter, who was in the same year as my client at Old Manor. Dr Winter was lying and Claire would not have died had she not been given this information.

'My client's recent discovery of the truth behind her sister's death drove her to act out of character, which is understandable, but something she now regrets deeply.'

The jury also convicted Lincoln of possession of an offensive weapon and threatening behaviour towards Donald Bloom, chair of the Allensbury Historical Society. She acted after finding out that Mr Bloom had discovered her sister's love of history and encouraged her to write a pamphlet on the Burns family after an essay she wrote won a society award. Lincoln previously admitted the assault on Maisie Barratt, Secretary of the Historical Society, in a bid to recover a pamphlet written by Claire.

Detective Inspector Jude Burton, who led the investigation, said: 'These were cold-blooded crimes perpetuated long after Miss Lincoln's sister died. Dr Winter's part in Claire Lincoln's death does not excuse Miss Lincoln's actions. Professor Randall had nothing to do with her sister's death, but Miss Lincoln killed him to protect herself. His family will never recover from that.'

Della Winter, Jayne's mother, said: 'I can't believe that I've lost my daughter like this. Jayne would never have maliciously given this girl false information. She's been made a scapegoat and killed by someone who was misguided. No parent should have to bury their own child and, for that, I can never forgive.'

The family of Professor Randall has asked to be left to grieve privately.

Mr Bloom said: 'I'm horrified to think that my actions in encouraging a young person to follow their interest could have resulted in her death and started this chain of events. The treasure hunt was supposed to be a fun game for families ahead of the museum anniversary, and everyone at the society is devastated by the events of the last few weeks.'

Sentencing will take place in six weeks at Tildon Crown Court.

***

ARCHAEOLOGISTS DISCOVER BURNS FAMILY TREASURE

By Dan Sullivan, Allensbury Post reporter

Evidence has, at last, been found in the hunt for the Burns' family treasure.

In comparing a plan of the Old Manor Hall site in Allensbury Museum with one held by the county records office, experts discovered what they believe to be an ice house in the grounds of the house.

They believe the ice house was sealed by Simeon Burns, with the treasure inside, to protect it from his family.

Dr Lula Blackthorn, Head of Archaeology at Allensbury University, said she was delighted to have obtained funding to dig at the site.

She said: 'For many years, there have been rumours circulating that Simeon Burns had left behind treasure hidden from his family. However, most people believed these to be false, as there has never been any actual evidence.

'Now we have found this hidden ice house, and geophysics testing suggests there is an underground area. We don't know, as yet, what the treasure will be, but we are very excited to be working on this site.'

Dr Blackthorn credited Dr Jayne Winter and the *Allensbury Post* for bringing this to her attention.

'Jayne Winter's meticulous research into the death of Simeon Burns, now believed to be murder, gave us a great start in the next steps of our work. I only wish she could be here to see the fruits of her labours.'

Dr Winter had spent many years researching the Burns family, after being inspired by an essay set while she was a student at Old Manor Sixth Form College. As she dug further, she became convinced that Benjamin was murdered by his sons, Simeon and Nathaniel, who wanted to protect the family inheritance.

Maisie Barratt, Secretary of the Allensbury Historical Society, is planning to use Dr Winter's research as the basis for a book on the social history of Allensbury.

She said: 'I only met Dr Winter briefly, but I was really impressed with the work she's done already. I'm very grateful to her family for allowing me to use it.

'I believe there may be some skeletons in the Burns' family closet, given what we now know about the death of both Benjamin and Simeon Burns, and the appearance of Elias Hannigan, Benjamin's half-brother. This angle forms the basis of research into my family history, and I'd love to hear more from people who may have information.'

'We're also reactivating the society's Living History project to help us collect information about the history of the area. We think this is a fascinating time period and we'd love to hear your family stories.

'Who knows, we might find a few more skeletons rattling around in closets.'

A note from me....

Thank you for reading A Deadly Legend. I hope you enjoyed the book.

You can find out more about the rest of the series and sign up to my newsletter by visiting www.lmmilford.com

I can be found on Facebook, X, Threads and Instagram under the handle @lmmilford

I'd love to hear what you think of the book.

Research resources

A Deadly Legend has taken more research, probably, than the previous four books combined. Once I'd added a historical element through Jayne's work, I needed to make sure that everything was as accurate as possible. As ever, I've taken some liberties, for the purpose of the story, but most of the information is correct.

I've created a bibliography of the sources I used so you can see for yourself the background to the history of the Georgian and Victorian periods covered in the book.

While I didn't specifically quote from Who Do You Think You Are magazine, I did find it useful for background and I recommend picking up a copy. Absolutely fascinating stuff.

For general history:
What the Industrial Revolution Did for Us, Gavin Weightman (BBC Books, 2003)

Tracing Your Kent Ancestors: A guide for local and family historians, David Wright, (Pen & Sword Family History, 2016)

For Victorian wills and inheritance:

Queen Mary's, University of London's website provided this:
https://www.qmul.ac.uk/geog/news/2017/items/keeping-it-in-t
he-family-inheritance-in-victorian-and-edwardian-britain.html

In addition, when Dan refers to how much Simeon Burns' inheritance would be in today's money, I used this website https://
www.officialdata.org/uk/inflation/1858?amount=600

For cholera and poisons:

A is for Arsenic by Kathryn Harkup

https://www.webmd.com/a-to-z-guides/cholera-faq#1

https://crosscut.com/2010/09/arsenic-victorians-secret

Local newspapers:

All Victorian newspapers were local papers. Not everyone was literate, so those who were would read out to those who couldn't. That could be at home, in the pub, coffee house etc.

Find out more here: http://backinthedayof.co.uk/victorian-n ewspapers or http://www.newsmediauk.org/History-of-British -Newspapers

About the author

LM Milford is a crime fiction author who writes the Allensbury mysteries, covering the exploits of local newspaper reporter Dan Sullivan.

A former newspaper journalist, Lynne's experience has influenced her work, although her stories were never as exciting as Dan's.

Lynne was born and brought up in the north-east of England, but now lives in Kent with her husband and far too many books. She loves cooking, baking and holidays in Spain. She's partial to a good red wine and plates of cheese.

Acknowledgements

It's always difficult to write this section, because so many people play a part in getting a book from idea to shelf. There's always a risk of leaving someone out.

I'd like to say thank you to my editor Donna Hillyer for her fantastic advice and guidance, my proofreader and good friend Victoria Goldman for her support and skill, and to Jessica Bell and Emily Reading for yet another beautiful cover design.

My writing colleagues continue to provide endless support and entertainment through their own books and also when we meet at events. Thank you to those who were able to read and review. Your hard work is much appreciated.

And, as always, thanks to my family – for never saying 'you can't do that' when I announced at a young age that I was going to be a writer and for keeping me going when the going gets tough.

www.ingramcontent.com/pod-product-compliance
Lightning Source LLC
Chambersburg PA
CBHW010422170726
48283CB00011B/3010